Forth from Eden

Mark Stay

PublishAmerica
Baltimore

© 2010 by Mark Stay.
All rights reserved. No part of this book may be reproduced, stored in a retrieval system or transmitted in any form or by any means without the prior written permission of the publishers, except by a reviewer who may quote brief passages in a review to be printed in a newspaper, magazine or journal.

First printing

All characters in this book are fictitious, and any resemblance to real persons, living or dead, is coincidental.

PublishAmerica has allowed this work to remain exactly as the author intended, verbatim, without editorial input.

ISBN: 978-1-4489-7821-2
PUBLISHED BY PUBLISHAMERICA, LLLP
www.publishamerica.com
Baltimore

Printed in the United States of America

To God

Special Thanks To

My mother Nancy

My friend Mandy

All others who supported and/or
helped me in this quest

Chapter 1

From the outside looking in, Eden was a perfect paradox.

Its location on the Snake River Plain made it one of the most open and therefore most liberating areas in the entire mid-mountain west. Its surface, unlike the miles of jagged mountain country which surrounded it, was as flat as a lake, though not of water, but of hard black rock, covered only with a paper thin layer of soil. Indeed, Eden sat atop a land of pavement—a smooth, wide boulevard spanning hundreds of miles.

Yet in the midst of these open miles, the inhabitants of Eden found themselves strangely confined. The power behind this confinement was subtle, almost undetectable to them, for they went about their lives in perfect contentment. It was a subconscious power that guaranteed that they would always come back to the place, that they would live out the years in the midst of the ghosts of not only their childhood, but their parents' and grandparents' childhoods as well. They would live and die under one sky, and not think twice about it.

Michael J. Christiansen, himself, had done twenty-five years to the day in the place—twenty-five years of barrenness and solitude and endless work that fell onto a plain of monotony much akin to the landscape. It did not, however, seem to wear on Mike. Even as he stood up and straightened himself from his work, the look on his face was not one of repression, but of pure contentment. Holding the small of his back in unconscious soreness, he looked around to review his work. To his satisfaction, the plot of tomato plants in front of him had considerably less weeds choking them. With a nod of approval and a quick swig from his thermos, he bent back down and recommenced the task at hand.

The calendar, indeed, marked his twenty-fifth birthday; it was nothing but a simple formality to him. There would be cake and ice cream later, and presents were a probable commodity as well, but in the mean time, it was just another day outside. The work did not go away, and he would rather have been outside chipping away at it than inside sitting idle, "celebrating". So he continued on, just as he had the day before, just as he had for as long as he could remember.

Mike pulled himself up from the plant only to hunker down, curl up, and sneeze. He sneezed again, smiled at himself, then recommenced his work. There was dust everywhere. Summer rain in Eden, Idaho, was a rare commodity, and this year was no different. The whole world highlighted a collage of blacks, browns, and golds, interrupted only occasionally by sporadic trees, houses and grazing cattle. Above all, raced the sun, whose sublime luster dominated. Its golden rays constantly penetrated the landscape and had a habit of drying up any moisture that the soil may have attempted to retain.

Not that its presence bothered Mike. The scorching heat was simply the nature of things. He had known nothing else, and figured there was no use complaining because nothing would ever change. He simply donned a hat, filled up his thermos, and dealt with the heat as it came. The sun was doing its job, and that would not stop him from doing his.

As the only child, Mike had grown accustomed to working long, working hard, and working alone. He did so as his livelihood, but he saw it as much more than that. The spritely edge in his hand could not deny his passion. He worked because he enjoyed it, thus he had built and furnished this vegetable garden for his mother. He loved the earthy feel of the dirt between his fingers, as well as the minty essence of the tomato plants as they grew. He loved cultivation, taking charge of the life of another, and watching its progress from his effort. He loved tasting of the freshness of the evaporating dew on the cooler mornings, watching it glisten on the leaves before the sun burned it off. Mike loved the work for what it was, but the main reason for his love stemmed from the time the work gave him to daydream.

There were certainly no limits to such a pastime. In the blink of an eye Mike could be anywhere, ranging from the depths of the ocean to the tops of the highest mountains. He could be lazing away on some distant beach or in the middle of the World Series. He could be whoever he wanted, whenever he wanted, and such was a freedom that made his otherwise unseasoned life quite tasteful.

Mike, like many of his townsmen, had never actually left the mid-mountain west. He had visited Boise a few times as well as the Utah border at Bear Lake, both of which were a few hours away, but those brief trips were the closest he ever got to traveling the world. All of his daydreaming was just what the word implied—simple dreams. He had seen pictures of remote parts of the world in movies and issues of National Geographic, but the full experience of being in the places he read about had never been his. Los Angeles was as foreign to him as Venice, and New York as foreign as Bangkok.

Mike surveyed the tomato plants once more and smiled. They were now completely devoid of weeds and were now left to grow unimpeded. Considering the time of the year, they would start boasting the beginnings of green fruit soon. It would be soon afterwards that his work would pay off in the forms of bright red jewels.

Mike took one last swig from his thermos and pulled off his gloves. Instead of walking back toward the house, however, he headed the opposite direction, walking through the fields of hay until he reached a line of drooping willows at the opposite end of the property. The willows sprouted from the little brook that bubbled through the property and still boasted a constant flow of water even in the heat of midsummer. As he reached it, he yanked off his boots, rolled up his pants, and, after descending the slight knoll, waded into the stream. Finding a dry rock in the middle, he sat down and proceeded to soak his feet in the cool, clear waters.

He took a deep breath. This little nook was one of his most favorite places. There were no disturbances to the quiet stillness except for the constant bubbling of the stream and the occasional rustling of willow leaves. Mike watched with mesmerization as the water flowed around his bare feet and wiggled his toes to feel the coolness in between. This was his gift to himself, and though he willingly gave it on days other than his birthday, he thankfully received it just the same.

It was here, in the quiet solitude of nature, that his mind was left to wander and ponder the things of life and family, of death and God, and of everything in between. Mike had been taught by his parents and had listened in church concerning the purpose of life, and he felt like he had such things more or less figured out. As far as he knew, he was on the right track to obtaining his place inside the pearly gates; all he had to do was continue with the life he was living, and all would be settled. Mike's mind became passively submerged in such thoughts at this moment, toying with nature as the wind blew over his tan face and rustled his short sun-bleached hair.

Eventually, Mike's feet became pruny; his gage of time was tolling its distant bell. Suppertime was approaching, and he had made it a habit to try to be showered in time to help his mom prepare it. He got up, waded out of the water, grimaced as he put on his sweaty socks and boots, and headed back toward the house.

Inside, his mother was preparing a salad. Mike greeted her and began to proceed to head upstairs to take a shower, but the now unseen voice his mother called out to him, stopping him and his dirty self. "You have a visitor, Mike, an elderly man. He left a package that he wanted you to open right away. I set it on your bed."

Mike furrowed his eyebrows and turned back in the direction of the kitchen. "A visitor?"

"I don't know who he is. He's out with your father right now. He wants you to open the package right away and read its contents. He'll be back in time for dinner."

Mike turned back, shrugged to himself, and headed upstairs to claim this unexpected prize. It was a manila envelope, lying sedately on top of his bedspread. Mike was eager to see what it was, but was even more eager to clean himself off. He decided to forego urgency of the directions until he had taken a quick shower, and felt only mildly guilty at it.

The opening was only delayed ten minutes, though, and soon Mike found himself staring down the return address. "Abraham Paul Augustine," he read. *Abraham—Abe. That's not a common name. But I remember hearing it recently.* The memory instantly flashed back to him—the memory of two months ago. It had been dusk, the end of a beautiful summer day. Mike had felt the urge to go four-wheeling out in the hills south of the interstate. As he directed himself away from his house, he could see a light already up in the dark masses before him. "I'm not the only one," he had thought. He remembered riding, watching the whitish-yellow of headlights rush onward ahead of him, then hearing the whizz of the semis fade behind him after he crossed under the bridge. With the interstate behind him, he had been freed, there had been nothing but him and the empty world ahead of him, and he welcomed its solitude. Again, he had been struck with the beauty of the night. The air had cooled, its fever breaking with the setting of the sun. Clouds had glowed hues of scarlet and indigo, reflecting the last colors of the daylight. The dew had promised to be particularly heavy that night—he could smell the sage in the air. As he approached the trail at the base of the hills, he noted the lights again, this time, almost directly above him. They sat in the same place they had sat before. Mike had not been heading in that direction, but after a moment of consideration, he had redirected his course.

"You're not from around here," he had called out as he approached the silhouette and his stalled ATV.

"I got lost and ran out of gas." The voice had been one of an older gentleman.

"I figured. It happens all the time up here to people who don't know their way around." Mike had approached the shadow by now. Mike had never before met him. "My name's Mike Christiansen."

"Abe Augustine."

Mike had pulled out a rubber tube and proceeded to siphon some of his gas into Abe's. "That should be enough to get you down the mountain. Where do you need to get back to?"

"My car's just parked off to the side of the road. This should be great. Thank you very much."

Mike remembered directing Abe back down the trail, the night now having become quite dark. He remembered looking forward, to the point where his headlights dissolved into the darkness, and looking back to make sure this man Abe was still on his tail. He remembered getting back down to the road, asking Abe if he needed anything else.

"For now, I'm good. My truck's just a quarter mile down the road. I really appreciate your help."

"No problem."

Mike had turned to leave when he heard the man call out, "I'll see you later."

Mike had returned the gesture, fully doubting the truth of it.

But now this man was fulfilling his prophecy. *Interesting that I should be getting a package from him, that he should be visiting.* Mike had not told him where he lived, but it would not have been hard for Abe to assume that he had been from Eden. He wondered what it was for, for he had not told him that it would be his birthday today. Mike pulled out his pocket knife and slit the envelope. As he reached inside, his fingers grasped onto a letter.

Dear Michael,

Mike thought it interesting that he was addressed as Michael. He had not introduced himself as that. Nobody called him that.

I have searched long and hard for you, and the events of a few months ago, if you remember them, have confirmed that you are, indeed, the one I am looking for. I want to briefly introduce myself in this letter so you know a little bit about me, as well as state my purpose for my pursuit of your further acquaintance.

Mike was not sure what to make of this. An attitude of estranged curiosity enveloped him as he continued reading.

My name is Abraham Paul Augustine. I was born in a cabin in the 1920's in West Virginia. My father was a backwoods pig farmer up in the foothills and was childhood friends with my mother. They married at 18 and I came along shortly thereafter.

Life as a child was good. There were several boys in the neighborhood and unlimited things to do. Day after day, we would tromp around through the wooded hills, hunting squirrels with our BB guns, fishing in the clear mountain streams, and filling our bellies with all the wild berries we could handle. Such times were tempered with household chores, but those were minimal, and since my father never bothered to send me to school, they did not get in the way of my world of adventure.

The only times when things were not good were when my parents went into town for social events. It was then that my father was transformed from a man who taught his son to read the Bible to a drunk who would come home and beat his wife. It only happened on occasion, but it set the stage for the disaster that happened the winter of my thirteenth year.

That winter, my mother got sick with Typhoid and died without a fight. My father fell into a deep depression and was hardly ever completely sober after that. I spent my nights weeping for my mother and hiding from my father, who seemed to look for any excuse to beat me senseless. The perfect world that had been created for me was quickly dissolving.

Then, ten months later, my father was arrested in town for getting into a brawl with a man and beating him to death. With his arrest, I was taken and placed on the county poor farm. I cannot say, however, that life there was any better than it was with my dad. The dorms were overcrowded and often stunk of unsanitary odors. We were often boarded with mentally ill adults, who were probably just as dangerous as my father. The days were long and the work was hard.

Mike looked up from the letter a moment. *What's going on here?* he questioned. *Why such a lengthy and detailed background?* Mike thumbed through the letter. He was not even halfway through it. Intrigued, he read on.

But by some act of providence, that nightmarish portion of my life was short-lived. Not too long after I got there, a newspaper article unveiled the horrid conditions of a similar farm and all of us kids were taken out and placed in boarding houses. As for me, I was shipped over to Charleston and was placed into a boarding house with 19 other boys.

It was there that I got my first taste of formal education and soon found that it was the perfect remedy for the depression I was suffering. My primary focus lie in literature and I spent the majority of my days in the local library. Every time I laid my eyes on words, I was thrown back to those times when my parents and I read from the Bible, to those times before everything fell apart. Since I had been used to the difficult language of the King James Bible, I had the ability to read most anything, which I did. I read the classics: Twain, Emerson, Poe, Hawthorne, Dickens, Shakespeare, Milton, you name it, I read it. Mostly, though, I read about history. The events of times past and how they affected their societies had always intrigued me. By the time I was fifteen, I was baffling the minds of everyone with whom I conversed.

Life outside of books continued though, and I was feeling the need to get out of the environment I was in. My life was not going anywhere, and in a few years, I would be turned loose without anywhere to go or any means to get by. And so I joined the CCC. Once again, I was back in the wild, planting trees, working in the National Forest, and building cabins for those in need. It reawakened a part of the world in which I had lived as a kid.

That did not stop me from reading, however. I was still able to gain access to books and read whenever I had a moment of free time. My knowledge of the world increased through those years and helped me understand the nature of cause and effect, such as the reasons to the stock market crash. This knowledge came out in my speech and conversation, and one day, one of our leaders pulled me aside and said, "How do you know so much Abe? You are too much for our conversations."

I told him of my love for reading and how it was all I did. The leader smiled at me and patted me on the back, telling me that the world needed more people like me. Then he looked me in the eye and said, "What would you say if I told you I could get you into West Virginia University?" I told him that it would be more than I could have hoped for. He simply smiled and told me that his brother was a dean there and that he could arrange for me to talk to him. He said that he was convinced that I would be able to get in.

Sure enough, the next year, I interviewed with his brother and found myself enrolled that fall. For the next six years I lived with that dean and studied history. It was during this stage in life, at the age of 25, while I was working on my doctorate, that I discovered hard evidence of the legend of the golden emblem.

The golden emblem was little more than a tradition handed down by history and archaeology buffs. It was a supposed object that was given to man to keep order and goodness in society. This emblem, when accompanied by six other supporting emblems, had the power to keep man's passions in check and had been held periodically throughout human history as a tool to create utopian societies. The last time that they were together was in Jerusalem, but when the Romans sacked Jerusalem, it was lost and became no more than a tale. With my discovery, however, I knew that it was more than legend.

The golden emblem? Mike laughed at the sound of it. He tried to think back on what this Abe Augustine had looked like. The night had been dark, though, and the memory came up blank. Again, he read on.

I had found my life project; rather, it had found me. The artifacts I stumbled upon gave me unprecedented leads. It was not hard to be motivated in such a pursuit. I thought back on all the horrors of my childhood and how none of those things would have happened with the emblems in order. All my life I have searched for the golden emblem, devoting all my education and money to it, and just two years ago, I finally found it. It is this emblem that brings me to you today. According to the information I've gathered, the emblem is very specific in its bearer. According to public records and what I've seen in you already, you meet these qualifications. I am writing to enlist you in a job opportunity that will last a few months. You will set the amount of pay you require for the project. I look forward to meeting you and speaking further to you on the subject.

Deepest Regards,
Abe Augustine

Mike raised his eyebrows. This was all quite strange.

"Mike," his mom called from below. Mike turned toward his door. "Come on down. There's someone to meet you."

Mike felt a sudden shiver go down his spine as he descended the stairs, still holding the letter in his hand. He reached the bottom and turned toward the dining room where, at the dinner table, he saw his mother and father sitting with a figure who, in the light, was only slightly familiar.

In that moment, Mike was able to fully absorb the appearance of this stranger for the first time. He did seem to be in surprising good shape for a man in his seventies but he still wore various evidences of old age. He cultivated a well trimmed beard and silver hair matted from wearing a hat. He clothed himself in a plaid shirt over which he folded his leather-skinned arms. On his nose rested a pair of spectacles whose lenses seemed way too small to be of much use. Abraham only supported this notion as he took his first look at Mike. Those blue eyes, which stared directly over the spectacles, seemed to beam with supreme elation.

"Mike, this is Abraham. He tells us that you two have briefly met before."

Mike nodded slowly, for after reading the letter, he needed to convince himself of the same thing.

Abe got up from the table and, with that same elation, approached Mike, who had remained stationary in the doorway. He held out his hand and Mike hesitantly shook it. "Mike, it's been awhile. You have no idea how glad I am to see you again."

Mike had a daunting feeling that that could very well be true.

"We'll have dinner ready in a few minutes," his dad said. "Why don't you two go wait in the living room."

Mike, torn between discomfort and curiosity, conceded and led his guest into the living room. Mike took a seat on the sofa while Abe commandeered the rocking chair directly facing him. Abe continued to beam at Mike, which only added to Mike's discomfort. Mike decided not to show it and instead gave him the attention he believed was due to every human. When Abe broke the brief silence by mentioning, "I hear it's your twenty-fifth birthday. Happy birthday," Mike smiled and thanked him.

Silence resumed, which Mike normally did not mind, but at this moment, his curiosity was bubbling over.

"So Abe—and please don't take this wrong, I'm just a little confused—how did you come to decide you needed *my* help?"

Abe did not answer right away, but continued to breathe in the moment. Then, silently, in almost a whisper, he said, "You're the chosen one."

If Mike had an inclination to doubt Abe's sanity from the letter, this statement only fed its flames. Mike glanced over toward the kitchen, but his parents had not seemed to hear. Mike felt quite alone in his awkwardness. Despite the myriad of thoughts running through his head, all that bled through to his tongue was a short phrase. "What?"

"You are the one chosen to bear the golden emblem. For two years I have searched for the one who matches up with the emblem bearer's criteria. I have read and reread its inscriptions and searched for a match. Two months ago, you completed the match, and now that search is over."

Mike was trying to let all of these puzzle pieces soak in, but his brain was already saturated. He still had absolutely no idea what was going on or why he was being dragged into it. Luckily for him, Abe finally absorbed the confusion Mike was feeling and proceeded to lay it on him. He did so without seeming to take a breath.

"I cannot explain it all to you now, but we need to take this emblem on a long trip, and you are the only one that can bear it—that is expressly stated in its directions. You must come with me on the journey, and I will pay you as my research assistant, but we have to leave right away, because until it is in the hands of its bearer, it is extremely susceptible to being stolen again. You would not believe what it has taken for me to retain it these past two years. I cannot afford to chance any more time. If it fell out of my hands, then all my life's work would have been for naught. Like I said, I cannot explain it all now, but I can let you know that if we succeed, the results will be glorious for you, for me, and for the whole world for that matter."

Mike figured that at the rate he was going, as long as he conversed with this old stranger who called himself Abe, he would be completely in the dark. The whole situation made him squirm. Mike resisted the urge to tell Abe to find someone else; he doubted that he would agree to such a thing so readily anyway. The man had been pretty insistent on finding him, and Mike was sure he would prod and push until Mike consented. Mike's head was starting to hurt, leaving him able only to ask a simple question: "What is this emblem's importance anyway?"

Abe was starting to grow agitated; he must have thought that he had explained himself sufficiently for the moment. "I told you I would explain all that later. It will take you a while to fully understand all of it. The key right now is immediacy. So will you, or will you not accept my plea?"

There was more than a hint of desperation in the man's voice, almost as if he were a mother with a lost child. There really seemed to be no option. Mike turned to the man. "Did you tell all of this to my parents?"

"I told them enough. I told them I was offering you a job as a research assistant. Why?"

Mike was searching for an excuse, any way to keep control of the wonderful world he had made for himself here. He did not feel right denying the man without a valid excuse. It came readily, though, and he replied, "I'd have to make sure they'd be fine with it."

Abe crinkled up his nose in confusion.

Mike seemed a little put out at his implication and addressed Abe a little more curtly. "I'm first obligated to my family and this farm. If my father needs me like I think he does, I'll have to turn you down."

With that, Abe opened his mouth, most likely to object, most likely to say something, but he stopped himself and sat back in his chair. While he broke eye contact and commenced rocking in the chair, Mike reigned in solitary triumph.

Dinner was soon prepared, and not a moment too soon. Mike's comment had ended the conversation in the living room, and the two had then filled the moment with looking everywhere, and at everything except each other. The air had become extremely unsettled in the stillness, and the sound of his father's voice, calling them to dinner, was a godsend. The two gratefully walked into the dining room, which held the aura of everything of which the meal consisted—a wide array of steak, vegetables, potato salad, and Jell-o. Everything was on special request for his birthday, and was a sort of *Best of Mike's Palate* collection. The four of them sat down and Mike's father offered the blessing on the food, after which he stated. "Alright, dig in. Every man for himself."

"Thanks again for having me stay for dinner." Abe stated politely after the food was claimed and halfway partaken in vocal silence. "This type of hospitality reminds me of home."

"And where is home for you?"

Mike pursed his lips at his father's comment, awaiting the same introduction he had been given. To his surprise, however, he simply said, "I grew up in West Virginia. I have been away from there for the past fifty years, doing archaeology and teaching history, but it seems your roots never leave you."

"That's for sure," Mr. Christiansen said with a laugh. "And in my case, I have never left my roots. This farm has been in the family for five generations." There was more than a hint of pride and satisfaction in his voice.

The comment was a direct cue for Mike to bring up the pending subject at hand, but he could not do it. He watched in stagnancy as the moment passed and everyone resumed eating. Not much was spoken for the next few minutes other than the occasional, "Pass the pepper" or "Could you hand me over the rest of that potato salad?" Despite the silence, Mike could not shake the matter that was weighing in his head. He was starting to lose his appetite. Fortunately (or unfortunately) for him, Mike's mom decided to take control of the situation.

"How, again, did you say you met Mike?"

Abe swallowed his food. "I was riding up in the hills and got lost. Your son came and rescued me."

"He's a good boy like that," his mom answered. "So did you just think of him when this position opened up?"

Abe nodded. "Considering the situation, Mike seemed to be a good fit. Some of the work will be quite physically demanding."

"Well that sounds like a wonderful opportunity for you, Mike. What do you think?"

Mike stopped chewing. "I told him that I wasn't sure the farm could do without me, that I wanted to ask your opinion on it."

His dad kind of chuckled at the answer, which confused Mike. "Why would you feel like you had to do that?"

Mike looked over at Abe, then back at his father. "Well, I have responsibilities that I am first committed to here."

"But is this something you want to do?"

Mike looked over at Abe, who was watching him with that same desperation in his eyes. The moment sat suspended, a million different encrypted trains of cause and effect dancing around his head. Abe stared at him, implanting his desire and desperation into Mike's mind. Mike's parents stared at him, opening a door to which he had hoped they would keep closed. Thoughts of selfishness and comfort whirled opposite feelings of charity and service, convoluting his mind and disrupting his knowledge of which way was up and which way was down. "Yeah, it is," he stated.

Mike did not believe the words even as they came out. However, his parents had destroyed his only excuse, leaving charity the strength to bleed through. Mike may not have fully understood what was going on (a colossal understatement), but he did recognize sincerity when he saw it. This man was genuine. He could sense it. And this man truly believed that Mike was a crucial part of what he was determined to do. No matter how much he fought against the idea of leaving, these facts controlled his lips and gave his leave. Mike wanted to curse them.

Mike's father looked over at his mother and performed some unspoken conversation with her that only a couple who had been together for thirty years could understand. What Mike did not know was that they had worried a long time about Mike's future, or lack thereof. They had been concerned that his staying on the farm was impeding him from where he needed to be in life. He had not pursued college after his home schooling; he rarely, if ever, dated, and did not seem to have any interest to either; and he felt perfectly satisfied to go on with life as it was. Although they appreciated his contribution to the farm, they felt his departure was much more important. They had never been able to arouse enough interest in him to leave, though.

"I think you should take the job," his father said. We'll be fine here." Then, turning from Mike's dumbfounded face to Abe's elated face, he added, "When will you be leaving?"

"It's all up to Mike," Abe stated, but Mike really knew what he meant. He was just too polite to say so.

Mike sat breathless, suddenly losing all interest in his steak. The condition of his parents' approval had been his ticket out of this situation, but they had ripped it up. He had never expected them to approve of it, let alone so readily. They had given their leave, and here was Abe, waiting for Mike's word to move things forward.

"I guess we'll leave as soon as I can pack a few things."

It was then that Abe's true emotions broke the surface and he responded by rapidly replying, "How long will that take you?"

"Uh..." Mike barely heard the words coming out of Abe's mouth through his swimming head. Slowly though, they registered, and he was able to respond, accessing his memory of the many overnight campouts in Boy Scouts. "I can get things together in about thirty minutes."

"Hold on," his mother said, "You must both stay for cake and ice cream first, and we have a few gifts for Mike to take with him as well."

The two events did not last long enough. Mike could not finish his cake and ice cream. The gifts lacked the luster that they should have had; a Fossil watch, a digital camera, and the .44 pistol at which he and his dad had gawked at the sporting goods store in Twin Falls. "You really might want to pack that, just in case," Abe whispered aside to Mike, quiet enough so his mother could not hear. The comment did not help Mike's comfort level.

Mildly shaking, Mike went upstairs to pack and in no time, found himself saying farewell to his parents, his house, and his entire world. Indeed, the world was spinning in circles, which made him completely sick to his stomach. Mike slowly slid into the black pickup like it was the black ferry of Styx. As the doors closed, he suddenly felt completely alone, for even Abe was in a different sphere. With an eager foot, Abe turned the truck around in the driveway and sped out toward the road.

And just like that, they were on their way.

Chapter 2

Mike had had a dream once when he was younger, a dream of sailing on a ship. In the dream, a storm had arisen and the ship had tossed him overboard. Mike remembered flying through the air, jolting, then waking up, having never hit the water. The dream came back to him now, and the feelings he had experienced while flying through the air mirrored those he felt at the moment, those he had felt for the past forty five minutes. He was waiting for the jolt, but knew, at the same time, that it was not coming. Instead, he was waiting for the moment when he would hit the waves, but not with a smile. Indeed, his mouth seemed totally incapacitated by the unfolding events, for it had yielded nothing but tense silence since they had left.

As they drove, Mike watched as the fields sailed past in the dying light, and could not help but notice what he was seeing was only a mirror of his emotions. Everything swirled in fast forward. *Where am I going?* he asked himself. *How did I even get on this?* Mike shifted positions, resting his elbow on the armrest. He only lasted a moment, then adjusted himself in his seat. His body seemed to want to keep up with his racing mind. *Where are we going anyway? Is he to drive me off the edge of the world?* Mike shifted again, shifted toward Abe and opened his mouth, but then slowly closed it in defeat. He mulled upon it a moment, repeated the action, and again, turned back in defeat.

Maybe ignorance is better. Maybe it's better that I don't know the details, yet. Mike sat back, exhaling all the fight out of him. *I guess I'll find out when I find out.*

Mike turned again to look at Abe. He had not seemed to notice Mike's wrestle with the seat belt. He simply continued driving on, uninterrupted in the expression he had worn since leaving Mike's place. Abe's expression boasted a sharp contrast to Mike's mood, for he was wearing a face of elation. Several times, Mike was sure that he was about to burst into laughter out of pure and simple joy. *And from his perspective, why would he not?* In Abe's eyes, Mike was a renegade puzzle piece that he had finally located, and with it he was one step closer to completing the puzzle and fulfilling some crazy life dream. It was interesting to note that Abe had really not said a word the whole way either, but felt contented to mumble random words to songs to himself and keep his eyes peeled on the road.

Mike thought back on the conversation that had sealed this. He had been floored when his parents had given him their leave. He had not expected the idea to go farther than the conversation that they had had. In the moment, he was at a loss for rational thinking and had agreed that it was something he wanted to do. That was when the restlessness had commenced. Mike opened his mouth again to end it, this time not being able to face Abe out of shame for wasting his time. For some reason, however, he could not get the desired words to come out of his mouth. For the last time, he closed his mouth in defeat.

Abe remained completely oblivious, and remained jovially silent all the way to Idaho Falls. "We are going to stop off at Wal-Mart to get some supplies, and then we'll be on the road for another hour or two before we camp."

"Okay," was all Mike could get out. He had no argument against it. The defeat had worn away into a blank slate; his body continued to fall and he was sure to hit the waves soon, so he decided he had better get used to rolling with the tide.

Mike had been to Wal-Mart once or twice before, but, as they pulled off the freeway, steered into the parking lot, and walked into the store, he realized he had forgotten how much of a zoo it was. He was certain that there were presently more people in the store than there lived in his entire town. Everybody dashed to and fro, rushing for the deals that they must have felt might not last. He and Abe slowly steered the shopping cart through the melee, using their best defensive driving skills to avoid any sort of collision.

"What a headache," Mike thought to himself.

Abe directed them over to the sporting goods section in the back of the store. "I hope you enjoy camping, because we're going to be doing a lot of it from here on out."

Mike found himself smiling for the first time since he met this character. *Camping is good. I can do camping.* Camping was familiar, even fun. In all this uncertainty, he needed that.

Abe took the smile positively. "Good, because where we are going, there aren't going to be any hotels around."

Mike chuckled. "Well, I'm more comfortable sleeping in a tent than I am in a hotel, actually."

Abe stared intensely at him for a moment in the strange sort of way that seemed to be characteristic of him. "I can tell. You don't exactly feel comfortable in places like this do you?"

Mike shook his head. "Places like this overwhelm me."

Abe, who was in the midst of dodging a young mother with her kids in her cart, stated, "Don't worry, you're not alone in that. I only came here because things are cheap and they can all be found in one place. I don't want to waste much time because I want to get as many miles under us as we can tonight."

Mike sighed as Abe handed him a packaged sleeping bag. "Hey Abe?"

"Yeah?"

"I know that I am still in the dark about all this, so my question might come off as a little stupid..."

Abe nodded. "Understandable."

"... but why is this so urgent?"

Abe looked at him, patiently reminding himself that he was speaking to his "chosen one", a thought which still made Mike uncomfortable. "I'll explain more tonight," he stated after exhaling. "Hopefully you can come to a little more of an understanding then. And when you do, I'm sure you will feel the same urgency I do."

Mike sincerely hoped so.

Two hundred fifty-one dollars and seventy-nine cents later, the two retreated from the battle scene into the cool night air and loaded all the supplies into the back of the truck. They had decked themselves out with enough provisions and snacks to supply an army. Mike felt like he was on another backpacking trip with the Boy Scouts; only this time, instead of his grandfather's ancient army gear, he was supplied with a brand new personal tent, sleeping bag, mess kit, water bottle, hiking boots, full-brimmed fishing hat, and flashlight. He could tell that the supplies were not the highest quality, but he was confident that they would work for their needs.

Abe reached into one of the grocery bags after they had pulled out of the parking lot and pulled out an orange bag. "You like Cheetos?"

"Yeah," Mike flatly said, although Cheetos were actually one of his favorite snacks, and he was eager to sink his teeth into the familiarity of their cheesy crunch.

"I'm a sucker for them too. Why don't you open them now—who knows when we'll get to have them again."

Had Abe not uttered that last comment, Mike would have been able to enjoy the Cheetos a lot more. He did his best to shake it off, though, and concentrate on the more immediate and pleasant matters in his hands. Mike did not want to put forth the effort to mull over the confusion now anyway. Silence was broken for the next hour only by the crunching of the chips. Whatever peculiarity was to come would be unveiled later on. The feelings of anxiety that had been so dominant for the past half day were pushed to the back of his mind by the cheesy fingers before him and the camping that was soon to come. These things threw Mike back into boyhood memories, which was something he eagerly grasped onto, and as the yellow dotted lines rushed past the car in the darkness, Mike felt, for the first time in several hours, somewhat comfortable.

Mike began to drift off to sleep, and may have even been out for an amount of time, for he was rudely awakened with a jolt of the car. Mike lurched and instinctively turned toward Abe, who was shaking his head back and forth. Mike looked at his watch and noticed that it was just past 11:00.

"You think we should stop?" Mike asked, although it was more of a suggestion.

Abe gave himself a few good blinks then shook his head again, this time in disagreement. "I'd like to make it a little further."

"Well, how much further do we have?"

"About a day's journey."

"Well, if we're not going to make it tonight, we might as well stop and get some good rest. Continuing to drive won't do us any good if you're just going to fall asleep at the wheel and crash."

Abe took a moment to silently absorb the simple advice before he stated, "Yeah. You're right. Sometimes I get a little too overzealous."

His safety assured, Mike took a moment to try and get a feeling of his surroundings. It was especially dark outside the car, and Mike soon realized that such darkness was due to the forest of pine trees which now surrounded them. They seemed to crowd the road as if they wanted to choke it, and the blackness they contained just beyond the first few rows of trees only added to their ominous presence. There were not nearly this many trees in central Idaho. Abe soon pulled off the highway and onto a forest access road which seemed even more choked. He drove down about a half mile and pulled off to the side where he killed the engine.

"Where are we anyway?" Mike inquired in bewilderment.

"We're in Targhee National Forest. I don't know if we're even allowed to camp here, but we're in a remote enough spot that the rangers won't bother us tonight."

So, without argument, Mike set up camp as Abe built the fire. Within no time, it was blazing brightly and warmly, and both Mike and Abe sat before it and stared at it with the usual mesmerization to which one always seemed to succumb around fire. They watched as it danced upward in its chaotic movements, casting an orange glow on the other's faces and on the trees above. Abe seemed to resume his state in the car, suspending himself between sleep and wake. Mike was fine with that now. His life was secure and the fire kept him company. While Abe seemed to doze without blinking, Mike sat there doing nothing other than occasionally pushing a stray cinder back in the fire or adding another stick. The smell of pine filled the air and reminded Mike of a thousand memories of the past, of the nights with his friends in Boy Scouts, of the times when they had simply had bonfires in the yard as a family. Mike smiled at the images.

Then it seemed that all at once, Abe awoke. "Well, I told you that I would try to explain a little more about what is going on here." The sound of his voice made Mike jump for a few different reasons. "I think the easiest way for me, though, is to draw you a picture. So why don't you bring your log over this way so you can see what I'm drawing."

As Mike moved around the fire toward Abe, Abe picked up a thin, but firm, stick off the ground and drew two circles side by side in the dirt.

"Alright," he started, looking up into Mike's eye and drawing Mike's attention away from the dirt. Abe wore a look of soberness, though the element of excitement was still in his youthful eyes. Such an expression, coupled with the dancing orange glow of the fire, gave him a slightly savage look. "What I am about to tell you may seem strange, but I'll let you know right now, there are a lot of strange things out in the world that only seem to be so because we have never encountered them before. It does not, in any sense, mean they are impossible. In fact, we often find evidence of these phenomena in the most common, everyday things. Do you follow me so far?"

Mike gulped and nodded. "I think so."

"Good. I want you to keep that concept in mind as I tell you what I know of the golden emblem."

"What you know?"

Abe nodded. "As extensive as my research is, there are still a lot of things I do not know about all of this. A lot of the knowledge comes from the inscriptions on the golden emblem itself. I cannot decipher all inscribed words right now," Abe confessed, "but I'm able to read enough of them to tell you about the emblem's origin."

Abe took a deep breath and explained on.

"When Adam and Eve partook of the forbidden fruit, God cast them out of the Garden of Eden, just as He had warned. After they left, Adam realized the degree of his loss. He noted that he had truly fallen from paradise into a cold, harsh world and succumbed to great sorrow and fear for the future. God took pity on Adam and Eve and decided to not leave them alone without help. He gave them a gift—the golden emblem, as well as six other lesser emblems to serve as supports." Abe drew six more circles around the circle on the right so they formed a hexagon. "This emblem," he said, pointing to the circle in the center, "along with these six other emblems of virtue: the emblems of knowledge, wisdom, love, meekness, courage, and sacrifice," Abe pointed to each of the other six, "were to give guidance to them and the society they were to create. In a sense, they were empowered to reconstruct as much of the Garden of Eden as possible, though it would only come with great faith and effort."

Abe then directed Mike's attention to the lone circle on the left. "The devil knew of the emblems' power to institute good, and so, in response, he constructed his own emblem—a burning branch—the emblem of fire, and commissioned six demons to take charge over it." With that, Abe constructed another hexagon of similar manner around the circle on the left.

Abe was methodical in his picture and contrasted sharply with the look that suddenly appeared on Mike's face. "Demons?"

Abe nodded soberly, once again standing up against Mike's skepticism. "These demons, the demons of ignorance, foolishness, hate, pride, cowardice, and greed were to counter each emblem of virtue and support the emblem of fire. They were to haunt each respective bearer of each emblem."

Mike hoped this man was crazy. He had to be crazy. *Demons? Magical Emblems?* It could not be. Mike thought back, though, on Abe's introductory words. This was all, indeed, strange, yet, at the same, not out of the question. Mike had seen documentaries on exorcisms. He had heard stories of friends with Ouija boards. *How could so many accounts be false?* Such evidences of the supernatural had to have some truth. On the other side of the spectrum, he had experienced times when he was sure he had felt God's presence. There were two sides to the story, and Abe was including both. Still, the whole concept made him shiver. He listened on to Abe's story, warding off a slight shaking that had suddenly come over him.

"The devil waited for the right moment to introduce the emblem of fire to the sons of Adam, and when he saw Cain working in his vegetable garden, he found his opportunity. The devil had seen that as long as Cain had been old enough, he had mocked the golden emblem and the power it possessed. The devil appeared to Cain and offered the burning branch to him. 'What is the purpose of this?' Cain asked. 'This will give you power to carry out your every wish,' the devil responded. Then, knowing of Cain's jealousy towards his brother Abel's flocks, he told Cain that he was now empowered to kill Abel and take his flocks. Cain agreed. He took the burning branch as well as the promise that as long as the fire burned, Cain would have the power to carry out any evil action he desired. And so as the branch burned off in the distance, Cain slayed his brother Abel.

"Cain realized the power of the emblem and, in order to immortalize it, created several dozen torches with its fire and passed them on to his family and everyone else that followed him. It was Cain's hope that the amount of cursed fires would be able to overpower the golden emblem and allow him to take Adam's throne, but the plan came to no avail. The strength of the emblem of fire could not compare to the strength of the golden emblem. In fact, as soon as the fire was introduced to the presence of the golden emblem, the golden emblem grew in power and uncovered all of Cain's crimes.

"Cain was cast out of the presence of Adam and his family. But Cain and his family took the torches with them and continued to try to spread the emblem of fire's power. They began to use them to light all of their fires for whatever reason they needed. The fires spread and that original burning branch indeed became immortalized in their wicked society."

Abe adjusted his seat. Mike continued to try to make sense of all of this.

"Unfortunately, at the same time, Adam's society, which had initially achieved the state of paradise, slowly decayed. The rising generations did not understand the importance of the emblems, and soon after Adam died, the emblems of virtue were scattered and lost. The emblems of fire were unimpeded in their rise to power and the society became decadent, evil, and motivated by pride and greed and hatred. The emblems of virtue were not gathered again until Enoch, hundreds of years later.

"The world has gone through these patterns numerous times—the balance of power has shifted back and forth from the emblems of virtue to the emblem of fire. Today, we live in a time where the power lies in the emblem of fire, where it has lain for well over a thousand years. Our mission is to do what has been done in the past—gather the emblems of virtue and restore order to society."

Mike's heart seemed to forget how to beat. His lungs seemed to forget how to breathe. Had his mouth not forgotten how to speak, he would have expressed the words, "Are you serious?" Abe must have taken the silence as awe, for he smiled and nodded to confirm the idea.

There were a million things running through Mike's mind, but he couldn't make sense of any of them. When he did again gain the power to speak, he spoke the thought that seemed to arise at the moment. "So how did the emblem of fire survive so well? I mean, surely there had to be a time when there was an end to all of Cain's fires." It was a question rather minute in importance compared to the big picture, but Mike had no control of anything right now.

Abe shook his head. "The torches became so widely used that the ashes from the fire spread all over the world. Today there is not any tree in any piece of soil in any forest in the world that does not contain the seed of those ashes of that original fire. Therefore, any wood fire that you create holds a small portion of the power of the original emblem of fire. If you add up all of the power of all of the present fires of each society together, the emblem of fire is thriving and always will thrive. The only way to fight it is with the golden emblem. Does that make sense?"

Mike pursed his lips. "I guess so. So you can't destroy the emblem of fire?"

Abe shook his head. "While you will physically hold the only golden emblem to humankind, you cannot, at any point, or in any way, say that you are ever holding *the* emblem of fire. Therefore, it is impossible to destroy or lose it."

As Abe paused to take a breath and re-collect his train of thought, Mike took the opportunity to note the expression on Abe's face. His eyes bore a look of utter intensity. Abe was spilling out his passion. Despite its utter insanity, he did not, in the least bit, take any of this lightly. Mike could tell from the way his frenzied mind threw out his explanation. Mike was floundering to remain afloat with it, and struggled with all his might to stay with Abe as he continued on without blinking.

"Now," he said, pointing to each of the six circles in the hexagon to the right, "like I said, each of these emblems has a bearer, and our job is to find these bearers, find these emblems, and restore all seven back to a central location, historically at the center of government."

"That's it then? We do that and our job is done?"

Abe let out a laugh that seemed to serve multiple purposes. Mike frowned. "It is not that simple, Mike."

Mike was starting to get a little frustrated. *Not that simple?* It had taken his entire brainpower to come to that conclusion. Mike's head wanted to explode. Visions of circles and Bible stories and flames and demons and gold and paradise and Hell churned about, swirling, making him dizzy, making him sick in its motion. *What is Abe suggesting here? Why am I still listening?* Yet he was. Mike felt jaded by his own compassion for a stranger in search of his dream. He gave in, yet once again, to defeat and cast aside the storm that raged inside of him.

"Alright then," he bade, "continue."

"What we are shooting to achieve is paradise, remember?—A genuine turning toward Eden. What we are shooting for is a world without crime, greed, dishonesty, a perfect Utopia." Abe paused to consider the thought. Mike did the same, thinking, ironically, that he had already possessed such a world and Abe had beguiled him out of it. At the same time, Mike knew that he was probably the exception. He heard repeatedly in church and from his parents of all the evil and discord in the world. There were continual wars, murders, and robberies going on in the world. People in Africa were constantly starving and fighting disease. There were class distinctions and prejudices that caused envy and hate. Families were falling apart. Mental depression was soaring. Such woes were causing people to live miserable lives, to completely lose touch with their identities. He had not experienced such woes, but Abe's introductory letter revealed that Abe, to a degree, had.

Abe continued, whatever vision he was seeing having now dissipated. "Remember, however, that the demons have controlled the world and formed it according to their principles. They will not simply sit back and allow us to destroy all the work they've created. We are in for a long hard road ahead of us, Mike. I have already experienced my fair share of the demon of ignorance and it's not over yet. We will watch as the other bearers face their demons, and it will take everything we have within us to pull through this."

Mike did not want to hear anymore. He suddenly felt very tired and wished, more than anything to be back home. He wished to open his mouth and go back on his word, to let Abe know that he had had enough. His mouth had seemed to separate from his mind, though, for it continued to pull him farther and farther in to this crazy escapade. He found himself asking with a gulp, "Abe, what's my demon like—what will *I* be facing?"

Abe looked him straight in the eye. Again, without blinking, and with a definite air of intensity, he said, "A little of everything, Mike."

Chapter 3

Mike did not get much sleep that night. Those haunting words had constantly pulsed through his head, warding off any ability to rest. He had lain awake in his tent, agonizing the minutes away with thoughts that repeated themselves in a vicious cycle. *What did everything mean? What would he be facing? Did Abe even know?* The vagueness of the situation only escalated his anxiety. *What* would *he be facing? Death, torture, betrayal?* The demons seemed to be tormenting him already, and even now, he could not decipher their nature.

Mike slept in short spurts, and when they came, they were feverish. The same thoughts blackened his dreams, but pulsed even more realistically. Mike woke up often, and each time he did, he held no exact recollection of what he saw, but the feeling of each dream lingered with daunting reality. Needless to say, he spent the night in a cold sweat.

But now the sun was coming up and the night was over. Mike sniffed the air and caught the scent of burning pine and bacon grease. Abe seemed to have been gracious enough to prepare breakfast. Motivated by the smell, Mike pulled his tired body and mind up, got dressed and walked outside. Abe hailed him and asked him how he had slept. Mike was not able to produce more than a dead look. Abe's smile disappeared and he simply nodded, seeming to understand. Both consigned to eat their breakfasts in silence.

Mike's mind remained anything but silent, however. The nightmares scattered like cockroaches as the light filled the damp forest air, and now more immediate matters came to mind. Abe's haunting prophecy had ended all conversation last night, and the dread of what else was to come today was hanging upon him. *Where would one start on a journey as colossal as this?* Mike questioned. *For all that Abe talked about last night, that subject wasn't one of them.*

His opportunity to find out came soon enough. Abe finished chewing his breakfast and said, "Well, let's get this place cleaned up and head out; we have a long day ahead of us."

"Yeah?" Mike had obediently set himself to burying the smoldering remains of the campfire with dirt.

Abe nodded. "We're headed up to Banff National Forest. The trip will be long, but it will be worth it. Because tonight..." Abe paused and smiled, "... you will be in possession of the golden emblem."

Yeah, and then the demons start harassing me. Excellent. Such were the thoughts going through Mike's head, but he decided not to voice them. For some reason, the midst of all the pressure that had been weighing down on him the night before had come to seem a sort of rite of passage. Its nature was cruel, to be sure, but through all of its cruelty came an unsolicited determination to continue. By all facets of logic, it was an act of insanity. They were chasing after some legend that claimed to create the ideal society, which had always seemed just out of reach. America, France, Russia, three countries in just the past 250 years. Two of those three had been bloody failures. America had seen the most success, yet Mike still could not deny some of its major problems.

Despite all that, he felt like he needed to do this. Maybe the motivation stemmed from the brainwashing with which Abe had provided him the day preceding. Maybe the motivation stemmed from his shame in never having turned his daydreaming into reality. Maybe, though, his motivation stemmed from something entirely different, something that lay unseen over the horizon.

Whatever the source of the motivation was, it was driving him, pushing him forward and through his shaking nerves. It was helping him pack up and get in the car. For better or for worse, he would keep going, and set his mind to the task ahead—like he had the time his father had left him to figure out how to uproot that oak tree in their front yard. At only fifteen years old, it had taken him the whole day, and as he had gone to bed that night, he had been dead tired, but he had done so in an atmosphere of glory and accomplishment. Mike hoped this journey would not prove to be different.

Before the sun was high enough to clear the trees on the east side of the road, the two were off again, heading north into the unpopulated ruggedness of Yellowstone country. Mike, who would have normally been enthralled by the scenery appearing before his window, had his eyes directed straight ahead. He hardly heard the Grateful Dead CD that Abe had since popped in, and to which he was now beating the steering wheel.

For what seemed like the first time, Abe turned over to survey the look on Mike's face, which had retained its dead nature from the morning. Abe interrupted his humming to soberly state, "I'm sorry what I told you last night came across as overwhelming. I'm sure that this whole escapade is a lot for you to take in, and I'm sure you are probably pretty nervous."

Abe paused to await Mike's confirmation or denial. Mike did not respond, but continued staring straight forward. Abe took the lack of response for what it was and continued.

"I feel it's important that you are as informed on the subject as I am, though, because, like it or not, you're the main character in this story, and after you have the golden emblem, you will be the one in charge of everything."

Mike gave Abe the pleasure of revealing a ripened look of concern. Abe simply laughed. "Don't worry too much—I will always be there to provide you with any information you need." Abe smiled weakly. Mike could not mimic the expression, for the reassurance only dulled the edge that had just been formed back to its original shape.

"So that is exactly what I want to continue to do now, if that is alright with you. I would like to let you know our plan of action."

Mike swallowed and cleared his throat. "Yeah, I would like to know."

Abe took a deep breath and settled into his seat. For a moment, he opened his mouth several times to begin, but stopped, seeming to be searching for the right angle. Mike did not take that positively. His discomfort stirred within him as Abe finally caught his tongue and ran with it. "I hope your mind is open to this, because this may seem extremely strange, but just keep in mind what I said about strangeness."

Mike smirked. "It does not mean it's impossible," he lazily chimed in unison with Abe. "Yeah, I know. Lay it on me, I'm ready for it."

Abe smiled. "Before anything, we must acquire more information—

information that has, up to this point, been impossible for me to gather. Now that you're here, and will soon have the emblem, that will change and we will be able to talk to previously unavailable people."

Mike did not appreciate Abe's ambiguity. "Come on, Abe, I told you I'm ready for it. You've already blown me away enough. Where are we going?"

Abe's smile continued to crescendo. "We are going back to the fifth century into the Northwestern Elfish Realm."

Maybe Mike wasn't ready for it, but he did not know how anyone with any sort of sanity could be. He felt as if every existent sense of logic and reality was being violently flushed out of his mind. With a look of disbelief, Mike turned to Abe. "What?"

Abe nodded to confirm what he knew that Mike had heard and said, "Yep. We are going back in time."

With that, the dam had burst. Mike threw up his arms in a flood of frustration. "Abe, hold on a minute. That's a little too far out for me. I believed you about the emblem. I believed you about the demons. I even believed you about me being the chosen one, even though I still have absolutely no idea what that means or why that has to be me. But time travel? Time travel is impossible. Man is not even close to understanding the concept of time."

Abe put his hand on the shoulder of his hyperventilating victim. "Hey, hey, calm down. Crazy as it may seem, it's true. It's got to be true. All of my research points to it. The fifth century, right after the fall of the Roman Empire, is a period of power vacuums and the best time to establish a proper foundation for Western Civilization.

"You're right that we do not understand the concept of time, but that does not mean we cannot work with it. How long has man understood the concept of radiation? Does that mean that anyone before did not benefit from the warmth of the sun? We don't have to understand something to make use of it.

"From what I have studied about the emblem, when it is in the hands of the chosen one, it will take him and all the other chosen ones with him back to the time where it is most needed. We cannot fix society as it now is with the emblem—the problems are too well established and too huge.

We have to go back in time to the setting of the root of the problem. That setting is in England at the time directly following the fall of the Roman Empire. As far as I know, when the Goths sacked Rome at the beginning of the fifth century, the final separation of the emblems, which had last been held by the Hebrews hundreds of years earlier, occurred, and that was when society went off the deep end. If all of the emblems are restored to a new center of civilization, say London, for example, a new history can be written, and through cause and effect, the entire western world can be what it always should have been."

"What about the elves, though?" Mike said, completely ignoring Abe's explanation. "Abe, elves are characters in stupid fairy tales. This is no fairy tale, Abe; this is real life. I'm not so sure whether you can differentiate between the two."

The jab did not seem to affect Abe. Calmly, patiently, he explained with a question of his own. "How well do you know your history, Mike?"

Mike shrugged. "Fairly well."

"How much does history speak about fifth century North America?"

Mike did not answer.

"Exactly. We know next to nothing about it. The sooner you catch onto the idea that our perception is extremely limited, the easier this is all going to be for you. I am a few steps ahead of you right now because I have studied these things my whole life. I know my history better than most anyone. I have a feeling that I know just about as much about the Dark Ages as I do about our modern ages. I am open to new information. I do not dismiss myths as quickly as the rest of the world.

"But as far as experiencing all of this, I'm in the exact same boat as you are. I don't know for sure if this emblem will actually take us back in time. I don't know if there is really a Northwestern Elfish Realm. All I can do is run with the idea that these myths are true based on the evidence I have received, and until I find out otherwise, my mind will remain unchanged.

"I'll tell you what, though. We will find out tomorrow morning whether all of this is true. If it is all a farce, I will pay you generously for your time, and return you to your family farm."

Mike sighed as Abe finished. Abe looked over at him soberly. "Does that sound fine to you? Or would you like me to turn around right now and take you back?"

Mike looked back over at his new partner. He knew how much this meant to Abe. It amazed Mike how much effort Abe had spent in pursuing something that he did not even know was true. *What if he was not right? What if all the writings on this emblem he had found were some colossal joke? What if Abe had spent his whole life devoting himself to something that yielded disappointment in the end?* The least Mike could do for such a devoted man was to continue on another few days, despite his fears and doubts. He felt like such a sincere man as Abe deserved such a chance. This, he realized, was the main source of his motivation.

"No, keep going." Mike conceded. "Explain why we need to go visit this *Realm.*"

Abe smiled. "My research states that we must find them so that they can guide us to the bearer of the emblem of wisdom, who will be our guide from then on out."

Mike almost chuckled in spite of himself but forced himself to take Abe at his words. "Well I guess that's pretty important."

Abe patted Mike on the back. "Thanks for sticking with me, Mike."

At those words, the conversation ended. Abe resumed his casual accompaniment to the music after a few minutes, seeming again to be carefree. Mike turned his attention back out toward the 70 mph scenery unfolding in front of him. Right now, the road was fairly straight and the surrounding countryside was relatively open around them, but there lay rugged landscape of mountains in the distance. Within no time they would be closed in by canyons and become blind, forced to witness a new scene at every turn. They would not be able to keep up their pace but would have to slow down and be more calculating in the turns and bends in the road.

Mike's thoughts rushed like the scenery, flowing into and out of his consciousness, repeating like a mad carousel. Today, he had been given a new subject to chew on. *Time travel? Was it possible?* Such a concept had been every sci-fi geek's dream ever since the concept of sci-fi had been dreamed up. The past was a limitless unknown, interrupted only by the meager histories provided in books. It was more than what such books could ever portray, for 1776 had been as real to George Washington as 2000 was to Abe or himself. It was this reality after which such dreamers sought, and it was virgin territory for the modern world of adventurers.

Sci-fi or obscure reality? Who was the judge on such a thing? If there was one thing that had stuck in Mike's head from the past twenty-four hours of craziness, it was the concept of man's limited perception. God alone could know of the reality or fiction of such things, and, based on past experience, He did not seem too eager to reveal such a truth to mankind. Nobody could ever disprove it; only give an affirmative, thorough experience.

Am I to break the barrier? Are we to be the ones who finally find out the truth of such dreams? Before yesterday he would not have hesitated to shake off the possibility as impossible, but before him sat a level-headed man claiming all of these crazy ideas—unheard of, unacknowledged by the rest of the world. *What other motive would he have? Has he grown to be so obsessed with this myth that the difference between myth and fiction and truth and reality has become blindingly obscure?*

Other thoughts turned upon himself and how he had been sucked into this. *Was I chosen solely for my sheltered, and therefore naïve, and therefore often gullible nature?* In the past, people had taken advantage of him for possessing such traits, and there was no reason that this case could be any different. But again, what was the motive? It seemed too big of a joke to play, especially on someone who was not even more than an acquaintance.

And the elves: little men in green suits, working for Santa in his workshop, feminine races of men who had special powers and supported Frodo's mission to destroy the Ring. Elves were the dream characters of bookworms and RPG nerds throughout the world. *Were they right all along? Was it fantasy or again, simple, obscure reality?*

Mike and Abe were pulling into the mountains again, and, sure enough, they were forced to slow down and take the blind curves as they came. Point-blank, rocky outcroppings replaced the openness of the valley plain as Mike wanted to laugh out loud at the whole situation. *Time travel. Hah!*

he thought to himself. *We're going back in time to the 'Northwestern Elfish Realm'. At least it will be an interesting next 24 hours, regardless of what happens. Even if it isn't true, Abe will be revealed for what he really is.*

Mike was only partly correct, for the first half of those 24 hours was extremely dull. The country heading up to Banff was beautiful, but not for such a long period of time. Mike's eyes remained riveted out his side window, but only because it was out of either that or out of the windshield. When Abe and Mike had raided Wal-Mart, Mike had not had the longevity of the trip in mind. What Mike would have done for a book of Crosswords or Word Searches would have been almost shocking. Neither of them were the biggest of talkers either. Mike tried to get more information on their reasons for visiting the elves, hoping to strike up conversation again, but Abe simply stated that he had told him all that he knew and the conversation was over as soon as it began.

Mike pondered on the nature of his new partner as the truck swerved in and out of the canyon curves. Abe seemed to be a man given to either extensive inner reflection or plain and simple mental apathy. Mike figured the former was more likely. Similarly, Mike, himself, was not the type of person to initiate long, invigorating conversations with anyone. They talked a little of music, and Mike found out that Abe was a large fan of bluegrass and jam bands, but the words had only broken the silence a little while. Again that conversation had ended as quickly as it had started and the cab had again reverted to its initial silence.

The sun cast long shadows as they commenced the ascent to their destination. The sun slowly, steadily set over the mountains to the west, creating a grand silhouette that overshadowed the thickly pined terrain of the northern woods. It was alien country, much different than the black, flat, Snake River Plain.

"Well, here we are," Abe stated matter-of-factly.

"Yeah, I guess so," Mike said. "Finally." Despite the casual nature of the comment, the butterflies were stewing in his stomach. This was the apex, the moment of truth. As Abe continued to wind through the park, fully intent on some destination within, Mike looked back behind them. *What if everything* is *true?* The pathway behind them revealed itself surely, constantly, predictably, *but what about in front? What's around the next bend?* There was a false comfort in looking back, because he knew that if there was an obstruction ahead, he would not know what was coming or when it would hit him.

Mike turned to face ahead again. "So is the golden emblem up here somewhere?"

Abe nodded. "I hid them as best as I could—less chance of them getting stolen than if I had carried them down with me to Idaho. For some reason, evil men have always been able to sense them, they've always been drawn to them."

Mike was confused, however. "Them?"

Abe simply smiled as Mike desperately struggled to put the pieces together. Up to this point, they had simply seemed to be revolving around each other separately. They retained their course, even though they stammered in an effort to bend toward each other. "What do you mean by them?"

"There is a certain order in which we are to gather the emblems, for one will depend on another. There is only one emblem that is not dependent on any other, and the golden emblem is not that one."

Abe did well to keep the pieces from bonding. He continued this liberty as he looked over at Mike. "Can you guess which emblem it is?"

Mike laughed in frustration, which was feeling ironically natural to him by now. "Not a clue."

"Knowledge, Mike. Knowledge. The emblem of knowledge is the primary virtue. Nothing worthwhile can be done in ignorance. We now have control of two emblems and tonight they will both be in the safe possession of their bearers."

The pieces seemed to jump into place for a split second but scattered again in the same rhythmic sequence they had been following ever since Abe had come into Mike's life. Abe was smiling. Mike frowned, thought a second, and looked around in the dying light. There was absolutely nobody around. "You've found the bearer of knowledge?"

"He's been with me all along. I just did not notice him at first."

Either Abe had conveniently left this man out of the story or... suddenly the pieces fit. Mike about jerked out of his seat. "Wait... you're..."

Abe smile evolved into a laugh. "It was the emblem of knowledge that I discovered while trekking in dunes in central Turkey, out in the middle of nowhere. I simply stumbled upon it, Mike, the first one to do so in 1500 years—it was destiny. I was to be the bearer of knowledge. I thought about it afterwards. Like I said before, the demon of ignorance had worked hard on me my whole life. It took my whole young life to overcome it. Why do you think I told you my personal history so extensively?"

Mike suddenly understood. Knowledge versus ignorance. Abe had qualified himself as the bearer of knowledge with his unique introduction.

At that moment, they again pulled off the main road and proceeded to hike down the knoll to a gulley touched only by wildlife, the occasional adventurer, and God himself before the departure of Eden. Methodically, Abe walked directly over to a rock and with a strength that only could have been fueled by his elation, lifted it to reveal a little manmade hole. He reached in and pulled out two six inch long, one inch diameter, baton-like bars of solid metal, one in each hand. The left he kept for himself; the other he held out toward Mike. Mike, now almost mesmerized by some force of its presence, reached out and grabbed hold of it. Its feel was heavy and surprisingly warm. Mike tossed it over his hands and felt of a sort of energy pulsing from within its smooth edges and minute engravings. Abe had been true to his word so far. He was now in possession of the golden emblem.

Chapter 4

Yawning, Mike unzipped the door to his tent and stepped outside. The cool of the morning left a mist hanging near the forest floor, and he could only see about forty feet into the forest before it became a background of solid white. A slight breeze blew in the air, moving the wisps of vapor through the camp in gentle waves. Mike smiled and soaked in the moment. Mist was like a holiday treat to a person from his parts, where the climate was always thirsty, and Mike took the moment to simply stand still and watch it progress across the scene. It was completely silent, and seemed to move as a ghost. Mike chuckled to himself. *Or a demon.*

Indeed, the stories of the past two days themselves seemed like ghosts to Mike now. They seemed lost in the past, for he had slept soundly last night, much more soundly than he had in a long time. *It's the fresh air,* he told himself. *There's nothing like sleeping in a tent to bring you back down to earth.* Mike recalled how the world had spun in circles for him the past two days. He no longer felt dizzy though. For some reason, he felt okay now.

Perhaps it was because nothing had happened after he went to bed last night. There had been no weird light sequences or spinning spirals or anything out of the ordinary that would have seemed to accompany the time travel that Abe said they could expect. Everything about him was just as concrete and tangible as last night. The sun rose upon the trees and would soon burn off this mist with its late summer shine; the pined woods echoed with the songs of birds; everything seemed to continue on in its normal course. Mike did not feel any different either, unless, of course he considered his change in mood.

His comrade was not up yet. Mike looked around. Either the man was still in his tent or he was off somewhere, invisible beyond the curtain of white. He could possibly be exploring or gathering wood for a breakfast fire, seeing that they had not made a fire last night. Either way, it was not important. Mike figured Abe would either be back or up soon. In the mean time, he would sit down on the log he had sat on last night, relax, and enjoy the morning.

Mike stretched methodically and set to looking for that log. After searching for a few minutes, though, he could not find it. *Funny thing*, he thought to himself. *Perhaps the mist is disorienting me a little more than I thought.* Mike smiled, shook his head disappointedly at his failure, and settled for a nearby rock instead.

The birds continued to sing as the sun slowly climbed higher in the sky. Mike focused his attention on a few ants moving methodically over the soft needles on the ground, carrying seeds and bits of other treasures to their hidden home. *They're quite interesting creatures*, Mike thought to himself as he placed his finger in one of the ant's paths. The ant stopped for only a moment, then sought out a detour. Mike smiled and did it again, watching the ant naively repeat itself. The entertainment only held Mike's attention for a little while, though, for his stomach was getting louder and louder in its demands. Abe was still not back and Mike decided to search out the snacks in the truck that still remained in abundance. With an insincere groan, he pulled himself up to walk over to where they had parked the truck last night—up the hill and just out of sight of their tents in the waves of mist.

At least he thought it had been parked just out of sight. Mike looked around him. There was no vehicle around. This time he was *sure* that he had walked in the right direction. He expressly remembered Abe parking at the edge of the hill and shining the headlights overhead on the leaves of the trees so they could set up camp. He could not even find the road now.

Only slight concern emanated from Mike as he went back over to Abe's tent and shook it. Mike waited a moment for a response. The shaken tent remained silent. *He must have gone somewhere. Why and where would he go without me, though?* Mike shook the tent again.

"Wha—" a voice groaned from inside.

Mike almost jumped out of his shoes. Quickly registering the meaning of Abe's presence, Mike answered in exasperation, "Abe, someone's taken the truck!"

Mike heard quick shuffling from inside the tent. Within a minute, Abe was frantically opening the door to his tent. After pulling his legs out, he quickly made his way over to the exact place where Mike had just looked. Like Mike, all he found was the same barren piece of ground. He ran a few steps one way, looked around, ran a few more steps the other way, looked around again, and came back. Mike studied Abe's face, hoping that he could shed some sense on the issue. The expression on Abe's face could not quite be described as exasperation or panic, but of curiosity.

"Where's the emblem?" he asked.

"It's in my tent," Mike answered, confused at both Abe's question and the calm manner in which he asked it.

"Go and get it."

Mike obeyed and ran over to his tent. He did not understand what the disappearance of the truck could mean, but it sounded like Abe had something on his mind, and he was not about to question Abe's commands. He reached inside his tent and into his bag, where he had placed the emblem the night before. After fumbling around for a few seconds, his hands grasped hold of it and he felt a wave of strangely surprising relief.

Mike brought it out to Abe, who took it from him and began examining it very carefully, rolling it over and over in his hands, studying its every detail. Mike did not understand. It looked exactly the same as it had the night before.

"What are you looking for?" Mike asked after a moment of confusion.

"It's happened," Abe said quietly. He had either failed to hear Mike's question, or he had completely ignored it.

"What? What's happened Abe?"

"All of it is true." Abe was now boasting a grand smile. "Everything I told you is happening."

Mike furrowed his eyebrows. "What do you mean? How do you know?"

"The emblem—" Abe started, "it's a lot less scratched. That can only mean one thing."

Mike's breath caught. Abe laughed triumphantly.

Mike felt something strange bursting and surging within him; whether it was fear, shock, or excitement, he could not tell. Abe handed the emblem back to him and he slowly took it. Now that he held and examined it, it did seem different. It seemed to be almost glowing. *Could all of this really be true?* Mike still searched for that first breath as he continued surveying the bar of metal with sweaty hands. In the mean time, his stomach was doing somersaults and his teeth were biting his lip. *Abe knows this thing better than I do; Abe would recognize the difference in the amount of scratches.* Though Mike laughed at the thought of the concept, Abe's proposal was the only logical explanation for the vehicle's disappearance. There had been absolutely no one up here the night before, and Abe had made sure to lock the doors and keep his keys with him. That led him to wonder.

"But why just the car?" Mike asked.

Abe held up a finger. "We don't know that. I'm sure if we looked around, we would find that other things did not make the jump. I'm guessing that the emblem brought only those things which would be of use to us."

Mike stumbled over to his tent and his bag, where he had shed his watch the night before. After dumping out all the contents of his bag, however, it was nowhere to be found. His camera and his pistol also seemed to be missing. All that he had just received was gone. In any other situation, he was sure he would have gotten angry, but now he simply fell back and shook his head in disbelief.

Although the mist had begun to disappear with the rising of the sun, it seemed as strong as ever now. After feeling much like a paperweight to his sleeping bag for a long moment, Mike pulled himself out of his tent and looked over in the direction of Abe, who was materializing out of the remains of the fog. Mike could no longer do anything but laugh.

"I guess it *is* true then," he muttered.

Abe smiled and nodded as if the concept was a common encounter. "Yes sir. Everything I told you is true. We are back in time." With that, Abe's mind seemed content to move on. He broke his expression and turned again to Mike, who sat with distant eyes and mouth slightly ajar.

FORTH FROM EDEN

"Are you hungry?"

Mike looked at him strangely. "Are you kidding?" he challenged, "I think I'm going to be sick to my stomach."

But his emotions did not show it. Mike was laughing again. The laughter was coming harder and harder by the second, though completely against his will. In truth he was horrified. He was scared out of his wits. There was no going back now—he had missed his chance. The ship he had climbed aboard was now out to sea and the water looked a lot more treacherous now than it did from shore. The reality of adventure suddenly seemed much less glorious than the prospect of it. Dreaming was safe back in the comfort of his Idaho farm. So was watching a movie.

This was different. The sun before him warmed his face. The scent of pine reached his nose. The dream was alive. Mike was in the movie. While he would not trade this particular moment for daydreaming, he had no control over the storms of the future. He shivered just thinking about it, for he would not be able to wake up from it or skip the scene. This was all real. He stood in a place about which he knew nothing, in a time about which he knew even less, with a man that he had just barely met, and in pursuit of a quest that he could never even begin to understand. There was no stamp of guarantee on this package; nor was there a return policy.

But here he stood even so, and there was nowhere to go but forward.

Abe joined Mike in his laughter, though Mike doubted that it could have been of any empathetic nature. "Sick, huh? Understandable. I'm not very hungry either." Then, without hesitance, Abe clapped his hands together. "Well, there's no time to lose then. Let's pack up camp and get going. Just remember, we can only take what we can carry. The emblem has screened us of a few things already, but we may have leave behind even more."

Mike simply looked at him. Abe, who seemed to be getting better and better at reading him, seemed to recognize the source of his hesitance. "Everything is back where we left it. There is nothing we can do about it now but let it all sit. Besides, things like the truck wouldn't have done us much good anyway. According to my research, we should be relatively close to the Elfish Realm—no more than a few miles."

"Yeah?" Mike asked, trying desperately to play along with this live fairy tale. "Did your research describe what this place is like?"

Abe shrugged. "One can only gather so much information in the modern times about the past. From what I have found, though, I believe the Elves to be the most educated and advanced society on earth at this moment. They have their own sets of emblems, and they have had them together and in order for a long time now. As far as I know, we will be staring at paradise, at what our society could one day become."

Mike discovered a slight twinge of excitement well up inside of his twisting vitals and his eyes widened slightly at the feeling. It felt good. He needed that. The whole idea, like everything else these past three days, was absurd, but he needed a line to hold on to. The idea of seeing paradise, whether it was true or not, was at least something. Mike directed himself over to his tent to gather up the few belongings he most desired to keep.

"Let's hike up to a point where we can get an all-encompassing view." Abe directed as Mike approached him and waited for his call. "I have a feeling that it will help us find something that will lead us to the realm then."

Mike agreed, for from where they stood, he could only see a portion of their surroundings, though by now, the mist had blown out. They could now see that the trees continued on in an infinite layer, sustaining the crystalline freshness in the air. Both Mike and Abe could now see, through minor breaks in the trees, exactly where they had camped last night. They stood on the side of a foothill, overlooking a transparent, blue lake in the valley below. Behind them, the Rockies rose to the sky amidst the eagles, and likewise touched the heavens with their bald heads.

The two proceeded to walk up the hillside on a floor of matted pine needles. Mike noticed that there were no paved roads in sight—his memory had not, in fact, served him wrong.

While they were walking, Mike turned to Abe. "So how did you find out about the elves in the first place? There's obviously nothing in written history about them."

Abe nodded. "That's right. I actually had no idea about them until I found the emblem of knowledge. It explains about them and their general location in the inscriptions. Here, let me show you."

Abe pulled out the emblem of knowledge, which he had stowed in his pocket. He held it out to Mike's curious eyes.

"If you take a look here, you will see very tiny inscriptions in the gold, tiny enough to require the use of a magnifying glass."

He handed Mike the tiny magnifying glass that he had also pulled out of his pocket. Mike put the magnifying glass up to his eye and pulled the emblem in close. He could only recognize one of the sets of characters, which seemed to be Greek.

"What are all of these characters?" Mike asked, giving it back to Abe.

"There're four sets of characters here: Semitic, Egyptian, Greek, and Aramaic. Each set stems from writings of the different civilizations which have held the emblem. Only the most useful information is written on it, for obvious reasons. Among that information is the location of Elfish Realm, written by the Hebrews, which were the last ones to put the emblems in order."

"So you know all of these languages?" Mike asked.

"I had to learn them after I discovered them on the emblem. The power of the emblem made it easy, though."

Mike nodded; things were starting to make more sense. "So there's information here regarding me, then."

"That information is on the golden emblem. It was actually written by the earliest Semitics. It was known, ever since the beginning, that there would be a time when the civilization of mankind fell like it had never fallen before. The Semitic leaders knew what would become of man even back in their time, 3000 years before Christ. The writings contain directions for a chosen one to redeem the goodness of society: what to look for, where to look, and how to know when he was found."

"What does it say?" Mike asked, pulling out his own emblem. He was more curious than ever now.

Abe reached out his hand to take the magnifying glass and emblem. He had to squint, even with the help of the glass, as he slowly began to translate. "*The chosen bearer is a male youth, and possesseth the name of both the archangel and the Son of God. He hath been raised in the roots of innocence and obscurity, and worketh the land. He liveth in the wilderness, the journey of a week north and west of a sea of salt. He will step out of his path to show mercy to his seeker, and though he will be hesitant, he will penitently pursue the mission not for his own glory, but for the glory of God."*

Mike looked at him. "So from that information you were able to narrow it down to me?"

Abe smiled. "The prophecy fits, doesn't it?"

Mike thought about it. His name, his household location, his upbringing, the night in the hills with the ATV's, his entire feelings toward this escapade—all of them were perfect matches. One thing did not sit right with him, though. "Yeah, but what about the time difference? Did they know that they were describing a person from the twenty-first century, even as they prophesied for the fifth century?"

Abe pursed his lips, but seemed to stand in firm resolve. "I don't know. Like I said before, I was the first person in 1500 years with access to the emblem of knowledge. The mission could not have occurred without it. Don't you see, though, Mike? Despite all that, it works. I did not travel back in time until the golden emblem was in your hands. You're the chosen one for the fifth century, regardless of when you were born, regardless of whether that was originally how it was supposed to be. This morning's events are proof of that."

Mike sat silent, not sure how to handle the flattery thrust upon him. He was inclined to cast it away like a hot potato, but he could not argue with Abe's reasoning. *How else could they describe what had happened this morning?* Whether he liked it or not, he had to run with the ideas as facts.

Mike wanted, more than anything, to scoff at it—it may not have meant him at all, but he had been a big enough sucker to agree to it. His hands gripped onto the object of his conflict, the golden emblem. What happened next was really bizarre. All of a sudden he felt strangely comfortable. He did not know how to describe the feeling, but it felt right. He felt as if he was in the correct place at the correct time; he felt as if he really was the correct person, though he wished, more than ever, that he was not, for the entire idea of what needed to be done also descended upon him.

Nevertheless, he had crossed a sort of threshold, and Abe seemed to be able to sense it. Abe smiled calmly. "See why this mission is so important?"

Mike turned to Abe. "Yeah, I think I do."

At that moment, they reached an outcropping of rock upon which they were able to get a full view of the valley below. It was sublime. Mike had heard of the beauty of the Canadian Rockies before, but this was larger than life. No photographer, no calendar could capture the awe and wonder that welled up inside his spirit at what he saw. The crystal blue lake looked even more magnificent in its entirety, and the deep green carpet of pines provided a perfect contrast to both it and the grey mountains that rose above it. The land seemed virgin, undisturbed from the way God had originally intended for it to be.

There was, in fact, one disturbance, though a very subtle one, which became apparent only upon closer examination. Squinting, Mike noticed a thin break in the trees close to the lake. The line was unnatural and constant, running directly north and south. Abe saw it just about the time that Mike did, and both of their eyes followed it first south, then north, trying to find evidence of any form of life. From what Mike could tell, there was nothing around.

"Looks like a road," Mike conjectured.

Abe nodded.

"What should we do?" Mike asked after a moment of examination.

"Let's walk down to it. Hopefully we'll run into travelers before long. Like I said before, I have no reason to believe that the emblem would put us too far away."

Mike nodded and the two started making their way down the hill to the lake below. All was very quiet, for not only were the pine needles under their feet all but completely silent, but they also muffled any other sort of sound. Mike looked around him, unable to utter a word. Although he had grown up in the country, there had not been too many areas he could go where ranches or fences or sounds of tractors pulsing and cattle lowing in the distance did not interrupt the setting. He wished he could have spent more time doing nothing but relaxing here, daydreaming, wondering about the world, but relaxation would have done him injustice, especially when he was living in a daydream.

It only took an hour or so to get down to the valley floor. The road appeared right where they expected it, down where they could smell the greenery of the lake. The trees suddenly broke to reveal a flat, stone-paved thoroughfare, about the width of a modern two lane highway.

Abe and Mike walked out of the trees, and both caught their breath at what they found. About fifty feet away lay gathered a group of people which were thin and short, yet very handsome and inviting. Both the men and women wore long, flowing robes of a uniformly plain, yet colorful, style that hid their legs and feet, as well as caps which hid their hair. If these beings were, indeed, the elves about which Abe had spoken, Mike was surprised that they did not appear any different from any other human being, other than their size and style of clothing, of course. Even so, Mike had never seen such a group before.

What struck him most, though, was their apparent lack of surprise at the two's sudden appearance.

Mike surveyed the group again in mild awe. There seemed to be one among them who did not appear particularly stronger than the others, but carried his presence as if he did. He was the one that spoke up first. But as he spoke, Mike immediately realized that there was no way to understand him. The language flowed as it came off his mouth, like a romantic language, with lots of vowels and unimpeded rhythm, but it all sounded like gibberish to him.

Mike looked over at Abe. Abe was enthralled by what he saw, but seemed to be just as lost as far as the language went. Abe looked back at him and shrugged, then turned to the man and said, first in English, then in Latin, "We do not understand you."

The elf, who seemed a little bit frustrated, not at them, but at the situation, tried repeating himself a little slower and a little more clearly, but realized as he was doing so, that the speed and clarity was not going to make a difference. At that moment, a very old looking elf who walked with the support of two younger aides pushed him aside.

"You do not speak our language do you?" the old man questioned in English.

"No, we do not," Abe answered meekly.

"That is to be expected. We know who you are, and we have been waiting for you."

Mike raised his eyebrows. *How would they have known that we were coming?* Mike and Abe had popped out of the future. *How do they know English?* He looked over at Abe, but Abe held a look of intrigue rather than surprise.

"I am Yolath, third brother of Gonali, Patriarch of the Northwestern Elfish Realm. He has asked that we come here to greet you on your journey and to provide for your needs. He then requests your presence before him at the royal feast tonight. Will you accept this offer?"

"We will, if it pleases you," Abe answered.

The old man named Yolath smiled. He muttered something to the foremost elf, the one who had first tried speaking with them. The elf turned, clapped his hands, and barked out an order to a group of youth carrying an empty litter. The young elves walked over to where Mike and Abe stood and let the litter down. The head elf then smiled and directed them into the litter.

Mike looked at Abe, who was climbing in without the least bit of hesitation, and followed him up. The litter was lightweight and practical, but, at the same time, shaded and comfortable. It was big enough for just the two of them, each sitting opposite of one another.

After that, the party wasted no time in making their way north along the road. The head man and Yolath got into the foremost litter and it led out, leaving Mike and Abe with relative privacy. As they plodded along on top of the backs of the elves, Mike chuckled and shook his head at what was happening to him. He watched as the temples of the youths beaded up with sweat. They had known Mike and Abe were coming. They had prepared themselves to receive them, and now Mike and Abe were floating along through the Canadian Rockies, being carried away to some paradise. For all the surprises that had descended upon him, this one was both the most intriguing, and the most cozy.

After a while Mike turned to Abe and asked him about the whole situation.

Abe seemed to be as amazed as Mike at it, but seemed to be able to offer some possible explanation. "It's the power of their emblems. I may be wrong, but I bet that that old man is their bearer of wisdom. From the research I've done, the bearer of wisdom is similar to what we would think of as a prophet. That must have been how he knew of our coming, and also how he knew our language." Abe paused and thought about the idea to let it soak in, and nodded after a moment. "In fact, that has to be the way, because English as we know it today was not even in existence during this time period. The English we know today won't be around for another 1000 years or so."

In any other situation Mike would have laughed and taken the English as a sign that their idea about time travel was a joke, but since there was so much else, he had to take Abe's words with relative gravity.

"So he's the one that will give us all the information we'll need," Mike projected.

Abe, though, shook his head. "No. He's not entitled to do so. His jurisdiction is over the Elfish World. We are on a mission for man. All he can do is guide us to the one that will bear the emblem of wisdom entitled to man."

"Do you think he already knows all of this?"

"Oh, I'm sure of it."

The mountains passed slowly on either side of the party as it made its way around the lake and into the range to the east. Mike did not mind the slow progress, it allowed him to pass the scene around in his mouth and suck all the taste he could out of it. The lake was still, interrupted only by the fish jumping out and touching the sunlight before falling back under the surface. Their ripples progressed outward to infinite yet infinitesimal size. The valley was silent, except for the occasional slap of a beaver off in the distance or the cry of a bald eagle overhead. Mike looked up at it and watched it glide swiftly, yet peacefully, through the skies. Everything had been moving so fast for him in the past few days that it felt refreshing to take some resting breaths.

Even so, the journey did not last more than a few hours. The sun had barely passed its apex by the time they ascended into the pass that Yolath mentioned would take them to their destination.

Mike fidgeted, feeling suddenly restless. Here he was, being carried to some ancient city that had never been known to the modern world. From what Abe had told him, the Realm of the Elves was as close to a perfect society as a society could get. He said that they *had it all together,* that their society was an actual El Dorado. *This is what will come to the world of men if we succeed in our mission*, Abe had told him. *And I'm sure that any hesitance or lack of devotion you may have toward this mission will dissipate as soon as you see what I'm talking about.*

Mike looked at each one of the elves in the group in a sort of reverent awe. Not one of them seemed to be a slave or even a servant. They all carried themselves with an air that demanded respect. They did not seem the least begrudged at their duties, whether it was walking alongside or under the litters. They all simply obeyed orders from the head man, who seemed to actually look to Yolath for his direction. Mike desperately wished that he could talk to each of them and ask them about their lives, countless questions about what he was shortly going to experience, but such could not be his privilege now.

"Are you excited?" Abe asked him, pulling his attention away from his surroundings.

Mike only let out a short, nervous laugh.

Abe chimed in with him. "You're not alone," he declared. "All my life, I have waited for this moment. And now, it's finally here and I can hardly believe it."

At that moment, he was forced to believe it. The party paramounted the rise and the sight of the next valley over was revealed. Mike's breath caught in his chest as he took in the view of the Northwestern Elfish Realm's capital city.

Chapter 5

For many long moments, Mike sat in the litter, looking out on the scene without even a blink. The party seemed to sense their feelings because they had stopped to let Abe and Mike take in the full view. It was not as if the city was anything spectacular by any modern standards. Mike had seen and knew well the skylines of Chicago and New York from pictures and movies, and this did not compare with the scale of those cities. In fact, none of the buildings were more than a few stories tall. It seemed fairly small to be a capital city, maybe big enough to fit 10,000 people.

There was something else in it, though, that caught Mike's eye.

The city seemed to be shining. At first Mike thought that the luster came from the sun, but soon realized that the source stemmed from the spectacle itself. Every building was of the purest white stone and perfectly clean. The entire city could have been a doll house, a handmade, showy, life size fairy castle. In the very middle of the city, there rose a central hall and courtyard of sorts that must have covered 20 acres. An aqueduct that flowed down from the mountains to the west drained into a great pool within, its cerulean glow reflecting the lightened sky.

Mike could not help but notice how green the city was as well. It seemed to be a living organism, breathing the freshness of its own air. Lawns of emerald grass complemented the buildings, and young, neatly pruned trees rose like silent sentinels above them. Even the rooftops breathed, being used as gardening spots, with small planters and hanging vines inching down the sides of the sparkling walls.

The roads were perfectly paved and emanating the same shade of white that the buildings boasted. They were extremely wide, giving the buildings enough room to breathe and allowing the sun to penetrate every corner. There would have been enough room for two lanes of cars, a bike lane, and two wide sidewalks on each side, although Mike did not see any evidence of vehicles. All he could spot were little specks, pulsing about their daily work with a passionate vigor.

From the scenery that surrounded the city, Mike gathered that most of the people that lived here were farmers. The valley which spread out before him was a checkerboard of wheat and cornfields, and endless lines of various orchards. It spread throughout the valley, fanning out from the borders of the city, uninterrupted save for a few stone service roads.

"It's amazing," Mike heard Abe say after a minute. Abe looked over at him and added, "Everything is in perfect order."

A slight grunt was all that Mike could get out in response. All other words had been drowned, like him, in the glory of the place.

The party had started moving again, and the view fell behind a cluster of trees. However, the two explorers, mesmerized at the sight they had just beheld, methodically turned their bodies in whichever direction the city lie, hoping to catch another glance at the sight. The city revealed itself again periodically as they descended, and even though their initial perspective of the city dissipated, their anticipation grew.

Within about an hour from the time the party reached the summit of the pass, Mike found himself before the gates of the city. They stood above him with open arms, beckoning him into their warmth. Mike's litter bade their request, and as he passed through them, he felt... *what could he call the feeling?* Excitement? Exhilaration? None of those words quite captured it. It was like coming home, but seeing that home through entirely different eyes.

As the party walked through the city, the people on the streets stopped to watch them pass. Mike took note that they all looked very similar in stature and clothing to the elves Mike had already encountered. Mike could not help but notice that the people did not bow down to worship the bearer of wisdom, like he had expected, rather they looked on at him in a sense of reverence and love. He returned warm smiles and waves to the crowd, not as subjects, but as friends. The people gazed on at Abe and Mike as well, no doubt due to their slightly different features, statures, and clothing. *Yet I don't feel uncomfortable*, Mike thought to himself.

They seemed to possess a love for them already; at least that was what came forth from them.

The buildings were just as grand as they had looked from afar. They were simple, yet beautiful in their simplicity. Mike could tell that the people took pride in the upkeep of not only their own homes, but of all of the buildings. Whatever industry took place inside was not apparent to the public. All of the grease and rust and dirt stayed in its proper place, if there was, indeed, a place for it at all.

It was not long before they reached the great building, or rather courtyard of buildings which marked the city center. The center was built up about ten feet above the city with great staircases highlighting each entrance, lending it a regal sort of presence. Pillars and arches marked the center's boundary as if a part of Greece. The party climbed the stairs without breaking stride as Mike peered out the side of the litter.

The southern end of the courtyard was open and boasted a great market of sorts, and Mike suddenly realized that this was where all of the commerce and trade of the city was carried out. People poured in and out of the square with baskets and satchels—some full, some empty. The place bustled with activity, yet it did not seem overly congested or dirty. *How can a place be so clean?* Mike asked himself again. *It's as if the grime can't even exist.*

The party walked on past all the clamor of trade. Mike would have liked to spend more time simply watching the people in the market, but it was not the market to which the party was heading. It was toward the great building that marked the north end of the market. "I'd assume that that is the main, governmental building," Abe said.

Mike nodded. Based on how this city seemed to be set up, such a statement made sense. "Do you suppose that we will be going to the royal feast right away?" Mike asked.

"I don't know," Abe said. "I never had access, of course, to any books on the culture of the elves, just legends. I'm not sure when they eat, what their habits are, anything really. I am as foreign to this as you are."

By now the caravan had stopped, and the grandeur of the main building, which looked to be a sort of palace, loomed before them. Its white stone seemed to shine with even more luster upon seeing it from up close, almost like it was on fire. Mike broke his open mouthed stare to notice that up ahead, Yolath's litter had been let down, and he was being helped over to where Mike and Abe's litter sat waiting. As he came to stand before them, he looked up at them with a hearty smile.

"I'd like to officially welcome you to what you would say in English is Utopia, the capital city of the Elves. You must forgive us for not having welcomed you at the gates, which is usually our custom, but we were given explicit orders to bring you directly to the Patriarch."

"Is this where he resides?" Abe asked in a sort of quasi-reverence.

"Yes, he is in his suite right now, awaiting your introduction. That time will soon come, but first, we will allow you to bathe and dress in Elfish robes, which I'm sure you will find quite pleasing. The high chief, Ganioid, will lead you to your quarters where you will find such accommodations."

The man who had initially tried to address them, Ganioid, bid them to follow but did not wait around to see if they actually would. Mike followed Abe out of the litter, and, after looking back at Yolath, who was still bearing the saintly smile he had initially shown, followed Ganioid into a sort of main hallway that bored itself into the core of the building's glorious face.

Mike and Abe walked down the hallway in silence, their mouths having been shut by the sights that met their eyes. The walls of the hallway were graced with artwork of the most ornate nature that had an air about it as old as time itself. The paintings and the carvings seemed to be a sort of history of the people: depicting wars and conflicts with beings much taller and more firmly built than themselves. Mike looked on as a story of silenced yells and cries of pain and victory arose like ghosts to his mind. A world of history that did not survive into the modern world sat before his eyes. *How much more happened that could not be depicted?* The lives of thousands had begun and ended in this society, each having its own battles, each having its own mural waiting to be painted. *So much more happened than this to make this place what it is.* Mike suddenly seemed to see that there were millions of stories undepicted that were just as important. The mural, however, did not fail to help Mike feel suddenly immersed into this world, a world that had overcome, a world that had everything important all figured out.

About fifty feet down the hall, Mike saw carvings of seven articles that looked very familiar, and these articles were brighter than any other object on the walls. They were each held by a regal looking elf, and from that point on in the historical mural, there were no more battle scenes, but pictures denoting the glory of cities, of families, of art, of education, of commerce and trade, and of scientific progression. Mike noted that Abe was just as drawn in as he was. The hallway ended and the three walked out, two of them feeling like they had passed through a portal with no return.

The great hall boasted three grand staircases—one directly in front of them, one to the right, and one to the left, which was the one to which they turned. As the group ascended its marble steps, the pure insanity of what Mike was experiencing struck him again. This was too vivid, too real, and too ongoing to be a farce. He was actually in the capital city of an Elfish nation, one that was seemingly perfect and far more socially advanced than anything he had ever seen in his life. He was actually entering his own private palace suite after having seen his partner enter the suite next door. He was actually stripping down and entering the pool of perfectly warm water to calm his muscles and purge his skin of the uncleanness that had built up in the past few days. Everything was completely true; the smell of wood smoke that fled from his now wet hair served as evidence—evidence from a fire that burned over 1500 years in the future.

When Mike had entered his suite, Ganioid had motioned over to what seemed like a sort of timepiece that ran off the sun and motioned when he wanted them to be ready. After examining how the timepiece worked, Mike conjectured that he had plenty of time to relax, for which he was glad. He finally felt that the initial terseness of the unfamiliarity of the situation had worn off, and he could finally breathe easier. It was not as if the situation did not still blow his mind, because it did, and he figured it probably always would to a degree. Nevertheless, he had come to peace with the matter, and all of the anxiety had given way to excitement and curiosity as to what would come next.

For the first time, Mike noticed a slight rose-like smell in the air. He looked to the side of the pool and noticed an open vial with a pink liquid in it. Upon seeing nothing else in sight, and highly doubting that the elves used only water to clean themselves, he poured a little of the liquid on his hand, mixed in some water, and rubbed his hands together. There was a slight lather, and as the scent of roses exploded in the air, his hands grew softer and cleaner than he could ever remember them being. The cleanliness, like a tingling feeling, increased gradually until the lather seemed to disappear, leaving his hands feeling like velvet. Upon such a discovery, Mike poured the contents of the bottle into the water and let it all soak into his dirty skin.

Mike took a deep breath and sighed slowly, inhaling the seconds with relish as they passed. In such a pensive state, he took the time to notice the room in detail. The bathhouse portion, a small eight foot by eight foot nook, was raised a few feet off the main part of the suite. The walls were decorated with softly shaped and cool colored patterns. In the ceiling sat two skylights that allowed the daylight to illuminate the room, as well as a vent to clear the steam.

Behind him was the actual bedroom, which was much more vibrantly decorated. The artwork was lively and bold, with oranges and golds and reds meshing together to give the room a sort of youth. The bed stood up against the wall opposite the bathhouse, and looked extremely comfortable. Off on the side of the room, next to the great window, was an open wardrobe that boasted a wide array of sizes and shapes of robes, whatever would best fit the needs and desires of the present guest. Other than these articles, the great timepiece on the wall opposite the window, and the couch directly below it, the room was relatively bare. The room, indeed, defied Abe's statement concerning camping versus hotel rooms, but, upon looking on his situation, Mike did not care.

Mike turned back around and let his mind slip into pure bliss. For all the stress and worry and sleepless nights and awkward days, this moment was worth it. Mike soaked himself for a noble amount of time, not bothering to think or wonder or worry about anything before pulling himself out and drying off.

After grabbing the cloth off to the side, which absorbed the moisture in a most efficient manner, Mike walked over to the wardrobe and surveyed what robe would be a best fit for him. Upon closer examination, he found that there were some robes that were heavier than others, most likely intended for the harsh winters. It was summer though, and quite pleasant at the moment, and so he chose the lightest style he could find—a dull, dark blue fine twine—and slipped it on. He felt a little awkward at first, for he had seen no signs of underclothing, but the robe fit well enough and he soon did not notice the difference. In fact, the whole robe was quite comfortable and gave him unimpaired movement of his whole body. *These elves have sure mastered the concept—the technology—of comfort,* Mike thought to himself as he walked around the room to get the feel of it all.

Mike was donning the cap in the same way in which he had seen the elves wearing them when a knock was heard at the door. Ganioid entered, not having waited to make sure whether Mike was dressed. He gave Mike a look as if to ask if he were ready, and upon Mike's affirmative return gesture, motioned for him to follow.

As Mike walked out into the hall, he found Abe bearing the same manner of garb as he. As the two marched down the hallway after Ganioid, Mike turned to Abe. "How are you doing?"

Abe could not help but let out a laugh. "I have never felt better. That bath has seemed to cure all the arthritis I used to have." Then, turning to Mike, he added, "These robes are not too bad either."

"Yeah, I think we look pretty good in them. It's just amazing they had our size."

Mike looked down to note that the robes did not quite reach the ground like they had on the elves.

"I'd imagine it's a size that isn't too common."

At that, Mike couldn't help but laugh at the truth of that statement. Mike could not help but notice that he had not seen one elf over five feet tall, more than a foot shorter than himself. At that moment, they re-entered the main hall, where Yolath waited for them with his ever-present smile. "Ah, I see you've found your robes. They were made especially for you. How do you find your accommodations to be?"

"They are very fine, thank you," Abe stated politely with a bow.

Yolath seemed distant from his gratitude and instead looked confused. "Why do you bow? Is this a custom of respect among your people?"

Abe seemed at a loss of words, for while it really was not a custom in America to do so, it almost seemed the appropriate thing to do, as if they were ambassadors to a Far Eastern country.

Yolath noticed the silence and proceeded to set Abe straight in a parent-like fashion. "It is not proper to bow to each other, for we are all equals. The only one to which we bow is our God. He is the only one that deserves our reverence. Instead, we look each other in the eye and simply give a slight, modest smile, which the receiver returns. Such gestures show mutual love, equality, and brotherhood towards one another."

Mike proceeded to carry out the eye contact and the smile. The smile came naturally, for it was a reaction to Abe's sheepish expression. Mike figured, however, that his time of embarrassment would come too, and so he did not poke too much fun at his partner. Yolath himself seemed to be understanding, for he completely dropped the issue as if it had not happened. Instead, he complimented Mike on his correctness.

"Good. Now you are ready to meet with the Patriarch. You have your emblems I presume?"

Abe proceeded to pull his out from a fold in his robe, while Mike suddenly got a sick feeling in his stomach. He had been so enthralled by the scenes that he had seen that he had completely left his backpack in the litter, the backpack which contained the emblem that Abe had worked so many years to try to find. Mike looked over at Abe, painfully recalling his explicit directions never to let the emblem out of sight.

Yolath must have seen Mike go pale, because he pulled out Mike's golden emblem. "I felt its presence in the bag you left in the litter. You have no need to fear, Mike; as long as the emblem is in the Realm, it is safe, but I must warn you, once you step out of these city gates, things will be different. So take good care of it."

Mike could not help but notice Abe's slightly nervous stare as Mike reached out and again took hold of the talisman. *He is completely justified in worrying,* Mike chided to himself. As Yolath bid them to follow him, Mike turned to Abe and said with all the soberness he could muster. "I promise that that will never happen again."

"That's what I like to hear, Mike," he replied with understanding. "Your apology is accepted."

As the two walked into the great dining hall, an overwhelming scent of food flushed over them, although none was yet visible. Instead, there sat a great, horseshoe-shaped table which seated a little more than two dozen elderly men and their wives, including Ganioid. There remained three empty seats, one of which sat right next to the man and woman in the center. The other two empty seats were found at each end of the horseshoe. Yolath proceeded to make his way over to the seat in the middle, and the two women on either side of the other two empty chairs stood up, pulled the chairs out, and motioned for Mike and Abe to each sit in one. As they proceeded over to their places, Mike noticed that a young boy had begun to accompany him. He looked over to see that another boy had done the same to Abe.

No sooner had they sat down than the man in the middle, who seemed to be the oldest, stood up and started speaking. Immediately, the boys began to translate into modern English. Mike looked over at his translator, who seemed to be about nine or ten. He wore an emotionless face and reiterated each word clearly and without accent:

"As Patriarch of the Northwestern Elfish Realm, I, Gonali welcome our guests of honor. They have been anticipated for many years now, and recently Yolath has declared that the time has arrived for them to come. They are to set forth on a divinely appointed mission to reclaim the virtue of our distant brothers across the ocean, men of the European World. We wish them all of our hospitality and comfort until the time arrives for them to depart on their journey."

For the first time, the Patriarch looked directly at each one of them and gave them that slight smile of which Yolath had spoken. Mike returned the gesture. Gonali then continued, and the translators relayed: "What do you call yourselves?"

Mike deferred to Abe, who stated his name. The Patriarch repeated the name and was then followed by the rest of the party. Then he turned to Mike and the same occurrence ensued.

"Welcome, Abe and Mike." The patriarch had stated this in English, and though there was a slightly slurred nature in his words, the meaning was distinct. That was the extent of his knowledge with their language, and as he continued in his native tongue, the translators were re-employed.

"Please accept this meal as our token of welcome to you, and afterwards, my brother and I shall like to meet with you privately."

At that moment, a whole parade of waiters marched into the room carrying hoards of breads and various boiled grains that could be compared to cooked rice or oatmeal. The platters were placed first at the places of the Patriarch, Yolath, and their wives, and afterwards at the places of the others. Mike thought it interesting that he and Abe were the last ones to be served, even though they were supposedly the guests of honor.

"Food is first served to the patriarch, the chiefs, and their wives," the translator told him, reading his thoughts. "The guests come next, and then the rest of the people." Mike looked up at him in surprise, astounded. "But since nobody else is here, you are served last."

Then, upon further examination of Mike's face, the boy added, "I presume your customs are not the same as ours."

"No, they aren't," Mike said in bewilderment. Then, feeling comfortable to speak his mind, asked, "How do you know my language?" The question was a poor representation of what he was really getting at, for it was the tip of an iceberg of questions that had arisen about this boy in the last five minutes.

"We are the students of Yolath," the boy stated matter of factly, referring to both himself and his peer, who presently conversed with Abe. "As of now, Yolath is the master of wisdom, but it is his responsibility to make sure there is a replacement for his position when he leaves this world. The emblem gives him one student every two years to personally tutor, and I was picked five years ago. Ever since he chose me, he has been teaching me your language, so I could be of service to you when you arrived."

"Well, you speak my language very well. What is your name?"

"Hanoth," the boy stated.

"Well thank you very much for your service, Hanoth. I appreciate it a lot."

The boy gave a strange sort of look, and did not seem to understand the practice of verbal gratitude, but he soon passed it off as another cultural difference and let the matter go.

Mike decided to dive in on the food, although he felt extremely guilty about eating in front of the boy, who simply stood there and watched him. His resolve only lasted a few minutes before he found himself offering him a slice of bread from his plate. To Mike's surprise, however, the boy adamantly refused. The more he insisted, the more the boy seemed offended at the offer.

"My time to eat is later. It is disrespectful to eat out of turn," the boy repeated, over and over, trying to help Mike understand that the offer was completely taboo.

Mike looked at the boy and saw a sincere look in his eyes. The offer had not even tempted the boy, despite the heavenly smell steaming out from it. "You really respect your elders, don't you?"

"It is treason to do otherwise."

"Treason?"

"Our family is our government. The Patriarch is my great-great uncle, the oldest uncle of my grandfather on my father's side. Yolath is also my great-great uncle."

"So this whole city is one big family?" Mike asked in astonishment. As good as the food had been, he found himself turning away from it to listen.

The boy nodded. "We all come from my great-great grandfather and mother Ganioid and Benala."

"But there must be ten thousand people in this town!" Mike said.

"Eight thousand, seven hundred and seven, as of yesterday," the boy iterated. "Ganioid had twelve sons."

"Wow, I'm the only child in my family," Mike said, although he was thinking out loud more than anything.

Nevertheless, Hanoth heard him and his eyes nearly popped out of their sockets. "The only child? That would be a disgrace in our culture."

"Really," Mike voiced, "That's the least of everyone's concern in my culture."

Mike's words got the boy's curiosity going. "What do you mean?"

Mike looked at him, trying to decide whether he really wanted to give him the details. "My culture's family situation is very different from here. Divorce happens casually, it is common for teenagers to willfully rebel, and the amount of illegitimacy is rising."

The boy was shaking his head now, trying to deny that such a thing could happen, and Mike suddenly felt sorry for having mentioned it. "You cannot be serious," he retorted. "Don't tell me they are that common, at least not without punishment. Such crimes can oftentimes be worthy of banishment here."

"Banishment?" Mike repeated. This education of differences seemed to be enlightening to both of them. "That seems pretty harsh."

"Why do you think so? The ruin of family order is the ruin of everything here. Our entire society would crumble if such actions became so common."

Mike let the words sink in as he thought back on his own distant world. He decided that it would probably be better if he ended the conversation with Hanoth. He did not want to put a rainy day into the kid's life, especially since he seemed perfectly content with the sunshine—him, along with everybody else in this place. Even as he thought such things, he could not help noticing all the laughing and jovial storytelling that was going on. From what Hanoth described, this society seemed to have very strict rules and standards by which to live, but ironically enough, they seemed perfectly happy—more so than he'd ever seen in anyone else. Of course, this lifestyle was all they knew, and a two-sided perspective could have changed things, *But would it really change in this case?* he thought. Mike felt a strange sort of attraction toward this society, even with his two-sided perspective.

Mike resumed his eating, for which Hanoth seemed glad. Mike could tell that he was feeling uncomfortable with the ideas Mike presented and did not want to pursue any further enlightenment on the subject. Mike joined the group in their feasting and he found the entree to be amazing. The breads and the meals of grain were fresh and sweet, and the courses of fruits and vegetables, followed by meats were delectable. Mike strove to take his time and let his tongue enjoy the taste, but ended up failing most horribly. As the meal ended, the chief that sat near Mike, a big, muscular being as far as elves were concerned, said something to him and laughed, as well as those who were in close proximity.

"He says that you have the appetite of a high chief," Hanoth said, laughing. He seemed glad to be back in the midst of his own culture. Mike smiled weakly with the face of an overstuffed child and turned to the chief to acknowledge the compliment. The chief laughed and heartily slapped him on the back.

As the plates were retired, the Patriarch stood once again and addressed the party. Hanoth resumed his post as translator.

"Sons and daughters, you are now excused from this feast. We must allow for the private departure of myself, Yolath, Mike, and Abe."

At that, everyone stood and proceeded out of the hall, talking and laughing to each other while they all went their separate ways. Within a minute, the only ones who remained were the Patriarch, Yolath, their personal helpers, Mike, Abe, and their two interpreters. Yolath summoned Mike and Abe over and dismissed the two boys. "I will be their interpreters. Go to the kitchen and help yourselves to as much food as your stomachs can handle."

Remembering what Hanoth had stated concerning verbal thanks, Mike consciously gave him the slight smile of gratitude, for which he had seemed to be waiting. Hanoth returned the gesture and ran off with his little comrade.

Abe and Mike then proceeded to walk over to where the two old men were standing. Yolath smiled and inquired, "Did you enjoy the meal?"

"Very much so," Abe stated. "Thank you very much." Yolath simply stared at him while Mike once again gave the customary smile. Again, he was not the one feeling the awkward gap between culture, and he admitted to himself that it felt pretty good. Mike would, however, make sure to enlighten Abe about the elves' feelings toward verbal gratitude that night.

"Well, we are glad," Yolath stated after a brief moment of silence. "We will now like to take you to the emblem room, and discuss your plans of action."

As they slowly followed the two men and their aides out of the room, Abe smiled over at Mike. This was the moment for which they had both been waiting.

Chapter 6

The two were slowly led down a hall which jutted off the main banquet room. The progression was slow, since both of the elves walked with the help of canes, giving Mike and Abe time to stop and gaze at the paintings that lined the corridor. The paintings here seemed to emit a different tone. They seemed a lot calmer. There were pictures of merchants selling their wares, of animals pulling wagons of grain, of people working in the hayfields, of students reading, of walks in the orchards, of celebrations and holidays. There were pictures of a type of sport they played here that looked almost like rugby. There were also depictions of funerals and of weddings. Birth, marriage, death. They were all depicted, each with a different beauty. They brought a warm smile to Mike's face, and feelings of excitement suddenly welled within his heart.

"I see that you are noticing the paintings," Yolath said without even turning around. "They were painted about a hundred years ago by our grandfather, Yanforn. He was a master of wisdom like myself, and is still revered to be one of the wisest elves of all time. He passed the duties of bearing the emblem of wisdom on to me, but I am afraid that I have not lived up to the reputation he left for the position."

Mike and Abe looked at each other and shrugged. In all honesty, they both seemed to be blown away at what they saw in everybody. At least, that was the way that Mike felt.

As they neared the end of the hall, Gonali spoke and Yolath translated. "My brother gives his apologies for the slow movement. He says that it has been harder to move around these past ten years."

"It's alright," Abe stated, though Mike could sense some tension in his voice. Mike had detected a slight restlessness in Abe ever since they separated to go to their rooms to get ready. If he had to guess, he would conjecture that within fifteen minutes of getting in that tub, Abe was out and dressed in his robes, sitting on his bed in between moments of pacing the bedroom.

Mike, however, was just the opposite. These last few hours had helped him forget everything else, including his anxiety about this whole mess, and this meeting would be sure to bring it back to mind. Mike finished Abe's sentence where Abe could not. "Just take your time."

"Mmm," Yolath mouthed, and laughed. "We are almost there anyway."

They turned a corner to find a burly elf, one of the burliest Mike had seen yet, standing beside a little room about six feet square. He smiled at the party, seeming to have been expecting them. Gonali gave the standard greeting, and then he and Yolath dismissed their aides and stepped into the room. Mike and Abe stepped inside as well, and immediately, the room began to rise. Mike, slightly startled, looked below to see the burly elf pulling down on a long rope. It was a man powered elevator. But even as burly as the elf looked, it did not seem...

"How is that elf supporting our weight?" Abe interrupted Mike's thought process as they rose higher above the ground. He seemed just as intrigued as Mike.

"Can't you see? He's really strong," Yolath said, laughing in a jolly sort of way.

"There's no way that..."

"We feed him the best foods," Yolath said again, continuing in his banter. But then, he stated, "The contraption is connected to a system of pulleys and sprockets that give him a 1:8 weight ratio. He is only supporting, as far as my guess in your weight system goes, about 100 pounds."

"Amazing," Mike said.

Immediately afterward, he regretted having given the elevator such glory, for what met his eyes at the end of their vertical journey made the elevator plain in comparison. As it came to a stop, Mike peered into a room that was glowing. Natural light came into the room, but it seemed like natural light emanated from the room as well, like the city, only more luminescent. The glory of the room only complemented this choreography of light. The walls were a jungle of vines of gold and silver and colored glass that formed intricate, continuous patterns, and the floor was a gentle sea of white velvet, glistening in its purity.

In the center of the room sat the emblems of the Elfish Realm arranged in a hexagonal shape and glistening in their glory upon a large, round table of glass. The golden emblem, a bar that resembled Mike's, ruled in the midst of the hexagon. Below the table burned a torch and gave the table an orange glow. This glow seemed to creep up into the emblems and cause them to shine—the same shine that fed the room—the same shine that fed the whole society.

"As you can see," Yolath started, "this is the room of the emblems. Here each of the seven emblems of virtue has sat for two thousand years, bringing virtue, and therefore keeping order and unity to the Realm of the Elves in the Western Hemisphere. You have seen the result in our society. This society is the longest running of its kind, and the facets of those virtues have been strongly interwoven into its culture.

"What you have seen here in the Realm, Mike and Abe, is what you need to achieve for mankind, who has never been able to hold such a standard for more than a few hundred years. Man is much more carnal by nature and very susceptible to the demons of the emblem of fire, which you see here below the table. Since the golden emblem and its satellite emblems are present, it is virtually powerless. It is only here to provide an opposition, and therefore a more complete definition, to the virtues that emanate from the emblems above."

At that moment, Yolath picked up the golden emblem and tossed it to Mike. Mike panicked as he instinctively reached out to catch it, fully expecting it to burn his flesh. To his great surprise, however, there was only a slight warmth to the emblem. In fact, Mike was not even sure it came from its temperature, for it seemed to supply power to his entire body.

"Intriguing," Abe mouthed as Mike tossed the emblem back to Yolath.

Placing the emblem back on the table, Yolath continued.

"I do not feel like it is necessary to outline the reasons of why this mission is so important to your society. You have lived in it. You know the issues that you are facing. I can tell that you are fully invested into the cause of reforming it. All I will do concerning this is salute you for your desires, for the task will certainly not be easy."

Mike was right about the reversion to anxiety—a little too right. He shifted uncomfortably back and forth in the pause that followed and could not help but notice that as Yolath had been speaking, his eyes had been directed solely toward him. *"Like it or not, you are the main character to this story."* Abe's words pounded through Mike's head, and he felt a headache coming on. He was the one upon whom the sole responsibility rested. Abe was there to help him; Yolath and the entire Elfish realm were there to support him; but it was to him that the glory or the blame would be accredited, depending on the events that would unfold.

Suddenly Mike began feeling very hot, and sweat began pouring down his temples and forehead. Yolath noticed the effect that the information had on him and motioned for him to sit down on the carpet. "It is only appropriate to feel the way you do, Mike. But remember the help that you are given. You have Abe, the bearer of knowledge, to help you with the cultural and societal barriers. He knows the way the mission is supposed to be run, and can let you know if something seems out of place. Also, before you do anything else, you will have your own bearer of wisdom to direct you and advise you as well."

Mike knew all this, but that knowledge still did not help his condition. He felt sick to his stomach. "You can breathe easily, Mike, for it is too late in the year to make the journey you need to make. You and Abe will wait here until the spring."

Mike could not, in his mind, determine whether that fact was a blessing or a curse. He did not know if he could stand the anxiety of waiting that long. The task would restlessly weigh upon him until it was finished or at the very least in progression. Even so, Mike did find himself breathing a little easier. Spring was many months off, and if he was to live as he lived today, he could accept holding off on the job. He could accept it quite calmly.

Abe, in the mean time, had taken on Mike's recently shed edge of tension. "Spring?" he asked. "There is no other way?"

Yolath shook his head. "It was to be this way from the start. You need some time learn about where you're going first."

"Where will we be going?" Mike asked.

"Across the land to the great ocean of the East. There, one of our ships will be waiting to carry you to the eastern hemisphere, down a river its people call the Avon, and into a village that bears a new stone church."

"That must be Bath," Abe interjected, thinking aloud.

Yolath smiled. "You will know it when you see it. Just outside the village you will find a young man—a farmer like yourself, who bears the name of the great Roman poet, Virgil. He will be painting a picture of wheat fields when you find him."

"Painting a picture of wheat," Mike repeated.

"But that is not important right now," Yolath reminded herding both of their wandering minds back to the Realm. "Pay attention to what you can learn from Abe. Abe will be your teacher."

Then turning to Abe, he said, "Abe, teach him the language of the men of the Avon. He must be able to communicate with the bearer of wisdom. Teach him about the culture and customs of the people. Help him understand everything he needs to know to fit in with the ways of the people with which he will be dealing."

Yolath then turned to both of them. "Aside from that, pay attention to what surrounds you. The more you experience this culture, the more you will be driven to succeed. You will find, if you immerse yourself in this culture here, that you will experience more happiness in these next few months than you ever have before."

"And the language?" Mike asked.

"Feel free to try to learn the language of our people, but know that it is not a priority. You will always have your interpreters with you when you need them."

Yolath turned to his older brother and asked him a question in the Elfish tongue. Gonali responded his in usual manner: shortly and curtly. Yolath turned to the two. "Gonali states that it will be best for you to keep the emblems here. That way, you will not have to worry about keeping track of them. You may access them any time that you wish."

Abe pulled out his emblem and handed it over to Yolath. He seemed almost relieved to do so, having felt the pressure of losing both of the emblems for quite some time now. Mike pulled his out as well. At their offer, Yolath, as well as Gonali, smiled warmly. "If you have no questions, you are dismissed at this time."

As Abe and Mike walked back, Mike felt caught in a tidal wave of emotions. They swirled about in feverish fashion, blacking out his perception of up and down, and even light and dark. The weight was certainly burdening his shoulders. He could feel the resistance in his legs as he walked forward. On the other hand, as he and Abe walked back to their quarters, they were again given the delight of viewing the paintings and grand architecture of what Yolath had told them was properly called the Patriarchal building. Mike was again struck by the utter beauty and perfection of the environment it provided. As Mike turned to glance at Abe, he could tell that Abe seemed to feel the same. Abe turned to Mike with elation in his face, "Well, what do you think so far?"

Mike laughed, "About what?"

Abe smiled. "Well, everything, really."

"It's all overwhelming."

Abe laughed and nodded. "I could have guessed that. What about all of this?" he asked, waving his hand panoramically to indicate the walls through which they were proceeding.

Mike shook his head sheepishly, not knowing quite what to say that would have done the place any justice.

"Hard to believe, huh?"

"Everything seems too perfect. How can we ever achieve this?"

Abe's smile suddenly morphed into the educational expression that he wore when preparing to teach. Mike had come to recognize it even in the short time that he had been with him. "Like I explained a few days ago, Mike, it has been done before. Think about the Bible. Can you think of what I'm talking about?"

Mike strained to think of all of his Sunday School classes as a child. "No, I can't."

"There are only a few verses about it—in The Book of Acts as the apostles of Jesus Christ established the church." Abe pulled out a small pocket Bible he had stowed in his robes. "Turn to Acts 4:34-35 and read it."

Mike took the Bible from Abe and turned to the passage. *"Neither was there any among them that lacked: for as many as were possessors of lands or houses sold them, and brought the prices of the things that were sold, And laid them down at the apostles' feet: and distribution was made unto every man according as he had need.*

"I don't remember ever reading or hearing about this before," Mike commented, looking up from the book; "That state must not have lasted very long."

Abe and Mike had come to the main hall and headed across to the staircase that took them to their rooms. "It didn't," Abe confirmed. "It is a very small detail of the Bible, but a very important one, because that was the last time in which these emblems were all present and in order for mankind."

"So what happened then?"

"Chaos. Ultimately, a draw toward outside influence began undermining their culture and the society began to unravel. Outsiders learned about the emblems but were ill-informed of their natures, and eventually each emblem started disappearing. Without the order of the emblems, the people started adopting the corrupt traditions of their neighbors, and within a matter of years, the society had failed."

"So the emblems all disappeared after that?" Mike asked.

Abe nodded. "The Romans seemed to have some concept of their importance, and recovered all but the emblems of meekness and sacrifice, but then Rome, too, could not hold together, and all of the emblems were scattered for the last time."

"So how do you think that this society has lasted so long?" Mike inquired motioning to his proximate surroundings. "From what it sounds like, this society alone has existed longer than any of mankind's utopias put together."

Abe shook his head. "I don't know for sure. It seems to me that Elves are more observant by nature. They can recognize the vices that the emblem of fire controls and seem to catch them before they begin causing disaster." Then, as an afterthought, Abe added, "I think that their government helps as well."

"Yeah?" Mike inquired. "I've never heard of anything quite like what I've seen."

"It's not unique. It was the form Adam set up under God's direction through the emblems, and there are still secluded societies in our day that practice a Patriarchal order, but they are usually small and considered primitive in Americans' eyes."

"Now what exactly is a Patriarchal order?" Mike interjected. "I think I have an idea of what it is, but I'm not sure."

"A Patriarchal order is a rule by family. You see it on a very small scale in the home. The father and mother rule over the family. When a decision needed to be made when you were growing up, would your parents bring the decision to a vote among all the members?"

Mike laughed at the idea and the consequences it could have brought at certain times. "No, not at all. If it had been like that, I would have had as much say as either my father or my mother."

Abe chuckled. "Exactly. Now this place is run in the exact same manner except on a much larger scale. The oldest male member of the family is the Patriarch and presides over the city, though I assume that his wife has just as much say in the decision making. They make the decisions and the high chiefs, who are younger and much more able-bodied, make sure that they are carried out. It is a beautiful system really."

By now, the two had reached their bedrooms, but since Mike was held in intrigue, he followed Abe into his quarters instead of retiring to his own just yet. Again, he was caught by the flood of colors that bombarded his eyes. They were violent with activity, yet it somehow still calmed him. It was a feeling unknown to his senses. *The only other times I've felt this way have been in some of my most pleasant dreams,* Mike realized, *but when I would awaken from such, the source material for such feelings would dissipate.* This scene, however, remained. The dance of the colors continued on around the wall as Mike took it in in full. They almost seemed to move along to the rhythm of his eyes, pulsing at his tempo, doing whatever his eyes most wanted to see.

Mike was held suspended in silence before the question he had on his mind was able to surface again. "Why do you think such a government works so well?" he asked going back to the previous conversation.

Abe's face signified that he had actually been pondering on the very thing at the moment. Mike watched him in intrigue, wondering whether Abe was even capable of traveling the same artistic journey he had just taken. "It seems to me," he started slowly, as if trying to feel his way through his thoughts as he spoke them, "that it is a government wherein the leaders have the people's best interest in mind." Abe paused, mulling over the implications of his own words. Upon being convinced that he agreed with himself, he continued. "Remember that this is all just one big, ideal family. It is much easier, if not completely natural, to love one's kin. When one leads out of love, he is able to focus on the needs of the people, and everyone is satisfied."

"That makes sense." That was all Mike could get out, though, for a new whirlwind was flying through his mind, having pushed the initial one completely out. Abe's words had stimulated realizations in him, realizations that scared him to death. *I am completely inexperienced at life. I'm to be that leader. I've never been in charge of anyone in my life. How am I to start now? How can I tell people how to live their lives when I don't have the experience they do? How am I to lead out of love when I don't even know what that word means?*

Abe watched Mike studiously as Mike sat pondering such things next to him on the couch. Finally, Abe exhaled a chuckle and patted his partner on the back. "It's been a long day, Mike. Why don't you go get some rest now? Life should be a lot more relaxing for the next little while."

Mike nodded. *It has been a long day.* The fact did strike him that just this morning, he had awoken in the mist to find that their car was gone. It seemed like a world of events had occurred since then. Mike found it hard to believe that three days ago, he was working in the vegetable garden of his parents' house in Idaho, no more than a farm boy making his way, day by day on the land, working hard and content to have no destination in sight. How suddenly the ebb had turned to a flow.

The two lingered in silence for a few moments before Mike announced to his partner that he was going to head back to his room. He exited, entered the next door over, and proceeded to flop exhaustedly down on the bed. It had been a rough battle of two opposite emotions today, and as he lay back and pondered upon the outcome, he heard in his mind the call for no quarter. Its sound was melancholy, and as he let his breaths fall back down to resting pace he realized that the worst part of it all was that after all the effort spent, he felt even more conflicted than before.

The bed, however, offered a softness and comfort unmatched by anything he had ever felt before. The materials were of such a nature that they were present and provided warmth, but were almost indistinguishable to his sense of touch. The bed created a feeling of perfect bliss, and once again, he was struck by how advanced these people were when it came to the technology of comfort.

As Mike felt himself falling helplessly back into a perfect world of dreams, he smiled to himself. Maybe the call for no quarter would soon be obsolete. He figured he had eight months here before he had to worry about anything. His anxiety to complete what was placed before him was slowly beginning to accept that. It calmed slowly, and with his waning consciousness came a more comforting feeling. *Eight months here in Paradise.* Mike allowed the possibilities to sweep over him and wash away all remaining tension. He held his smile as he yawned and commenced letting consciousness go. He had faith that the next several months were to be filled with countless new experiences, and he had a feeling that it would all be unforgettable.

Chapter 7

The gentle songs of the frogs in the nearby marshes marked one of the many evidences of the arrival of spring. There sat a subtle charge of electricity upon the air which energized every being that took the pleasure of breathing in its sweet breezes—zephyrs that swept down upon the city and filled the valley with life. It was a life long hoped for, a life that had been continually anticipated throughout the months of a dark winter—the months of entrapment in coldness and slumber.

Mike opened the window to his room. There again was that gentle breeze which seemed to swell up and strike his self in more ways than one. It boasted an aura of fresh, flowering trees which was so distinct he swore he could taste it. This moment was one for which he had lived in continual anticipation—one in which every care in the world seemed to be washed away into the throes of pure insignificance.

What a perfect end to a perfect day, Mike thought, and for that very reason, he almost did not want to snuff it out with sleep. He knew, nevertheless, that even as he slipped into restful unconsciousness, the breaths of God that he tasted now would continue to flow in through the window and continue to sweeten the world of his dreams.

Mike took one more deep breath and changed into his night clothing. He hung up his summer robe, which he had worn for the first time in a great while, and crawled into bed, situating himself deep within the covers, for although the air outside was mild for the year, it still necessitated the warmth of the layers upon his bed.

Before he drifted off, however, Mike could not help but think with regret what the coming of spring also meant. Indeed, his time here in the Northwestern Elfish Realm was drawing to a close. Tomorrow, Abe and

Mike were to meet with the Elfish council, where they would receive directions concerning their journey. Truly, the departure was a pity, notwithstanding the importance and glory of their mission, for his eight months spent with the Elves had, indeed, far exceeded any expectation that he could ever imagine.

With such thoughts in mind, Mike turned to the nightstand beside his bed and pulled out a journal. Soon after his commencement with the elves, Abe had suggested that he keep a journal of all his experiences. Abe had said that journals had always helped him remember experiences, facts, and education that he had received and thought that keeping one would be beneficial here. Mike had readily agreed, and had since become quite comfortable in his writing. Each night, he had recorded the experiences that he had encountered in the Realm, and had, at times, spent over an hour doing so.

With a hint of nostalgia emanating from his fingers and the prospect and appeal of sleep quickly fleeing, Mike opened the journal. Immediately a world of memories broke forth in his mind. His mind was bombarded with the smells, sights, songs, and movements that defined the society. Flashes ran through his head, filling his heart with warmth like the winter hearth fires, like the distant laughter of children playing in the snow, like the stories of the elderly on those dark and stormy nights. Mike thumbed through the pages, reading and remembering each experience as if it were still warm in the ground.

Day 2

The dawning of the sun awoke me this morning, and as I got up from my bed and undrew the drapes, a new world opened up to me. I had slept better than ever before, and this only added to my eagerness to go out and experience this newfound wonderland. I bathed myself again, once again experiencing the magical transformation of the rose-scented liquid that sat replenished on the sill. I don't think I will ever tire of it. I met up with Abe for breakfast, and he told me that today was to be the first day of our normal schedule in the Realm, as if normal could justly describe our situation. In the morning, Yolath took us on a tour through the town, something

I had been hoping for in the first place. Yesterday was spent completely in the Patriarchal Building, which gave me just enough of a taste of the culture to make me want to leave it and go out amongst the daily life of the people. So I was eager as we again mounted the litters and began our procession first through the square, then down the steps and out into the main city.

"I want you to get to know this place as soon as possible," Yolath explained. "Try and spend as much of your time as you can out here."

After seeing it, I don't think that will be a problem. I saw that everything is as smooth as clockwork yet as humane and down to earth as home. There are so many new things that I noticed today. I could not help but note the constant smiles on the faces of the people, along with the constant sounds of laughter heard on the streets. They're a beautiful people. It would be wrong to say that they are all fit to be supermodels, for there are elves of all shapes and sizes, along with Elves with handicaps or impairments, but they all looked very healthy and extremely happy. Everybody carried himself with an air of genuine self-confidence, regardless of who he or she was.

The city was spotless. I caught glimpses of only occasional garbage in the street, but I also watched as elves walking by picked it up and threw it away. There were no dilapidated buildings; they were all kept in good repair. Yolath pointed out the ages of some of the buildings in town, including some of the original dwellings, and I was floored. Some of them are over a thousand years old! The industrial district was well tended; the yards of the houses were well groomed and inviting; the city itself seemed to breathe life. I wanted to take it all in at once, and came away slightly disappointed that the feat could not be done.

We took a break for lunch at about noon, and commenced education directly afterwards. Abe explained that he will educate me in the language, in the history, in the culture, in the church, and in the daily lives of all levels of fifth century British society. Abe explained that while the emblem will help in the education I receive in the next several months, I will still need to work hard and take good notes. He said the lessons will be intense, but I am looking forward to them. He is quite the good teacher, and already I feel like I've learned a lot from him.

Abe is insistent on me learning both Latin and Anglo-Saxon, for he says that I will be speaking both of them when we leave this place. I noticed that in just this first day, my language acquisition was phenomenal. There are distinct differences in the length of vowels between Latin and Anglo-Saxon, and Abe said that my pronunciation was almost perfect. When I told him my surprise at its easiness, he told me that the presence of the golden emblem made my senses and abilities much keener than they could ever be on their own.

He also started teaching me the history of the Roman Empire. I already knew most of this stuff, but Abe places a distinct focus on the details that most people do not learn, for in modern-day cases, they are not very important. However, for two men like us, who will be fully immersed in the culture, he says that every detail is crucial. Abe explained that he can probably only cover three quarters of everything that I need to know due to the scarcity of records written about the time period, but he says that that amount should be enough to get us by until the other quarter comes into play.

Abe was right about the intensity of the lessons, though. They lasted five hours today. Tomorrow will be no different.

Tonight, we ate dinner with Yolath and Gonali and their wives while our interpreters stood by. The meal was not to the scale it was yesterday, but it was still grand. The food was plentiful and delicious, and reminded me of a small Thanksgiving dinner, not only in matters of food, but in matters of goodwill found across the table. The chiefs and their wives conversed back and forth in their own tongue, laughing, carrying on, not worrying about proper etiquette. The dinner seemed as much a social gathering as a time to eat. They lengthened it out for about two hours.

Hanoth stood by my side the entire time, and though he started out seeming a little distant from me, he started to open back up, especially after I spoke of all that I had seen that day and said nothing of my own world. By the end of the meal, we had formed a warm friendship, driving Hanoth to walk up to Gonali and ask him if Abe and I could come visit his family with him. Gonali smiled, patted Hanoth on the head, and gave his permission.

We made the walk to Hanoth's house and were bombarded by a platoon of energetic children. I found out Hanoth is the third oldest of seven children, soon to be eight children. What surprised me was how they seemed like many families which I knew back in Idaho. Unlike my initial perception that everyone here is perfect, I noticed that the families here are just as prone to consist of wild and disruptive kids as everywhere else. For example, when we were talking to Hanoth's parents through Hanoth, one of his little brothers loudly interrupted and tried to pull him away to play some game. Hanoth lashed back angrily and shoved his brother away, knocking him down and telling him probably something similar to "bug off". The mother gave Hanoth a dirty warning glance that made him apologize immediately, both to his parents and to his brother. Then the mother seemed to chastise the younger son in a tone that no kid ever wants to hear. The kid ran off like a sulking puppy. Other similar situations ensued during the evening, and both of the parents apologized to us several times.

Something I noticed, however, was that although the kids were far from perfect, they were extremely obedient to their parents, true to what Hanoth said. They made mistakes, but it was ingrained into them to accept their parents' chastisements. And the parents knew how to chastise their kids. Most of the punishments were verbal, and although I could not understand the spoken words and Hanoth seemed to have no desire to translate them, I could see that they were effective. Only once did we see the father get up and deliver a mild smack to one of his children—but only at a time when the chaos was at its peak. At that, the chaos immediately dissipated, and the child, more stunned than hurt, immediately stopped what she was doing.

Overall, although today was calmer than yesterday, it was still fairly eventful, and I am tired out. I am fighting back the yawns even as I write. I'd better finish this up, because Abe tells me that tomorrow we will be going out and doing more or less the same thing—going out to the marketplace in the morning, then coming back in the afternoon for lessons. If such is the case, I cannot afford to stay up any longer.

Day 7

    I still cannot believe that it has been only a week and a half since I was back on the farm in Idaho and without a care in the world. I know I say that a lot, and Abe is probably growing tired of it, but the concept is always on my mind. How can it not be when I have learned so much? Abe and I can already have a basic conversation in both Saxon and Latin, and the culture of the elves is becoming more and more alive to me each day.

    I'm not used to such intense learning, and so when Abe consented that we go out to work in the fields, I was more than ready to consent. I had grown to miss being out in the sun all day, working with the land. Hanoth seemed surprised at this, and when I asked him why, he stated, "You just don't seem the type to like to do that."

    I told him, "I've done it my whole life, though. The fields are really all I know."

    He did not completely believe me until he saw my eyes light up at the sight of the field and the people harvesting the corn. For the first time since this whole crazy escapade began, I felt at home. I sniffed the air and caught the scent of chaff dust. Bodies appeared amidst the otherwise uninterrupted sea swinging away with sickles in their hands. I only took a moment to observe them to get the idea of harvesting by hand before finding myself dashing forward to join them.

    The elves worked like titans. Their sweat watered the earth as they swung away, their movements almost seeming to take on the hum of a machine. They only took brief, periodic stops to grab a drink of water from the numerous nearby vats, then they resumed rhythm, swinging away with relish. I had to pause in my own work at the sight. None of these elves groaned or complained, rather they laughed, joked, even flirted. I would have thought that they weren't even working at all if it weren't for the visible dividends their sickles produced. The male teens, especially when around the females, seemed especially keen on seeing who could reap the fastest and piled up bunches of grain almost as quickly as the girls could collect it.

After working a great while, I noted that there was no overseer. I could not believe it. These elves worked with no manager, yet they seemed to need none at the same time. There was only one exception to this, and I laugh even as I write about it. About mid-morning, one of the teenage boys grabbed one of his peers and dunked his head into the water vat. I paused in my work to watch him hold it there for almost a minute. He was laughing deviously, and the laughter was contagious. I watched in humor as the other kid struggled to fight his way out, knocking over the whole vat in the process. One of the older men, possibly a father or uncle, grabbed both of the boys by the arm, handed them the vat, and ordered them to get more water from the aqueduct in town. The boys walked off with the vat, by then both laughing.

I had Hanoth ask a man what it was that motivated everybody. I don't know if I phrased myself very well, because he gave me a sort of quizzical look. Assuming that I was the one to blame for the confusion and not Hanoth, I rephrased my question.

"You seem to take a lot of pride in your work. What is it that makes you do so?"

The man seemed to understand this a little bit better. He stated, "Without us, the city does not eat. We harvest all the grain. Our people are healthy because of us. In fact, it is my team that has been given the award for highest production. Each month for the past five years, when our team has reported our output to the high chief, he has rewarded us.

"What is the reward?" I asked him.

By then, he had to have realized who I was, for he did not look at me with quite the same perplexity that he had initially given me. Instead, he took on an air of honor in being able to be the one to explain what was simply common knowledge to the whole community.

He said, "We are given the greatest portion of the community's profits. After everybody's needs are taken care of, there is always an amount of excess." The man then shook a bag that sat at his side and the contents inside jingled. "Since we contributed more, we receive more of the profits."

He spoke of a monthly report to the high chief. By that point, the pieces were coming together for me. It seems like the government holds each person fully accountable for the economy of the community. There are managers, but they work for the community rather than for separate companies and they determine the reward according to the person's efforts. The leftover profit seems to fall into a currency system wherein the more faithful contributors are able to buy more. This is the reason that there is still a market in the town square. People are able to buy luxury items that are not automatically provided for them.

"So are there still class differences then?"

The man looked confused. "What do you mean?"

"I mean," I expounded. "Some people are not able to do as much and so will not be rewarded, like those who have handicaps."

The man then laughed, an unexpected reaction to my explanation. "Those are some of the people with the most. Everybody makes sure they are comfortable and usually give much of their extra substance to them of their own free will."

He must have seen my shock at their ready charity, for he added, "I would much rather see them comfortable and happy than have the things myself, and I am no more charitable than any other elf here."

My attempt to soak that in temporarily stole my breath away, but when I had recovered, I asked him one more question that pressed upon my mind. "From what you said, I know this would never happen, but what if someone did not contribute like they should?"

The man seemed to think long and hard before saying, "Our system is, of course, dependent on the integrity of the people, but I guess that case actually has happened a few times throughout my life. When it's happened, the suspect has gone before the high chiefs and pleaded his case. If it was just, he was let go. If the lack of production was due to idleness or some other cause that he could have helped, he would have been given a warning. If it happened three times, he and his nuclear family would have been exiled from the community."

I would explain more, but I am tired and that was the main part of the conversation. At any rate, the day was enlightening.

Day 23

I wish I could properly describe the breadth of the smile that became glued on my face today, for I feel like I saw the true nature of the Realm. I learned, upon spending the first week here, that these elves don't let the goodness of life pass them by. I have never seen harder workers in my life, but I can tell that, at the same time, they don't let the work consume them. The whole community, other than the necessary medical and safety staff, works the same four days a week. The other three are open for doing things that I have often passed by in my own life. These are the days for sports, hobbies, recreation, and socializing. And here in the Realm, one particular sport rises above all of these.

The sport is called Sevina, and the best way I can describe it is a mixture of rugby and life size foosball. I was interested to note all of the pick-up games around the city contained almost an equal number of girls and boys. Upon seeing this, I was intrigued—I had a feeling like they had different roles, but I could never quite tell. That feeling was confirmed today when I went to the championship game against another Elfish city.

Yolath had personally invited Abe and me, and so we were able to obtain some of the best seats in the stadium just outside of town. The place was filled to the brim, and the atmosphere, even before the game started, was on fire. Arbitrary cheers careened through the arena, beginning in one spot and flowing to consume the place in a matter of seconds. Words were chanted by all present, and though I could not understand them, I felt shivers sail down my spine.

Before I knew it, the game had started. The tide of cheers again consumed the stadium as the ball was put into play. For the first time, I understood the general rhythm of the game. The ball was passed, held, passed again, rolled forward, blocked, stolen. The pattern repeated, over and over, the crowd rising and falling in energy. The ball was stolen, rolled the other direction, sent down the line, stolen *again, cleared through the lines of the opponent, scored. The crowd erupted in chaos. I found myself joining them before the stadium settled down and play resumed. I watched and noted the different players. The women passed with precision and ran back and forth with grace and dexterity. The men blocked and hit and struggled, using their weight and power to fight for superiority and allow the ball through to their lines of women behind them. I noted that the men and women stayed separate from each other, in respective zones like a foosball table, yet depended on each others' strengths and roles to succeed.*

I could not tell who was more passionate, the players who ran and hit and sweat and struggled, or the crowd who erupted in intense, however appropriate support. At any rate, I realized as I observed and cheered beside them, that this was what they lived for, whether they were a player or a fan. This was their passion. This was what made everything they did those four days worth it. I was taken into a different world today, a world in which every struggle could be cast aside for a few hours of fiery bliss.

After walking back from the game, which our city ended up winning, I turned to Yolath and expressed how fun it had been. I wanted to thank him for it, but kept my mouth shut, knowing their feelings on verbal thanks. Instead, I commenced making light conversation about it. I turned to Yolath and said, "It seems like the whole town was there today."

Yolath nodded. "I wouldn't doubt it. There are very few that don't take at least a little interest in it."

"So everybody that wants to go can?" I asked.

It was then that Yolath gave me a confused look. "Yeah. Why wouldn't they?"

"Well, what about paying to get in? Paying to get the better seats?"

"Paying? They don't have to pay anything. Who would get the money?"

I then started feeling the familiar discomfort when encountering a distinct cultural difference. Still I continued. "I don't know—the players maybe."

FORTH FROM EDEN

Yolath laughed. "The players aren't compensated at all for this. This is all nothing but fun and games. The honor of representing your town is payment enough, don't you think?"

To that I could do nothing but nod. It's hard for me to believe that it is what he says it is, though, when the explosions and cadences and movements and flow of the game still pulse through my head even now. I think of some of those plays; the flashes of unexplainable execution and herculean displays of strength linger in the eddies of my mind. I was truly taken to a different world today, and all as a simple pastime.

Day 103

There have been very few times wherein disillusion has helped me sleep better at night. I have always encountered it with a wary eye. Today, however, Yolath helped me see it in a different light. Today, his words to me helped me understand a little bit more how all of this is possible.

Abe was not feeling well today and was not able to lecture me this afternoon. He was hesitant, despite his condition, to retire to his quarters for my sake, but Yolath politely told him that he would take care of my lecture today and that Abe did not need to worry. Frankly, I think Abe worked too hard this morning. We spent the morning hauling firewood with a few other elves and I think he did more than his old body could handle.

In any case, I think Yolath wanted the time with me anyway. After we made sure that Abe was well settled back in his quarters, Yolath bade me to follow him. We walked very casually, not moving very fast—even for someone of his age, and I soon figured that the destination was not important. As we walked he spoke without turning to face me.

"I'm an old Elf, Mike," he said, "If you can help it, don't ever become one."

I simply laughed and replied, "I don't think I'll ever have to worry about becoming an old elf, Yolath."

Yolath smiled at that. "Mmm, true. But I don't know if becoming an old man is too much better. Either way, you become slow and wrinkly. If you can imagine, I used to go out and work in the fields too. Now my only redeeming quality is that I can yell at people without retaliation. Nobody wishes to fight back against me anymore."

"They don't want to kill you off," I chided. "These people love and need you."

"Hah," he droned. "Just like my wife needs me. Two old people get tired of seeing each other sometimes, but they're so used to each other, they can't live without them. It's not like my body can even turn her on anymore."

I couldn't help but laugh at that, and Yolath joined me, but only for a moment. I could tell something else was on his mind.

"I suspect something has been weighing on you for the past little while, Mike," he said.

I shrugged at that and said, "Nothing that I can think of. My time here has been like a dream. I've fallen in love with this place. Hanoth's family has taken me in as one of their own. I don't think I've ever been happier."

Yolath, however, did not buy what I thought was my honest opinion. "Oftentimes we block out what is bothering us instead of confronting it, Mike, simply because it is easier and gives us temporary relief." He paused to catch his breath and gather his thoughts, then turned to look at me directly in the eye. "But ignoring the problem neither resolves the issue nor allows us to learn."

I understood what he meant. For the first time, I realized that there was something, though it lay buried deep within my soul. I noted Yolath's piercing stare and dug to find it.

Yolath watched me intensely as he said, "Think deep and be honest with yourself."

I then realized what it was. With anyone else, I think I would have been afraid to mention it, but with Yolath, I felt the comfort that I had encountered the very moment I first met him. "It just seems all too perfect to be real."

By now we had walked out onto a balcony of what had been a hanging garden in the summer. All of the perennials were dormant *now and drooped down in melancholy brownish-grayness. I looked out on the city, for most of it lay below the level at which we stood. Its shine persisted, like always, re-energizing my heart with joy despite the absence of greenery, despite the absence of the sounds of children playing and the smell of sizzling meat, despite the crisp air, despite the oncoming winter.*

Yolath smiled and stated, "I think you put us on more of a pedestal than we deserve."

I was shocked to find him serious as he continued. "The environment we have achieved here has taken centuries, and, despite what you think, it is not out of reach for your society. Man has done it before and man can do it again. Everything depends on the emblems of virtue."

"I understand all of that," I told him hesitantly, "It just seems that everybody here is so happy that it seems like just a fairy tale."

"Happily ever after, huh?" he said.

I nodded to this, noting his modern-day cultural allusion.

"Why don't you explain yourself a little better?" he suggested.

I hesitated, struggling to think of what I was trying to say. "Well," I processed, "there is never any pain, any crime, or any sadness."

Yolath stopped and faced me again. He gave a glancing stare, the turned away from the view and resumed walking. "There is no such place," he countered. "That ideal is impossible on this earth. But the fact that we still encounter those things does not mean that we cannot generally live happily ever after."

"So these people experience such concepts?" I continued.

Yolath laughed and said, "Of course. Remember the presence of the emblem of fire. The people are very aware of pain. Think of how much love these people possess for one another. Love must be coupled with pain, because every person that we love must one day depart from us, whether they permanently leave us in death or whether they get married and move away to another town. Even though most of us believe our society has continuance on the other side of death, that belief does not resolve the loneliness that occurs in the mean time. And marriage? You may not know this, but when a girl marries, she almost completely cuts ties with her family to be adopted into her husband's family. Visits are rare, since travel can oftentimes be difficult and costly."

Yolath's concept of pain did not seem complete to me, though, and I made it known by saying, "I've dealt with that though. I know those situations are hard, but I also know that they cannot be compared with the amount of pain that occurs from war and crime."

"Would you wish such pain on anyone?"

I immediately felt a little sheepish and responded that I would not.

"Then, what's the problem? We've encountered these things in the past, and we will most likely encounter them in the future. Right now, while we don't have them, we should be more happy, shouldn't we?"

He had me on that one. I stood there silent until he continued by explaining something else to me.

"Consider the heartbreak and depression, and the sickness and physical injury from which these people cannot escape. Consider the little misunderstandings and prejudgments and differences in personality and opinion that end up in hurt. These people are not robots, Mike. They are living creatures who are extremely similar to every human being that you've encountered. They make mistakes; they get off track; they create hurt; the only difference between them and you is that they usually resolve their issues before the consequences get blown out of proportion. They've been raised to do that. Occasionally, a very foolish elf will fail to make such reparations. It is then that a punishment is decided upon by the high chiefs."

"How do you punish them?" I then asked.

Yolath laughed and responded by stating, "I do not believe it's necessary to give you all the details. I only believe it's necessary to let you know that the punishments inflicted satisfy justice to those afflicted and teach the perpetrators the seriousness of the crime."

"They are harsher than the punishments of my country, huh?" I scoffed.

Yolath did not answer directly. "The criminals know the laws when they break them. They are simple enough principles. Their rebelliousness is what motivates them. The punishment effectively teaches that such *an attitude is inexcusable. If they do not feel that such a philosophy can fit in their lifestyle, they are more than welcome to leave."*

"Why is crime so low here, though? I still don't think I understand."

It was then that Yolath put an arm on my shoulder. "You will see a lot of bad acts and bad things happen in your life, Mike, but remember this: Men and Elves are not, by nature, bad. They are not born with evil in their hearts, but born with potential to grow and excel in any direction they go. But also remember that Men and Elves are, by nature, creatures dependent on structure. If their structure is good, they will excel in goodness. If their structure is evil, they will most definitely excel in evilness. It is up to people like you to lead out and create those structures. It is then also up to people like you to determine the nature of those structures, whether they'll be good or evil. If you keep that idea in mind as you perform your mission, you will most definitely succeed."

The words, even now, resound as distinctly as when Yolath said them, if not more so. They have run through my mind over and over again, cycling more and more clearly each time through. I feel that Yolath is right. He must be.

Day 181

There have been a lot of joyful days in this community, but the air today held a different tune. A week ago, four boys went missing up in the mountains. They had been hiking up in the snow when a sudden storm struck. They did not come back when they were supposed to. The community sent out a search party the next day, and after two days, their bodies were found frozen in the snow. This tragedy shocked everyone, for these boys were all young and healthy—it was a blow to the flame of life of the entire community.

Today was their funeral, or what I would refer to as a funeral. Although I did not know the boys very well, I still found myself attending the practices of everyone who did, including Hanoth. We were standing in a long line waiting to pay tribute to the memory of the boys, which had been given its place on the wall. The wall seemed to serve as a sort of memorial, similar in idea to the wall in

Washington DC, but instead of names, there were portraits. Three fresh portraits sat on the wall today.

"We do not have any formal ceremony, like your culture," Hanoth had told me before we left. "We believe that such a ceremony holds the person's soul back in this life and does not allow them to move on to the next."

To that, I had looked over at Hanoth, who by now, is adept at knowing when I need cultural education.

"We never bring the bodies to the funeral like your culture does, either," he added.

"So nobody gets to see them?" I asked.

"Only the immediate family, for identification and a final goodbye, before the person is buried out in the mountains toward the east. The only other person to see the body is a painter, who paints a live rendition of the dead body. You've probably seen these paintings on the inner part of the city wall before."

I recalled these words as I stood up on my toes to catch another glimpse at how far away the paintings were. I was happy to see that we were coming closer, but wished that the line would move a little bit quicker. The day was sunny and beautiful, with freshly fallen snow, but the temperature and biting wind made the air brittle. I shivered once again and pulled the hood of my winter robe tighter to my head.

"What do you think of the next life, Hanoth?" I asked, speaking the thoughts in my mind.

I have since learned that this culture is deeply religious. Each week, they have a holy day—a day in which they do not buy or sell or work, but spend time in religious services and in their homes with their families. I have written about many of my holy days with Hanoth's family wherein we have sat around and feasted, read, told stories, conversed, and shared experiences. I have always been a little bit confused about their beliefs and I decided that today was as good of a day as any to ask about it.

Hanoth shrugged in response to my question. "For now, I'm not quite sure. Yolath has spoken with me on many occasions about it, *and everything he says seems logical enough to me. He says that he has seen visions of it. He says that the next life is definitely something worth working for. Yolath has explained to me that God has prepared us a place similar to what we have down here, but without pain or death. He has explained that as long as we do not rebel against the emblems, such a place will be ours."*

"And if you do rebel against the emblems?"

"Then you obviously do not want the joy that they give. We know of the difference in happiness that they make. We are taught this in school. Such things are an integral part of our education."

"So they teach you religion in school?"

Hanoth toyed with the idea for a moment, trying to decide if such a statement was accurate. "We are not taught how to believe, or what to believe, but to believe in something. We are taught that the power of virtue from the emblems is real, and we are given the possibilities for why that concept might be true. There are some elves in the community that believe that that power exists of its own accord, and that is fine, but most believe what they teach in the churches, that the power comes from God, which not only makes more sense to me, but gives me a greater motivation to live according to the emblems' principles."

By then, we had reached the paintings and I caught a glimpse of a tear coming to Hanoth's eye as he placed his small gifts alongside the other tokens of endearment. I had to remind myself that Hanoth was only ten and these were probably boys that he had looked up to.

Hanoth surprises me sometimes, and I saw a fine example of this in the wisdom that he showed in his words today. I could tell that he had taken a lot of time to weigh such matters in his mind and had come up with his own conclusions based upon what he was taught in school, what he noticed himself, and what he gathered from those he respected most: his parents and Yolath. I know that this astuteness will make Hanoth a great master of wisdom someday.

Mike closed the journal and sat back on his bed a moment, letting all the memories soak in. There has been so much, he found himself thinking. How can I ever leave such a place? Mike was suddenly thankful for the journal, which had set such a world of dreams in stone. The hour was late, but he wanted more. Smiling, he opened the journal again and directed himself to the entry of a week ago. This entry accounted what had to have been his favorite memory in the entire eight months he had spent here in the Realm.

Day 251

Oftentimes, I have not realized a memorable experience for what it is until time has sealed its stamp upon it, but such was not the case today. Even as I lived the moments of these past several hours, I have dwelt in a joy and reverie unmatched by anything before. And I'm sure that the sights, sounds, and smells of today will sing to my recollection for many years to come.

The first of all the wedding ceremonies that would occur all year happened today. The elves hold weddings every full moon from the spring thaw to just before harvest. We just missed the last marriage of the summer when we first arrived here, and so I did not have the pleasure of such an experience until now. I may have thought that weddings were a big deal back home, but they are nothing compared to the ones they have here. These seem to be the focal point of the entire elfish community, of an elf's entire life. If not, the ceremonies are deceptive.

This morning, the whole city gathered for this day-long ordeal. Even though everyone was off work, the entire city was fluttering by mid-morning. Everyone rushed this way and that to gather up their offerings to the bride and groom before laying them in a great pile in the central square. The calls and shouts of the adults were augmented by the shrieks of their children, running around and playing. Some of them had to be too young to understand what was going on, but somehow they still knew that the day was something special. Yolath had told us just as much and directed Abe to break his schedule so we could participate in the activities. So instead of making the walk to the emblem room this morning, I made the walk next door to Abe's quarters so that we could watch the square from above.

The ecstasy of the populous increased, and I would have thought that there were a whole lot more than four couples getting married. Tiny clusters congregated and gossiped as others made their contribution to the mountain of food on the north of the square. It consisted mainly of fruits and breads and it was being freely handed out to anyone in search of a bite.

At noon, we decided to descend and lose ourselves in the crowd, for even though we had a much better perspective in our quarters of what was going on, we could not resist the magnetic pull of the energy below. We longed to be a part of it. Yolath had encouraged us to be a part of it. We were being pulled into its current, and we did not resist.

Just as we got down there, a hush arose and Gonali got up and spoke. Hanoth, who was most likely with his family, was not there to translate so we were only able to understand a few phrases that we have since picked up. That was fine with me, because the electricity of the cheer that arose out of the crowd after the speech was invigorating enough. I soon realized that the speech was made to welcome in the brides. These brides led the groups of families and peers that had come from the other Elfish towns. The conglomeration of gifts that all of the people had gathered were presented to the families, and then, amidst resounding cheers, the grooms were each introduced into the square to join their brides.

The ceremony itself lasted about an hour, with the Patriarch making long speeches to each of the four couples. The speeches seemed personal, mainly directed at each couple's success, but given in a loud and public manner. I then wished I could've fully understood what was being said, for there were times when the crowd laughed, cheered, and even made suggestive coercing noises, but I understood enough to get the idea of it.

As captivating as everything had been up to this point, it was nothing compared to what came next. The couples were carried out of the square on the shoulders of some of the stronger young males and led through the streets of town. The entire city followed, making a mad rush as if being chased by a herd of bulls. Abe gave me his leave to run on ahead, telling me that he would find me later. I joined in the wonderful melee of the younger, more athletic elves who followed closely behind the couples. I rushed with the party through town enveloped in a din of yelling, shouting, and banging of drums.

It wasn't until the bride and groom were brought out to a large open field at the edge of the mountains that the procession stopped. Within what seemed like a few moments, the music commenced—quick, bouncing melodies formed atop endless, pounding rhythms. And the dancing that followed—I have never seen such dancing. I stood to the side and looked on as thousands of bodies threw themselves into the mass, connecting up to the sound and the rhythm. Even the brides and grooms, now shed of all their lavish clothing down to their light summer robes, joined in, being thrown by the others into the very middle. The shouts and cheers sustained, though in a more periodic fashion, falling in line with the beat. I stood there for several moments doing nothing but looking on at the sight with my mouth slightly ajar and my emotions stimulated.

It did not take long before a slender, light-footed, warm-natured female elf approached me and introduced herself as Wenala. With a giggle, she beckoned for me to join her. I told her, "I don't know," but she shook her head and wouldn't accept rejection. I have never been a very coordinated dancer, but there was such an energy in the air that I soon could not help but begin moving my body. I witnessed myself quickly getting sucked in, and I soon gave up trying to fight it.

The female by the name of Wenala stuck with me and I did not deny her my company. We danced and bounded in sync with the rest of the mass, and whether my skills lived up to her expectations did not seem to matter. They did not seem to matter to me, even as I look back on it. I became lost in it, and did not realize until a long period of time had passed how tired I was becoming. I was able to communicate this to my partner and fully expected for us to take a break, but she, without seeming to be the least fatigued, pulled me by the hand and bounded over to an area where two large vats held a certain liquid on tap. She got herself a drink, and motioned insistently that I do the same. I did so, tasting the pure, sweet richness of the nectar, and, within a few seconds, I felt strangely re-energized. It was almost like a stimulant, only it enlivened my mind as well rather than clouded it, like a drug would do.

Whether it was a drug or not, it allowed the girl and me to dance until the sun had set and the moon began its ascent overhead. It was then that I realized that the intensity of the music had gradually quickened over what must have been six hours. Still, the nectar kept me energized—no crash—

no aftereffects of any kind. At this point Wenala bid me farewell with a kiss on the forehead and both cheeks and left me for her family. Left alone, I went out to find Abe. I noticed that everyone was gathering around fire pits into their individual family units.

I found him with Yolath and the other elders who had been present at our welcome feast. Abe and I caught up on the events since we parted and I told him how I had been chosen by one of the females. "I saw you," he commented. "I also saw the way she was looking at you." I could do nothing but chuckle with mild embarrassment. "I asked Yolath about the practice," he continued. "He explained that along with displaying celebration, the dancing is there to initiate friendship, induce mutual attraction, and spur the young to desire to marry. He explained that it is the most effective opportunity to meet people from the other cities, and that it initiates 90% of the marriages." I gulped at the thought that I was being searched out, but did not worry too much, seeing that I would not be here too much longer anyway.

It was while Abe was relaying this concept to me that the feasting commenced. Boys of about twelve brought limitless amounts of food around to the fire pits, always offering to the family leaders first and then to everyone else. Unlike our first feast in the Realm, which was served in courses, everything was served all together and in rotation. By then I was aching to replenish myself. Countless amounts of delectable meats, vegetables, breads, cheeses, and were placed in front of me; I consumed a fair amount of everything.

Just as Abe and I and seemingly everyone else were about to explode from consumption, I heard the drums strike up again and noticed that there were several mid-aged, bare-chested men gathered up on the hillside. It was there that the performances commenced. Acts of strength, bravery, skill, and culture were placed before my eyes by both male and female elves, offering them wonders yet unfathomed. They continued for hours, though the time seems to have been only a few moments. I will never forget it. These people take real pride in their achievements, I continued to tell myself. Apparently, this was their moment to which they looked forward. Abe mentioned to me, as we watched, that the dancing was left to the childless while this moment was left to those who were older.

The performances lasted long into the night, and when it finally concluded, everybody quenched the fires and followed the brides and grooms, again carried on the backs of others, back to the square, pressing forward to that again, constant, pounding rhythm of drums (I do not think that pounding will ever leave me. Even as I write now, they are pulsing through my head). The group watched and cheered as the couples were led into the Patriarchal Building to the honeymoon suites—suites at the very top of the building.

Then, after the brides and grooms were taken care of, the whole crowd dispersed in almost the blink of an eye, leaving the square in shambles, abandoned. After everyone dispersed, I came back up here to my quarters and immediately started writing all of this down, even as physically exhausted as I am right now. It must be four o'clock in the morning, and my eyelids are finally drooping. I feel grateful that the town does not begin cleaning up the city until tomorrow afternoon because I am pretty sure I will sleep far into the day.

It was not until Mike finished reading through these entries that he finally noticed the distinct lump in his throat. There were no tears, though he was sure that they would come later. Soon all of this would be no more than words written in his journal and memories fading in his mind. Mike thought back on that last entry of a week ago. He had already read it at least a half a dozen times. He was thankful that he had recorded it, as well as all the other experiences. The entries served to bring back the smells, the sounds, and the sights that his memory held. Even now, that constant pounding continued to course through his head. *I hope it never ceases*, he mused to himself. Mike feared that it would, though. He feared a lot of things now. Already, the sights outside his window seemed to be fading into the darkness beyond.

And the fact that he knew that his road was rocky ahead only added to the hesitance he held toward his departure. This mission was not going to be easy. The fact weighed upon his consciousness as an iron chain of events that ultimately lay ahead of him. Mike could feel it, even though its nature still lingered in obscurity. *I would rather stay here. I would rather never face it.* Mike knew with responsible regret, however, that that privilege was never meant to be his. Tomorrow, despite all his most innate desires, he and Abe would leave these mountains, probably never to return.

Chapter 8

I wish time would have stayed still. I wish spring would have never come.

Mike felt the presence of Abe's stare as Mike plodded forward on the trail. He looked over to see Abe staring at him and realized he must have voiced his thoughts. He had not meant to, for he had taken an informal vow of silence ever since this morning when he had last set eyes on the shining city he had called home for the past eight months. Up to this point, he had held true to the vow, though his thoughts had been coursing endless cycles. Finally, the culmination of them had seemed to escape.

Abe is cooking up some adage in his head. Mike knew it and, frankly, did not want to hear it right now. He knew Abe's feelings on their departure; he had seen their evidence in the gleam in his eye. Mike doubted the words Abe was to say next would be comforting. There would be something about duty, something about the greatness of the mission.

Abe kept quiet, though, at least for a minute. He let Mike have his moment. When he did eventually speak up, his words were of a different nature than Mike expected. "You know, Adam was never meant to remain in the Garden forever."

Mike looked over.

Abe nodded to confirm himself. "He might as well have been tormented by the demon of ignorance, for he was no better off anyway."

"Yeah, but he had everything right at his fingertips."

Abe shook his head. "Not quite. There were things he could only learn and do after he was kicked out."

Mike walked on a moment without response. When he had been a kid, he had pricked his finger with a thorn. The tip had broken off inside his skin and he could not get it out. For months, it had lain lodged, continuing to wedge itself in, reminding him of its presence with a dull ache that kept returning. He turned his shoulder to look behind him, as he had done no less than a dozen times today. He felt that ache again now, but the ache seemed to consume his entire body. It hurt to walk, though Mike was sure that if he turned around and began walking back, the pain would be alleviated soon enough.

Mike knew Abe's words were true, and more than for just Adam and Eve. Even so, they did not help to take away the pain. Mike wondered if Adam had felt the same pain. *Was that his first struggle?* he pondered. *Certainly it had to be one of his greatest.* It was one of Mike's greatest struggles, for he felt like with the Elfish city, he had left behind a part of himself. A few wrinkly robes sat unused in a closet. A vacant place sat at the table in the great hall. A lively Elfish dance partner waited in some distant city for further communication and courtship. All she would get would be a ghost. All the robes and vacancy would get would be a ghost. Indeed, a part of Mike's soul would always haunt those halls and streets, and he would be aware of it just enough to know it was not with him.

Mike looked up and around him. All that he could recognize now was the mountains, whose sight he had come to know so well and love so much. He thought back on when he last laid his eyes on the valley of the Realm, several hours ago. He had kept his eyes on it for as long as he could, and then it fell lost in the shadow of the mountain. Their trail had directed them rapidly downward toward the plains after that, and Mike's knees had struggled with the steep descent. Yolath had explained that they would come out of the mountains tomorrow, then a few days after that, the mountains, like everything else, would disappear. Mike regretted that day even as it lie in the future. From that point on, the Realm would remain behind them forever, nestled in the clouds of some of the most perfect country he had ever seen.

Mike allowed himself to think back on the place, though it effectively shoved the thorn deeper into his side. The experience had soothed him like an eight month massage, but instead of the beautiful soreness that was supposed to be felt afterwards, he felt only numbness. Mike yearned to be able to taste of its fruits of perfection once again. He knew that such was his goal for mankind, but Yolath had explained that it had taken generations for the Realm to reach its present state, and that was with the seclusion that these mountains offered. Mike knew all too well what that meant. Even if they succeeded in their mission, they would not live to taste of the same sweetness.

It was hard to accept the fact that life was a downward journey from here on out, but he could not see how it could be any other way. *That was as good as it is going to get.* Mike thought on the words Abe had used to describe the state of Britain at the present moment. It made him shudder, even tremble. What scared him most was the length of time he would have to spend there. Abe had said a few months. Abe had already been proven wrong already. Even now, eight months into the mission, the end was nowhere in sight.

Mike had not noticed that the wind had begun to blow down from the canyon behind them. There were always breezes in the canyons, but this one had an unfamiliar feeling to it. Mike sniffed the air. It sustained a taste of the Realm, but there was something new—something dusty. The air pressure was dropping. He could feel it. A storm was coming. Mike paused to take note of it. The air held an eerie silent note, and the sudden ceasing of songbirds only added to its discord.

Mike wondered if he was the only one that had noticed it. The elves who served as guides did not seem to be moved, but continued trudging onward. Without feeling like he had the authority to call the party to halt, he followed behind them, shivering at the wind.

The afternoon grew darker and the storm made its entrance. The clouds enveloped the sky, the mountains, and then the party as they continued in their descent. The dark grayness brought with it a light, but piercingly cold, drizzle. Mike pulled the comfort of the Elfish cloak's hood over his head and finally called over Hanoth, who had gotten clearance to join them on the journey, a break that had at least softened the rock that lay at the bottom of his gut.

"Hey, do you want to go ask the chief when we're going to stop?"

Hanoth nodded and ran up to the front of the procession, returning only a moment later. "They said that there are a few caves about two miles ahead where we will settle in for the night."

Mike nodded, but said nothing more. Instead, he concentrated all his efforts in wiping up his misery. *Man, this rain is cold.* The cloaks proved to be relatively waterproof, but Mike knew that that would not last forever. His feet were already wet anyway and quickly becoming numb. The rest of his body anticipated numbness, which was just as harsh. Mike shivered, struggling to fight off the water on his cloak.

The procession reached the caves no sooner than Mike could have hoped, and he selfishly went to work shedding his wet cloak and shoes and trying his best to get warm under a blanket. Abe settled in next to him, and with no more than a few words, both set their eyes out on the now pounding rain in the dark, both wishing they were miles back, in the comfort of their suites.

The following days were all the same, although the weather dried up considerably as they traveled east and left the mountains far behind them. Each day, the sun commenced lighting the world. It would make its round, rising, warming the landscape, then falling again, leaving everything cold and dark. Over and over, time and again, the pattern repeated in a never ending cycle, and each cycle would find Mike and Abe at the same activity, walking across the never ending plains.

Occasionally, the elves would allow Mike to come hunting with them, a daunting adventure in which they snuck up alongside herds of grazing buffalo, but Mike never brought himself to do more than watch. Living in the Realm for eight months had done little to spur his adventurous spirit, and now that he was thrown back into the cold, very real world, he was uncomfortable and homesick, not for Idaho, but for a secluded valley up in the Canadian Rockies.

Abe and he still continued his studies while they walked, and he was becoming quite fluent in the Latin and Saxon languages. Abe told him that although his accent was not perfect, it was good enough to get by. From what he learned, it did not matter much anyway, for there were so many misplaced foreigners in Europe that nobody would know the difference.

Mike often thought of the concept—having encounters with these foreigners. It all still seemed very distant. It seemed like it was just as distant as the day they left the Realm. However, over time, the grass became longer, then gave way to patches of trees, then thick forest. Two months passed and they were encountering several lakes a day, and Hanoth explained that it would not be long until they would not walk anymore. "How far are you going to go with us?" Mike asked him one day as they trudged around another lake, swatting mosquitoes and sweating profusely in the humidity of the midday.

"To the great fresh waters," he answered. That is as far as Yolath has allowed me to go. He told me to make sure that you were safely on an Elfish ship, and then to part with you."

Mike looked at him with a sad sort of loneliness. Hanoth had come to be a godsend in more ways than one throughout their association. They had shared countless days in each other's company playing up in the mountains with the other Elfish youths. They had feasted together until they could no longer move; they had laughed together until their sides had hurt. They had shared stories, ideas, and experiences that had bonded them in the short ten months of their friendship. Hanoth had been Mike's breath of fresh air these past two months especially, always sporting a smile on the days that Mike had desired to go back to the Realm or even the safe, blissful confines of his Idaho home. Mike did not want to see the time come when they would have to part, probably to never see each other again.

Nevertheless, the day came—another hot, humid, mosquito-filled day. Mike had been able to feel the change in the freshness of the air. It was milder, as if coming off large body of water, and soon, it smelled of freshwater fish and seaweed. They plodded forward still until, as quickly as Mike could blink, the trees cleared to reveal a blue-gray mass of water, larger than any body of water he had ever seen. Mike took a deep breath as the waves lapped placidly along the rocky shore. *This cannot be a lake,* he muttered to himself. The mass seemed to drop silently off the edge of the world. All that lay ahead of him was the water and the sky, and his peripheral vision only revealed a fading coastline on either side.

"Lake Superior," Abe said. "I've walked along these shores before, although they were studded with the sidewalks and parks of the cities of Superior and Duluth."

Down the beach, Mike could see five other elves rigging a boat about forty feet long. It was then that Mike first felt sick to his stomach. The time had arrived. He was not ready for all of this. He held his sides as he followed the rest of the procession over toward the boat, and as they approached, the elves rigging the boat jumped down, into the water, and over to where they stood. As they presented themselves to each other, the familiar greeting was given, followed by animated, excited speech in Elfish.

Within a moment's time, however, their attention turned from each other to Mike and Abe. The chief beckoned them forward and Hanoth followed faithfully beside them.

"The chief wants to introduce you to Farnoth, the captain of the ship," Hanoth repeated, translating the words of the chief. Abe gave the smile of approval. Mike forced it. "He doesn't speak English, but he is confident that all needed communication can successfully occur with sign language."

"Tell him that that will be fine," Abe said.

"Furthermore," quoted Hanoth, "He said that there is no time to waste, because the winds are favorable for speedy travel right now." At this, Hanoth looked up at Mike. He pulled Mike close to him and hugged him. Mike had long since learned what a hug meant in this culture. They were not used freely. The gesture, though cherished, made the moment even more difficult.

"Thanks for everything, buddy," Mike said, with tears welling up in his eyes.

Hanoth seemed to appreciate the verbal thanks even in its foreign nature to his culture. He squeezed Mike tighter. "Yolath says that one day I will possess the ability to see what has happened to you. I look forward to it."

"I wish I could possess the same ability," Mike returned. "But I'm afraid it wasn't chosen for me. I'm sure that whatever I'd see of your future would please me though. You are an amazing person, Hanoth."

The two parted. Mike looked down at Hanoth as he felt Abe's hand rest upon his shoulder, urging him to board. Slowly, reluctantly, Mike turned away and climbed up the ladder to the deck. As the crew set the sail and the ship was drawn off the beach, Mike riveted his eyes on Hanoth and the rest of the Elfish clan. They grew smaller and smaller in the distance, separated by the strong favorable winds of which Farnoth had spoken. It was then that the wells of tears began to freely flow.

FORTH FROM EDEN

Mike did not feel very well the rest of that day. He remained quiet, and could not eat much of the food that was served. He spent the entire afternoon staring off the edge of the stern, not moving; not saying anything. After approaching him, watching him, getting no reaction from him, Abe decided that it was not a good day to continue studies, and so he let him be. It was not until the evening, after dinner, that he approached him again.

"You did not want to continue on, did you?"

Mike looked over at him. Abe leaned against the railing, letting his hair, which now lay in long silvery locks, blow in the breeze. His face was calm and more one of concern than of sorrow. Mike did not feel like he could respond. He looked out on the waves beyond his partner. Abe shifted and added, "It's hard leaving something that makes you that happy, isn't it?"

Mike could not help but give out a short laugh. "You have no idea." Even as Mike said this, he knew the words were hollow. Abe settled in next to him so that they were both staring off in the same direction. Out on the horizon, the sun was setting in glorious hue, bejeweling the skies with a circus of reds and purples and oranges. Mike could not enjoy it like usual. Out of the corner of his eye, he caught Abe opening his mouth. Mike pretended not to be irritated. What followed, however, was not at all what Mike had expected.

"When I was about your age, I traveled to Turkey to do some research on the Byzantine Empire. I was working on my master's degree and was determined to get it within the next year. I was only there for a summer, and had a lot of work to do, but that did not stop me from interacting with the people.

"It was in my apartment complex that I met a young, beautiful girl by the name of Esmeralda. She spoke little English, and I spoke little Turkish, but somehow we were able to communicate. It all started when a piece of mail that belonged to me was accidentally dropped in her mail box. As she returned it to me, we made eye contact, and something strange happened—an anomaly that I had never felt before. It was almost as if we could read into each other's souls. There was a spark in her countenance behind a face of innocence, and I immediately knew that she was to be a special friend. That was the first time I ever remember being in love.

"In the next few months, we exchanged little favors for each other, anything from giving little gifts to making each other dinner to surprising the other with potted plants to decorate the window sills. Like I said, there were never many words exchanged—nothing but simple words and phrases in the other's language—but there was always that feeling. And that smile—her smile always took my breath away with its beauty. It was as an instant remedy to any gloominess and I would do anything to get a glimpse of it as often as I could. Those months were some of the most splendid of my life."

Abe beamed even as he told the story. Mike could tell that such feelings had never left him. Mike waited for Abe to go on and reveal the fairy tale ending, but it never came. Upon recollection, Mike realized that Abe had written nothing of her, or of any love for that matter, in the letter.

"So what happened?" Mike asked.

"In the same summer, I found the emblem of knowledge. Upon learning what it was, and what it meant as an artifact, I had to make a choice. I could not stay with her and pursue this mission at the same time. So on my last day, contrary to my utmost desire, I left without saying good-bye, or leaving a U.S. address for her." Abe spoke these last words with deflation. He then added, "All my life, I have wondered what has become of her."

"You never talked with her again?"

Abe shook his head. "I never got around to it. It's a good thing, too, huh? I would not be here with you if I would have started a family."

Mike thought back on the conversation that sprouted this story. Mike was not sure that Abe was not trying to convince himself, as sure as he made himself sound. There was definite regret in his voice, regret for a thousand unborn joys that could have been his. Abe did have a point. Mike may not have been here if Abe had chosen his alternative. And Mike could not defend that alternative justly, for he had no experience in pursuing love either, but something still did not sit right with the whole situation. Abe seemed to know it too; he seemed to have known it for a long time, but he did not voice it now. Instead, the two stood in relative silence until they could no longer see anything on the horizon.

FORTH FROM EDEN

A sudden crash and jolt brutally interrupted Mike from his sleep. He had been dreaming of the night he had first met Abe—the night wherein Abe had been no more than a shadow and a pair of headlights. Mike dreamed of leading him back down the trail, only in the dream, he had not been able to see a thing. His headlights illuminated only the next few feet before him, yet he was traveling at a deathly speed all the same. The turns had been sharp, and his arm muscles had strained to keep the ATV on the trail. The trail had been bumpy, throwing his body around like a rag doll. Yet he had no control over anything. All he could do was struggle, spending every ounce of energy he had to stay alive. Even in his dream, he felt deathly tired.

A return to consciousness revealed the reason why. The boat was rocking and rolling like a frantic animal caught in a trap. It was worlds from the gentle rocking to which he had long grown accustomed from the nearly two months on the ship. Almost immediately, he heard cries from the Elves up on deck. The cries were frantic, of a tone which sent shivers that chilled to the bone through Mike's body.

Never once, in almost a year of association with the elves, have I ever heard that tone. Mike was terrified at the source of the fear, but even more terrified of being entirely clueless of it. Such a mindset, in all the rolling chaos going on, moved Mike toward the ladder of the deck, whispering silent prayers in his lips.

As Mike popped his head out of the hatch, he instantly noticed that the sky was much blacker than he had ever remembered. Then, in shock, he realized that what he had turned his head to see was not the sky, but the churning angry sea instead. The ship was not sitting high atop a plane of water, but being swallowed in the jaws of its monstrous, foaming surf. Mike threw himself back into the hold just as the boat wrenched. There was the sound of wood cracking and water rushing, and the terrible absence of screams. Water poured in and flooded the floor below.

Mike regained control of his balance, then sloshed through the hold to achieve the hatch again. In ultimate surprise, yet horror, Mike looked toward the control deck, where four of the crew had held on and were yelling orders at each other, but seemingly without rhyme or reason. Mike's heart collapsed as he finally caught sight of the source of the crack. It was the helm; one of the crew spun the wheel rapidly and much too freely to starboard into the wave but the boat was sliding heavily to port. They were entirely without control in this churning Hell.

Lightning crashed and revealed the waves in their full, terrible glory. They were as good as dead, Mike thought, though his wits were lucky to squeeze out any rational thought at all. Suddenly another titanic wave crashed down on the deck and again drenched Mike in seawater. The force of the water pouring down into the hold ripped Mike from the ladder and threw him back down below. He ignored the force with which he hit the ground, and focused instead on anywhere to which he could hold for security. It was a useless cause, for the ship was now in a merciless barrel roll.

It was amazing that the ship was not capsized, but it might as well have been. The bodies of Abe and the other elf in the hold, now very awake, were being thrown around the room like rag dolls right alongside Mike. They were utterly helpless, splashing and crashing in now over two feet of cold seawater.

Suddenly the biggest jolt happened yet—a sharp crash that sent all of the inhabitants below flying into the bow of the ship. Mike hit the walls hard, stunningly hard, seeing white flashes course through his brain. He did not lose consciousness, though, and seemed, after a moment of shock, to be somewhat intact. However, the boat was filling quickly with water. Frantic, Mike looked around in the darkness for a solution, but he was like a deer in the headlights. Water was now up to their chests, and would soon be over their heads.

Such a train of thought was interrupted by a sudden squeeze on his shoulder. "Find the emblems!" the source yelled. It was the voice of Abe.

The ship was now completely stationary and the only impediments were the complete darkness and fast depleting air. Mike quickly heeded the order and made his way, mostly swimming now, to the other end of the ship, where he had been sleeping. He could not help but notice that the incessant crashing of the waves and coursing of incoming water were the only sounds now. There was neither time nor energy to think on it, though, for Mike's mind was consumed with the instinctive energy toward survival and obedience to the only voice remaining. Taking a deep breath of air and a deep bite of faith, Mike dived down into the numbing water to feel around the hammock. Sight was useless, and in frustration, Mike used up the air quicker than he could afford. He came up to the surface and found that there was only six inches of airspace left in the hold. Sucking in all he could, he made one last dive down and frantically moved his hands about. Had he been in the right state of mind, he would have realized that it could have been anywhere with all the tossing around the ship had done. But now he was all actions. His air depleting, he ventured out a little further from his hammock, quickly losing hope both for the emblem and for his life by the second.

But suddenly when he thought that he could not bear holding his breath any longer, his hand fastened around a cylindrical piece of metal, when, upon contact with his hand, suddenly felt warm. Mike suddenly felt that he had an added supply of oxygen and set himself to finding a way out of this wooden cage. He swam up to the ceiling and over to where he guessed the middle of the ship was—where the hatch would be located. After feeling around for a few seconds, his arms felt a hole and he surged up through it and into the ocean above.

Mike broke the surface to find himself quickly churning toward a colossal rock—the same rock that must have finished off the ship. There was no escape from the lethal crash that would come and Mike started to brace himself the best he could, but then saw the rope. He took his chances and grabbed on with his free hand, hoping to all that was good that it would hold him. The rope tightened and Mike could feel his Elfish clothes being ripped off him in the vacuum of water.

As the backlash occurred, Mike abandoned the rope and swam with all his might as far away from the rock as he could. He had never been a strong swimmer, but somewhere, either from the emblem or from the unknown reserves of his own body, he was receiving the needed strength.

Mike turned to see a towering wave crash down upon him, and he tumbled and tossed in the water, helpless to do anything but let the force of the wave carry him where it would.

Its power subsided and Mike re-emerged simply to be carried upward by another towering swell. As he peaked it, lightning flashed in the sky, revealing a ghostly coastline off in the distance. Again, Mike started swimming, neither rejoicing nor despairing in the sight, for he was completely without emotion—only a creature fighting for its life in a fiercely unbalanced battle.

The swimming was futile and Mike left it to simply focus on staying afloat. Again, through everything, he noticed the warmth of the emblem in his hand. He fed off it, absorbing all the energy and warmth he could get, for his body had been pushed beyond its limits.

Wave after wave came, some carrying him up and over, others crashing down upon him, every time twisting and contorting his body. Each swell was a battle, and each battle was fought not for victory, but for survival. The enemy kept pressing, and Mike was positive that it would last forever. But every time lightning struck, he could see the coast growing steadily closer, and hoped that the waves would continue to carry him there. A rocky death might then ensue, but there was at least that chance that it would not. Mike could do nothing but cling to that chance as he was tossed around: cling to that chance and cling to the emblem with all his might.

Each wave whittled down more and more of Mike's hope, but right as he sat at the threshold of futile submission to the sea, his body hit sand. With an added sort of motivation, Mike commenced swimming as soon as he gained partial control again, and when lightning struck, he found himself staring at a narrow beach backed by cliffs, which wetted with the especially big waves.

Before Mike knew it, he was being dragged across the sand in the shallow tide, and before the undertow could suck him out, he dug himself in and held his ground. Between this and the next wave, he crawled, scurrying up the sand and up the cliff, just enough to reach a ridge in which the waves did not reach. There he collapsed, cold, naked, and, aside from his iron grip on the emblem, without a speck of anything left in his strength.

Chapter 9

Lights seemed to be flashing methodically, periodically as consciousness slowly, cruelly materialized. It came with a pounding that set to work like a jackhammer against Mike's head, forcing him to keep his eyes closed. Mike's mind, refreshing itself with activity, for he had not even dreamed in his unconsciousness, struggled to make reacquaintance with the flesh with which it was tied. Everything had shut down. Every muscle remained still—legs, arms, neck—and Mike wondered how long he had been out. His ears seemed to work fine, filling with the far off rush of the sea—his former enemy now retreated back to its original borders.

Mike's skin was hot. Instead of the icy water, he was now enveloped in a blinding, burning sun. It had warmed his body up, and then it had baked him. He struggled to wet his chapped lips with his tongue, but failed, for it, too, was parched. Mike gave out a long, unreserved groan.

He rolled onto his side, feeling the sandy ground as he did so. The shift would allow his eyes to open in more moderate light. They opened slowly, painfully, but successfully even still. After blinking a few times to allow in the proper moisture, and squinting in the daylight, Mike remained lying on the bank for a little bit longer, slowly taking note of the day. The daylight moved in patterns of bright and brighter, clouds periodically intercepting the sun's rays. The clouds were fluffy and white and moved quickly in the summer air, showing no signs of previous hostility. The sun peeked through them when it got the chance, and caused Mike to turn away and look out on the blue-gray sea of glass.

"Where am I?" Mike voiced out loud. It was only one of a myriad of questions now racing through his mind, all of which caused him to bolt up and instantly go dizzy. Mike grabbed his head with a wince, squeezing it until it regained equilibrium. He then sat up slowly and looked around at his surroundings, subconsciously hoping for some answers but knowing, in reality, that the tide had driven them far out of reach.

Before getting up, he looked around the ledge upon which he had dragged himself. The golden emblem lay a few feet away, as his iron grip had expired and released it some time ago. Mike reached over and grabbed it, then stood himself up and lumbered down the ledge and onto the sand. The emblem was all that he presently possessed, literally. All of his clothing had been ripped off of him, leaving him completely naked. Mike felt lost, abandoned, confused, and exposed. He felt dead inside—like his identity, too, had been stripped away in the storm. He wanted to cry, but felt no capacity to do even that.

Remainders of the ship were strewn all up and down the beach, some washed up on shore, others floundering in the shallow surf. All combined to remind Mike of what had happened last night. Mike surveyed the beach, up and down for any signs of anything that he could salvage. There was nothing. There were no signs of trunks of clothing, or food or water for that matter. Mike's tongue felt like sandpaper. He knew he was dehydrated—his splitting headache revealed it—and knew that if something did not appear soon, he would have survived a shipwreck only to die a slow, painful death from thirst.

It was then that he heard a voice from behind him. "Mike! Mike!"

Mike turned around to confirm with his eyes what he already knew with his ears. He saw Abe running toward him, about a hundred meters away. He was naked as well, but seemed uninjured. Mike ran over to meet him, finding in doing so, that his left leg was slightly bruised, but other than that, he, too, was physically unharmed.

"Mike, you're alive!" He looked breathlessly down at Mike's hand, which held the emblem. His eyes lit up even more. Mike noticed that Abe had his emblem in his hand as well. "I have been searching for an hour for you up and down this beach. Where were you?"

Mike pointed over to where he had dragged himself the night before. "Up on that ledge over there."

Abe nodded, realizing why Mike had escaped his attention. They began walking down the shoreline.

"That was a wild storm," Mike mentioned as they walked.

Abe nodded. "Yeah. It's amazing we survived it."

"I could feel strength coming from the emblem as I swam."

"Yeah. Me too."

The water washed over the toes of the two as they walked. "What about the others? Did they survive?"

Abe shook his head. "They're all dead; all five of them drowned. I dragged the bodies up onto the beach." His tone was despondent as he motioned for Mike to follow him over to where he had placed the bodies. Despite the news, Mike's mood was unaltered. Although his body was warm, his soul was still too numb to feel any remorse. When Mike caught sight of the bodies, he did not shed a tear, although the elves had served them selflessly for the past two months. When he focused on their cuts and broken bones and blood, his stomach did not squirm. Their death was only a mere fact. It was intermingled with the fact that he and Abe were still alive, but without a thing in the world.

"I don't even know where we are," Abe stated, looking up and down the beach.

Mike realized that he, on the other hand, did, although he could not explain why. "England," he muttered.

"England?" Abe said in surprise.

Mike's mouth sat ajar, having been just as surprised as Abe had been at his response. Yet somehow he was certain of it. "Yeah, England," Mike confirmed after a slight pause.

"How can you be so sure?"

"I don't know," Mike said. "It just seems right."

Abe looked down at Mike's hand. Mike followed his eyes down to the emblem, which he noticed seemed to glisten ever so slightly brighter. Abe did not protest any longer, but set to moving toward the bluff.

"Where are you going?" Mike questioned.

"We have to find somebody to provide us with clothing, food, and water. We won't last too long in this condition." Abe had suddenly seemed to gain inspiration at Mike's confirmation.

Mike looked back at the bodies, but only for a second before abandoning them for more urgent matters. He followed Abe and started climbing the bluffs at the edge of the beach. They stood about a hundred feet high, and both realized just how famished they were. Hopefully there would be some sort of inhabitant nearby that could help them out.

They reached the top with shaky legs and wheezing, dry lungs and made their way over to a nearby boulder to sit down upon. As Mike rested, he took note of his surroundings. The landscape was relatively temperate and very green, with rolling hills of blossomed fields interrupted by groves of great deciduous trees.

It was all calm and quiet, and very excluding. There were so many groves that they seemed to form a curtain—a curtain that blocked out an entire island beyond them. Mike could only see about a quarter of a mile in each direction before his eyes were veiled. Each direction, that was, except for the sea. It seemed like the trees were closing in on them, trying to push them back into the watery monster from which they had just escaped.

The two sat there a little while longer in silence before Abe suggested that they move inland. Mike got up and followed, stepping lightly to protect his delicate feet from the unknown contents of the field floor. Mike's stomach was now growling insistently and his head was throbbing like mad. From the way Abe messaged his temples every few minutes or so, it seemed like Mike was not the only one.

The edge of the field gave way to the curtain, which seemed almost as impenetrable from up close as from afar. Before them loomed a great mass of oaks, lined below with thick underbrush. The two paused to find the best possible way to breach the wall, then pressed on, away from the beach and into the shaded world of unknown. They moved through the trees slowly, cautious to keep their exposed bodies from getting too scratched up, but they did not have much luck. The bushes seemed to close in and latch on to them like jaws.

As they plodded forward, Mike's emotions were beginning to thaw out and add to his general discomfort. Every word that Abe had said about this place was coming back to him slowly. *A wild land at the edge of the world,* Mike thought to himself. *Who's to say if it is much better than the sea?* Mike thought on the culture of the Celts, of their practices within trees like this. *Who's to say that those rites weren't performed in this very grove at one point in the past?* The thought made Mike shiver. Much of that culture was gone, destroyed by the Romans, but Mike was not positive that now was a much better time. From what Abe had told him, England's history was rocky, just like its coast, and would not get any better until long after they'd be gone. Mike looked back toward the beach. Despite the severe pounding in his head and growling of his stomach, he was having second thoughts.

It is, indeed, an ocean away from the Realm, Mike thought, and as he did so, a realization struck him in the chest like a wrecking ball. *My journal.* It had been placed below his hammock the night of the wreck—he had been mulling over its bright contents before he had fallen asleep. It was surely destroyed now. Mike's stomach wrenched. He wanted to vomit, but there was nothing inside to excrete. For the first time since they had arrived here, tears came to his eyes. He suffered in silence, sparing Abe an extra burden, and continued to plod along, away from everything he had known to be good and into an island of uncertainty.

It was not long until they did, indeed, come upon a road, if it could justly be called so. It was extremely narrow, just a break in the trees a few feet wide and could have almost passed as simply a game trail. It was too ordered to be natural, though. Both Mike and Abe sighed as they exited the trees, then looked left and right for their next move.

"I don't see any difference," Abe stated. "It seems that one way is just as good as the other way." They made a random decision and turned toward the left, hoping that it would lead them to some proximate habitation.

It was not until they must have traveled a few miles down the road before they saw the cottage. It was crude—a small circular hut made of stones and mortar—but cozy looking and kept up. Alongside it ran a gentle, trickling stream. At first, Mike hesitated, worried of the friendliness of the inhabitants, but that stream pushed that to the back of his mind and Mike started forward to it. Abe read his mind and grabbed his wrist. Mike looked back to see that Abe was shaking his head and pointing over to the field upstream from it. Mike noted that several sheep were grazing in the field, and drinking and standing in the water.

"It's better just to wait on it, Mike. Let's see if these people are home."

Mike regained his composure and inched toward the door behind Abe. He noted that his legs were shaking, and not just from hunger.

Abe knocked on the door as Mike stood by, waiting and hoping. There was no answer, and Abe tried again. Looking over at Mike, he shrugged, "Maybe they've gone off somewhere." He opened the door slowly and peaked in to its one room. All seemed to be silent as Mike peaked around to get a glimpse as well.

CRACK! Out from the hut, a resounding din of a wood staff striking stone rattled Mike's ears and nearly sucked the life out of his heart. He jumped and fell backwards onto the ground, as did Abe. They looked up to see the door swing open and a short but burly, fair-skinned man directing a flint spear at them.

The man posed a question that neither Abe nor Mike understood. The man waited a moment for a response, then asked, this time in Latin, "Who are you?" This time, his tone was lighter, and Mike hoped such was due to his realization that they were harmless.

"We're travelers who were shipwrecked," Abe answered. "We mean no harm, but only ask for some food, water, and clothing and a place to stay.

"Where are you from?" the man asked, again in Latin.

"We're Britons, from Londinium," Mike blurted, trying as casually as he could to state a friendly origin.

The man lowered his spear. His features lightened as he offered his hand to help up first Abe, and then Mike. "Come. My name is Antiochus."

Antiochus led the two into his cottage, where his wife and three grown sons were gathered into the far corner, opposite the doorway. The three sons also held their spears, ready in case of a violent confrontation. "Please, sit down," he invited. Then, in what Mike now guessed was a Celtic dialect, he motioned for his wife to dish up whatever meat had been left over from their meal.

"You must forgive me for my initial violent confrontation. We had not been expecting anybody and there have been lots of rumors running around these parts lately."

"It is not a problem," Abe told him. "We simply appreciate you taking us in." By now the sons had brought a couple of wool blankets and draped them over the two, which made Mike feel a lot more comfortable, especially since they were in the presence of a woman. The wife had also given them some mutton, dark bread, and ale, which Mike would have never drunk had it not been that there was nothing else. The taste was horrible, but Mike dealt with it the best he could.

"I'm glad to do anything for my countrymen, though you do not look to be either Celtic or Roman. Is Latin your only language?" The question seemed to imply an inquiry on their ancestry as well.

Mike was about to answer that they spoke Saxon as well, but Abe was quick to answer instead. "Yes. I was born on the continent. My parents spoke both Latin and their native tongue, but only Latin was beneficial to me, especially when I married a citizen. That was the only language I passed on to my son."

Antiochus nodded. "I have a similar heritage, as you can probably tell from my name, though in my case, my wife only spoke Celtic, so our children know both."

Mike studied the man astutely as he spoke. He looked tired, but from so much more than the day's labor. Mike studied his sunken eyes. There were thousands of untold stories in those eyes—stories of a different life in a completely different world. It told of something far different from his own world, far different from the Realm. Indeed, Mike had passed through a veil into the heart of fifth century Britain. He learned more about this world at that moment, as he looked into those eyes, than he had in the entire year that Abe had taught him. At that moment, Mike appreciated Abe's inability, for the feeling he felt now in his heart about what he was up against would have changed his entire mindset in the Realm.

"I'm afraid that the Latin is becoming less and less important every day, though," Antiochus added. "Five winters ago, I got word that the chieftains made a last appeal to Rome for help, but got none. I have also heard word that the entire empire is in shambles, and I fear that they will never be coming back now."

Abe only nodded. Mike watched him. He watched how Abe held back from stating all that he knew of this portion of history. He watched how Abe did not assure them of Rome's complete abandonment. Mike could tell that these people still held to the glimmer of hope that the retreat of soldiers was only temporary, that better times would come and they would be back to guarantee protection again. Mike knew that they were not coming back. Mike knew that Abe knew they were not coming back, yet he watched how Abe decided not to destroy that glimmer of hope in them. Abe seemed to feel it was more important than the truth at the moment. Mike respected Abe for that, especially when considering how Abe usually was with such things.

The conversation continued into the night, until Antiochus could see that Abe and Mike were struggling to keep their eyes open. He had his wife prepare bedding for them and invited them to retire. "I'm sorry that we do not have any clothes for you," he apologized as they lay down. "But I will have my wife set to work tomorrow on making you some from our finest wool. And I will have you stay no less than a week."

"Thank you," Mike uttered as he bedded down and wrapped the blanket around him. Antiochus smiled then headed over to his wife and lay down beside her. Soon they were both breathing gently, as well as Abe beside him. Mike however, remained awake. The mutton and bread filled his stomach, along with the ale, giving his body relief. There was not, however, relief for his soul. Moments of the evening conversation coursed through his head. Much more had been spoken on the state of Britain, or rather, rumors of the state of Britain. Such were the best that these people could get. In reality, they did not have any more idea of what was happening than Mike did.

Outside, Mike could hear the wind blowing through the oaks. Those oaks held secrets in them, secrets of the past, secrets of the present, secrets of what lay beyond and could be the future. They closed them in, held them in their leafy palms. As grateful as Mike was for Antiochus' hospitality, he wanted out of here. He wanted, more than ever, to return to the Realm and knew, with a tear, that that was not possible, especially now. Mike wanted to run, but he did not have any direction to point himself. Either way would be more of the same. In such thoughts, Mike drifted off to the surreal world of sleep.

Mike was happy to be on the road once again, for the week spent at Antiochus' was like a cage. By the fourth day, their bodies had recovered, the elves had been buried, and their clothes had been made, so Mike had seen no reason to stick around and burden these people any more. Abe had silenced him, however, explaining that he did not want to go against their host's hospitality.

"He's done so much for us," Abe had said. "The least we can do is honor his request."

It had been hard to believe him. The whole thing had seemed backwards to Mike, especially in a world such as this one. Antiochus had close to nothing, his whole family had to work hard just to stay alive, and the world itself seemed to be closing in on him, yet he was so determined to bleed for them that Mike was thrown off guard.

"It's just the way these people are," Abe had further explained. "You would be insulting him by leaving early. Enjoy it while you can, too, for we may not get too many more opportunities like this. There are a lot of people like Antiochus, but there is also a lot of fear going around right now. I think it would have taken a lot more convincing to gain entry into his house if it weren't for the fact that we had absolutely nothing."

Mike had realized that for himself. Several times in that week, Mike had gone out with the sons to watch the sheep. While there, Mike was inundated with stories, stories of monsters and dragons. At first, he took them as just that, but it did not take long to figure out that these men were serious. "They're out there," one of them had explained. "They're like giants—hairy, horned creatures with razor sharp arms that can slice an oak in half in one swing. They're well over seven feet tall and come out of the sea at night to feed on human prey."

Mike had listened to the stories in silence, caught in between 20th Century skepticism and the spirit of the world into which he had been thrown. *There can't be anything of the type. Nobody has any evidence of such things.* Yet the brother had been sincere. Mike had waited for the punch line but there was none. When Mike had inquired whether he had ever seen one, the brother had shaken his head but added, "A traveler who once stayed at our house said he had seen a herd of them from far off. They came out of the trees from the other side of the clearing, and he had to run for his life."

Mike had desperately tried to shake off the story as ignorant folklore, but it had stuck with him. He remembered having gone to bed that night stiff, cognizant of every sound that came from the outside. Even if the stories had been tall tales, there had to have been some inspiration for it. They would not have materialized out of thin air. And any sort of inspiration for them could not have been too much more positive.

The days had been easier to deal with, at least from that aspect. Despite the stories, Mike had gone out several times to swim on the beach, simply for lack of something better to do. Sitting around was driving him nuts, like it had been while being on the ship. He found his mind constantly reverting back to the Realm, to the days when he did not have to worry about a thing. It was becoming more and more apparent every day that he would never be able to experience that again.

In a last ditch effort to fight the limitations of his memory, Mike also used his time to reconstruct whatever he could remember of his journal. The materials he had were primitive—bits of wool that the family was able to spare and juice from berries—and the entries were detached and lacking in imagery, but Mike was satisfied enough in the end. Luckily, he had read the journal so often that much of it was still vivid in his memory. He had gone into the reconstruction with a slightly lower standard than the original, and he honestly felt like he achieved it. The project seemed to be a godsend on the one hand. On the other hand, it was a great tease, a horrible torture device.

Ahead of him lay not the spirit of the past, but darkness yet unfelt. Mike knew that he would soon be facing it, and he could already taste it in the air. It was like those storms of last spring, coming in across the Plain from the west. Those seven days spent in the company of Antiochus and his family were seven days of anticipating the storm—the only thing worse than experiencing it.

So when the day had come, exactly seven days after they had landed ashore, when Abe had announced their departure, Mike was more than ready to go.

"We will take our journey to Aquae Sulis, where we have relatives," Abe had announced to the family. "They will be able to take us the rest of the way to Londinium." Antiochus had then pointed them in the direction of Aquae Sulis, or Bath, and had given them provisions for the two day trip.

"I wish you God-speed, my brothers," Antiochus had said. "I hope, one day, to see you again."

So they had set out and had been walking along the Roman road for a day and a half now.

"How are we going to approach this master of wisdom when we find him?" Mike asked as they set out from another village into the wild, unaltered country again.

"I'm not sure," Abe responded. "I assume that we will tell him many of the same things that I told you."

"Do you think he will buy it?" Mike retorted with mild skepticism. "I mean, I know I did, but it wasn't easy. And from what you say of the times, he would have no reason to trust us."

Abe seemed to roll that comment over in his head for a few moments. "That's a very good point, Mike," Abe finally declared, "however, I just know that we have to hope for the best. I hope you notice that everything else has worked out perfectly for us so far, and I simply cannot understand why we would be able to get this far just for it to collapse in on us. I have a feeling that we will know what to do when the time comes."

"Do you even suppose, I mean, because we wasted all that time at the cottage, that we will find him as Yolath described him? What if he had been out painting a week ago and today is twenty miles away?"

"We'll just have to hope," Abe repeated. "Everything will be fine."

Mike was still not convinced, however, and quite far from comfortable with the whole situation as they approached the hills surrounding Bath the next day. He did not like starting something without knowing exactly what he was doing.

However, even at the moment as they walked, Mike got an inkling that they needed to stray from the road. It was the same inkling he had felt a week ago when he had assured Abe that they were, in fact, in England. That had proved to be correct, and looking down at the emblem, he noted that it held the same shine that it had on that occasion. When he voiced his opinion to Abe, Abe had simply stared at him and nodded.

"How come you believe me so easily, Abe?" Mike asked as they turned off the road and started through a wheat field.

"This is the way that it is supposed to work," Abe responded, "at least until we meet up with Virgil. He will be our guide, but for now, you have to be the one making the calls. Like I said before, even though I am the one who initiated this voyage, I was never meant to lead it."

Don't remind me, Mike thought to himself as they traversed the sea of grain. It was midsummer and the crops were about waist high, and Mike held out his palms to feel the seeds move across his skin. It was the only calm sign that Mike was giving, the remainder of him was shivering.

Yet he kept being guided, the golden emblem becoming more and more distinct in its warmth as they moved. At times, Mike felt prompted to change their direction—to climb over a certain hill or to turn at a grove of trees, and, each time, Abe followed unquestioningly. The whole situation was beginning to unnerve Mike, and he was beginning to wonder if he had simply gone crazy and they were walking in a direction that would get them lost forever. But suddenly, as he was about to suggest that they turn back to the road, they mounted a rise and caught sight of the view below. And strangely, though Mike had never seen this place in his life, it seemed incredibly familiar.

Down below, a river flowed lazily along, denoted by a gently curving line of trees. Up a ways sat a village with a stone church in the center. Mike surveyed the landscape. *This is right,* he assured himself. His eyes continued to scan, looking for the one missing piece to the puzzle. Then, he caught sight of it. Off to the right of them, about a quarter of a mile away, across the fields and just up from the bank of the river, stood a solitary man with his back toward them. Behind the man seemed to be a large, partially painted rock. A sudden rush came upon Mike and he started running down the hill and through the fields toward him.

"Wait up! Wait up!" Abe cried, calling out and running after him the best he could.

Mike slowed to let Abe catch up to him. He could not have done it without him anyway, for it seemed like his whole body was shaking. Abe caught up to him, panting, and together, they walked toward the man. The man did not turn around, though, even when they were almost on top of him and were sure that he could hear them. They could now see that the painting had some sort of field on it, though the man's body hid the majority.

Mike and Abe had now stopped, just ten yards short of the man. Mike could now make out that he was young, fairly tall—about six feet two inches, with a bleach blonde mop of hair. Mike waited for the man to address them, but he continued on in his painting undisturbed. Abe nodded for Mike to announce themselves, and swallowing hard, Mike peeped out in his best Saxon, "Um, excuse me, sir?"

The man did not, however, turn around. Mike took a few more steps forward and said again, this time in Latin "Sir?" Still, there was no response. *Is the man deaf?* Mike wondered. *Oh, please no. But why wouldn't he respond?*

Mike advanced until he was practically on top of the man, practically breathing over his shoulder. He could now see the full contents of the painting, and what he saw made him gasp.

"I've been waiting for you," the man proclaimed in perfectly enunciated Latin.

What Mike saw in the painting were two figures which held the exact resemblance of themselves.

Chapter 10

The man said nothing more for five more minutes, but directed his attention toward the rock instead, alternating between pensive stares and paintbrush strokes. Mike and Abe gathered on either side of him, watching his progress on the near to completed painting. Neither of them moved, or attempted to start a conversation, for they were still shocked into paralysis from the strange greeting.

With a last brush across the rock face, the artist seemed satisfied. He glanced at the depiction, then at his recently arrived models, and gave a nod of approval. He promptly began packing up his things and turned around to start up the hill. Mike and Abe stood still, watching him as if he were an opportunity silently floating away from them. The man turned around, motioned for them to follow, then did not wait around to see if they did.

"I assume you want to know how I knew of your coming," he said as they caught up to him. Upon seeing both of the men's faces, he chuckled to himself. "Your looks give yourselves away. My name's Virgil."

"Yeah," Mike responded, looking at Virgil and then at his emblem in a sort of disbelief. "We figured that's who you were. I'm Mike and this is Abe."

Virgil paused in his ascent to study them closer. "So I guess I'm not the only one with foresight of this meeting." Even so, he seemed far less shocked than Mike and Abe did. Mike looked over at Abe to note a particular bounce in Abe's step. *He is eating this up,* Mike thought. To Mike, however, it was extremely surreal, and even after all through which he had traversed, he still found himself in revered silence.

Virgil led them up to the top of a hill on the southern bank of the river that towered over everything else. Upon the crest sat a few small boulders upon which they took rest. Virgil retained his relative silence, not bothering to rush into the answer to his original question, but taking time instead to gaze off at the day. The weather was not unlike the first day they had arrived ashore. A slight breeze blew and a periodic smattering of clouds swept the sky, keeping the heat to a bearable degree. The surroundings themselves were almost of a postcard, and did not at all display any evidence of the monsters or dragons purported to infest the land. Everything looked innocent. Nature continued on in its usual course, either oblivious or apathetic to the vile dealings of its inhabitants. The trees sifted the breeze, baying slightly at its coercion. The fields and flowers of daisies, too, moved in perfect synchronization to the freshness of the air. Everything was most vibrantly green—Mike supposed he had never seen such vibrancy. Despite everything that had run through Mike's head from the moment of shipwreck on, he had to admit one thing, the landscape here was more alive than Eden.

Although such a panorama was most definitely familiar to him, Virgil did not seem the less intrigued by it. He, too, stared off in silence, inhaling passionately, passing the fresh air around in his mouth before exhaling again. A serene smile had since materialized upon his face.

It was Abe, who could not hold in his thoughts any longer, who ended the moment.

"So what was it?" he spilled forth. "How did you know of our coming?"

Virgil simply smiled, though for what reason, Mike could not exclusively determine. "This," he said, waving his arm slowly out toward the unfolding landscape. "This is how I knew."

Mike could tell, without even a glance, that Abe was starving for a more concrete explanation. The tension created between Abe's anxiety and Virgil's ambiguity resonated through the air, causing a welling up of blood in Mike's chest. It did not last long, however, for Virgil decided to relieve the moment. "I come up here often, and I hope you can tell why. Up here, the cares and struggles of the daily life, which so often burden us, seem to fade away into oblivion. Up here, it's just me and Mother Earth. Up here, I find myself lost in the pensiveness which it intends for me.

"Within the past year, I have begun to have dreams—dreams which have been sweet, but confusing at the same time. For weeks, I searched for a way to comprehend these dreams, but could find none, until one day, I came upon some paintings in a nearby cave. An idea struck me, and I immediately set to work scraping out my memory and transposing the dreams on to boulders. I cannot explain just how the figurative nature came out in such a concrete manner but it did. My hand painted the feelings that I received from each dream and they came out as objects."

Virgil led the two over to a nearby boulder, where, painted in bright greens, yellows, and reds, resided a most stunning depiction of a group of people with seven golden sources of light. Mike gasped. Abe continued on fidgeting like a little child in church.

"Just today," he continued. "I felt inspired to paint my latest dream, which turned out to be the two of you. As I painted, I became more and more sure that the figures in my dream were real, and that they would arrive soon. The impression got stronger and stronger until I heard rustling behind me and your voice speak up."

He stared at Mike and Abe. Noting their looks of intrigue, he added, "It's all true, though I have no idea how it's all happened."

Abe's energy level, like a volcano, had been growing steadily as Virgil related his narrative, and, as he finished, Abe could not hold himself in any longer, "It is because you are the master of wisdom."

Virgil looked over at him with a slightly confused look on his face. "Excuse me?"

Abe, blushed, found his usual self again, and spoke in a more civil tone. "There is a reason that you have been having these dreams. There is a reason you knew of our arrival, and there is a reason why you did not reject us as strangers or thieves or assassins.

"My comrade Mike and I are on a quest for humanity. You are to be our guide for that quest. For some reason or another, by powers higher than our own, you have been chosen. And with your help, we will be able to restore order to humanity."

Mike felt a lump form in his throat. The initial delivery to Virgil had not been any lighter than it had been to him. *What must he be thinking now?* Mike asked himself. *Surely, the whole idea must seem entirely ludicrous not only to him, but to this whole world.* If Abe had educated him accurately, this part of England had already seen years of invasions from the Picts and the Irish, and it was likely that many of the people here, possibly including Virgil, had seen friends, relatives, and countrymen mercilessly cut down. *Indeed, the stories of monsters have their truth to them,* Mike realized. *How can a few lines and a strange, preconceived introduction convince him that we have the power to end them?*

But Virgil continued to stand there. Mike studied his face in bewilderment. Virgil seemed to understand, and even believe Abe. It was as if an unsolved equation had been completed in Virgil's head with that one bit of information. The calm smile on his face seemed to reveal it all.

"Tell me everything," Virgil said.

The three dove into an intense conversation of explanations, memories, questions, and answers. Legends were shared, as well as histories, projections, and promises. Virgil was given, in a matter of hours, everything that Mike had been given over the course of a few days. Abe told him his life story and of how he came upon the emblem of knowledge. He told of his search for the golden emblem, and then for Mike. He explained the origin of the emblem and the concept behind it. He concluded by speaking of the visions of the Elfish wisdom bearer Yolath, and of how they were commanded to come to Virgil and enlist him in the cause.

"I was extremely overwhelmed when Abe told me all of these things," Mike related. "That was, until I saw the Elfish Realm." Mike then spoke of his experience around the elves and the vision of paradise that they had planted in his head. A smile grew on his lips as he resurrected the sights, colors, sounds, smells, and spirit of the Realm. Virgil listened intently, never straying from eye contact with Mike.

"You are the master of wisdom," Abe repeated at the end of everything. "It is your calling and duty to guide us in our journey. Your emblem is close, and though you are not yet in possession of it, it has been inspiring you with dreams. These will be the dreams that you will continue to receive to guide us. Without you, we cannot go anywhere or do anything."

Abe finished and Virgil did not say anything for a moment, but seemed to look out again at the landscape. Their stories had taken up the afternoon, and their surroundings were progressing far into dusk. The long shadows had now become one to form a continuous dark shadow over the once green landscape. Stars had begun to appear and all that lingered of the daylight was a slight orange glow that hung over the western horizon. Accompanying those stars emerged a giant orange globe that quickly began to reveal itself on the eastern horizon. It rose in full wax and boasted its own contribution of light as it commenced its own journey across the night sky. Nevertheless, Mike and Abe could only see a silhouette as they watched Virgil for a concluding response.

"It's getting late," Virgil stated finally. "We should probably get back to my hut." And without saying a word more, he turned and started walking back down the dale, leaving Mike and Abe wondering if they had wasted their breaths.

Despite all of this, Mike had a good feeling. The emblem glowed warmly in his hand, emitting an actual light by which he could guide his steps. It seemed like the pieces fit. This man seemed to be everything Mike had imagined he would be. The way he seemed to live his life seemed to transcend even these lofty hills from which they all descended. He was a man for the clouds, apparently for dreams within the clouds. Virgil led onward, leaving Mike and Abe behind to follow him, entrusting everything to him.

The night was quickly getting cool and dew was beginning to form on the blades of grass. The air smelled of damp hay that sent Mike into a familiar, delightful nostalgia. The crickets sung out their melodies, and the lights of what Abe fondly described as fireflies danced in the air. Even in the blackness of the night, the world was filled with life, and for the moment, even the threats of monsters and demons were pushed to the back of Mike's head.

The light of the circular hut shone brightly against the black of the evening. As the group approached, Mike sensed something in the bushes behind him, quickly squelching the feelings he had just experienced. Without time for another thought, he heard the bushes rattle sharply and looked, to his horror, a figure rushing at full speed towards Virgil.

"Look out!" Mike yelled.

The figure hit him not a split second after Virgil, too, turned his head.

The now almost horizontal foe sent Virgil flying off the path and into the brush. Mike was about to rush in after them when he stopped at what he heard. It was laughing. On closer look, he realized that it was a boy of about fifteen that had tackled him, and was now pinned under Virgil's somewhat recovered body.

Upon helping himself and the boy up, Virgil led them into the hut where his whole family was now present. The room smelled strongly of oven-baked bread, which made Mike's mouth water. Although they still had provisions left from Antiochus, his stomach was grumbling, and he was eager for whatever they had for him, especially if it was fresh and warm.

"The soup is ready whenever you are, Virgil," a young lady proclaimed, and without any more delay, Virgil grabbed a few clay bowls, two of which he handed to Mike and Abe. He then proceeded over to the pot over the fire and dished out soup for each of them. The soup looked to have carrots and onions and cabbage in it, but little else. There was no meat, which, Mike imagined, was not an everyday commodity for these people. There was fresh bread and cheese, however, which Mike gratefully took from the hearth before sitting down beside Abe and the others.

"Brutus, Apollus, Claudia, these are my guests, Abe and Mike," Virgil said as they all sat down. Turning to his guests, he added, "Brutus is my brother, Claudia is my sister, and Apollus is my brother-in-law. The pitiful rascal who tried to take me down back there is Brutus' son Peter."

"Tried?" Peter challenged, "I succeeded."

Virgil laughed. "Maybe for a few seconds at least."

"Where are you both from?" the older one, Brutus, inquired, ignoring his son's bragging and focusing instead on the two guests and his food.

Abe and Mike looked at one another. They were leery to tell the complete truth but they knew that they would eventually have to come up with a good reason for asking for their brother's leave, if, of course, he was willing in the first place. Virgil, however, picked up their hesitation and answered for them.

"They are on errand from Rome and have come to me seeking guidance through Britain."

It was a rather poor story with lots of holes, but everyone seemed to believe it. No other direct question toward the matter was posed as the family continued to converse over their soup for an hour or two longer. They did ask a lot of questions, mostly about Rome, wherein both had to draw from book knowledge to answer, but Mike was fine with that. Luckily for them, their limited knowledge still exceeded the families'.

Abe then asked a few questions of the news of the land, but nobody had anything more than second-hand stories and rumors to offer. As they were shared, Mike felt the original feelings he had had here creep back into his chest. With all the excitement of finding Virgil, as well as the journey of serenity upon which he had taken them, Mike had almost forgotten where he was. The stories and rumors shared, much along the lines of those of Antiochus, brought it all back to the surface, though. "There has been talk of strange man-like creatures coming off the coast to the west," Apollus stated. "We have not seen any such thing yet, but from what it sounds like, we cannot avoid seeing them for too much longer."

The words haunted Mike, especially as the household lay down to sleep. Mike was exhausted, but his mind was, again, fully awake. *How can they live in this fear I feel now?* Such a sustained feeling had never been in Mike's heart before, and his body did not know how to handle it. The only solution it had conjured so far had been insomnia, and, despite everything Mike did in the next few hours, his body seemed intent on it.

The room left Mike behind in the steady breathing of slumber. Mike envied them, for they could be taken away, out of this world for even what seemed to them as a few short moments. Mike was left behind in it, abandoned, but still victim to whatever nightmares might have appeared in sleep.

Mike turned over again on his bed roll. His mind reverted back to home. He wanted to think of what his parents were doing at this moment, but, truthfully, they would not be alive for another 1500 years. *There's definitely no way back now,* he concluded. *I am no longer a part of that world anymore.* Yet his mind still longed to be so, especially now. He longed to be with his family again. He longed to be back on his farm, in the midst of those tomato plants, in the midst of familiarity and safety. He longed to come in after the day and only have to worry about overeating. All of it was futile, though, and the more Mike thought on it, the more frustrated he became.

Mike started at the sound of a stirring outside. The air that had a few moments before been silent, save the ever present droning of the crickets, was now filled with the slight, almost nonexistent hoot of an owl. Mike sat up. *Owls would not make such a racket,* he muttered to himself. Then he caught sight of a shadow quietly get up and walk toward the door. There was enough light to identify it as Virgil.

"Hey," Mike whispered to get his attention.

"Mike," he responded, "you're still awake, great. Put on your shoes."

"Where are we going?"

"You'll find out soon enough. I promise you, however, that it will be great."

A little confused, but curious at the same time, Mike followed Virgil's lead and exited the hut. The only thing Mike could think of was the sight of the stars. Virgil would have been, after all, a grand admirer of such things. *But of the rustling?* Most definitely it was another person, or a group of people. He doubted that they would come over to do something as simple as stargazing. Sure enough, outside waited two male peers that greeted Virgil with a slap on the back.

"Hey, Virgil, good to see you again," one of them said.

"Yeah, it's surprising that it's been a month already."

"But it sure hasn't come too soon," the other said, and all three laughed. Mike, in the mean time, simply stood there, trying to discover a clue at what could be going on, but with no luck.

"Comrades," Virgil said, putting his arm around Mike, "this is my friend Mike." Then, turning to his friends, exclaimed, "Mike, this is Lucius and Arwulf. Two of the best men in Britain."

"Just because we let you in on our little secret," the one called Lucius exclaimed.

Virgil shrugged. "More or less." The other two chuckled and shook their heads in insincere chide.

Mike watched the trio converse back and forth, growing more frustrated by the moment. He doubted very much now that they were speaking of stargazing, or any other innocent pastime for that matter. The sky was quite striking tonight, with the stars burning brightly alongside a full moon, but Mike soon realized that it would have been nothing out of the ordinary, especially to these people, who had lived in the darkness of night their whole lives. His anxiety began to rise, but the three started walking off, and he felt somewhat compelled to follow.

The group paraded through the night, moving forward with an energy that seemed somewhat savage. Mike followed, panting behind them and considering at every moment to turn back. He desisted though, and for several semi-conscious reasons. A lump was beginning to form in his chest; he was seeing a shade of Virgil that had not been apparent in the daylight. Something had changed him, whether it was the bluish-purple sky of the full moon, or the dark trees of the gullies through which they ran. He was no longer the pensive prophet they had met earlier.

The group ran deeper and deeper into the wilderness, beyond the limits of civilization. Mike shook as he ran behind, struggling to hold his composure. *Where could we be headed?* He wondered. *It might as well be the edge of the earth.* Then, all at once, the trees opened up to a clearing which harbored a dark, abandoned building below. It was to this building, which looked to be an old Roman villa, to which the group had directed themselves, for after stopping to catch their breath for a moment, they ran with greater zest down to its silent gate.

"Mike," Virgil sounded, opening the gate with a clanking creak, "prepare to feast upon a grand treasure."

Mike, his curiosity peaked, followed the three into the courtyard in dread. The entire place seemed to have been dead for quite some time. Paint peeled off the mortared walls. Spider webs dominated in every nook and corner. The place was stunningly silent. Mike, however, seemed the only one cognizant, or at least concerned, about the haunt. The other three gingerly directed themselves over to the shadows on the south side of the villa and into a room glowing with the light of the moon. The blood drained in Mike's head at what the moon revealed. The entire room was filled with glass bottles. "Some of the best wine in the land," Virgil announced to Mike, "imported from the continent and abandoned by some Roman for our taking." The three commenced tapping into it like a group of wolves.

Mike stood there and watched in horror, now knowing way too much and not wanting to know what was to ultimately follow. He refused, again and again, their invitations to join. The world was spinning in enough circles for him as it was. Mike watched as the spirits rose to their heads and planted even more fire in their eyes. They carried on like banshees, laughing and cursing everything within the night, including the ghost of the Roman who had supplied them.

Mike wanted out of it, but he had no idea how he could escape. He had no idea where he was. He would be strangled in the darkness of the night if he tried to make it back on his own, for the pathway back was treacherous in its obscurity. What was to come next, however, was an alternative far worse. Before the end of the night, Mike would find himself choosing that obscure pathway back anyway, fumbling along it alone and shaking, and trusting in faith to guide him.

Chapter 11

By some act of providence, Mike had been able to find his way back to the hut, even as unfamiliar with the terrain as he was. The night had become much blacker since the villa, for the moon had fallen behind a front of clouds in the sky, but Mike's emblem was able to provide enough light. He stumbled into the hut after catching sight of it and running to it with his mind racing like a sickening rollercoaster.

He entered the darkened room, feeling like he had made an epic journey, for although his feet had only been walking for half the night, his soul had seemed to have traveled to Hell and back. Monsters, demons, ghosts: they were as real as ever in Mike's mind now, but of an entirely different nature than he would have thought. *They have always been here. They're rooted in the land.* Apollus had spoken of invading monsters. There were already monsters native to the woods, dancing in the moonlight under the shaded groves of yews.

Virgil and the others had ignored Mike's pleas to return to the hut while at the villa. They were so far off in their own twisted, horrid world that Mike doubted his words even reached them. Instead, they led him to the trees, where a great midnight gathering had congregated. Mike recalled all too vividly what he had seen. There had been a fire. Yew branches had burned and cackled in the mist, augmented by the beat of giant Celtic drums and the cries of naked bodies coursing round it. They were not human. They could not have been. Some metamorphosis had been undergone to transform them into creatures capable of such ghastly movements. Virgil and his friends, already transformed by their previous actions, melted right into churning energy.

Mike recalled seeing others. They wore fear on their faces, just like him. But unlike him, they sat tied up in the middle of the grove. Mike had looked on from the edge, daring not to venture in any further for fear the fire would melt his heart. Mike knew, without even asking, for what those beings were intended. That moment was what caused him to turn and run.

Now he collapsed onto his mat, feeling more tired than ever before. He wanted to alert Abe, but he did not have the presence of mind, nor the energy, to do so. Instead, he collapsed onto his back and into unconsciousness, his body ordering his mind to desist.

Mike did not wake until late in the morning, and when he did, he found Abe sitting a few feet from him, staring at him. Mike wiped his eyes and felt for his head. Whether it was the stress from last night, or the altered sleep schedule, Mike now had a pulsing pain in his temple. Abe handed him a cup of water and some bread. Mike took it and ate, wondering how he could tell Abe what he had seen.

Abe brought it up though. "I notice that you slept much later than usual, and that Virgil's not here."

It was then that Mike told Abe everything, down to the last detail. It made him lose his appetite.

Abe listened to his entire account without breaking eye contact. After Mike finished, he asked, "Is he still there?"

"For all I know," Mike replied.

Abe nodded. "I'll talk to him when he gets back."

Virgil did not come back until late afternoon. Mike and Abe sat around the vicinity of the property all day waiting for him. Nobody was working. When Mike asked about it, Virgil's nephew said it was the Sabbath. Mike could not help but note that although they were most definitely resting, they did not attend any sort of church services. From what Abe had taught him, though, Mike doubted that there were any services to attend.

The family seemed to hold no opinion toward Virgil's actions. Mike had pried his sister concerning his absence, and she simply shrugged. "It's the full moon. He always goes out with those guys. He'll be back soon."

"Do you know what he does with them?" Mike had not told her that he had been out with him and had seen everything.

"No," she had answered with apathy, "nor do I really care, as long as he does not get himself killed or incite other families against us."

Mike had walked away in a complete daze. He could not help but wonder how he had been thrown into such a world and what he was up against. *How is one to make paradise out of this?* he sat pondering. It overwhelmed him, especially when he thought that the man that was to guide them fell right into the nightmare.

The images still flooded his mind, even in the bright noon sunlight. The drums, the fire, the prisoners, the endless dancing and chanting and ranting, the grove of trees filtering the light of the full moon, the endless pounding of those drums. Mike held his pulsing head as he sat under the shade of an oak. The scenes had taken up residence in his memory like a parasite and would not leave, no matter what he did to divert his thoughts. Mike tried to turn his thoughts to the beauty of the day, but the sky was gray and fields and songs of birds seemed only skin deep—a cheap covering for the dark secrets that the cursed land held at night.

Early afternoon found the wayward man returning along the trail. He walked with heavy steps and was holding his aching head while shading his eyes from the sun. As he approached Mike and Abe, he smiled a weak smile.

"Mike, you missed out."

Mike did not say anything. He could not even return the fake smile with which he had intended to welcome him.

Abe, taking on a professional tone, stood up. "Virgil, can we have a talk?"

Virgil chuckled weakly. "Yeah, sure. When?"

"I was hoping about right now."

"Now?" Virgil repeated, groaning. "How about later? I'm not feeling too good right now."

"Yeah, now."

Virgil shrugged. "I guess if it's that important, we can."

Abe led Virgil away from the house where they would be out earshot from the rest of the family members. He had not invited Mike along, but Mike followed at a distance anyway, feeling, for some reason, that it was important that he heard the conversation.

When they had reached the shade of a solitary tree at Virgil's pitiful request, Abe started into him. "Mike has let me know what you have been up to, and it is simply unbecoming of your calling to do such things."

Virgil simply looked at Abe and laughed in spite of the accusation. "What are you talking about, Abe?"

"Your behavior last night. Your reveling was about the worst thing you could have done." Mike stared at Abe in wonder as he spoke; he was laying it on pretty thick. He believed that Abe had good intentions, but knew, at the same time, that Abe's education and ambition ruled over him, placing in him passions beyond his control of emotion. This was one of those times, for he was getting red in the face. Abe continued in his barrage. "Your calling is one of meditation and deep thought, of prayer, of fasting. It is about receiving truth from a source greater than us all. That cannot be done when you are in drunken fits of frenzy."

Virgil furrowed his eyebrows. "Hey, I am just living my life the way I always have." Mike started back at the strength of Virgil's rebuttal. "Who are you to come along and to tell me what I should or should not do? You don't understand our lives here. I have seen the land you come from. You don't know the life that constantly falls into question. I am holding on to the moment as it comes, because I don't know if it will be there tomorrow."

The tension was building. Virgil was now facing Abe head on and staring down into Abe's eyes, which now matched in intensity. The two were squared off, ready for battle. Mike thought that he should do something, but he feinted from action, fearing he might simply make things worse.

"Have you committed yourself to our cause?" came Abe's real question.

Virgil retained his intensity. "I don't know. Now I'm not so sure I want to if things are going to be like this. I cannot ignore the dreams, but now I don't know if they're worth the chastisement."

Abe was now waving off his hands in frustration and defeat. He pointed down at Virgil. "I'm not going to deal with this. You let me know your decision by the evening one way or the other so I know whether we should stay the night, or journey off and sleep somewhere else."

With that, Abe walked away without turning back, leaving Virgil slouched under the tree staring coldly out at him. Mike looked on from his original spot, still unnoticed by either two. *I have to do something.* Mike still did not move. *I don't want to look like a busybody, though. And how can I approach the man after instilling this attack on him?*

Mike felt for the emblem in the fold of his cloak, a nervous habit he had since picked up in the past year. Again, it was warm to the touch. He thought back on the other times when it had been warm—when he had needed to take some sort of action, such as escaping the waves or deciding where to go. It required action out of him again, and the feeling was no less vivid than before. *How can this be right, though?* he questioned. *This man is not what he needs to be.*

Regardless, the answer was the same. The emblem did not back down in its intensity, independent from Mike's doubt. Mike suddenly got the feeling like the mission was in jeopardy and he needed to act now. *He is the man,* Mike realized. *Without him, the mission is dead.* Mike had to face his petty fears. Slowly, he uncovered himself and approached him.

Virgil saw him when he was about ten meters away. "Mike," he simply said, though his tone implied that he was not too excited to see him.

"Virgil," Mike timidly responded, "Can we talk?" Mike could feel his legs shaking; he almost wished for a negative answer.

"If you are planning on regurgitating what he said," Virgil retorted, pointing in the direction in which Abe had stormed off, "The answer is no."

Mike found himself continuing on in his words. "Abe is not a very personable man. He does not always know how to express himself."

"Or it is in his nature to be a knave," Virgil said. Then, after a few breaths, he added, "And you. Why would you do such a thing?"

"I didn't mean to make anyone angry. Please, Virgil understand that we do come from a different culture—one in which such practices are abhorred. The sights shocked me. I didn't know what to do."

"Well, I don't understand. Why would such things be bad?"

Mike did not know where to start. He had no idea how to bridge such a moral gap. Yet, the words came like manna, and Mike found his knees were discovering a more solid stance. "It's a lot like Abe said. I know we haven't explained very much to you, and it was completely unfair for Abe to explode at you in your ignorant foolishness, but it was foolishness, just the same. I hope you'll let me explain."

FORTH FROM EDEN

The words flowed boldly out of Mike's mouth. For a second, he feared that it might create more anger in Virgil, but instead Virgil seemed interested in what Mike had to say and looked on for Mike to continue.

"I cannot explain exactly why, but the emblems of virtue are governed by a class of laws that are higher than all of us, regardless of our culture, class, or society. For example, Abe's emblem will not function in its role as the provider of knowledge unless Abe himself puts forth the effort to educate himself through reading and experimentation. It simply will not work. It is the same with you. You do not have the emblem of wisdom yet—I imagine it is up to you to find it—but when you do acquire it, it will not be of any worth unless you embrace the laws that govern it. Abe has taught me the nature of such laws, and I feel it's my duty to pass them on to you."

As Mike spoke, truths were being revealed to him as well. He realized that it had never been Abe's responsibility to speak with Virgil, it had been his. Mike recalled Abe's words from that first night on the mission. He was to bear a little of all of the demons. Up until this point, he had not had to face that issue, but now Virgil's foolishness was calling him to action. Mike suddenly understood why his emblem had been glowing and was now motivated by the assurance that he was doing exactly what he was called to do. He grasped the emblem tighter and drew in another breath with a bit more evenness.

"Your emblem is arguably one of the most important ones out there. Without it, we cannot be directed on where to go, and we cannot know what to do in certain situations. Your emblem is the source of truths beyond the reach of what books can teach Abe. It is the consulting of a power greater than our own, and for that reason, your role is one of gravity and reverence. I know that you may not hold the same beliefs as we do, but you have to try things our way; you have to look to the emblem's source—the God of everything in heaven and earth. In order for you to do this, you must refrain from drunkenness, you must give yourself over to your passion of meditation. You must fast and pray to this God. Only after this will you be found worthy and prepared for the dreams to come at will. Are you willing to do that?"

Mike watched Virgil intently as he weighed the matters in his mind.

He could tell that Virgil was teetering on a pinnacle, probably not having realized before this point what these two foreign strangers had been asking him. Mike could almost read the thoughts as they went through his peer's head. He was debating whether it was worth the sacrifice and wondering what reward would come to him. Mike could tell that Virgil was looking back with longing on the life he was living, desiring, more than anything, that he and Abe had never come to him.

Yet Mike could also almost sense an air of nobility in him. Somehow, Mike was able to read into the man—down into his very core. Despite his actions, there was something special down there inside. Mike had a feeling that at this point, the man simply did not realize it.

Mike continued to watch him for some moments. Virgil's silence was pressing. The moment began rebuilding the strength of Mike's previously waning anxiety before Virgil broke it. "Do you think I am the right man?" he asked.

"I do," Mike said, forcing himself to forget the horrid scenes of last night.

Virgil nodded, taking this into account. "Then I'll do it. But I hope you will be the medium between Abe and me. I don't really have any desire to associate with him."

Mike was so relieved at the words, such a request seemed miniscule. "Yeah, I'll take care of it. Right now, concentrate on getting a hold of your emblem."

Virgil smiled weakly and nodded. Mike slapped him on the back and exhaled for what seemed like the first time in several minutes.

Abe sat off about a few hundred yards, staring off into the sky under the shade of another tree. Mike had sought him out immediately after he had parted from Virgil, who lingered on in quiet pensiveness. *That's good*, Mike had thought to himself. *That's exactly what he needs to be doing.* Now, as he approached Abe, he prepared himself for the next leg which, in comparison, seemed a downhill stretch. Preparing tactfully what needed words were to be said, Mike called out to Abe, who turned his head to look over.

"Mike," Abe started before Mike could say anything more, "I don't know what to tell you. That boy is simply not qualified for the job. I have no idea what this means about the mission."

"He is fine," Mike reassured, now standing over his partner.

"I just talked to him, though," Abe interjected, furrowing his eyes in confusion at Mike's words, and especially at the tone with which they were carried. "I don't know if you heard us, but he's not willing to cooperate. It seems like the emblem misled us."

"I heard it all," Mike stated, "But I talked to him as well afterwards. He is fine. The emblem was correct. It was us who fell short. It was never your duty to speak with him; it was mine. Everything is okay now, though."

Mike's words seemed to get through to Abe. After he finished, Abe simply turned his head downward and said, "Mike, I'm so sorry."

Mike could think of nothing else to do but shrug it off. It was a mistake that had been made out of ignorance and would not be repeated in the future. However, Mike added, "It's important that you two make amends, though. The last thing we can have is disunity in the group."

Abe nodded. "Yeah, I think you're right."

Abe struggled to get up and Mike reached down to help him. The two silently walked back to the hut, which continued on uninterrupted in its usual rhythm. Everybody in the family lazed around, drinking ale out of sheepskin flasks and watching the day go by. They gave the two a nod of recognition, oblivious to the battle the two had just fought, and Virgil's sister told them that there was food inside to be had at their leisure. The two took the food, but did not sit down, for they were eager to find Virgil again and re-instill some sort of unity. But after looking around a while, they realized he was nowhere to be found.

They came up to the top of the rise near the house and scanned the horizon, but, again, the figure of Virgil was undetected. Abe looked over at Mike with an air of skepticism, but Mike remained calm. "Don't worry, Abe. He's the right one. You have to believe me."

"So where do you think he is?"

"I could take a guess, but I'd rather not bother him. It's not where he is that's important anyway, but what he's doing."

Mike had been right in his assumptions, though it had taken all his willpower to remain confident in them, especially when Virgil did not show his face for a week. Abe expressed more than once his failing faith in the man. "He's gone—he's not coming back," he had conjectured most audibly to Mike. Mike, however, parried off his remarks, keeping a silent steadiness about him.

The family worried, but did not, or rather could not do anything about it. Food still had to be provided, and that would not come without work. They had made short searches at night, including the place where he and Mike and Virgil had originally gone—the promontory of boulders—the place where Mike had originally thought he would be—but they had found no trace of him. The family pried the two for answers, and Mike told them all he could without unveiling the whole mission, but it came as no surprise that all the information he gave them offered little comfort or direction as to his whereabouts.

In the mean time, there was nothing else to do but wait and work. Twice, Mike traveled to town with Virgil's nephew and brother-in-law to help barter their bread for more grain and other foodstuffs. The work was hard—they had to pull a crude cart weighed down with everything back and forth—but at the same time, it was very satisfying. With all of the emotional drama that had occurred in his life for the past few months, it felt good to have a good, hard sweat.

Eight days had passed when they again caught sight of Virgil as he strode spritely down the knoll. His sisters, at his sight, ran up to hug him, and he received their hugs warmly. His face wore the look of a thousand years, but his eyes remained bright. Mike could see something amazing had happened since they'd seen him last. He watched as Virgil allowed the reunion to occur. Virgil only tolerated it for moment before resuming his walk down to the hut. He headed directly toward both Abe and Mike, reached into the fold of his tunic, and pulled out an object that was gold and glowing. The glow reflected in their faces as well as in their comrade's as he triumphantly stated, "I have it."

Chapter 12

They were to leave first thing tomorrow morning. Virgil had announced this to Mike and Abe just before dismissing himself to sleep. Both men were surprised at the announcement, for Virgil had looked like he needed a full week to recover from whatever he had been through while he had been away. His body swayed from fatigue even as he talked. Mike asked if he wanted to wait a few extra days, but Virgil adamantly opposed the idea.

"No," he had argued, "we are to leave tomorrow. Don't worry about me. I will be rested enough."

"What about your family?"

"I'm sorry that I have to leave you to let them know, but I cannot stay up any longer."

Virgil had all but collapsed after that, leaving Mike and Abe more curious than ever at the journey Virgil had taken. "He seems to be fully invested," Abe said. "I guess he is to be trusted on the decision."

Mike nodded. "Yeah, I guess you're right."

It was then that Brutus approached them and joined them in looking into the hut. "Did he go lie down?"

Mike nodded. "Yeah. He looked like he could not survive another moment." Without even looking, Mike could tell what was coming next. It had been avoided for long enough now, and Virgil's strange disappearance then reappearance would be enough to draw the family's curiosity out to the open. Brutus retained his silence for only a moment longer before turning to Mike.

"Will you tell me what's going on?"

Mike knew that he had to tell as much of the truth as he possibly could.

Luckily, the words came to him as he spoke. "You know as well as we do that the Roman way of life has been in jeopardy here in Britain for years now." Brutus nodded with sober eyes. "We have been sent here to assess the problems and come up with a solution. Virgil fits the type of character we need in order to carry this out and he has agreed to help us. We must leave tomorrow morning, though."

"Tomorrow morning?" Brutus challenged, staring up into Mike's eyes. "How long will you be gone?"

Mike bit his lip. "Unfortunately, this could take up to a few months. Virgil will not be back in time for the end of harvest. I hope that you are not too inconvenienced by this."

"Well, if it is for Rome, then you have my leave," he stated, though with some hesitance. "It is good to see that they have not completely left us behind."

Mike cringed inside, knowing that their cover-up had given Brutus a false hope. Even though he may not ever realize the falsehood of such a hope, Mike felt sick for him and his kin all the same. Here they were at the very edge of civilization, always having lived with a slight inner twinge of desperation at the prospect of the creatures in their closets waiting to strike out at them. Rome had given them limited security, but they did not even have that to fall back on anymore. And they never would again.

Mike had studied all of the limited history of this time. He knew that there would be nothing for the next several hundred years. England would be racked with invasion and shifting authority for generations after these people lived. Future times would bring monarchy; England would rise out of the dust to become the greatest nation on earth, but the future had no applicability to these people. Theirs was an England of chaos and warfare. People would die; blood would be shed in the name of honor, and only the victor would be recognized. There would be no flag atop the caskets with a twenty-one gun salute. People would be lucky to get any burial at all.

Mike wished that he could tell these people the truth—the truth about Rome, the truth about the invasions, the truth about what would become of the days that they spent so deliberately. It would come up as a blank spot in history. There would be no praise, no stories or heroes, nothing but legends. Mike wanted to shed the light on these people, but it would do no good. *What could they do differently anyway?* They could only do what they had been doing their whole lives—work their hearts away and hope to God that the day would turn out as peaceful as the last one.

Mike thought on such things later that night as he helped Peter wipe out the earthen bowls from which they had been supping. *Maybe we will change all of that. Maybe our actions can write a different, much more pleasant course of events for these people.* Mike thought again on the implications if their mission succeeded, on the murals of paintings denoting the elfish history. He thought of what good he was chosen to bring to the world, of what good he was chosen to bring to these wonderful people. It was often easy to get so caught up in the events of the day that such a perspective fell out of focus. Everything that had recently happened with the shipwreck and Virgil had seemed to do that for him. But such thoughts tonight reset his vision. An itch to act was suddenly re-inflamed. His sight suddenly fell in line with Virgil's. They needed to quit this place and move forward. Immediately.

The three departed from the hut the next morning before the rays of the sun were any more than a light blue glow in the eastern sky. Virgil seemed re-energized, yet shockingly calm at the same time. The sleep he had allotted himself had, indeed, proved sufficient. Still, he did not say anything of his experiences of the past week, neither did he say anything more than what was necessary. He simply led out, walking confidently as if he had a specific, proximate destination in mind. Mike and Abe followed behind him in curiosity, wondering, among a million other things, where they were directing themselves.

They headed west, over the hills of trees and fields, feeling the cool breeze of the morning wash over them like rain. Abe threw out an inquiry as to their destination, but Virgil only answered by stating, "We're almost there. I want to show you what I saw while I was gone." Abe looked at Mike, and both shrugged and continued on walking.

Silence reigned until they reached a small glade near the top of another hill. Virgil directed the party over to a boulder which lay exposed above the ground. Mike could see that there was a painting upon the rock, though it was not quite as concrete as the first one they had encountered. In actuality, the brushstrokes looked much like typical petroglyphs: scattered and enigmatic. Mike took note of six main components. The first was a conglomeration of what looked like houses. Enclosing those houses was a giant heart. Through the heart ran a straight line which was headed on the bottom by three distinct dots. Off to the side lay a castle and above everything looked to be the big dipper constellation. Mike could not make sense of it at all, but it had apparently been enough for Virgil, who proceeded to explain. "I saw these things in a dream three nights after I found the emblem off in those trees over there. After putting them down on this rock, I discovered that we are to travel north along the road to a village just south of York. There we will find the next member of our mission."

"The bearer of love?" Abe asked with energy.

Virgil smiled. Mike looked over at him. The smile had a distinct nature to it, as if there was something else, something deeper on the subject that required further explanation. Mike found himself waiting for it, but if Virgil did in fact have something on his mind, he did not voice it at that moment. Mike furrowed his eyebrows.

Abe, in the mean time, seemed to be sent to an entirely different world. He paced back and forth, muttering phrases to himself in pure excitement. Then, all at once, he looked up at the two. "Well, why don't you say we get a move on with it then?"

Mike looked over at Virgil, who did not seem to hold the same urgency as Abe at the moment. Virgil opened his mouth to respond, but as he did so, another voice was heard from across the clearing. Mike turned to look, and what he saw tied a knot in his stomach.

It was Arwulf. Dozens of memories that Mike had struggled to push out of his mind suddenly revived, sending a shiver down Mike's spine. He could not help but recall how he had seen this man last, something that he had not dared let past the gateway to his conscious mind. This man had tormented his subconscious in the form of nightmares for the past week, and Mike had thought that he would be able to leave them behind at Virgil's hut. Yet there they were, entering his life again, strolling through the field as if nothing at all was wrong in the world.

"Who's that?" Abe questioned.

Virgil, the only one of the three who did not seem surprised, was the one to answer. "That's my good friend Arwulf."

"He looks like he's prepared himself for a long journey," Abe noted.

Mike's eyes widened. Arwulf was almost on top of them by now, definitely in range of hearing, but still, Mike said, "Virgil, can I talk to you alone?"

Virgil greeted Arwulf with a hug. Mike repeated himself. Virgil looked over at Mike for a second, then nodded and excused himself. "Arwulf, this is Abe," he motioned, walking aside with Mike. "He is coming on the journey with us."

"Arwulf is coming on the journey with *us*?" Mike questioned softly but strongly, turning Virgil away from the other two.

"Yeah, Mike. What's the deal?"

"I was about to ask the same question."

The serene expression on Virgil's face promised harmlessness. "After I finished the painting, I urgently needed something to eat. Arwulf's hut was nearby, so I decided to stop by to eat and tell him that I was leaving. He asked me where I was going and I let him know, and he told me that he could take us there."

Mike did not say anything for a moment, but bit his lip and turned away. It seemed like Virgil could read his thoughts, for he asked, "Was that wrong to agree to that?"

"Wrong?" Mike looked over at Arwulf, who was chatting lightly with Abe. "I'm sorry, but my only impression of that man is of the most terrible kind."

Virgil set his hands to steady Mike's temper. "We had a long talk about it, Mike. I told him your feelings on it. Actually I told him much of the same things you told me. He seemed to agree. You have my word, nothing of that nature will occur."

Mike rolled the issue over in his mind, denying Virgil the benefit of an immediate response. Aside from Mike's genuine dislike of the man, something seemed wrong, but he could not place his finger on it.

"Mike," Virgil stated again, looking for a response.

"I don't know," Mike stated. Again, it did not seem right. He was not one of the party. Then again, they had had the elves to guide them away from the Realm, without which they would have been lost. There was no guarantee that they now faced the same risk, for, in all likelihood, Virgil did not know the countryside any better than he or Abe. The idea of a guide made sense, but one matter lingered in his head.

"Those three dots were us, weren't they?"

Virgil detected Mike's direction with the comment. "Yeah, and I took that into consideration, but I've done so much for him in the past, and he's always felt indebted to me. I want to give him this chance to rectify himself. I figure that we probably could have found our way to York on our own, which is what was probably originally planned, but it will be easier and faster, and safer for that matter, with someone who knows the way and has connections all over Britain."

"Connections?" Mike asked.

"Arwulf's father is a Druid and a bard, one of the most influential on the island. He is known as the great bard of the Celts, and Arwulf himself seems to be following in his footsteps."

Mike was still hesitant. He felt for the emblem but could not tell whether it was hot or cold. But maybe it did not matter. Maybe this was not a big decision. After all, it was only a means to an end. They would get to where they needed to go either way. And they would get there faster with Arwulf along.

Then there was the safety issue. In all honesty, Mike was scared to death of traveling long distances through the countryside. The rumors must have had an element of truth to them. Mike was still anticipating with dread the day when they would be proven true. There were most definitely yet unencountered monsters in the land; he could feel their presence. It was almost as if it was a sort of coldness in the air.

Even if Arwulf hadn't known his way, it would be beneficial to have an extra body around. "You say it's safer with connections?"

Virgil nodded. "Even though I would have made the journey without his offer, I would have been terrified."

Again, Mike understood. He shuffled his feet in further consideration. "How long will it take to get there?"

Virgil shrugged. "I've never been farther than a few miles from our hut."

Mike tried to think back to his geography lessons to imagine how big England was and where Bath and York fell in relation to one another. It was useless, however, since the drawings could not capture the reality of the size, especially when they would be traveling by foot. At this moment in particular, the land seemed especially big, overwhelmingly big. He felt like he was an ant, about to take a journey into the heart of a dragon's lair, without any weapon whatsoever. Mike looked over at Arwulf. He carried a long spear in his hand and had a sling strung to his side. Those were commodities that Mike suddenly felt he could not pass up.

"Alright, but he leaves as soon as we get there."

"I would doubt that he would stay longer than that."

Mike nodded, telling himself that it was the right decision. He felt the emblem again, but again there was nothing. In a way, it was comforting though, knowing that he had made a decision after weighing the alternatives, instead of depending on someone, or something, to simply tell him what to do. Maybe it was supposed to be that way after all.

Mike smiled as they both turned around and started walking back to the hut. "Alright, but you have to promise that your pasts are behind you."

Virgil smiled. "It wouldn't be worth it anyway, unless, of course we found another abandoned villa with a stash of Gaulish wine."

Mike shook his head, laughing despite his sincerity. "Well don't go searching for it."

Virgil returned the laugh, but then immediately straightened his face. "I already gave you my word. I am giving it to you again."

Mike looked at him and knew that he meant it. He patted him on the shoulder and replied, "That's good enough for me."

Chapter 13

The sun did not rise the next morning. At least it was unseen to the party as they ventured forth on a road in an east-northeasterly direction. The clouds drooped as a low, thick blanket, rolling across the sky in a series of semi-connected folds. The cover provided a welcome shade, but where the brightness had subsided, the humidity almost compensated. The party was breathing the moisture that enveloped them; soon the folds would close in and soak them.

Mike had not gotten much sleep last night. They had slept near the roadside, and Mike could not shake the thoughts out of his head. He had known that he would have to learn to deal with his fear, but up to this point, such had been a task beyond his capabilities. This morning, Mike was surprisingly awake. He would see if the fatigue would catch up to him later, but for now, he was able to enjoy his full senses in the gardened surroundings. For the first hour or so, they walked alongside the Avon River, listening to its steady current wind its way down to the sea. Wildflowers pleasantly interrupted greenery near the roadside and filled the air with striking aromas.

The other members of the party were silent for one reason or another for the majority of the morning. It could have been that their moods mirrored the weather and kept them suspended in silence, or it simply could have been that they were tired from last night and the prospect of the days ahead. At one point however, when Arwulf was leading the party, Abe ran up to catch up with him and initiated a conversation about something, most likely Arwulf's culture and role in society, if Mike knew Abe at all.

Mike smiled at this; he was glad to see that Abe was willing to accept Arwulf. Mike had explained the situation of Arwulf to Abe, fearing that

Abe would utterly refuse his company and thus reignite the contention, but he had seemed to be understanding. Now it looked like Abe was actually taking advantage of having such a man around.

That left Mike and Virgil. As the two heard Abe let out a chuckle at one of Arwulf's comments, Mike opened his mouth to speak. "So did you have any dreams last night?"

Mike looked over to see Virgil respond with a nod of his head. "Yeah. Mostly flashes of images, really. I'm going to meditate about and inquire into them again in the next few nights."

"What were the images?"

Virgil paused a moment to consider the answer. "People. Groups of people interacting with each other. I cannot put my finger on more than that. But it specifically had something to do with you."

Mike was not surprised. That was nothing out of the ordinary. This whole mission seemed to be centered around him for one reason or another, much more than he would have liked. "Well, you'll have to let me know about it when you get a clearer answer."

"Yeah, I will."

They continued in silence, leaving Mike to wander off into the unexplored corners of his imagination. The possibilities concerning his fate in the next few months were numberless; he had no idea where to even start exploring. The foray was pointless anyway—he knew he would have to wait for Virgil to receive more clarity—yet he wanted to try to imagine what might be in store for him anyway. Mike had a feeling like something big was about to happen, not only for the mission, but for himself as well. He could almost feel it, like the density of the humid air. It lingered, suspended before his face, yet, at the same time, it remained completely invisible to his sight.

The party passed by a little stone cottage which either contained no occupants or which did not reveal any. It was the only sign of civilization they had seen in a while. The rest of the world around them was completely in God's hands and sang, uninterrupted by the woes of man, melodies that must have been sung in the original Garden.

There were, of course, their conversations. Mike's and Virgil's had paused for a few moments, but Abe's and Arwulf's strode in continual movement. A slight head breeze had been initiated, allowing Mike to catch a few words of what they were saying. They were, indeed, talking about the Druids, more particularly concerning the actual religious beliefs they held. Abe was struggling to understand the logic behind it, but was obviously having a hard time with it. Mike could only imagine a man as practical as Abe, who would normally even have problems understanding aspects of Christianity, trying to understand the logic behind paganism. Even so, he saluted Abe's efforts.

Virgil must have caught tidbits of the conversation as well. "So tell me more about Christianity," he posed. "I've heard of it my whole life, but have never known too much about it."

Mike shuffled his steps a little bit more. "Well, I'm not sure where to start. I've gone to church my whole life but have never been much of one to explain it to others."

"Well, start in the most general terms. Where do you even get the name Christianity?"

"Well that comes from Christ. Jesus Christ. He lived about two thou—, four hundred years ago."

Virgil nodded. "Yeah, I've heard of his name before. Who was He?"

"He is our God," Mike answered. "Him along with His father and the Holy Spirit."

"Holy Spirit? Father? So you have three different Gods that you worship?"

Mike chuckled in frustration. He already felt he had dove in over his head. All he could do was tread water the best he could and hope that Virgil did not hold him under.

"Sort of, I guess. They're three, but They're also one."

Virgil stared at him. "That doesn't make sense to me."

That makes two of us, he admitted to himself. He tried to think of Them, though, in comparison to the pagan gods with which Virgil was more familiar. "They all work together for a common goal. I've always kind of thought of them as a team—several members, each with their own job, all working together for a common goal."

"Huh," Virgil noted, seeming to make sense of it. He thought about it a moment, which gave Mike time to catch his breath. Virgil then resumed the inquiry. "So tell me more about this Jesus Christ. People say that he actually lived here on earth, but they also say, as do you, that He is God. Why would he do that?"

Mike had to take a moment to organize his thoughts, for everything was completely interconnected, and he was sure that if he was not careful, he would confuse Virgil even more. Of course, he would then fit in with the majority of Christianity, but Mike would do his best to avoid that.

"Well, he started slowly, "I guess because God the Father loves us and wants us to live with Him in heaven after we die."

"Heaven?" interrupted Virgil.

"Yeah, heaven," the facts seemed to be coming easier now, "—a place where everything is perfect and where you can be happier than you've ever been before—a place where there is no more pain or death. And so you can see why someone who loved you would want you to get there." Mike paused to take a breath. "The only problem is that God is so good that we are unworthy to be in His presence. We need to be purified first. That's where Jesus Christ comes in."

Mike then jumped into the one thing that did make sense in his head. "Jesus was sent down by His father to pay for our mistakes. He suffered pain and death so that we do not have to suffer the full consequences of our wrongdoings. All He asks in return is that we show our devotion and love to Him through following Him and His teachings to the best of our abilities."

Virgil seemed genuinely interested in the things Mike told him, and, through some act of providence, Mike was able to clearly answer the ensuing questions that he posed to him. Virgil asked about the commandments and right and wrong in general, and seemed to catch on pretty quickly. It seemed to make a remarkable sort of sense to him, despite Mike's feebleness in explaining such things.

They talked for a great while as they traveled on about living life according to Christian principles and how that had been specifically beneficial to Mike. Mike spoke of the positive outlook he carried in life, not to mention the rather apparent satisfaction he took in whatever was dished out to him. "Oftentimes, it's the hard times that are there to make us stronger," he told Virgil.

During their conversation it had begun to rain—a light sprinkling at first that soon became a torrential downpour. The company quickly sought shelter underneath the first tree that offered sufficient cover to wait out the storm, though by looking at the clouds, it did not seem likely to end soon. The four men took the time to eat some of the food they had packed and Mike and Virgil continued on in their conversation. Abe and Arwulf were content to stay more or less silent and listen to the other two.

Though Arwulf periodically scoffed at the Christian principles, he was not bad company. In fact, after the religious conversation dropped, Arwulf did well to keep the company in high spirits. He was a definite benefit to have along while stranded underneath a pine tree in the middle of a rainstorm. They were not able to move from the spot the rest of the day, since Arwulf could not remember any abode in proximity, but the rest was needed, and the stories that Arwulf told were much enjoyed.

To everyone's relief, the next day cleared up to reveal, once again, a cerulean sky, interrupted by a few white leftovers from the night. The group, which had remained surprisingly dry, was, however, anxious to move on, for it had not been the most comfortable of nights. Mike had found himself, as well as the others, warding off exploratory spiders among other bugs which had seemed to also have found likings to their tree, and such had prevented them from truly falling into a good sleep.

But it was a rather uneventful following two days. They walked along the roads, which Mike was finding were still relatively well kept up. To his surprise, they only ran into occasional travelers, who were spread thin over the land. The groups exchanged looks, but not much more than that. Although Mike had come from a place where such a thing was unusual, he seemed to understand now. Frankly, he found himself in company with them, for there was no guarantee of who the strangers were or who the strangers thought them to be.

Luckily, due to Arwulf's connections along the way, they spent the next two nights in the hospitality of his acquaintances. Upon their arrival, Arwulf's usual gravity turned up into a grin at seeing people with which he had not had the chance to associate in what he said was probably six or seven years. He knew the people by name and called them out as they approached, and in both cases the party was received warmly.

As they left the second house, Arwulf turned to the man and asked, "Has there been word of any strange occurrences lately or things we should watch out for?"

The man thought a moment, but then shook his head. "Just stories and threats. But I've seen no evidence of anything out of the ordinary around here."

"Yeah, that's all we ever get back in Aquae Sulis, too." Arwulf replied casually, remaining steadfast in his lack of wariness. "Well, thanks anyway. Hope to see you again."

The man smiled. "Same to you, friend. You know that you are always welcome in my abode." The two embraced before Arwulf turned and followed the others back to the road.

As they started off, they noticed that there was a slight drizzle in the air. Mike was worried that they would not be able to travel that day, but at the time, the weather seemed perfectly satisfied to remain at its present intensity. It was certainly warm enough that the rain was not a nuisance, and so they traveled on, resurrecting the motions and the mindsets that they had been holding for the past three days.

It was about mid-morning when they came to the cross-road. There had already been a few such forks, but, up until this point, they had led in almost completely opposite directions. This one, on the other hand, had a fork that sent two roads off, more or less, in the very direction they needed to go. Arwulf, who had not had a problem up until this point, paused a second.

"Do you remember which one to take?" Abe asked.

Arwulf bit his lip. "Well, here's the thing," he posed. "I've taken both roads and both lead to the same place. I am pretty sure, though, that this one to the right is faster and a little bit easier."

Mike looked at the distant horizon. The road to the left seemed to eventually take them off into some hillier, more forested areas. The decision made enough sense to him, and so he started to follow Arwulf off to the right, as did Abe. Virgil, however, lingered. His voice was heard from behind, calling out, "Hey, does it make much of a difference, Arwulf?"

Arwulf stopped and turned back to look at him. Hesitantly, almost confused that Virgil was even questioning such a thing, he replied, "I don't think so, maybe half a day's journey at the most. Why?"

Virgil shrugged. Mike could see him rolling around his emblem in his tunic. Mike passed it off as a recently acquired nervous habit, for he found himself doing the same thing every once in a while. "I don't know." Virgil answered. "I kind of think we should go this way." Then, after a slightly awkward pause, he added with a smirk, "You know, there'll be more shade this way."

Arwulf seemed to be a little bit perturbed at the holdup. Slowly he turned to Mike. "It's your choice, you know, since you're the leader of this trip." Mike could tell, though, that Arwulf would only approve of one answer.

Mike looked back and forth at the two options and the two people presenting it. Slowly, without making a decision, he turned to Arwulf. "You say this way is shorter?"

Arwulf nodded. "A little bit easier, too. This is actually the road that most people take, the road that was originally built by the Romans. They added that one later on to access some of the smaller villages and lumber in the forest. It is a little less developed than this one and could be pretty rough in some spots from rain erosion."

Mike then turned to Virgil. "Shade?" he questioned, wondering if that was the only reason.

Virgil paused once again, looked at Arwulf, who was staring impatiently at him, and then looked back at Mike. "Yeah. I was thinking, you know, that if this rain ever leaves us, the forest would be a little bit more pleasant to walk through, and I don't see any particular rush."

Mike thought back, however, on Virgil's initial feeling that the need to depart was immediate. "Well, we'll go Arwulf's way. I don't want to take any more time than we need to."

Virgil hesitated once more, then agreed, and the party continued their journey, enjoying the cool of the rain. Mike found himself falling back into his usual trains of thought: of the mission, of the Realm, of the emblem he held in his hand. It was an endless cycle that seemed to possess him, but in such a usual way now that it did not frighten or aggravate or even call his conscious attention.

Somewhere along the line, as the sun, a light orb in the clouds, slowly made its descent towards the hill in the northwestern distance, Virgil, who was walking in front, stopped. Arwulf, who had been telling Mike and Abe a story quite animatedly, continued the few paces, catching up to him before he noticed. With his smile still plastered on his face, he turned to Virgil. "What's going on?"

"Do you hear that?" Virgil's face was rigid, like a statue.

The other three looked up ahead where Virgil had been motioning to notice a slight rumbling noise from behind the rise about a half mile ahead of them. Mike was not quite sure what to make of it. "Seems like a lot of people," he uttered.

"Yeah," Virgil replied, "that's what worries me."

Before they could react, about a dozen ghastly shadows came into view. They looked unlike any other Mike had seen on the island. They were bearded but not with red or black, but with light-blonde hair. They appeared to be huge, especially in the manner in which they were moving forward. They were not natives, nor were they Romans. Mike lost his breath.

The two groups saw each other almost simultaneously. And when the men, or monsters or whatever they were saw Mike's group, they picked up their pace. "Get off the road," Arwulf ordered, but the order was not needed. Mike bolted off the road with the other three and made for the edge of the trees about a quarter mile away. It would be close enough to make it well into cover, which was all Mike could think about as he ran faster and faster, his nerves about to burst inside of him.

He did not look over, but had he, he would have seen that the group, too, had broken off the road and were coming after them, cutting off the corner and dramatically shortening the time it would take to reach them. Mike could hear them yelling off to his side, and that only caused his legs to move faster. The edge of the woods rushed up at him, and he crashed through the wall of bushes, running inward, the adrenaline taking him straight through thorns and needles without more thought than to put as much distance between him and them as possible.

He paid no attention to who was behind him, though he was sure that he could hear at least one other of his group following him. About a hundred yards into the forest, he dove down to hide and looked back toward the clearing. Not two seconds later, another man plopped down beside him. It was Virgil.

The two tried to curb their hard breathing the best they could as they tried to make out what was going on. There was thick summer brush all around them, and they had to constantly fight the branches away to clear space for them to move. Mike moved some leaves away in order to get a clearer view of the green of the forest behind them, taking harsh note of the thorns in the branches as he did so. There was nothing to be seen however. Nobody was around. They had left all sounds far behind.

"What do you think they want?" Mike asked, speaking almost at a whisper between breaths.

Virgil shook his head. "I don't know. I've never seen such men before." He struggled to catch his breath. "I'm not willing to find out though."

Mike could not help but wonder if Abe and Arwulf had made it to the forest. At the time he was running, he had only one thing on his mind, but now, his nerves were risen almost to a panic. Frantically, he reached for the emblem, but upon finding it with his hand, he noticed the dead coldness of it. There was no life in it. For the moment, it was nothing but a clump of metal.

Mike stood up slowly, cautiously and made his way back a few steps to try to get a look. "What are you doing?" Virgil whispered harshly.

"I got to find out where Abe is," Mike said, though he trembled as he said it.

"Are you crazy?" Virgil countered. "What would you do? You have no weapon. You're outnumbered. You have no choice but to hide and hope for the best."

But Mike could not stop, at least not until he could see what was going on. He flanked out away from the path he trod to get a side view only to see a sight that made his blood curdle.

There stood three of the men at the entrance of the forest. The head man had Abe on all fours, stripped of almost everything. Abe was holding his stomach and the man standing above him was stating something in what Mike thought was Saxon, but it was coarse and Mike could only make out a few words. The man asked something about Abe's companions, and though Abe seemed to answer back in Saxon, the man was not pacified, but kicked Abe again and repeated himself. Mike grabbed his stomach, for it was wrenching in a pain of its own. He knew that Abe could not do anything to satisfy the man to the same degree that he could not do anything for Abe. He knew all too well that Abe was old, too, and could not take much of that abuse. Unfortunately, all he could do was stand there and watch.

But then, without hardly any warning, the head man was struck and fell to the ground, though by what, Mike could not tell. Then he saw it—another rock flying through the air. Its victim, the second man, saw it just about the same time Mike saw it, but it was too late for him, too. Mike then saw a blur move up and, in one motion, appear and swing his spear up and into the third man's stomach. It was Arwulf. He threw everything he had on him on the ground except for his spear and sling, picked up Abe, and ran with him deeper into the forest before the others could arrive. They would not be far behind now.

Mike appeared as Arwulf approached. "Is he okay?" he entreated.

Arwulf did not break pace to acknowledge Mike or answer his question. Instead, he continued running and yelled out, "Drop your stuff and run."

Mike obeyed, welcoming an idea on which he did not have to make the decision. They ran in farther than before, splitting up and trying not to make such a disturbance. Mike did not know how far behind they were or how far they would pursue, but he took no chance in stopping until he reached another clearing about five minutes later. He then dove in the grass and turned around to watch the edge of the trees for any sign of life or death.

Mike bowed his head and breathed hard, trying desperately to catch his breath and calm his senses. Again, he had lost all the others. In vain did he try to curb the wild possibilities pulsing through his head. *What if they have all been caught?* Surely those men would not show any mercy after finding two of their men down and one mortally wounded. *Is Abe okay? How can I find out? How long do I have to wait?* Mike dared not move now. There was no use in running any further. The next cluster of trees was too far without cover to reach. The grass provided as much as he needed for the time being, at least as much as he was willing to move to.

There was no way to measure time, but Mike figured that he had been lying in his spot for over an hour without seeing any sign of life. He could not see the sun, for it was behind the cluster of forest through which he had run, but from the amount of light, he could tell that it was progressing on to late evening. Mike changed his position for the hundredth time since he got here and a tear came to his eye.

Just as the panic was about to become unbearable, Mike heard a rustle in the bushes ahead of him and saw, to his relief, Arwulf coming through. "Mike," he called out, though not loudly.

Mike stood up, slowly, and with overwhelming relief. As Arwulf caught sight of him, he smiled weakly. "Mike, it's okay now. They're gone."

Chapter 14

"I can get up fine," Abe insisted, batting away Mike and Virgil's hands to help him up. "I'm not doing too badly."

It was obvious that such a statement was not entirely accurate. Indeed, Abe had been caressing his ribs with both hands and periodically wheezing out half breaths, half moans when Mike had come back to him. Abe had tried his very best to curb them, but with little success.

You're not the age you used to be," Virgil stated matter-of-factly. "Your ribs could very well be broken, and your body cannot handle that very well anymore. You would be a fool not to let us carry you to our next stopping place."

"I'm okay," Abe again cut. "I don't need to burden any of you."

He tried to rise, but the motion sent a pain through his torso that caused him to collapse back to his original fetal position. He tried his hardest to keep any audible sign of pain inside, but it was useless. He let it all out, and a loud whimper ushered forth from his lungs.

"You are a greater burden to us trying to move on your own than you are on our backs," Arwulf stated. "I'll carry you. We only have a little ways to go anyway. I have a good friend just a league or two down the road. He has a farm and a nice, cozy hut that you can stay in until you are healed enough to keep going."

It took a considerable amount more prodding to get Abe to concede, but after a few more dramatic failures to get up, he finally agreed. Reluctantly, he was helped onto Arwulf's back and the party cautiously set out back to the road, which was now ghostly silent. It seemed like the marauders had moved on, having become satisfied enough with what provisions they could get from Mike and Arwulf's abandoned bags. Even so, Mike found himself looking all about him, taking especial note of all that moved or sounded within range of his senses. He could not wait for the extra company of Arwulf's friends.

"Who were those men anyway?" Mike voiced in a timid, hushed tone as they again reached the road.

"Saxon mercenaries," Abe answered, holding his breath then exhaling quickly. "They were summoned here to guard against the northern invaders, but they are not much better company themselves."

Mike remembered such things from his studies with Abe. They were reported to be fearful, war-mongering men who did not hold respect for anyone other than their own kin. They would sack villages and homes, taking what they wanted, mostly because they could. They were burly animals with advanced weapons and armor for the day. Mike imagined that they had not planned on getting in a fight that day and so Arwulf's attack had caught them off guard. At least one of their men had died, and Mike did not know how they would feel about that—whether they would be back to take revenge or whether it was not important enough for them to waste their time searching for their brother's murderers. They had taken the body, so they would at least be occupied for a few days with their funeral rites. That gave Mike a little comfort.

But then again, Mike did not know how long Abe's condition would incapacitate them. One thing was for certain: Abe could not do the required walking necessary for today and most likely for tomorrow and the next day. Mike shuddered to think that he might have to face those men again, like a rabbit in its hovel, having been chased in by a fox. They knew where Mike and his party would be. All it would take would be a little patience. Mike wanted to leave this place, to leave this whole island. But with Abe the way he was, both were far from possible.

It was quite dark by the time they reached their destination. Mike expected a warm welcome as they approached the hut of Arwulf's friend. Alas, there was nothing—no smell of cooking food, no sporadic exchanges of words, no little children running about in the summer night, no activity whatsoever. Mike remained optimistic, however, until he saw the definite lack of firelight inside and the absence of a door. He looked over at Arwulf, who seemed equally confused.

FORTH FROM EDEN

The party walked through the threshold and strained their eyes to see within the shadows of its inside corners. Mike's heart welled up in the trepidation he had felt all too much today, realizing that the same men who came after them would have passed right on through here. As his eyes adjusted he feared he would find it ransacked and laden with dead, bloody bodies. Again, however, his expectation was wrong. Instead, it was completely empty. No hay, no articles of clothing, no earthenware, no ale vats. It seemed like nobody had lived there for quite awhile.

"They must have headed out," Virgil surmised solemnly.

Arwulf pounded his fist on the doorframe in frustration. "Not even a speck of food either. How much do you have, Virgil?"

Virgil shrugged. "Maybe enough for one regularly-sized meal each."

Arwulf massaged his beard as he surveyed the situation.

"It's probably a good thing that this place did not have any provisions," Virgil added. "They probably would have come straight back here if it did."

Arwulf grunted his approval, but added nothing more. He looked around once more in search of anything useful, but again, he was disappointed. He then turned to Mike. "Come with me outside."

Mike hesitated, then followed. Again, he found himself shaking, and realized that he had not stopped doing so since the raid. He knew that it was not logical that those men were waiting outside to attack, but it was hard to tell that to his pounding heart. Once he had found out that the hut, though abandoned, was safe, at least some of the fear had subsided, but outside, where he did not have the fortification of walls, was a different story. As Mike walked out the doorway and followed Arwulf around to the back, he could not help but notice the numerous dancing shadows in the last bits of the twilight. He jumped at every one of them and scampered up to join Arwulf at his side.

"We're going to need to have two people keeping guard tonight," Arwulf declared as he surveyed the field in front of him. The field was filled with hay, but the hay was overgrown and ridden with weeds. *They must have left sometime in the past year*, Mike conjectured, *and there must have been a fairly good reason for the urgency*. Mike did not blame them. He was sure this party of Saxons had not been the first to pass on this road. "In the mean time, though, we need to find something soft to lay Abe on."

Mike nodded in agreement. They ended up simply pulling hay out and gathering it in piles. They would be enough to give Abe at least a little cushion from the packed earth floor. They each made three trips with piles in their hands and left the arranging to Virgil.

"Virgil, why don't you get some rest," Mike said as they laid the last amounts down. "Arwulf and I will keep watch."

Virgil had placed the majority of the blades under where Abe now lay, and Abe was quickly falling asleep. Mike could tell that his friend's body was worn out even from riding on Arwulf's back. There would have been no way that Abe would have made it here on his own. Virgil himself had taken the remainder of the blades and placed them under his head, and was quickly beginning to follow Abe's suit. Mike and Arwulf watched the two for a few seconds in silence, then went out the doorway and settled themselves near the road.

The stars were beginning to appear, one by one, in the night sky as the last twinge of orange disappeared on the western horizon. Mike noticed that the hut was strategically built; it was placed at the crest of the road, and one could get a fairly clear view for a good mile and a half in each direction. It would be easy to see anyone coming, which made Mike wonder why Arwulf had wanted two people out there, but soon after they had settled themselves down, his intentions revealed themselves.

"Out behind the back of the hut was a stack of wood," he said. "Beside that pile was a long walking stick. I want you to go get that, as well as a rough rock and bring it back here."

Mike did not understand, but Arwulf seemed sure enough in what he was doing that Mike did not question it. He made his way around the hut once more and found what Arwulf was talking about. Mike then succeeded in finding a rough white rock on the ground and returned just a moment later.

"I'm going to have you make yourself a spear," Arwulf explained. "For now, a very crude one will have to do, but it will do the job until you can get the right materials to make a good one."

Again, that anxious heartbeat resurfaced in Mike's chest. Arwulf's statement was only a reminder of the encounter they had had that day. Only Arwulf had had weapons, and his performance with them had probably saved Abe's life. Even so, Mike had never wielded any weapon before, even for hunting, and truthfully did not have any burning desire to break with the tradition, and so he stated, "Do you think I'll need to use it?"

If a "Quite possibly" would have daunted Mike, the "Most definitely" that Arwulf voiced froze his soul. Mike looked over at Arwulf, who, at this moment, stared at him with quiet intensity. "This isn't the Roman world it once was, Mike. Even as a kid, my dad told me how the Romans were being seen less and less. I would not be surprised if they have completely abandoned us. Even with the Romans, it was common for invaders to come. You can only guess the degree that are coming now."

Mike nodded. This was all common knowledge to him. He realized, though, that up to this point, he had never internalized it. Now he felt like it had come alive, like a waking dragon. All of the history was real. It all applied directly to him. He suddenly knew that whether it was here or elsewhere, he would have to face the Saxons again. He could not simply hope to avoid them just as he had in Western Britain. He felt sick to his stomach. *What's to say that I, too, could get injured, or even killed out here?* Mike had originally assumed that the emblems would keep them away from danger, but that had not been the case with Abe. *Why could it not happen to me as well?*

Making the spear that Arwulf pictured for him was no different than Mike already imagined. He set to work stripping the bark and smoothing out the knots with the rock before moving on to the end to create a point. The work was slow, since the roughness of the rock had limited effect, but he had time enough. If for nothing else, it kept him awake and able to keep watch on the completely silent, still night.

Arwulf and he talked as he worked, but of nothing of consequence. Arwulf told him a few stories from his childhood, of playing in the woods, and Mike answered back with childhood stories of his own. It was interesting to note that despite the difference of origin, they shared many of the same types of childhood experiences. They had both spent a lot of time outside, making up games and imagining they were grown up. *How things have turned back on themselves since then,* Mike thought through the mists of nostalgia.

Mike could not help but note, however, that Arwulf had tried at no topic of consequence—nothing that Mike would have guessed that he would have wanted to know. He had not asked about Mike's background. He had not asked about Mike's reasons for coming here. He had not even asked about Mike's abnormal stature. Mike was sure that he or Abe had said something out of place that would have hinted that they were grand strangers, but apparently it had not been great enough to initiate in Arwulf a desire for explanation. Maybe Abe or Virgil had explained everything already. Either way, Mike did not feel any desire or necessity to go into such an intense conversation at the moment. He had had enough with the cares of the present for now.

Later on, however, the present was brought back as Arwulf turned to Mike and said, "Hey, are you done scraping that stick yet?"

Mike smiled and shook his head. "Not really. It's pretty slow."

Arwulf turned away from the road to look at the piece of work in Mike's hands. "That's good enough for now. I'm falling asleep here. Why don't I instruct you on a few ways to actually use that thing."

Mike agreed, welcoming the idea of doing something active as well. In truth, in the last hour, he had made hardly any progress at all due to his fatigue. It would feel good to move around a little. The two stretched as they got up, and Arwulf then set to work on showing Mike some defensive blocks and some thrusts that would give Mike a slightly better advantage than waving the thing madly in the air. Arwulf was knowledgeable and skilled in wielding the spear and also seemed to be able to teach it well.

"Have you ever had to use this, other than yesterday?" Mike asked as they slowly and carefully sparred with each other.

"No," Arwulf answered, "other than to hunt. Some friends and I will occasionally do what we are doing right now, and fight with the blunt end of the spears. But that experience today was a first for me as well. Our people are not prone to go out and go to war. At least they are not now—they used to be out of necessity. But we have never needed to see it in our neck of the woods."

At that moment, Arwulf struck Mike's fingers as they grasped onto the spear. He instinctively abandoned grip of the staff and grabbed his hand in pain. Rather than letting up on him, however, Arwulf brought his staff down hard on Mike's shoulder, and jabbed the blunt end of his spear into Mike's stomach, knocking the wind out of him and sending him crumbling to the ground. He stood over Mike as Mike wrenched back and forth in pain, trying to catch his breath again. After a moment, he was able to wheeze out, "What did you do that for?"

Arwulf, however, remained untouched by Mike's condition. "You dropped your spear. Right now you would be dead because you cared more about your fingers than your life."

"I'm just a beginner, though. You didn't have to show me that so roughly."

"Those men did not care whether you were a beginner or not. They would treat you the same as the next guy. The only difference they would see in you is how long it would take to kill you. I did not get you as hard as they would. You'll be okay. Now get up, let's try again, and if I get any part of you, keep on going if you can. Go until you disable me. Worry about your pain only after that."

Mike did get up; he was okay; and although his fingers were hit several more times in the next few hours, he bit his lip and swallowed the pain until he could suffer safely. The reality of Arwulf's words slowly emerged into perspective, and Mike was almost glad that he did what he did, mostly because he was absolutely right. That was what kept Mike going even when he was out of breath. That was what kept him determined to get Arwulf at least once. And he did—it was a nice blow to the side of Arwulf's ribs that disoriented him enough to allow Mike to sweep Arwulf's legs out from underneath him and bring him to the ground. Arwulf absorbed the pain, massaged his side, then smiled up at Mike. "That's the way it's supposed to happen. With your size, you will become a great warrior."

Mike laughed weakly, painfully, and helped his comrade back up. It was then that he noticed how utterly exhausted he was. Arwulf noticed it as well and patted him on the shoulder, where a bruise from a few good hits was forming. "Go in and get some rest Mike. It's getting lighter now and Virgil should be up soon."

"Should I wake him up and send him out?"

"No, that's fine. Let him sleep a little bit longer. I can stay awake until he gets up on his own. No one will be coming at this time anyway."

Mike was a little hesitant, but again, decided to trust Arwulf's judgment. He stumbled back inside where the two men remained in sound sleep, lay down beside them on the hard earth, and was soon fast asleep himself.

Mike woke up several hours later to find that Arwulf and Virgil had switched spots. It was now Arwulf lying beside him snoring quietly with his head on the little bundle of hay. Just beyond him, he still saw Abe in his same place, and worried a moment that he fared worse than they originally thought, but Mike found, on further study of his face, that his complexion was more full of color and there was a more peaceful look on his slumbering face than there had been last night.

All the tiredness had departed from Mike, and after lying on the ground for a minute, he pulled himself up and walked outside. There he found Virgil, casually sitting on the grass in what looked to be the early afternoon light. The sun was indeed back out, thereby making the stagnant air hot and a little humid, but Mike did not really care. It gave him joy to see his surroundings again; it made him feel just a little less vulnerable.

"Mike," Virgil said without turning around as Mike drew nearer. "Could you grab my lambskin in the hut and fill it up in the stream back in those trees there? It shouldn't be too far; I can hear it distinctly."

Feeling the pangs of thirst himself, Mike obeyed and walked along the edge of the hayfield to the cluster of trees at the bottom of the hill. He tried to ignore the soreness all over his body as he walked, primarily telling himself that he was sore, but not injured, and secondarily that it was for his own good. As he drew nearer, he could hear the water himself, and could tell that it was not a very big stream. He entered the trees, cleared away the brush with his hand, and slid down a slight drop into the shallow water.

The water was amazingly clear—the clearest he had seen since he had arrived in Britain—and he soon found out why. Looking over, up the hill a little, Mike noticed that the water suddenly appeared as a spring and flowed down in purity until it reached a small pond surrounded by what seemed a few other abandoned huts. Mike walked over to them in curiosity, but found, like up on top of the hill, that they had been empty for some time.

FORTH FROM EDEN

With the skin filled, as well as his thirst, Mike walked back to where Virgil was sitting and handed the skin to him so he could drink as well. Virgil guzzled from its mouth for a good thirty seconds before he came up for air, then handed the skin back to Mike and thanked him. "That was good water," he said.

"Yeah, there was a spring back there. There were also a few other huts, but I didn't see any life in them."

Virgil nodded. "I don't blame them. Especially after what we saw yesterday."

Mike looked over at Virgil and studied him. Through everything—even while they had been hiding in the bushes yesterday—he had retained the same calm look on his face that he always bore. Mike had wondered if he had been the only one severely affected by the experience and Virgil's comment was the first sign that he was not alone.

"How are you doing with all of that?" Mike asked.

Virgil looked over at him with a deep expression. His following words bore the utmost gravity, taking Mike back. "Scared like mad," he said. "I've been that way for a long time, and the experience was no better than the anticipation."

Mike could do nothing but nod, and nothing more was spoken on the subject. It seemed that the desire for silence on it was mutual.

The two sat there in silence for a few moments both filled with thought. Mike's thoughts turned toward Abe, who lay in the hut in a condition unknown to him. Mike kept looking back behind him, but only to find the structure in a constant state of silence.

"Abe came stumbling out here a few hours before you woke up, in case you're wondering," Virgil said.

Mike was mildly surprised. "He did?"

"Yeah, he came out and sat with me for about an hour, and although he didn't say much, I could tell that he was doing at least a little better."

"So he went back to sleep then?"

"Yeah, I told him to." Virgil paused then added, "Sometimes I don't believe that man can take care of himself. Kind of ironic since he knows so much."

171

Mike smiled and nodded, thinking all the way back to the first day he had met him and Abe had nearly fallen asleep at the wheel.

"He was anxious to get going again," Virgil continued, "But I told him that there was no chance for at least another few days. He spoke of the mission, but I told him that there was not enough rush to warrant his risk and pain."

"No?" Mike asked.

Virgil shook his head.

"What about the revelation to get going right away? Was that correct?"

Virgil shrugged. "Correct enough. There was nothing for us back there. There was no reason to delay the mission any longer. This, however," he mentioned, pointing back over his shoulder to the hut, "is a legitimate reason. Besides, I don't think she will be going anywhere."

"She?" Mike asked, confused.

"Yeah, she." Virgil turned to face Mike in the eye. "I've been able to spend some time meditating these past few days, and the images have started to become more distinct. I now know what we, or, more appropriately, what you are supposed to do when we get to where we're going."

Mike shifted to a more comfortable position. "Oh yeah?"

Virgil smiled, the same smile that he had given a few days ago when the future had still remained cloudy for him. Mike eyed him carefully, as if he were a serpent about to strike. Had he known what Virgil was about to tell him, he may have turned and run from him, but curiosity had its way of coaxing him into stillness. Mike waited for the answer, not knowing that he was about to add one more knot into his consciousness. The mission was about to draw him farther in than he would have ever thought possible.

Chapter 15

It might as well have been raining. The dark pensiveness that came along with such weather would have complimented Mike's mood a lot better than the present environment did. The sunshine, the mild temperatures, the singing birds, the dancing wildflowers in the field across the road, the green backdrop of broadleaf trees: all did well to mock Mike's state. It was all too innocent. Even the underlying anxiety that came along with the constant threat of seeing those Saxons again, an event that had remained no more than just that for the past two days, seemed more appropriate right now.

What Mike now faced was something that he had never needed to face before. He had actually let out an involuntary laugh when Virgil first told him, but it had not been out of humor. He could have just as easily shed tears.

Mike laughed again, just now, at the thought of it. Ever since Virgil had laid the instruction on him, he had barely spoken a word to anyone. The thought had been on his mind constantly, nagging at him, tearing away at any feeble sprout of comfort he had found in this place. *This is more than I bargained for*, he thought to himself as he looked off on the still road.

"I really had no idea, Mike," Abe had said after approaching him in between naps yesterday. Somehow, he had found out about Mike's and Virgil's conversation.

Mike had simply shrugged in reply to Abe's apology.

"Are you still up to the task?"

Mike had chuckled without smiling. "What other choice do I have, Abe? I'm way too far in now to do anything but move forward."

"Well, I just figured that this is more than I ever asked you to commit to."

Mike had turned to Abe with sober intensity. "I appreciate your concern, but my commitment to this mission is far too deep now to go back on it."

"Well, for that I am glad," Abe had responded. "But still, if there is anything I can do, let me know."

Mike had simply shaken his head. "No. I have to do this completely on my own."

Mike watched the road, though he saw nothing more than he had seen for the past two days. There were no travelers, no soldiers—it was as if the world had been completely washed of its inhabitants, ever since the dark storm had blown through. It was a rather eerie stagnancy, which, in any other situation, would have made Mike feel deftly uncomfortable, however, considering the possible alternatives and knowing now of their natures, he accepted things as they were.

Still, he was anxious to get moving again. This land had proved its savagery, and like hot sand, it felt better to keep moving upon it than to stand still. Yet they found themselves bound to a stagnancy of their own, and were left naked to be acted upon by the land's undercurrent threats. They could do nothing here, yet they could not move. Arwulf continued to teach him skills in fighting, but that was not the reason Mike came to this place. Regardless of what he was able to do here, the mission was not moving forward.

Needless to say, Mike had paid great attention to Abe's condition. Abe had continued resting more on than off for the past few days and was getting better. Mike could tell that it took his body more time to repair itself than, say, him or Virgil or Arwulf, but luckily Abe's relative fitness worked to his advantage. Mike figured that within three days Abe would be fine, and that they could finally continue on.

Yet he realized that it was a wish to jump from the pan and into the flame. Again, the next required events leaped to the forefront of Mike's mind, and he squirmed. Mike got up and paced around a bit. It was amazing that with a little more light shed on what he needed to accomplish in his role as the bearer of the golden emblem, his enthusiasm to move forward had suddenly changed to dread.

Such feelings were contrasted deeply by the moods of Virgil and Arwulf. The present idle nature of the party had seemed to cast a different sort of disease over them. Though they still performed the necessary tasks of finding food, they did it with an air that set Mike's nerves on edge. Virgil was not retaining the stoic maturity required of him. The past few days had cultivated several bouts of frenzied laughter in the two. Though Mike knew that such was no great sin by any means, it still seemed to whisper that something important inside Virgil was quivering.

Mike pulled out a piece of dried fish and chewed on it, mulling over its contents as the thoughts mulled over in his head. *I criticize Virgil for that, and yet I don't know if I'll even be able to perform my next duty.*

He heard someone approach him from behind. The steps were uneven, and Arwulf and Virgil had stated just an hour ago that they were going to go hunting for deer, so Mike did not bother turning around as he opened his mouth.

"Abe, I have no idea what I'm going to do."

Abe came and sat down next to Mike, wincing only slightly. "What do you mean?"

Mike thought for a moment. "I don't know, really. I just feel so lost when it comes to all of this. How am I supposed to find and marry the bearer of love?"

Abe laughed. "Mike, you'll be fine. You are a caring, sincere person. I will almost bet that it will be completely natural to you."

Mike looked at his comrade with a smirk on his face. "I can't say I hold the same confidence."

"Look," Abe started, "I'm not exactly the expert either." Mike nodded, thinking back on Abe's miniscule experience. "But I know what love can feel like. Tell me, Mike, have you ever had feelings for any particular girl?"

Mike shrugged. "I think so; not since high school, though."

"What did you feel?"

"I guess like I wanted to see her, because it made me happy when I did."

"Okay. So did you ever do anything about it?"

Mike shook his head.

"Why not? Was seeing her good enough?"

Mike did not seem to have a clear answer to that question. "Probably not, but I don't know. I was always too scared to do anything."

"Scared?" Abe repeated, smiling.

Mike gave him a defiant look. "Yeah, scared."

Abe laughed, but placed his hand on Mike's shoulder. "You're not a coward, Mike, otherwise you would have bailed out of this mission a long time ago. I think you are a lot stronger than you think. You've encountered so many new experiences in the past year that this one will be just another bend in the road."

Abe paused to slowly sit himself down. "Don't think about it too much," he added with a sympathetic sigh. "Just let things happen."

The two sat silently for a moment or two. The words seemed to have some wisdom in them, although they sourced from a man of nearly unfounded experience. Mike wished he could follow the counsel; he wished he could get his mind off the thoughts, but it was a mountain for which he was not fit to climb. He wanted to further confide in Abe, but Abe was not much for that type of conversation.

Which was why Mike was so intrigued at how patient Abe had been with this entire mission. He had waited all his life for these things to happen, and when the time finally came, it had been fraught with delay after delay. The few months that Abe had originally planned on using to complete his goals were long past and lost in the blissful memories of the Elfish Realm. And although Mike could see that Abe had gotten restless at times, he had never shown physical frustration at how all of this was turning out.

It was a good thing that he had been able to master the virtue too, because Mike had no idea how long this next step would take. *Man,* he thought to himself, *I don't even know if it's possible at all. It would be a miracle for such a thing to occur.* Mike wondered again at whether he was really the right man, or if Abe had been misled in his pursuit of a bearer. All of the other evidences that proved otherwise seemed insignificant right now.

Mike looked on to the field in front of him while these thoughts raced in his head. Its serenity had since been interrupted by two figures carrying a mid-sized doe on a stick while wearing smiles comparable to young schoolboys at recess. Beforehand, Mike had overheard Virgil bragging to his friend that he would be the one to bring down the doe. Arwulf had scoffed at that, and took Virgil's words as a challenge. Mike wondered who had won.

"Look what we got," Arwulf boasted to Mike and Abe, "and guess who took it down."

"Man, if I hadn't flushed her out, you wouldn't have gotten her," Virgil retorted.

"Right. That was exactly what you were thinking when you chased after it... and missed it with your stone."

Virgil's expression suddenly seemed to take on an air of exposure. "It was a team effort. We both got her."

Arwulf simply laughed. "Have it your way; I know the truth."

Virgil decided to change the subject. "Maybe you can come next time Mike, have Abe keep watch. It will at least keep your mind off *her*."

Virgil was the only one that thought his comment was humorous. He chortled at his jab, then slowly faded into silence at the lack of reaction in the others. The other three stared at him, but it was only Arwulf that stared out of complete ignorance. He had suddenly become interested in something other than his victory.

"Wait, what is this Mike?" Arwulf chided. "Who's *her*?"

Mike shook his head, not wanting to talk about it.

"Is this why you've been aloof the past few days? Are we going to visit one of your wenches?" Arwulf playfully nudged Mike in the shoulder. Mike remained silent. "I thought this was all about Rome. Hah! Great cover up, though I have to say, I do feel a little insulted that you did not tell me about this before."

Without intention, Arwulf had suddenly created an awkward atmosphere in the group, and Mike suddenly realized that Arwulf was still completely ignorant about the whole mission. Virgil must have used the story Mike and Abe used with Virgil's kin when he told Arwulf about the trip, and it seemed as if Arwulf had not figured anything else out. He knew nothing of the emblems, Virgil's calling, or the weight that their actions could have on the world. He was utterly clueless.

It only took a few seconds of shuffling feet and avoidance of eye contact for Arwulf to figure out that things were not as they seemed to him. His smile slowly shrunk away to match and then surpass the degree of sobriety of the looks on everyone else's face. He looked around, waiting for something, but nothing came, so he decided to take matters into his own hands.

"Something tells me that I don't know a lot of what's going on here." He looked at Mike, who, again, avoided eye contact. "What's really happening here? You two are not really from Rome, are you?"

Mike found it hard to make out the tone in Arwulf's voice. It almost sounded aggressive, but it may have only come from frustration on his ignorance. Arwulf seemed to feel he had been left out of something, and was trying to figure it out. Mike was not sure that he wanted to fill him in. To his severe discomfort, however, Abe did not seem to hold the same opinion.

"Okay," Abe stated, slapping his hands together. "I'm going to tell you, but I want you to take all I say seriously."

Arwulf nodded.

"You're right. We are not Romans, but men from a far away land and time. We're from 1500 years in the future."

"Wha—" Arwulf blurted, looking around humorously, as if the man was crazy, but the serious looks on everybody's faces made him lose the face and go pale. He shut his mouth and turned back to Abe, almost in fear.

Abe continued. "We are on a quest to redeem seven magical emblems that control the virtue of society. If we succeed, all war and evil will cease in the world. We already have three of the emblems: the emblem of knowledge, the emblem of wisdom, and the golden emblem, which controls them all."

Abe pulled out his emblem to display it to Arwulf, and motioned for Virgil and Mike to do the same. Mike did so hesitantly, a sudden sick feeling to his stomach. He felt as if he was revealing his deepest secret to a complete stranger. Arwulf surveyed the three small cylinders individually, then let out a nervous chuckle.

"You're not serious are you? You cannot be serious."

Abe nodded, though, and continued. "We are on our way right now to recover the fourth emblem—the emblem of love. In order for its power to be fully unveiled, it must be joined in union to the golden emblem. Rather, the two bearers must be joined in union. That is the girl that Virgil was talking about."

Arwulf was shaking his head. "You guys are crazy. The future? Emblems? Missions? Changing *this* world? I don't believe this."

With that, he stormed away and disappeared into the hut. Virgil looked after his friend and began to follow him, but decided to stop himself. "I was worried about that," he said.

"We should have never brought him," Mike stated. "It just makes things that much more complicated."

"Don't worry about him," Virgil said. "He'll leave after we reach our destination. There won't be any harm done."

Mike wasn't convinced of the harmlessness though. He remembered Virgil's description of his dream. Three people, not four. *Was that significant, or an extraneous detail?* Although Arwulf was not an important part of the mission, his skeptical presence dampened the optimism of the other three. There would always be a certain discomfort around him. *He doesn't belong here*—the thought coursed through his head, screaming out accusations against an alien piece.

"We just won't talk about it around him and everything will be fine."

Mike looked over at Virgil, then nervously over at Abe, who returned his gaze. He sure hoped so.

The party was content to engage itself in other activities that evening. Abe, who was still feeling quite well, volunteered to take the watch until dark. The other three agreed, happy to see him both physically and mentally better.

The other three took upon themselves the task of gutting and skinning the doe. They worked in relative silence, each thinking the same line of thoughts, each avoiding the vocalization of them. Luckily for them, the skinning process took much of their attention, especially since Mike needed their constant instruction. He volunteered to do almost everything, feeling like it might be a good skill for the future, and the other two were content to let him do so. They watched, critiqued, and smiled as Mike made the belly cuts with a shaky hand, pulled out the innards with a turned up nose, and peeled back the skin with a wince and a grunt.

The whole process, with the three of them, took a few hours, especially with all the cutting of the meat, but Mike was glad for it. For those short hours, everything about a daunting task and a misplaced man was thrown to the back of his mind and replaced with the rush of accomplishment and the aroma of sizzling meat over the fire. It did well to bring Mike out of his thoughts and back into the present. Worries could be put off for tomorrow. Tonight, they could all sit down and enjoy the hum of crickets, the flashing of fireflies, and the rich zest of the roasted venison.

"You're looking a lot better, Abe," Virgil mentioned amidst bites of food. "You don't look as tired out."

"Yeah, I'm feeling a lot better too. I feel more energetic."

"How're your ribs feeling?" Arwulf asked.

Abe nodded. "They're doing better. We may have to take things slower, with a little bit more rest than usual, but I think that I am ready to get going again."

Virgil nodded. "Excellent. We'll probably rest one more day—that will allow the deer skin to dry as well—and then be off."

Not much else of consequence happened the rest of the night. Everyone, especially Abe, held a sort of quiet determination to get as much rest as possible so they could be back on their journey and reach their next destination. Mike did not know quite how he would fare, but there was only one way to find out, and sitting stagnantly like this would kill him if he did it for too much longer. He needed to be out doing something, progressing, even if it meant the undesirable task that he was to face next.

Arwulf followed Abe's watch that night, and took his turn to sleep the next day. The whole next day was filled with sitting around, eating more deer meat, and waiting for time to tick by. Mike spent the morning constructing a new journal, separate from the reconstructed journal of the Realm. He had held off on the act, hoping that he could resume the habit with more happy entries, but he realized now that the other side of the spectrum was important as well. Having run out of wool from Antiochus, he was forced to use deerskin, but it still worked.

Later on in the afternoon, when Arwulf had woken up and was in a much better mood, Mike asked him to spar with him again. Arwulf readily agreed and the two jousted for a while, making light conversation about everything at hand but the mission.

"So is your spear your weapon of choice?" Mike asked as he parried Arwulf's lunges and, in turn, made a few lunges of his own.

"Nah," Arwulf said between heavy breaths. "Spears are only good for fishing and hand to hand combat. We took down that doe with slings."

"Slings," Mike repeated. "I'd like to learn to hunt with a sling."

Arwulf laughed. "We can make you a sling, but it usually takes years to become adept enough with a sling to hunt. There are only a few places on a deer that you can hit that will take them down. You might as well leave the hunting to us."

Mike did not like that idea, though he did not know why. Fighting was one thing—defending oneself was completely necessary in a world like this one—but hunting was completely different. Arwulf probably had a good point—there was a small chance if any that he would ever be good enough to use a sling, but that did not stop his desire to learn. Then a thought of a different nature came to him.

After he and Arwulf had had enough, Mike took a walk out into the woods. Abe had instructed him on the English longbow while they had been in the Realm, and Mike had spoken of the desire to have one. Up to this point, they had had no time to make one, but such was not the case now. For a good hour, Mike scoured the trees for what he was looking—a young yew sapling. In time, he found one, then set to work cutting it down and shaping it into the design to which Abe had instructed him. The other three watched in interest as he did so. Both Arwulf and Virgil, who had only heard about bows and arrows, were impressed. Abe made occasional comments on both its history and its abilities.

The process, including securing the proper sinew for the string, consumed the rest of the day, as well as the days in which they finally resumed their travels. Mike performed test shots and made adjustments, growing in excitement on every improvement that was made. At the end of the second day on the road, when Virgil gave word that they would arrive in the village the next morning, Mike had himself a crude, but effective, weapon.

Chapter 16

The warmth of the golden emblem pulsed through the veins in Mike's fingers as he nervously fiddled it around in his pocket. It had become a part of his hand now—an extra metallic appendage attached to his fingers and vital to his soul. He needed its full power at the moment, for although nobody else noticed, his stomach muscles were shaking, and he felt sick. Which symptom was the cause and which was the effect, he was not sure.

The party was still quite a great distance off from the village—maybe two miles—but their position atop the promontory upon which they stood gave them a full view of what would soon become a part of their daily lives. In the center of the clearing lay a feeble smattering of small huts which, at the moment, shed their shadows and took on their full, yet ever dull color with the rising of the sun. The party noticed, upon further survey, numerous dark interruptions in the golden continuity of the grain. They were out at the crack of dawn and in the fields, battling survival yet another day, having neither found nor given quarter the day before.

"She could be one of those dots," Mike thought to himself, and the sickness temporarily gained strength.

The four stood looking at the dozen or so huts in silence. Mike was sure that an array of thoughts and emotions were racing through each member's head, though he could only guess what they were. He was sure, however, of his dread of moving forward.

"That's your village?" Arwulf blurted after a moment. "Good luck with your task, Mike. I don't envy you."

Mike did not acknowledge Arwulf's cutting break of silence. Ever since Arwulf had been enlightened on their true mission a few days ago, sarcastic comments toward the whole idea had slipped out of his mouth, sometimes getting laughs, but most of the time getting uncomfortable shuffles. It was now certain that Arwulf did not have any faith in what they were doing and thought the mission completely absurd. He was bound by his word and his friendship to continue with them, but Mike almost wished that he had not.

On the one hand, Arwulf had been a great help. He had taught Mike how to use a spear, and yesterday, Mike had speared his first fish, though no doubt with help from the power of the emblem. In addition, Arwulf had known people along the way who had provided shelter and provisions for them. Most importantly, he had been a great aid in helping Virgil and Abe establish a fairly good relationship. The two talked like old friends now, not showing any sign of any rocky beginning.

But Mike had since realized something that he had not before. Something that had been subtle, yet had caused enormous consequences. He had been an extra ingredient that had set them off course and almost caused disaster in the party. It was the first of what could be many nightmares, nightmares which Mike hoped would never have the chance to materialize.

The party had started walking again, descending down into the little valley where the village lay situated. It did not seem long, especially to Mike, before they found themselves walking through the fields where scattered workers toiled, harvesting the grain. They worked like the elves had, though their motivation from them differed completely. Mike could tell from their demeanor. There was no laughing or joking, merely grunts and sighs and occasional communication when necessity called for it.

Mike felt exposed as they walked past the fields and caught the bewildered, careful stares of the bodies closest to them. Mike only made eye contact with the creatures for a second, then he turned his head straight forward to avoid their gazes. His party seemed to have become a death parade, and the village, no more than a haphazard collection of huts centered around the road, seemed to be the executioner's block. *It seems as if they do not welcome us,* Mike muttered to himself. He bit his lip and curbed the desire to turn back to the countryside. *How can this be the right place?*

The party entered the gathering of huts in stale silence. Again, they were given dead stares from those who were too old or too young to work in the fields. An old man stood with a menacing look in the doorway to one of the first earthen huts they encountered. He remained silent, though Mike almost wished he said something to break the stagnancy of the air. Little children ceased playing and stood perfectly still, like deer after catching the scent of trouble.

"We need to find someone to talk to here," Mike mentioned softly to Abe in English, more so the people would not understand than their counterparts.

"Yeah, but I assume the leader is out in the fields somewhere," Abe replied.

The group passed through the conglomeration of buildings in a matter of only a few minutes. Ahead lay more fields and beyond that a continuation of the wild, empty world. Indeed, the village sat like a small ship struggling to stay afloat in a turbulent sea bigger and deeper than life itself. Mike and the others stopped and turned to look behind them. The villagers continued to stare at them, most likely wondering if they would continue on.

Mike turned back and approached a lame man in the hut nearest them. "Excuse me," he said in Latin, "my name is Mike and I was wondering where I could find your leader."

The man held the same defensive glare that the old man had held. "Leader? What do you mean? What do you want?"

Mike gulped nervously. "Don't you have a village leader? We've been displaced from our land and have come to seek the refuge of your village."

The man stared at Mike studiously, intensely enough to seem to burn a hole in Mike's eyes. *Who could blame the man?* Mike thought. They did not exactly look either Roman or Celtic, especially with his and Virgil's size. Virgil himself seemed to be a giant image of a Saxon, perhaps a Saxon general. Mike did not know how much contact, if any, they had had with the Saxons, but he was sure that rumors were just as, if not more, rampant here than anywhere else.

"What do you plan on doing? Eating all our food? Living off our hard work? We barely have enough for ourselves. It will be better for all of us if you continue on to York."

"We plan on nothing but contributing to your village," Abe cut in. "We are farmers ourselves, and will help in the work here. We offer our weapons of protection. I swear by my honor that our intentions are innocent and we will do nothing else."

The man's features softened slightly, and he looked over at the other two, who now stood behind them. Though the motive may not have been strong, the man seemed to consider Abe's oath.

Mike turned back to Virgil. "Virgil, offer the man some venison."

Virgil pulled some of the meat out of his bag and approached the man. The man looked at it, then motioned for the group to enter his hut.

As the four ate the remnants of the deer, the man introduced himself. "My name is Magnus. I broke my leg a month ago, and so I have not been able to work out in the fields. Your coming is timely, for if you mean what you say, you can help the others make up for what I cannot do."

"How many people live here?" Virgil asked.

"About fifty," Magnus replied, "but only eight are able bodied men. Like I said, there is more work in this village than they can perform."

"Well, we mean to provide that help," Mike said, "at least through the end of the autumn."

Mike happened to glance over at both Virgil and Abe, who were looking at him quizzically, though Mike did not know why. If they were expecting this to be an in and out sort of ordeal, they were set for rude disappointment. With fifty people in the village, and only eight able-bodied men, it would not be hard to narrow down for whom he was looking, but the act of doing what he needed to do was not going to happen in a matter of days. That act was simply beyond his capabilities.

Mike offered their help in the fields after they had finished eating. Magnus offered him his sickle, but did not have any tools for the others. "Go anyway," he pressed. "They will have work for you to do."

Abe started forward as the three began to leave, but Virgil turned him back. "You are not fit to work, you'll kill yourself if you don't get some rest."

Abe turned back hesitantly to Magnus, who motioned that his house was welcome to him. "Please, I'd be honored to have you keep me company. I'm sure you can update me on a lot of what is going on around the island."

As the three left, Virgil turned to Mike and Arwulf. "That man cannot take care of himself."

Arwulf laughed. "I agree. The man is a bit too ambitious, especially when it comes to such unimportant tasks, such as coming out to work in the fields."

Mike had a feeling that Arwulf really wanted to say something else, but had decided not to voice it. He took note that Arwulf was heading out to the fields with them and had, up to this point, made no hints as to his time of departure. It made Mike a little anxious, especially since Virgil seemed perfectly content to keep Arwulf by his side.

The fields were dusty, much like Idaho. Rain had not seemed to have fallen up here in at least a few weeks. The air was hazy with the dust that the workers were throwing up and it hid the three until they were almost upon the main cluster. As they finally became noticed, the workers stopped, one by one, and stared at the newcomers.

"Who are you?" one of them asked.

"Countrymen," Mike said. "We've been displaced from our homes and have traveled seeking new residence. We have already spoken with Magnus back in the village and are now come to work with you."

The workers studied the three. They took note that the three were all armed, but their weapons were not drawn, and Mike did his best to make the sickle visible enough to show that he was sincere. Still, the workers kept silent. They seemed to neither accept them nor reject them. Mike had no idea what they were thinking. They may as well have been thinking nothing at all, waiting for someone else to take the initiative of dealing with them. Whatever the case, the ice was thick and not easily broken.

"Do you understand me? We are here to work. Where would you like us to go?"

A man off to the side finally stated, "We can use a few men to put bundles together over here, and you with the sickle can thrash over there."

A decision having been made, everyone broke their stares and resumed the work they were performing. There were no welcomes, nor were there any introductions. Directions were given once and not seen through to be executed. Mike studied the group in intrigue. No smiles, no conversation, simply work. He noted that the women and teenagers worked alongside the men, bending down, sweating, blending in with the group almost autonomously with the ragged clothes and dust covering their dirty bodies.

Mike looked over at the others and shrugged. He then proceeded over to his directed spot and began the task of reaping alongside everyone else.

Throughout the day, a few of the people seemed to warm up to them a little, perhaps because they saw that Mike's words were genuine. They saw that all three men were good workers and did more than their sufficient share of what they would owe to the community, which seemed to be called *The Haven*. A few of the people posed wary questions directed toward them; Mike did his best to give superficial answers when they were directed toward their origins. He did fill them in on their encounter with the Saxons, which seemed like a familiar occurrence with the workers—one about which none seemed incredibly eager to talk.

Of course, he was not able to deny the thoughts of the girl he was supposed to find here, and he found himself looking around at more than just the fields. As he did so, he grasped the emblem tightly, for he was confident that it would radiate the same heat it always did when he found himself on the right track. There was no such heat today, though, only the heat from his hands. Mike did not fret. Perhaps it would not work so easily—perhaps he would need to get to know the girls personally before the emblem filled him in on anything. He was also not in full sight of everyone since a few worked on the other side of the village.

They worked until sundown, stopping only to grab swigs of water from their skins and to eat a morsel that their children brought out to them. Mike, Virgil, and Arwulf were given pieces as well, but it did not seem to be nearly enough. Mike knew Virgil had jerky in his bag, and he looked over at him as they finished their allotment. He knew that Virgil knew what he was thinking, but Virgil did not act upon it. They could not have fed thirty people with it.

When they finally turned in for the night, the three men walked with exhausted limps, despite their experience in hard work. Two days of travel and one day of harvesting was a little bit more than their bodies could take. Luckily for them, Abe and Magnus had a nice lit fire which sizzled with bits of roasting meat when they came back. Magnus' welcome was much brighter this time.

As they ate, Magnus and Abe continued their conversation about Rome and its ideals. Mike, Virgil, and Arwulf were content only to offer comments when asked as Abe spoke of democracy and law and order, of technology and architecture. He described Rome to Magnus, though it very well could have been Rome as it was two hundred years ago. Regardless, Magnus stayed attentive and absorbed whatever was given him with great earnestness.

Despite all the discomfort that had occurred that day, Mike had left the fields with a calm look on his face. To him, the work was a reversion to old lives, lives that now seemed to have been paved in gold. He had since become adept at the art of the sickle, and he was glad to reawaken the action. In addition, the physicality of the work allowed him to do more than sit and think about what was ahead of him. Aside from all that, it helped these people, who seemed to be in need of all the help they could get.

Mike hoped that that act would resonate loud enough for the people to hear. Somehow their frigidity would need to melt.

Such thoughts seemed to continue on uninterrupted as they lie down on the dirt floor, fell asleep, and woke up with the first rays of sunlight again. With a groan, Mike, turned over and lifted himself up. The initial eagerness of helping out the community did not have the strength this morning as it had the day before.

As he dragged himself out to the fields to continue on, a wave of loneliness washed over him; Arwulf and Virgil said that they would set to work on building a hut so that they would not have to depend on Magnus' hospitality. Abe, unable to both work in the fields and build the hut, had decided that he would go into the woods and set up snares for small game. Nobody had objected to that. It was hard enough keeping Abe from coming out to harvest, and Mike figured that his present task would be easy enough on his old body. Even so, it would have been pleasant to have him to talk to.

So the day started relatively quiet for Mike. The other workers silently fell back into their routine, seeming to be as much strangers to each other as they were to him. Mike studied them all as his arm moved back and forth through the blades of grain. *They may as well be machines,* Mike thought, scanning them. There was no emotion, either of joy or sorrow, nor was there any passion, either of ecstasy or spite. They were simply extensions of the tools which performed the work. Throughout the day, he even made efforts to strike up conversation with some of the women, but never got farther than shallow introductory conversations.

It continued like this for the next three days, and Mike was thankful when Arwulf and Virgil had finally finished the hut, for he would at least have people with which to converse. They came out to the fields on the fourth day and livened things up a little, and so the three stood out among the others together.

But having the other two there only changed the nature of Mike's discomfort, and to a much more disconcerting degree. Arwulf's presence reawakened Mike's initial fears concerning his threat to the mission. Almost a week had passed since they had arrived in the village and it seemed as if Arwulf had no intention of leaving. After Arwulf had failed to leave upon arrival, Mike had thought that he was simply there to help his friend build the hut, but that did not seem to be the case either. Last night, when they had moved their few belongings into the hut, Mike had heard Arwulf comment, "Hey, our place turned out relatively nicely, didn't it?" Mike had looked over Abe with consternation, but Abe seemed confused with Mike's reaction.

Mike had spoken with Abe in private later that night after everyone had fallen asleep. Abe had fallen asleep as well, but Mike gently shook him and bade him to follow outside. The night had spelled serenity, with the nearly full moon silently keeping watch over the huts and the crickets singing in rhythm to each other, but it was all nothing to Mike at the moment.

"What is it Mike?" Abe had asked in English.

"It's Arwulf," Mike had replied with a sigh, "I think he needs to leave, but I don't think he has any intention of doing so."

Abe had again given him the confused look he had given earlier that night. "Why do you say that?"

Mike had stared at his companion and had realized that Abe had not taken the same notes that he had taken. "It doesn't feel right having him here. He never should have come with us."

"What do you mean?" Abe had replied. "He has been invaluable to us. Look at how he's built the hut, hunted for us, shown us the way. He saved my life in the woods."

"Yeah, after being the one that put you in jeopardy in the first place."

"How do you figure?"

"Virgil was supposed to be our guide on the trip. I'm now sure the emblem was telling him to direct us down the other road, where we wouldn't have encountered the Saxons."

Abe had thought that one over and had given no reply, but he still did not seem convinced. "So what harm is he doing now? These people need all the help they can get. We need him to stay, and until you come up with a good reason for him to go, I don't think I can support you in kicking him out."

With that, Abe had turned around and gone back to lay down in the hut, leaving Mike standing out in the night all alone. Abe had presented a few good points, and Mike did not feel like he had enough of an argument

Then again, he muttered into the night, *there is evidence of destruction that's beginning to show.* Virgil and Arwulf seemed to have started becoming more exclusive—Virgil was now spending more time around his old friend than he was with either Abe or Mike. Virgil's temperament was tending to be more and more carefree and less and less sober. Mike doubted whether he had done any meditating lately and could not help but notice that he left his emblem in the hut half of the time he went out to work.

This progressed through the next few weeks of harvesting, and as it did so, the fact that Arwulf was changing Virgil ate at Mike more and more. It was like watching a tragic play unfold, one in which he knew the ending and dreaded it. Several mornings, he had woken up, deciding that the day would be the one in which he would tell Arwulf to leave, but it never happened. Arwulf continued to work, continued to joke, and continued to poke fun at Mike, prodding him as to whether he had found his *wench* yet. Occasionally, Virgil joined in, and gave Mike a hard time about being poor womanizer. All the while, Abe seemed ignorant, expressing time and again, how valuable it was to have Arwulf.

But it was not until they had been in The Haven for three weeks that the evidence came out. The four men had all settled down to sleep and had been down for about an hour when Mike, who had always been a light sleeper, heard someone get up. He opened his eyes to a squint to note that it was Virgil. Virgil stepped outside the hut and proceeded to walk off. In any normal occasion, Mike would have shrugged the occurrence off, thinking he was going to meditate or to relieve himself, but, somehow, he knew it was something else. Mike paused a moment to make a quick decision, then silently got up and followed Virgil out the doorway.

The wind was blowing quite strongly, and Mike could see that great rainclouds were forming off in the distance. The sky remained clear, revealing a blazing sky of stars and half moon, and the temperature was still quite pleasant, but it had a sort of suspended feeling at the same time, like it teetered on the edge of a ten to twenty degree drop. Everything else—the grass, the trees, the bushes, and the eerie walking of Virgil about fifty meters in front of him seemed drawn into the commotion.

Mike walked briskly to catch up, but did not do so until Virgil had paramounted the dale that watched over The Haven. Mike surmised that Virgil had sensed him coming a while ago, for he had quickened his pace until he reached the spot in which he now stood, which was well out of hearing from the huts below. He then started speaking without turning around.

"I did not know that you heard me get up."

"It does not take much to wake me up," Mike said, still standing behind him.

Virgil turned around. "I'm scared, Mike. I know it does not look to be so, but it's true."

"Scared?"

"Yeah. Rumors are flying all over the place, from travelers especially, that Britain's being overrun with invaders. The people here have told me that they've been through twice already, and any man that has put up a fight has been cut down. Then just today, I saw black smoke off in the distance."

"Yeah, I saw that too," Mike said, recalling also the foreign stench in the air. "But what else can we do?"

Virgil looked Mike directly in the eye. "Take whatever girl will come with us and get out. What's the use in worrying about the correct choice if we're all dead?"

"Have you consulted the emblem on this?"

To that, Virgil did not have a direct answer. Instead, he said, "The call is yours right now. I cannot choose the girl for you."

Mike took a deep breath to calm his rising temper. All the thoughts that had been stewing in his mind for the past great while were rising to the surface, and he had to fight the urge to let them explode like they wanted to. He paused a moment, then looked Virgil directly in the eye. "Do you even have your emblem with you?"

Mike knew the answer to the question even before he asked it. He had noted that the emblem had been sitting beside Virgil's bed of hay when he had left the hut. Again, Virgil did not give a direct answer, but instead turned the question on Mike. "Do you?"

Mike pulled out the golden emblem from his pocket and displayed it to Virgil. He then boldly continued, strengthened by his minor victory. "What is happening to you Virgil? Lately, you have not been the man we first knew. Have you forgotten who it is you have been called to be?"

Virgil broke the eye contact and shuffled his feet. "No, I haven't. Have you? Have you forgotten what you are supposed to do here? I have not seen you make any effort whatsoever to find this *bearer of love*. Arwulf has even less confidence in you than he did when he first found out about this mission." Virgil was flailing any weapon he possessed at Mike, but in its frenzied manner, it could not do much harm. Mike was hurting, but only from the rapidly disintegrating loss of hope of unity between them.

"Arwulf," Mike repeated, returning the defiance and feeling everything break down even more. "Is he the one where your attitudes stem from? Arwulf isn't even supposed to be here. He should have left a long time ago."

"Then why have you not told him to go?"

This time, Mike did not have an answer. Instead, he stood there in jaded emotion, realizing for the first time that he was alone in his opinion of Arwulf. He suddenly felt incredibly empty inside, like he was no more human than the people from the town. It was a shocking feeling that disabled him. He stood there looking at Virgil with wide eyes, but with nothing else. Virgil did not break his frown, but seemed to emanate triumph even so. Without saying any more, Mike turned away and retreated back down the hill in defeat.

Chapter 17

Nothing was done about Arwulf. He stayed, and along with him, Mike's feeling of a churning disaster. On the surface, he was a great help to have—he worked like a machine and hunted and even helped Mike fine tune his bow once he saw how one worked. He was welcome comic relief, especially when the rest of the community seemed to be stunningly stagnant of humor. Mike therefore understood why the other two wanted to keep him around, but he stuck to his initial feelings about the whole thing. Rather, they stuck to him.

In the mean time, they worked through the days. As they worked, Mike started taking note of the ways of the people around him. They did not seem to hold any particular sort of unity other than the fact that there was strength in numbers. They were nothing more than a school of dumb fish, living in a group but existing alone. In asking one of the nearby workers about the nature of the community, he simply shrugged and said, "It was about four months ago that everyone started congregating here. If you would have been here a year ago, you would have only found three huts."

Mike had asked him if he were one of the original families to which he shook his head. "But I was the first one to arrive. I guess your experience was pretty similar to mine. I was displaced from my home to the north by marauders. My whole family was killed and I had nowhere to go but elsewhere. I saw these fields and approached Magnus' hut to see if I could join him and the other two families, and he agreed."

"So who are the other two families?" Mike had asked.

"One is Julius' family, who was the man who first asked you who you were, and the other is gone."

"Gone?"

"Yeah, gone. Even The Haven is not safe from marauders, especially since it lies on the main road."

The man spoke of it unemotionally, and Mike tried with all his might to view it the same. He could not help but recall Virgil's comments to him the other night. Virgil was most definitely referring to the stories of these people, and he now seemed to be haunted by the ghosts of their whispering dust and dried blood. Up to this point, Mike, on the other hand, had fought their influence. He had desperately tried to keep those ghosts out of his head and in their graves, but they continued to shake at the ground, ushering forth muffled screams that his fate would soon be the same. It was getting hard to ignore them, especially with the black smoke that continued to linger in the air.

It was hard to think of his duty here with such things on his mind. Even so, he continued trying to at least rotate his proximity in the field to different persons, especially the girls, each day. There was not much luck for him, though. The attitude of everyone here was sunken, almost to a robot-like level of humanity. It seemed like the people worked to eat, and ate to live, but were capable of no more than that. The others often found Mike's attempts at conversation odd, and put up their own respective fronts, returning his comments with monosyllabic answers.

There was one exception to the populace, however. Julius had a daughter named Aeola that had spoken to him more than anyone, and, underneath the dirt on her face, she was actually quite beautiful. It had taken a several days for Mike to see through that, since he was not culturally accustomed to it, but once he did, he found her absolutely stunning. Mike thought, more than once, about making an attempt to move forward with her, and often worked alongside her, but, at the same time, something did not feel like it fit. It wasn't the emblem, for the emblem remained cold regardless of which direction he headed with it, but something else. Mike could not explain it, but, at the same time, he did not want to fight it. It was all really frustrating.

On the brighter side of things, the minor scuffle between Mike and Virgil seemed to pass within those few days. Nothing more was said on the subject, and although the next day progressed with relative silence between the two, Virgil seemed just as willing on the following day to laugh and joke with Mike as he always had. Mike accepted the reconciliation without bringing it up, and did not worry any more about the breach in friendship they had encountered. Despite the fact, Mike could tell that he was still on edge, though, and eager to get out. Frankly, Mike could not blame Virgil, for he, as well as everyone else in the town, feared what tomorrow might bring. The black smoke in the distance did not cease and filled the air with an acridity of which Mike did not wish to know the cause.

What was not apparent was whether the smoke arose from a closer source today than it did the day before. The conversations overheard in the fields revealed that this ignorance was consensual, and Mike could detect nothing that signified that anyone meant to remedy it. The villagers simply continued to work, living in the idea that the moment was still peaceful regardless of what lay before them.

Mike felt different. The idea that invaders could be just over the rise without anyone knowing it ate at him with greater and greater intensity. Like Virgil, he wanted to run. *But where would be safe?* he kept asking himself. Mike knew his history. Foreigners were coming in from all fronts. They could continue to run, and take their chances with the others, but eventually, the Saxons would drive them into the sea, whether on the north or on the west. Mike knew that running was not an option. He had known, even from the early moments in the Realm, that he would be entering a lion's den. For the longest time, he had fooled himself, making himself believe that battles could be avoided. That belief was quickly dissipating. All he could do was to avoid it as long as possible, and perform the mission to the best of his ability in the mean time.

Still, his eyes kept reverting back to the sun, trying to make out any sign that the degree of smoke was increasing. Arwulf, who worked alongside him and Virgil, took note of this.

"Mike," he piped up soberly, turning Mike's attention away from the sky. "What's on your mind?"

"I think you know," Mike said, "I think we've all had that thought for the past few days."

Mike looked over at Virgil, who did not say anything, but looked down to the ground. It was amazing to Mike that the same man who had so stoically prophesied of everything up to this point could have such a pitiful look on his face. *This cannot be the persona of the bearer of wisdom,* he thought. Mike had noticed that the playfulness had stopped, and that he had resumed bearing his emblem, but he also noticed that Virgil still had not left Arwulf's side and could not seem to shake the fear he had so ardently expressed that night he spoke with Mike on the hill.

"It seems like these people are only waiting for it to come," Mike continued.

"Yeah, kind of pitiful really," Arwulf replied, straightening himself and looking at all the villagers toiling.

Mike stared at Arwulf in amazement. He did not understand the man. Mike turned and made his way over to Julius.

As he approached, he saw Julius look up and stare at him in silence. "Hey, have you noticed that smoke's getting closer?"

"Yeah," Julius said as if it were no big deal.

"Are you going to do anything about it?"

Julius looked at him as if he were a fool. "What's there to do? They obviously outnumber us; we have already lost most of our men; and they have already taken all of our goods. We hide the majority of our harvest in the woods so it will not be found. We will just let them come through, take what they may, and go back to work. We don't fight them anymore. That has only ended up in tragedy."

Julius seemed to iterate the words with a particular bite in his tone, and Mike knew that he would not be able to change his resolve, but he felt that someone needed to take the lead here or more lives would be lost. Mike was sure of it. The emblem pulsed the warning throughout his body and engaged an anxious energy within.

Mike turned around and pulled Virgil away from where he was working, leaving Arwulf behind in confusion. Without saying anything, he held to Virgil's elbow and started walking back toward the huts, back toward the source of the smoke.

"Hey, where are we going?"

"Toward the fire," Mike replied curtly. "Is your spear and sling back at the hut?"

"Yeah, why?"

"You might need it in case we're discovered."

"Mike, what's going on?"

"Just follow me." Mike let go of Virgil's arm and quickened his pace back to the hut. Virgil hesitated, then jogged up behind him and did not say anything more. Mike, mildly surprised, kept moving forward in silence. Mike did not want to say anything anymore anyway. They had talked enough. They had speculated enough. Now was a time for action, for if none was taken, they could end up dead by the end of the day. Mike grasped tighter to the emblem and quickened his pace even more.

They reached the hut and made for their weapons. Mike looked down at Abe and Magnus and told them to prepare to leave quickly. Abe looked at them queerly, but did not say anything. Mike was glad. He would not have stuck around to explain anyway. After grabbing his bow and arrow, and urging Virgil once again to grab his weapons, they set out northward on the road at a jog.

The source of the smoke was a lot closer than Mike thought. They had not been jogging long when they discovered flames behind a cluster of trees up the way about half a mile. It looked like a hut and the fields behind it were on fire.

Almost at the same time they noticed this, they heard the screams of girls. Mike instinctively darted off the road into the tall grass of the field and hastily advanced to get a better look. He already had one of his crude arrows drawn and held in his left hand, for although he was still not proficient from a distance, he could do some damage from up close. The screams which came again caused him to wince.

They came from the proximity of the huts, which, by now, were only two hundred meters away or so. They could now clearly see the flames, which paled in comparison to the horrific scene occurring with the sources of the screams. Two young ladies, maybe in their teens, were being wrestled to the ground by two or three men each, men who seemed to emerge directly from the nightmares that had terrorized him since that first day on the island. Again, he was reminded that the nightmares were more than just farce. They could exist in his waking hours. Mike knew he was awake now. There was no escaping them, nor how they were treating those girls. He feared they would witness something that he had hoped he would never have to witness, but to his surprise, the screaming abruptly stopped and the clink of iron was heard on the wind, along with the Saxon word for slave. He then noticed the whole group of men, who numbered about a hundred, coming out of the smoke to add two more prizes to the menagerie they carried with them.

Instantly, Mike turned his eyes back to The Haven in horror. A gold mine was waiting there for the monsters, and they probably knew it too. Mike knew that although he had not witnessed anything yet, things would happen to those girls nonetheless. He did not wait around any longer, nor look back to see if they saw them, but started retreating out across the field back to The Haven, the anxiety carrying his legs faster almost than their sounds of alarm.

"Make for the woods!" he cried as he frantically banged on all the huts. He could almost feel their advancement behind him and was now too frightened to look back. Virgil had run on ahead, hopefully to forward the warning. Mike could not spare the time to see if there was any response at any of the huts, for they would be on top of them within minutes. He had to warn everybody.

Mike ran for the fields. "Make for the woods, they're taking slaves! They're taking slaves, they're almost here!"

Mike found himself pausing to notice that everyone was staring at him like he was a maniac. Virgil had not seemed to forerun him, but had simply seemed to inform Arwulf, and together they had taken off. "They're just over the rise," he reemphasized. Still, there seemed to be no response. Mike was getting desperate. Abe had caught up to him by now and was antsy to move forward to the woods himself.

"Mike, come on. We cannot force them."

Mike knew that to be true, and instantly, for the first time, the thoughts for his own life kicked in. He made for the woods off to the west of the fields. And to his joy, he found that the people were following him, picking up momentum as they went. Mike breathed a little more steadily, but still did not look back again until he reached the cover of the trees.

The villagers followed close behind him and Mike urged them to keep going deeper into the woods. "Don't stop until it's too thick to pass," he ordered. Mike however, stayed near the edge to make sure the others made it safely. Beside him he found Julius.

"How far away are they?" Julius asked, his tone surprisingly different than it had been only half an hour ago.

"They were right behind me," he wheezed. "Hopefully there's enough dust in the air so that the rest of these people make it without being seen." The last of the elderly and young were now approaching the forest. Mike could not tell whether the enemy had entered the valley yet.

"Have you seen my daughter?" Julius then asked.

Mike recalled that he had not. "Is she still out there?"

"I sent her to refill my skin with water from the stream." Julius' face had lost its color.

"The one on the other side of the road?"

"Yeah, but you cannot risk it now; you'll be cut down."

Mike did not listen. Rather, his legs did not listen. He found himself running back out from the safety of cover to where he knew the stream to be. As he ran out into the field, he noted that the dust was settling. To the north, the dust was rising. Relapses of his encounter with them flashed in his mind, but again, his mind no longer dictated the actions of his legs, which carried him farther out of the woods and more into the open.

"Mike!" he heard Julius' voice call out from behind him.

"Make sure everyone keeps moving in," he yelled back. "Do the same yourself."

With that, he was alone. He ran out across the road just as the hoard reached the huts a quarter mile away. Mike ducked low into the grain to get out of sight, but moved as fast as he could toward the hill that led down to the stream.

In no time, smoke suffocated the air as the huts burst up in flames. Mike imagined that the Saxons would have spread out by now to search for the villagers. Under the screen of the smoke, Mike stood up, looked around, and not seeing nor hearing anybody in close proximity, started off again at a sprint.

He had scarcely done so then with no warning at all, a burly silhouette appeared in front of him. There was no way to avoid it, and out of some sort of primal instinct, Mike charged and leveled it, then whacked it over the head as hard as he could with his spear. He did not stick around to see if he completely disabled the thing, but kept running for the shadow of the trees where he knew he would find the stream.

At the moment he heard another female scream, his foot caught on what must have been a root or rock and sent him tumbling down the hillside. "Who is that," he heard a gruff Saxon voice call. Mike, who now lay on his stomach halfway under some thorny bush, turned to see that about ten yards away, a Saxon sat poised over Aeola, whose face was one of utter helplessness and fear. The man could not see him, but the sound his crash had created had diverted the man's attention. Mike scurried out of the bush, ignoring the countless scratches that came to his face, pulled out his bow and an arrow and fired. The shot was quick and amateur, but sunk itself deep in the Saxon's leg, deep enough to send the man wrenching back in pain and off of his victim, who scurried away at a safe distance.

Mike dropped his bow, pulled out his spear, and charged the wounded man. The Saxon remained on the ground but held out his sword in defense. Mike ran on complete animal instinct. His actions were not his own, for his own would have sent him into pitiful retreat. Somehow his actions had taken on that of a warrior. He was fighting just as he had with Arwulf, and as he parried the blows of the now limping foe, he found his muscles knew their movements. There was only enough presence of mind to note the only difference lie in the direction of the deadly point on his spear.

The warrior was no doubt experienced, but Mike had the advantage. He was taller than the man, and the man was wounded. Mike backed him down the hill toward the stream, though the fighting continued as intensely as ever. Blow after blow, jab after jab kept coming—one at his stomach, a swipe toward his legs, both parried, though not without painful gashes. Mike continued on, blocking out the pain, focusing instead on delivering much more vital blows to his opponent.

Then it happened. Mike caught the moment of weakness—an unsure step with the man's strong leg. The Saxon shifted his weight to keep balance. In a quick blur, Mike knocked his opponent's weapon aside and jabbed at his chest. The spear sank deep—the force of the jab had been Herculean—and the Saxon fell backward onto a rock and breathed his last.

Mike's eyes widened as he stood there, and, suddenly, he felt sick to his stomach. He wrenched over and vomited at the sight. For a moment, he could do no more than breath hard and spit. Then, remembering where he was, he pushed the sickness out of his mind, straightened up, recovered his bloody spear, and looked around. Nobody was near except for Aeola, who was sobbing quietly over to the side.

Mike pitifully wiped his mouth with his arm. "We have to get out of here," he somehow managed to say, though without strength. "We have to get farther into the forest."

Aeola did not say anything as Mike retrieved his bow, took her hand, and quickly led her across the stream and deeper into the trees. He knew that that other Saxon would be awake by now and coming this way. Mike did his best to navigate them through the bushes as quickly and carefully as possible. The thorns still scraped them up, but he could not care about that now.

When they had run for a few minutes and had found a good place to hide and look back on their trail, Mike stopped, tucked his companion back behind him, gave her his quiver to hold, and held his bow and arrow at ready position. "If anyone comes," he commanded in a whisper, "be prepared to hand me arrows quickly. In the mean time, keep silent."

Nobody came, though. They sat there for a great while, but the sounds of the men were far off. Mike shifted his position, and, for the first time, he was able to reflect on what had just happened. The Saxons had attacked. He had directed the entire village into the trees to the west. He had run before the Saxons across an open field and now he and Aeola were in the trees to the east. He had incapacitated one man and killed another. He had killed a man, killed him close enough to hear his breath exhale and feel the impact of his fall in his feet. His spear was stained with the man's blood. The sickness in Mike's stomach was back again, but he breathed hard to keep down anything that was battling to come up.

"Are you okay?" Aeola asked, disobeying Mike's command and breaking the silence at last.

It was now safe enough though that Mike did not care. With a hard exhaling breath, he looked down. "Yeah. I think so."

Aeola looked at his expression, then down at the rest of his body. "Your leg is bleeding pretty badly."

Mike followed her gaze to survey his wounds for the first time and realized he must have looked like a disaster. Blood had run down his leg, covering it in a violent hue, but the blood was not gushing, nor did it hurt incredibly badly. "It's just a graze," he assured. "He did not get me hard." Mike grabbed the corner of his tunic and dabbed the still wet blood on his leg. He also reached down his tunic to feel his stomach, but that was not bleeding too badly either.

"Thank you," she said and forced out a smile.

Mike looked back at her and simply nodded. His head was in too much of a hurricane to do anything more.

They waited in their spots until dusk, until the forest was dark and the silence had presented itself for a great long while. Mike pulled himself up and got the circulation flowing back into his legs. Aeola followed suit. For the first time, Mike noticed the thorn scratches all over his face and back. He rubbed his hand over his face and found dried blood.

As they walked up the hill and into the field, the sky had cleared itself of all the smoke. The waxing gibbous moon lit up the valley to reveal charred remains of all the huts. A few of the villagers who had returned earlier huddled around a small fire off to the side while others walked to and fro, scavenging the remains. Julius noticed them as they approached and ran up to embrace his daughter. Mike simply collapsed onto the ground, and within no time, was asleep, not even having had enough energy to seek after the well being of his fellow friends.

It was not until the next day that Virgil, Arwulf, and Abe caught up with him. The gray sky was well lit before Mike woke up, and as he did, he found his back sore and his face and leg stinging. As he stirred and opened his eyes, the three, as well as Julius, who were sitting nearby, turned to him.

"We're glad to see you are alive," Abe stated soberly. "Julius told us how you went after his daughter."

"And my daughter told me how you saved her," Julius stated in earnest thankfulness. "You do not know how I am indebted to you. She is the only one I have left, and if it weren't for you..." Julius trailed off.

Mike did not reply with anything but a groan. Then, gathering his strength, he asked, "Do any of you have any water?" That was all he could think of right now. His lips were parched, his throat was dry, and his face was burning.

Virgil reached over, grabbed his skin and gave it to Mike, from which he drank until the skin was almost empty. "Thirsty, Mike?" Arwulf exclaimed in usual humor.

Mike grunted and sat up for the first time to look around. They were encamped just south of the hut ruins and just east of the road. For the first time, Mike noticed that the remainder of the fields was burnt. There was absolutely nothing left. The huts were charred piles and all of their contents were gone. The only things Mike saw were the living corpses that slunked about.

"How did everybody fare?" Mike finally found the strength to ask.

"The Saxons found five women," Julius stated without emotion. "They're gone. Magnus is dead. He did not make it far enough in. A few of the elderly said he would not go deeper into the forest until everyone else had gone before him. They seemed to cut him down with little resistance."

For the first time, Mike noticed how affected Abe seemed. As for himself, he felt much like Julius, very much the same way that he had the day they had found the elf bodies on the shore after the shipwreck.

"Get everybody together," Mike said. "We need to leave here as soon as possible."

"And go where?" Virgil asked.

"I don't know," Mike stated. "Somewhere off the main road. Somewhere that no one will encounter us."

The group was gathered together before long, and since there was nothing at hand to eat, they promptly set off away from The Haven and off to the west. Mike led out with Virgil, Abe, Arwulf, and Julius. He did not know where he was going; he just wanted to get away from this place as fast as possible. He wanted to leave this valley and its concentration of horrid memories behind.

The next two weeks were spent building huts, hunting, and grinding all the grain the villagers had recovered from their storage into flour. There was no more harvesting—there were no more fields to be harvested. The group had traveled for about a day until Mike found a satisfactory spot—a bald promontory surrounded by trees on all sides with a clear stream not a quarter mile away. From atop the promontory no road was to be seen, only endless rolling hills covered in fields and forests. The base of the hill had three different clearings that would serve as good field lands for the next year. As Mike stood atop and surveyed the place, he commanded that they would travel no more. They called the place Newhaven.

Since that fateful day of attack, the villagers of The Haven had begun to look to Mike for the decisions. It seemed to him that they had inwardly suffered from a vacuum of indolence for so long that when someone took the initiative to fill it, they were ready to follow him. Mike executed the necessary decisions, but did so unwillingly and with a heart of hesitance. He felt out of place ordering the people around, but he knew that nothing would happen without it. Even so, he kept the decision making to a minimum.

During these few weeks, Virgil had a new thing to keep his mind occupied. Ever since Mike had risked his life to save Aeola, she had opened up to him extensively. She always found an excuse to work by him, and he did not refuse because she was a good, able-bodied worker, not to mention pleasing to look at. Mike knew he was, indeed, quite attracted to her, and once she began feeling the same way about him, a sort of magic that she held within her seemed to emerge. The magic seemed to draw him in, charm him so that he would listen when she talked to him, sometimes for over an hour. He often returned the conversation, and did not deny that being around her gave his otherwise gray life a little bit of color. Yet still he hesitated. Something was amiss. He struggled to place his finger on it. At times she seemed rather juvenile; at times she seemed a little too tempting. It all scared Mike half to death.

"Take her, Mike," Virgil told him for the hundredth time one evening as they skinned a deer together.

Mike, like before, simply shook his head.

"Will you give up on her so easily?"

"I don't think she's what I'm looking for," Mike reiterated. "What am I supposed to do?"

"Make her be," Virgil insisted.

Mike turned away, just like he had done before, ignoring Virgil's rash suggestion fed from fear.

Mike had tried to talk to Arwulf during this time, asking him whether he was the root of Virgil's continued anxiety. Arwulf denied having to do with anything, but Mike could not bring himself to believe so. He and Virgil were more aloof than ever. In fact, the only times Mike or Abe ever saw them was at night in the hut. They seemed to disappear during the day.

It was not until Julius approached Mike, however, that things got really bad.

After three weeks, not much more could be done other than hunting and gathering the last remaining bits of honey from nearby hives. That left a lot of time for Aeola to visit Mike and drag him away from everyone else. One day, as Mike was sitting back, outside his hut, sipping from his skin, Aeola approached him.

"Come, Mike; I have to show you something down in the pasture," she requested.

Mike followed her off down the hill at a rapid pace. She bounded down the hill like a hart, laughing as she almost lost her balance near the bank of the stream. Mike followed behind as she crossed and continued to beckon him on. "Almost there," she assured.

When they had progressed to a green pasture out away from everything, she stopped, turned around, and smiled a grand, alluring smile. Mike watched her, caught, paralyzed by her magnetic gaze and upturned lips. Suddenly, she threw her whole self on top of him, almost knocking him back into the grass. He felt her body press against his, as well as her lips. Mike felt fiery feelings well up inside of him, and knew exactly what she wanted. Her power was stunning, and his very carnal self begged to let everything flow on in its course.

Mike, however, was able to get a hold of himself. He grabbed her shoulders and pushed her away in horror.

He stared intensely at his aggressor, who seemed shocked and hurt. "Why will you not have me?" she questioned.

Mike could not answer for a moment, but kept staring at her in disbelief both at what she had just done and what more she wanted.

"It's not right," he stuttered. "It's not right."

Tears streamed down her face and she ran back up toward the hill, leaving Mike standing alone in bewilderment and utter confusion with himself.

It was not long after that that Julius approached him. "My daughter has related to me your refusal to her."

Mike nodded. He was sitting in his hut during the heat of the day, braiding a new bowstring out of deer sinew.

"May I ask why? Is it another girl in the community? She has held onto this hope for three weeks now, and you have let her down."

"Julius, your daughter has formed a hope in something futile. Please don't take offense, but I've already determined that she and I are not meant for each other."

Julius stared down hard at Mike. Mike very well knew that he could have insulted the man, but such a chance could not sway his decision in a matter as important as this one. "You know there are not very many men left in this community," he cut back. "Most of those men have families already and I do not see that you have conversed with any single lady more often than my daughter. It is your responsibility to take her. You have proved yourself worthy in both my and her eyes. Tell me you have another lady in this community in your sights and I will be silent. Otherwise, I will not let the matter rest."

Mike took a deep breath. His dislike for confrontations had not left him, and this one was an extremely uncomfortable one, but he could not change his mind. The emblem was dead cold in his hand as he firmly stated, "I have no other girl that I'm seeking right now, but I cannot accept your daughter. She's a good friend but can be nothing more. I wish I could explain it all to you, but I can't."

Whether it was Julius' respect for Mike or simply his realization that Mike would not be swayed, Mike did not know, but Julius said nothing more at the moment. Quietly, he left the hut and let Mike back to his braiding. Mike sighed heavily and shook his head.

The fact that one person's news was everybody's news in a small community became very evident in the days following. Mike became aware of this fact with a renewed array of attacks from not only Virgil, but from Abe and Arwulf as well. Mike was to find that their hut would turn into an interrogation room that night. The other three sat opposite him staring him down as the subject was brought up.

"Why did you refuse her, Mike?" Abe interrogated.

"Yeah, Mike. It's obvious she loves you," Arwulf added.

Mike curbed his temper. "My own inclinations deny her, and the emblem seems to have no objection to that."

"If the emblem has denied it," Arwulf scoffed, "why has it not instead produced for you a shining goddess? Mike, like it or not, that girl is the best you're going to find. I don't know how it is where you come from, but you must be expecting a dream. You should have told me all this earlier so I could have taken Aeola for myself."

Mike had lost his patience. All the tension that had built up from all the fear, all the drama with Virgil, all the work in this village, and recently all the whispers and urgings from everyone around him could not be held in any longer. "Take her, for all I care. After what she's shown herself to be, you two would be perfect for each other."

"Excuse me, Mike," Arwulf defended, stepping back with palms upturned, "I didn't know you felt that way about me."

"You've been on thin ice with me for a while, now," Mike returned coldly.

"Gentlemen," Abe intervened cautiously. "Let's calm down. If he doesn't feel it right, it's not right." Abe turned to Mike and smiled weakly. "That's good enough for me."

Arwulf did not listen, however. "What have I done that has deserved such words?" he inquired forwardly. "I have sat around patiently for you to do your thing, whatever it is you're supposed to do, and have not said a word to you about it. This is the first night that I have brought it up and you explode on me."

"You're not even supposed to be here anymore," Mike countered. "You never even belonged with us. You never believed in this mission. Whatever happened to leaving after you led us here?"

Arwulf went wide-eyed. "I did not know that I was not wanted anymore."

Abe put his hands on both men's shoulders to calm them down. Virgil simply sat in silence. Mike took a deep breath and tried to recover from his short outburst. He sat back and instead set out to soberly say what he had meant to say for a long time.

"Arwulf your help has been appreciated. But you cannot stay here anymore. I want you to leave tomorrow."

Arwulf did not reply vocally. He simply looked at Mike for a moment, then at Abe, then at Virgil and lay down. Mike exhaled silently and did the same, for he suddenly found himself extremely tired, and in that manner, the night's conversation ended.

Chapter 18

How different life can seem to be at momentary relapses in our existences. We continue on in various circles, though they may more appropriately be called spirals, for although our orientation returns to a previous location, our position is not the same. Upward or downward—there will always be movement; there will always be change.

Mike paused in his writing and looked out of the open doorway of his hut in order to renew the ideas he was recording in his new journal. The writing did not come as easily as it had grown to come while in the Realm, for Mike simply had not possessed the same motivation to write in it. As opposed to his original journal, the entries had been superficial and spread out. He had only pulled it out today because he could not help noting that today and this time last year juxtaposed each other perfectly.

The turbulent weather had brought on an untimely chill in the air, and Mike could not help but be reminded of his last autumn. According to his reckoning, the Realm would be past fall color by now, and the elves would be breaking out their warm robes. More time would be spent indoors commiserating and telling stories and feasting on the various goods of harvest. This time last year, Mike was basking in the warm goodwill of all his compatriots in the Realm.

Mike was alone now. He had been all day, for everyone had been gone when he had woken up. The small beeswax flame that he used to light his writing did not echo the warmth of the blazing elfish fireplaces. There were no stories to be told, except for the one that he was living in now, lost atop an English hill among people that he hardly knew, with little knowledge of what nightmares could lie ahead.

FORTH FROM EDEN

The hut strained at the wind, just as the flags had atop the Patriarchal building. Mike pulled his deerskin cloak tighter around him and walked outside. The clouds were frenzied, dark, and moving sharply northeast. They had, as of yet, to shed their contents, but Mike could sense the air could not hold out much longer. The sun still shone somewhere hidden behind the gray, though Mike doubted it would be up for too much longer. In reality, it was hard to tell, for on a day such as this, when neither sun nor stars were to be found, time lost all of its order. At any rate, the world around him had darkened early, and all that could be seen now were the shadows of the trees down the hill.

The huts were the only things that interrupted the continuity of the landscape, for all of Newhaven's inhabitants were huddled inside them. Mike had only seen a few of them all day and wondered, for the first time, to where his companions had disappeared.

Mike walked over to Julius' hut where he found the man sitting with his daughter, (with whom he avoided eye contact), and a few of the widowed mothers and their children. They were talking of something in grave tones, though Mike did not hear much of it before Julius stopped and turned to him.

"Are you looking for someone, Mike?" he questioned, having noticed that Mike had immediately surveyed his guests upon entrance.

"Yeah," Mike started slowly, "Abe, Virgil, and Arwulf. I have not seen them all day. I had thought that they might have been here, but I guess I was wrong."

"Sorry. Have you checked the other huts?"

"No, but I will. I cannot imagine that they'd still be outside."

Mike exited and started making his way to the five other huts, but each time, he came away without luck. He thought it especially odd that all three of them were gone at once, since Abe usually stuck relatively close to the hut and did not breach the pair Virgil and Arwulf made. Mike furrowed his eyebrows and looked up again at the sky. The clouds had been gathering for quite some time now, and they should have been making their way back. He returned to his own respective hut.

It was not long after his return that the rain finally fell, and when it did, it came down in a torrent. Mike looked up to his ceiling as the rain mercilessly charged down and struck with a pounding barrage. He worried that it would penetrate the thatch, but the thatch held firm and kept him dry. Mike sighed at his comfort but did not relax. Such a feeling could only make him think more on his friends that were still outside in the storm.

Mike had lived in England long enough to know that such clouds were dense enough to sustain more than a passing storm. Lightning and thunder raged in waves ebbing with darkness and rumbling and flowing with cracking flashes. An hour passed and the rain continued to fall just as violently. Mike looked at his emblem, but it was as cold as stone. Then, making a decision himself, Mike again pulled close his deerskin cloak and readied himself to brave the melee. The three had still not returned, and Mike was worried.

As Mike ventured forth from the hut to an unknown destination, the wind, which still continued to howl, magnified the raindrops' icy stings. In no time, his face was threatening numbness. The deerskin cloak was relatively waterproof, but that did not prevent him from getting drenched almost right away. He knew the escapade was crazy, but it was the only way to ease the relentless tension that had built up in his chest. Something was wrong.

Mike briskly walked, almost ran, down toward the trees surrounding the stream. Again, he had no idea what he was doing, for the three could have been virtually anywhere. The trail was extremely slippery, and twice Mike lost his footing. He became completely covered in mud and was wet even under the security of his cloak, but that was near the last thing on his mind.

At the bottom of the hill, the stream rushed as if in a death race at a level fit to warn off anyone that dared challenge it. The waves rapped at the dead tree they had emplaced to traverse it and forced it to sway in subjection up and down. Mike hesitated, then bent down to cross it on his hands and knees. The water thrashed at him from both sides now, struggling to knock him off his path of safety, but he withstood its forces and crossed safely to the other shore.

He then continued on for an unknown time, no longer noticing the ungodly pouring, for he was soaked to the bone from the river. He forged on ahead, keeping his eyes open only enough to see what was directly in front of him. Then, what met his eyes made him gasp. There lay Abe, on the ground, cold, soaked, and motionless. Mike ran up to him. "Abe!" he yelled. A clap of thunder challenged his voice. "Abe!" He yelled even louder.

As Mike approached, he noticed a skid mark behind where Abe lay. *He must have slipped,* Mike realized. A nearby rock indicated he could have hit his head. Mike yelled out to Abe once again, and this time, he heard a groan emerge from the body before him.

"Abe, can you hear me? Are you alright?"

"Mike, Mike," Abe muttered. His eyes remained closed, but Mike could tell that his mind was awake. Mike knew that Abe very well could have been injured, and it was a risk to move him, but he would surely die if left out here. He picked up Abe's very cold, very wet body—a task since Mike was near to numb himself—and turned around.

The trail back was even more difficult and the crossing of the stream well nigh impossible, but somehow Mike accomplished it with Abe on his back. Abe was breathing, but not much more. Mike also realized he was trying to say something, but lacked the energy. "Hold on, Abe," Mike called out to his friend as thunder drowned everything else out. "Stay silent. Wait 'til we get back to the hut."

Mike found that the trip took several minutes longer than it should have, though. He did more sliding back on the hill than anything, and yearned to give up in frustration at one particularly steep point. Mike lay in the mud, almost in tears, catching his breath. Then pulling himself and his load back up out of the mud, he barreled forward and overcame it. The sight of the huts soon presented itself and Mike thanked his God in heaven for them.

Within minutes, Mike had shed all his wet clothes as well as Abe's and had wrapped Abe, as well as himself, in dry deerskins. Mike then set to work lighting a fire to heat up their wretched dwelling and started rubbing down the blanket that contained his friend to get as much frictional heat in his body as possible. The task was long and tiresome, but it warmed Mike up as well and seemed to revive Abe.

"Mike, Mike," Abe blubbered feverishly, yet with little to no energy. He seemed either delusional or disturbed about something, but either way, the quiet, almost whisper in which Abe performed the mutterings sent chills down Mike's spine. Mike gulped at the lump in his throat at what he was seeing—his friend in such a state—but there was absolutely nothing he could do but what he was already doing.

"Shh, it's okay," Mike answered, "be calm." The advice, however, was just as much for him as it was for his friend. Both the adrenaline and numbness had since worn off, leaving Mike to find himself in a state of panic. *Abe is in bad shape,* he avowed to himself. *Really bad shape.*

Abe shook his head with all the energy he had. "No. They're gone. They're gone."

"What are you talking about?" Mike probed, though, with added horror, he felt he already knew.

"Arwulf and Virgil," Abe choked, "gone."

"Are you sure? Do you think Virgil just saw Arwulf off and is still getting back?" It was a stupid question. It warranted the stern look in Abe's decrepit face.

"I followed them this morning." Abe breathed hard. "I suspected them after hearing Celtic words outside the hut last night."

This last sentence had taken all of Abe's breath, and he struggled with ardent coughing to redeem enough energy to continue. Mike waited silently. A part of him desperately wanted for Abe to quit and save his energy, be he could not bring it upon himself to stop him. *Not with such important information on the line.* Mike's entire world was falling apart before his eyes, and he watched in helplessness, too stunned to panic and too shocked to cry. His head was swimming contrary to his actions, for all he found himself doing was quietly staring with wide eyes at his friend and placing his hand on his friend's shoulder to relax him.

"They heard me and told me they were hunting and to go back," Abe continued through deep breaths, as soon as the coughing had subsided. "I didn't. I followed them at a larger distance. They did not have their weapons drawn and were moving fast. Before I knew it, I had lost them in the forest and it was getting dark. I turned back to the trail. I started running. It started raining, hard."

Mike opened his mouth, but nothing came out. Mouth and tongue did not function. Abe resumed coughing, harder than ever now, and his body shook. At some point, Julius and his daughter came in and helped steady him with Mike. They made inquiries to Mike, but the words did not register, and Mike did not answer. Hard breaths replaced Abe's coughing, and flowing, silent tears finally made their appearance on Mike's face.

"Mike," Abe breathed, "I'm sorry. Take my emblem; it's yours to bear. I'm sorry."

"What? What do you mean?" They were the first words Mike had managed to get out in the last five minutes, and they had not come without difficulty.

Abe simply repeated himself, though, until his words faded. Along with his words went his breath and his pulse. Mike took two involuntary steps back and stared in disbelief as Julius futilely worked to revive him. Again and again he shook, but all he was shaking was a lifeless body.

Mike stumbled out of the hut and fell back on his backside. The puddle beneath him enveloped his bare body, now shed of its deerskin down to his already soaked loincloth, and gave him all too much of a reminder of where he still was, that he still was. Still the rain pounded incessantly, striking his face in icy stinging. Mike was immediately soaked again and now shivering, but did not make any effort to save himself. Instead, he laid back in the mud and let the storm consume him. It seemed easier that way, for the sky was sobbing for him.

All would have seemed better if all would have terminated right there—simply ceased to exist with nothing more than a simple dramatic finish—clouds in the sky that somehow spelled THE END, then afterward, a blank screen. That would have been the easy way. But time has a cruel way of continuing, and the pain of recovery boldly surpasses the pain of injury, especially since shock, the great anesthesiologist, delivers its numbing shot at the moment of crisis. The injury is almost nonexistent the moment it happens—quite possibly a frenzied nightmare at the most—but the cruelty lies when one awakes to find the nightmare resides in reality, in having to wake up the next day to find that recovery, if it can ever come, will be a long road through treacherous chasms of uncharted depths.

Mike reviewed the entry, then let his face fall silently onto its page in tears.

He knew he was to travel more than his share of that road. He had hoped that he would have woken up in the morning, back in the twenty-first century, in some English farmer's field. He had hoped that the emblem had aborted the mission and spit him back out where he belonged. He had hoped for the end to come, where he could move on and pass it off as an incredibly long, realistic nightmare. But his hopes had been etched in vain. There, in the morning, before his red eyes, was the wretched thatch of his hut. Alas, for some reason, the story continued, but with what plot, he had not the slightest clue.

What is one to feel in such a situation? Mike asked the question of himself. The answer was abstract at first—no denotation, no scientific classification—only pure and base feelings of wretchedness. Eventually the classification would come, and Mike would realize that what he felt was abandonment. Utter and perfect abandonment.

Much like the day before, he found himself here, all alone, squeezing out words upon his journal. He existed in a completely different sphere however. Today the feelings of loneliness became internalized. Mike looked down at the tear stained pages. They were now all he had.

Arwulf had been taken care of, but he had taken Virgil with him. They were not coming back—Abe had been right about that. Mike was sure of that as soon as he heard it come from Abe's dying lips. Abe had died in pursuing them, and due to Mike's lack of strength, everything was now gone.

Mike was all alone. Had he known that Arwulf's presence would have been the cause of the entire disintegration of all that he had worked for this past year or so, he would have had no hesitation in immediately turning the demon away. But again, the deed was done, time traveled a one way train, and there was no way that redemption could be made.

Abe was gone. Virgil was gone. Mike stared out into the nothingness that now consumed his life. Mike thought back on Abe's last words. *Take my emblem; it's yours to bear.* Even at the very end, when his work had been cruelly snuffed out, Abe had held confidence in the continuance of the mission. Mike did not see any possibility in it, however, especially with Virgil gone. Mike was sure that everything into which this emblem had led him terminated in dead ends. It had led him to the top of this paramount only to leave him naked, without any means to complete the task it had enlisted him to do. The road that it had caused him to travel ended up having no outlet, leaving him with no other purpose than to walk onward into the panoramic tabula rasa.

Mike did not stay in his hut all day. He could not. He spent the morning digging a deep hole beside the hut. His muscles worked in silence, methodically loosening the soil, then bringing it up, then placing it off to the side. The soil was damp—it gave way readily to welcome the end of Abe's physical existence. He worked tirelessly and refused any help from anyone who had since gathered around to watch.

When it came time to place Abe's body into the ground, no words were said, no ceremony was held. Mike simply nodded to Julius to help him lower the body, then instantly began replacing the dirt, leaving the body of his mentor, partner, and friend to return from whence it came, or more appropriately, from whence it would come 1500 years in the future.

The task did not take long, and Mike finished without taking a draught from his skin. Julius stood by him the entire time, but remained silent. That was perfectly fine with Mike, for he did not want anything said. After packing down the dirt, Mike picked up the nearby stone which had sat next to hut and placed it as a gravestone above Abe's head. Mike stared at its smooth plate-like surface, interrupted by the numerous chinks which Abe had faithfully made ever since arriving here. "It will be our calendar," he had said. "One chink a day, like in those prison movies, you know?" Mike rubbed his hands over those chinks. It had been Abe's contribution to the building of Newhaven. Mike silently made one more chink in its surface and stared at it for an unidentifiable amount of time.

Julius stopped by Mike's hut for the next few days with food, but rarely did he find Mike present. He would leave the food inside the hut and find it gone on the next visit. Mike, who gathered it up on sundry visits to the place, appreciated the gesture, and hoped that Julius knew he was thankful, for he did not find it in him to be able to express it. In the mean time, Mike spent most of his time down by the stream, for it reminded him of another stream that he had occasioned a lifetime ago.

I want nothing more than to be able to go back to it. Such thoughts ran constantly through his head, like the small bubbling of the autumn water through the stream. Such thoughts did not help his mood, for while he would daydream of home and occasionally nod off into sleep, he would wake up frustrated to find that he was not in his hammock, but in the tall grass which itched and festered with bugs.

"We know what you're going through," Julius mentioned to him one day when he happened to catch him in his hut. Mike went as far as to finally thank him for all the food he had received of him lately. "It's happened to all of us."

Mike sighed. He knew that what Julius said was true, at least concerning the aspect of losing a friend. These people had all been abandoned by Roman rule and order—left to the cruel buffetings of whatever monster decided to come in. It was a colossal game of cat and mouse. They did not have the capacity to fight back, simply to run to the holes and wait for the preying cat to give up on them. It was a pitiable state only made worse by the fact that many of their loved ones had not fared as lucky as they had and had fallen victim to their swords.

Or had the deceased been the lucky ones? It was the universal question asked by all humankind in wretched circumstances. Mike recalled the words of Hamlet in Act III and seemed, for the first time, to fully understand them, despite what he had been taught in church. He still believed in the doctrine, that the next life was to be glorious as long as he lived correctly in this one, and he knew he was not alone in his belief, even here among these people, who had occasionally revealed overtones of Christianity in various conversations he had had with them. *So why do they still hold on to life so tightly? Why do they still fight each day to wake up and keep up with the tasks that sustain them? Can there be joy in such an existence?*

Such thoughts perpetuated through Mike's mind, and he found, as they did, that he had started including himself in the questions. *They* had changed to *we*. For the first time, Mike felt like a member of this people. He finally conceptualized an understanding of why they had hesitated to run at his warning all those weeks ago. He finally felt the despair at knowing that no matter what he did to jump out of the hole he was in, his reach would be too short to catch the edge and he'd come crumbling back down to the bottom, more bruised and scraped than before.

"You just have to keep going," Julius added.

Mike snapped out of his thoughts, intrigued at how Julius had answered them. His comment, however, only brought the conversation to another level. "How do you do that?" Mike asked him.

There, Julius simply sighed. "I'm still trying to figure that out."

Chapter 19

The world itself seemed to shiver from the cold, arctic winds that blew in from the North. The sun refused to show its face, just as it had done for what had seemed like an eternity. Instead, its warmth remained hidden before the ever-present clouds, leaving them to shed snowfall on the colder days and an icy rain that pierced to the bone on the warmer days.

It would have been early April, though the isle seemed to have no awareness of such a fact. Instead, it seemed ignorantly stalled in February. Or maybe it was aware, yet obstinately resisted so as to put off, for as long as possible, the time when the plows would pierce its surface. After all that it had done to the inhabitants of this cursed land, that certainly would not have shown a change in temperament. It had sent them through the gauntlet; it had pushed them farther to their limits than they ever seemed to remember.

The stars, of course, held true to their cycles, but such truth only served as greater mockery to those cognizant enough to be aware. The world was past equinox, ordering the climate to pull out of winter. The days were getting lighter and longer, informing the people that their notions of an excessively long winter were not entirely unfounded. The orders, however, were ignored, and the information, useless.

Mike walked again into his hut, just as he had all winter. He sighed, looked down at the work he had originally planned to get done, and then shrugged it off. He meandered over to his hay mattress and plopped down, letting his body haphazardly slump and give in to the crunching of the material below him. As he settled, all fell quiet, even his thoughts. Mike stared up at the ceiling but did not take the effort to do more than that, physically or mentally. That required too much work. Besides, there was nothing to think about. His day had been much the same as yesterday, much the same as the past five months.

The thatch needs renovation, he finally noted to himself. It was an original problem that should have been attended to in the first place, but had been a small detail compared to simply getting the thing up. The thatch would not last, though, and so was yet another project for when the weather again decided to begin showing mercy.

Mike fell back into stupor. Such was the only thought that made it through, though it hardly even counted for anything anymore. Mike had made such a mental note dozens of times by now, ever since *that night*. Ever since the fire.

Mike had been more careful since then, but taking care did not take away the past, or rather bring it back for that matter. That event alone had both created a haunting memory, and destroyed a hundred others.

Mike pushed that thought out of his head, just like he had ever since the event had occurred. For some reason, although he had experienced so many other things much worse than it, it had gotten to him. Maybe it was the journal. Maybe it was the hundred memories that were now lost, only to be drowned out by the more present ones. They were fading quickly now, and although Mike had reached for them, although he had tried, a third time, to reconstruct them, they were beyond his grasp and left a trail of only a feeling—a feeling which he would no longer experience firsthand—a feeling that, in turn, seemed to cause, more than anything, a slow but steady spiritual decay.

Mindlessly, Mike turned over and grabbed for his living journal. He did not know why he did this. He knew these pages front to back. Maybe it was some stalwart part of his very inner soul still trying to grasp for some sort of happiness. If there, it was not very evident, and certainly did not reveal itself to Mike as he thumbed through the pages, for as he did so, he knew what he would find. There was nothing that would satisfy such a part. Even so, there was nothing else to do, so he turned to the page that contained the first entry after Abe's burial and started reading.

I cannot express how much I wish to have Abe back, even after over a month without him. His loss has completed my sorrow in every aspect possible. Laying aside the aesthetic desire of having so close a friend, and for that matter an only friend, I wish I had him here in which to confide in my sorrow, though his presence would negate the necessity in the first place.

I have just returned from a journey to Bath, though without success in my pursuit. Two weeks ago, I approached Julius and told him I needed to leave for awhile. When he asked where I was going, I told him I needed to find Virgil to take care of some pending issues.

"Do you know where to find him?" he asked me.

"Only ideas," I responded, "But there is no other way to know for sure than to leave."

Julius gave me his best wishes of luck, as well as his apology for acting so indignantly toward me regarding Aeola. "I hope you don't think I hold any sort of malice toward you. You have been invaluable to my well-being, as well as Aeola's, and I really don't deserve to ask anything more out of you."

I told him that the issue was dropped and that we could both leave it behind us. I then embraced him and told him I'd be back in a few weeks.

So I set out, back the way I had come with as little as I needed to survive upon. I had fully expected to find Virgil and Arwulf back at their homesteads, having returned to their old life. But after searching both at Virgil's dwelling and at Arwulf's dwelling, they were nowhere to be found. Virgil's kin was accommodating and insisted that I stay with them and rest for a few days, which I did, but they had not heard word of Virgil either. He had never returned, not even for a day. I told them what had transpired while they were with me and they listened with great interest. Upon hearing that he and Arwulf had abandoned me, they were perplexed and could not account for the possible reasons why he would have left us and not returned home.

I did not stay with Virgil's kin any longer than was required, for I was not in any mood to attempt to be accommodating to any form of hospitality. I took my leave of the abode, stating that urgent matters called me. I do not consider it a falsehood, seeing that I felt like I could not meditate upon the current unfoldings unless I was by myself, and I needed that time urgently. My mind entertained a flurry of questions that needed to be worked out. I feel like I am still battling them, but they are at least all laid out before me in a logical fashion.

The nights on the road were damp and cold. I did not feel that it was safe to light a fire, for I knew, more than ever, the danger and proximity of Saxons who would not think twice about cutting a lone wanderer down for no reason at all. Even after encountering the Saxons face to face, I cannot shed the haunting threat they continue to constantly pose in the back of my mind. The world around me seems larger and more daunting than ever, and the fact that Abe and Virgil have abandoned me only makes it worse.

To this moment, I cannot understand Virgil and Arwulf's reasoning. Where would they run off to if not to come back home? They had had an extra week, surely I could not have passed them and beat them. Had they been marauded and killed? Such questions still pulse through my head, unresolved after a week back on the road. No signs or stories from other travelers signified any account of the two, leaving me with absolutely nowhere to turn.

So here I am back in Newhaven, only because there is nowhere else to call home. The feelings of loneliness pry me apart. And from this loneliness comes the monstrosity of frustration. Even as I think about it now, it kills me. How foolish Abe had been to continue following after them. Why had he not told me in the first place? Why had he not turned back to Newhaven when he first suspected they were leaving? If only Abe had taken into account the limitations of his age. If only I could have woken up and stopped them, reasoned with them, talked them out of leaving.

If only—a term that does me no good. Unfortunately, no matter how much I think about all the ways I could have prevented disaster, I cannot do anything to change the past. Time has tread on and dealt me a hand with which I am confined to play or fold. Even as I write, the tears are flowing. I think I am done for tonight.

***

Life continues on much as it has for the past week and a half since I have been back in Newhaven, and I find myself once again writing the feelings that have prevailed upon me. It seems monotonous to return to the subject, but what else am I supposed to write? This thick black blanket has covered me ever since Abe's death, and I cannot see anything else.

It has been another day absolutely devoid of any activity or human interaction. Aeola came by, wishing to visit, but did not stay long after failing on many fronts to get a conversation started. In many regards, I respect her for her attempt, since her situation is no better than mine and she is trying to make the best of it, but at the same time, she has always been in such a state, whereas it has seemed like I have fallen from what now seems to me like paradise.

I am sure that the mission is now at an end, and I have slowly come to terms with the fact that I will have to live out my life in this land. I will never again see the golden hills of Idaho, or feel the wind coming in through the open window of a moving car. I will never again see my family or lay placidly beside my stream in my hammock. All prospect of again tasting the future is in my past. The rolling green hills of Britain are my reality now, as well as everything that they hold within them. The primitive agriculture, the saturated winters, the constant fear of annihilation—they all come along with this new reality. I can no longer be who I thought I was. I have no choice but to grasp onto this new identity and etch out what I can from it.

It is still infinitely difficult to grasp onto that fact, since I find that the more I do so, the more I feel inclined to slip into the depths of depression and apathy. I did not realize how much I fed into the American idea of self-made destiny until it was stripped from my reach. For even as I had toiled, day after day on my parents' farm, I knew that if I had wanted, I could have immediately abandoned it to pursue another horizon. That knowledge alone made me free.

From this point forth, my fate is set in stone. I am now tied to the land just like the rest of the people here—tied by necessity to belong somewhere in a cold, dark, dangerous world. My place is Newhaven; I will live out my life and die here. People will bury me beside Abe, and, like everyone else here, I will become forgotten to history. Perhaps I won't even have the privilege of being buried. There are, indeed, monsters out there that would wish a different end for me. I know; I've seen them in action. They have torn apart thousands of lives and turned the rivers to blood. They are hungry. Perhaps they will consume me as well. It is not out of the picture.

* * *

It is hard for me to lay a finger on what motivation I have in getting up each morning, for it only resurrects the emptiness of the day before and promises the same thing for another day. Today seemed especially cold and I found it hard to depart from the close proximity of the hearth. The fire served as my sole friend today.

The fact that life is hard has not changed, rather prevailed. Once again, I know that this is more of the same words as were written in my last entry, yet I cannot write other than that which I feel. Since my feelings remain unchanged, my words remain consistent. It does not disturb me much, seeing that this journal is for my sole benefit, and even more so since I am writing in modern English. Nobody would be able to read it even if I allowed them.

Even if this was a simple account of my actions for the day, it could not account for much more, for it seems as if I am stuck in a long, boring movie, unable to enjoy the experience, but unable to quit it at the same time. I am held captive in this limbo, watching the gray sky grow lighter in sole anticipation of it again returning to black. My one exception to this is my daily trip down to the river to gather water for the day. In the spring I think I will build a well for the community, but in the mean time, I rather look forward to this hour break in the day as my only diversion.

I find myself often turning to dreams of the future, when I quit this land forever, just as Abe has done. While the concept of death still remains a thing foreign to me, it has taken dominance over the memories of the past, which I used to dream about, for the past seems more remote than the future now, especially if the Saxons discover Newhaven, an event of which I am sure will occur.

The state of heaven perplexes me. I often wonder what Abe is doing, or if he is doing anything at all. I have been taught all my life that Heaven is a place of bliss and joy, and is something worth striving for. Being in the present state that I am in, I cannot imagine even Hell being much worse. But if all we do up there in Heaven is lie around and play the harp, I do not want it. I cannot see the point in directing my life toward that goal, for that Heaven does not seem any better than the present Hell I feel myself caught in. I can just as easily string my bow and pluck it like a harp here, but I would find no joy in that whatsoever. I do not think that any type of stagnancy could be anything but an eternal punishment.

For that reason I do hope that Abe has forgotten me, that he has gotten caught up in some heavenly work, whatever nature that might be. I hope that it takes his mind off of where he is not. I hope that he has not changed, that his mind will settle itself just as passionately upon some new task. He doesn't deserve to have what I have here. At least, I hope he is getting something better, for I am looking to his present state as my ticket out of mine.

* * *

I do not quite know how I am finding the presence of mind to write today, but here I am even so.

The fact is, I should feel more distraught than I am. As it is I am quite unemotional right now. I have realized that it feels better to be numb, for any pain that comes my way does not affect me any more than any other feeling or lack thereof. It is all a blanket white. I suppose that such an event as has fated itself upon me tonight would be devastating to most people, especially people of the 21st Century, but to me, it means no more than depending on the hospitality of others.

Everything is gone. Everything including my furs, my tools, my spear, my bow, my arrows. Only the two emblems and the journal in which I now write have survived. And had I not fallen asleep with the journal on my stomach, I would be left only with the two things that do me no good whatsoever.

Tonight I watched as my hut went up in flames. People gathered around me to witness the blaze, and we all simply stood there in helpless disbelief. There was nothing else we could do. Water was inaccessible and insufficient, and the hut seemed to burn like a pile of matchsticks. I did not cry, I did not panic, I simply stood there without reaction, which, now that I think about it, scared me more than anything, for although my life had been in dire jeopardy, I did not look toward my providential escape with any more fancy than the disastrous alternative. It is a scary thing when one realizes he has fallen into the pit of apathy towards life itself, yet as I write, I am looking up and there seems no distinct way out of it.

I have no idea how the conflagration began, but judging from the especially cold night, I imagine that I carelessly made the fire on the hearth a little too hot and a little too large. The closest thing to the hearth was my fur cloak, and that must have caught flame. I cannot say for sure because I had fallen into a deep winter sleep and did not wake until smoke had filled the room. I woke up after having dreamt a dream in which I felt like I was breathing in water. With every breath my body violently rejected what it took in with incessant coughs. I woke up in disturbance finding myself doing the same thing, only instead of water, it was a thick gray smoke.

Instantly aroused, I grabbed the journal that was lying on top of me and looked around for anything else I could salvage on my way out. My mind immediately turned to the emblems, which I had left on the back ledge of the hearth. In horror, I found them all too easily. To say they were shining, or even glowing, does not approach accuracy. The luster of their eminence was haunting, and cut through the smoke as if it presented no visual impediment whatsoever. I reached out for the golden emblem and grabbed it, almost expecting it to liquidate my hand, but it was surprisingly cool. However, as I reached out for Abe's emblem, I received some sort of shock or burn; something that sent me reeling backwards. In fear, I stumbled out of the blazing hut, retreating from the powers being cast within.

It was then that I remembered my other journal, the wool reconstruction of my memories of the Realm. By then, however, it was far too late. The thatch, completely engulfed in flames, sagged and moved to cave in on the place. All I could do was stare back at the destruction that unfolded before me. I could not move; I could barely even breathe, for I stared not only at the destruction of everything I owned, but at the destruction of every surviving word, image, and sense from my experience in the Realm. Despite the situation, I had to fight the urge to rush back into the collapsing hut, and I now shudder to think how close I'd come to giving in to it.

As the embers subsided, all juvenile hopes that somehow it had survived dissipated. I stared at the black charred mass in the early, pre-dawn stages of the night, shivering despite my inattention to outside matters. The emblem of knowledge alone remained in the wreckage, and mirrored the digression of the flames in its waning luminescence. I dared not touch it, even as the flames died out, but left it there to shine in the darkness. I waited until morning to retrieve it.

Julius stood by me the entire time, and invited me into his hut for the night. I did not fall asleep for a long time, though, passing my restlessness in turning the golden emblem over and over in my hands, feeling its distinct coolness, and reflecting, though not with much depth on the nature of the other emblem. Only now, as I sit in Julius' hut, staring at the emblem of knowledge, do I begin to wonder why it shocked me. It seems to be glaring at me, like a dog to a strange master, even after the fire has waned and its power returned to normal.

That is the least of my concerns right now, though, for I've lost something more important to me than the good graces of the emblem of knowledge. Even as I am concluding this entry, the tears are beginning to flow. Like a freight train, the weight of this tragedy is beginning to strike me. It is leaving me stunned, and I do not have the presence of mind to voice the myriad of emotions churning within me. I think it is best to end this.

* * *

The weather was warmer and drier today, (for it seems as if it has been raining or snowing all winter), but just enough to allow me to pull myself away from my newly built hearth and get out. The *opportunity was welcome, for it seems as if there is a sort of staleness in the air surrounding the community of huts, if such a thing can be possible out of doors and atop a hill where the wind blows constantly. The fever has been running rampant through Newhaven for the past two weeks, and it has already taken the lives of an elderly man and three small children. Since I do not take the time for much interaction, I have steered clear of the disease, and have only been involved in its effects when I have helped dig the shallow graves in the cold, soggy earth.*

The second reason for my desire to get out is that I had only used my new bow three or four times since I made it, and I was eager to test its full abilities. Up to this point, I had not shot anything with it and could not give it a full judgment on its quality until such a thing occurred. So at dawn, I exited my hut alone and inhaled the chill of the early morning air. Smoke arose from each of the respective huts and I issued forth a quick shiver, thinking of the burning fevers residing within them. I promptly turned away and ventured forth to put as much distance between me and them as possible.

The forests and fields were silent as I walked along the edges of the two, looking for tracks. The discovery of such would be welcome, but as more of a diversion than a necessity. In reality, we have enough food to last us until spring, as well as sufficient furs, for the game has been plentiful near the hill. Even without the tracks though, I felt fulfilled in my venture. It was the solitude and change of scenery that I most coveted.

My journey took me in an easterly direction with no interruption, and it was hard to tell how far I had come, but I know that I was in the middle of nowhere. The thought refreshed me, and I took a moment to sit down and relish in the moment. I cannot express how good it felt to be out of Newhaven, just for this short period of time, for although it is a place of refuge, it is almost too much of a prison to hold me in by choice. The sight of my hut and the smell of the hearth smoke and the sound of people coughing and children crying have fed my dark memories and kept them healthy enough to dominate my dreams as well.

Being out in the countryside today was different. I never found any tracks. Not much of anything happened either, so I cannot exactly describe why the experience affected me so much. Yet it refreshed me in a way that is giving me peace, even now, when I am back in my cell. I think that it was because the wilderness was new, fresh, and untainted. Out there, I could bear to live in the present, for the present somehow consisted of infinitely more out there than it does back here in Newhaven.

* * *

Today, for the first time in a great while, I had an experience that differed from the gray existence in which I have lived this past winter. It was an experience that teases my otherwise stationary mind with thoughts and possible actions to be taken. I do not know if anything will come of it, or even if it is plausible, but it is something to think about, which is more than I've seen in a long time.

I took the opportunity to go hunting again today, and the weather was much more tolerable than it has been, since the sun was actually out and the temperature was well above freezing. It was amazing that I had become so accustomed to such frigidity that what would otherwise be considered brisk was a welcome turn. I welcomed it today with eagerness.

Again, I decided to walk off toward the east, following the dull footprints in the mud I had created about a week ago, the last time I ventured forth. This has become my trail, the place I go when the melancholy of Newhaven becomes too great for me. I don't know from what it sourced today, for the fevers have since subsided after taking seven lives in total, but the overflow was there all the same, and so I shied away from it. I drew near to this path again for some reason, which seems ironic now, for while I came out here to escape the monotony, I found myself taking a path I have well trod.

In any sense, it worked to at least simmer down my depression and replace it with a subtle tranquility.

I continued on in the path I was taking, and, at length, I saw a line of disturbance in the grass before me. I approached, at first believing it to be caused by some sort of large game. But when I got a closer look at the tracks and realized what they were, my breath caught.

They were the tracks of another person. I took a moment and stared at them in mild disbelief. Aside from the inhabitants of Newhaven, I had not been aware that this land held any tenants. I had not seen anyone since Newhaven was established and had simply figured that the land was otherwise abandoned. The tracks led up north and so I debated a moment on which way I might go to follow them. They were fresh, for the grass on which they were imprinted was still rebounding. They were also distinct, with little drag in between, and so I figured that the person had not been walking long. I turned myself southwards alongside the tracks to see what I could find.

I had not traveled more than a mile when I caught a scent of burning wood in the air. I quickened my pace and soon cleared a line of trees to find a hut exhaling smoke. Behind, I could see a flock of sheep huddled together with their backs toward the clearing. I cautiously approached and held my bow and arrow ready, even though I did not believe the inhabitant to be home, or if so to be hostile.

I made it almost to the door of the hut before a young man quickly stepped out with his spear ready to strike forth. In surprise, I held my arrow in its notched position and brought it up, but only to bring it down again and stare at the man face to face. He was a short, darker man, but not in the manner of the Romans. He looked Celtic, though his menacing grimace matched that of a Saxon.

"Who are you?" the man asked in Celtic, keeping his eyes glued on me.

"Do you speak Latin?" I asked, eyeing him back with the same intensity.

"Yes, I do," the man stated, lowering his weapon. "What's your name?"

"Mike."

The man motioned for me to come inside from the cold. "My name is Marcus." I looked into the dark but warm abode to see an old man sitting inside, and I nodded a greeting to him. He did not respond but continued to sit, staring at me. "I am a sheep herder with my father here," he explained, "but bartering has been difficult lately, and we have struggled. I'm sorry that we have no food to offer you."

I told them that that was perfectly fine, that the warmth of the hut *for a few minutes would be enough and I'd be on my way again. We talked a little. He noted my foreign nature and asked me if I was Saxon, to which I denied. I kept my answers to his further inquiries regarding my origin ambiguous. He then asked me where I was living at present and how I had come to find his place.*

"I live out west of here," I stated, "with a group that used to call themselves The Haven."

At that, his eyes lit up. "You live with these people? Are Julius and Magnus still alive? I saw the smoke coming from that direction, and when I went to see what had happened, all was gone."

"Julius is still alive," I stated, "but Magnus is dead. He did not survive the attack."

Upon hearing that, the man called Marcus sighed, but did nothing more. "Well, it's good to hear that Julius is alive. He and I have had various associations in the past few years. I have traded wool for grain on occasion with him. Magnus was a good friend too, though. It's a shame they have not been as lucky with the Saxons as I have."

It was then that a thought occurred to me. My eyes perked up at it, and I strung more words together than I have in a long time. "Why don't you come to Newhaven," I suggested. "You will have people to barter with and more seclusion and protection. There is room enough for you and your father."

Marcus thought about it a moment and would not give me a clear answer. He told me that he had avoided their wrath so far and felt confident that he would continue to be able to. I conceded, but gave him my word that I would come back in a few days in case he decided to do so. As I walked back, and as I write, I cannot help but think that there are others out there in the same predicament as us all, and that it would be infinitely better to have everyone gathered in one place. If Julius knew Marcus, surely he must know others. Maybe if Marcus decides to come, I will talk to Julius about inviting others.

This last entry, the one in which he had found Marcus, was written five weeks ago. Marcus and his father never came. Mike had not been able to return for two weeks, for the weather drooped again and soaked the countryside with pounding sleet, but when he did, Marcus had turned him down, stating that they did not wish to move. After further expressing the idea to Julius, Julius had shrugged it off as a trite idea, stating it was too cold to do anything anyway.

This one bit of hope for purpose in life having been crushed, Mike had sunk into more bouts of depression. Not even his trips into the wilderness helped him anymore, for he had frequented them so much that they, like everything else, had become immersed in the reek of monotony.

Mike sighed, sat up, pushed the journal aside, and reached for a bit of bread he had left over from the night before. He ate, staring off into nothing in particular in the hut, then proceeded to dress and walk outside to relieve himself. As he walked round the hut, he could not help but notice Abe's gravestone and the dozens of tiny chinks in it. There was nothing different in it today than there had been every other day that he had walked out, but today it struck him in a particular sort of way, maybe due to the journal entries he had read last night.

Mike thought back on the entry of the fire and how things had changed that night. He looked at the tick marks, each representing a day spent in Newhaven. The rock was now grossly inaccurate, for the day his hut had burned down had been the day the tick marks had ceased to grow.

Outside, the wind continued to chill the world as, Mike felt, it would continue to do forever.

Chapter 20

Mike awoke with a start. The act spilled forth a strange sensation in him, for the present urge to get up seemed to wake him from a four month dream. He sat still and put his emotions on trial, but they seemed to plead innocent. Mike sat up upon his bed and shed his blanket, feeling the cool air of the hut touch his skin. He took a moment to appreciate the feeling, for he had not felt such a feeling since the Realm. Instantly, Mike searched his thoughts for a cause of all this. His mind reviewed the actions of last night. Nothing out of the ordinary had occurred. He had simply sat in his hut, staring at the hearth fire until he was too tired to keep his eyes open.

As his senses reawakened, Mike noticed a slight hum in the air that periodically rose and fell in volume. Mike strained his eyes in the morning light seeping through the cracks in his hut to find the source. It only took a moment to notice a solitary insect, a honeybee, exploring the limits of the building. Mike furrowed his eyebrows and watched it in peaceful silence. He had no desire to get rid of it. *I have not seen bees since before we arrived here in Newhaven,* he noted to himself. The bee hovered near Mike's head, investigating it, creating a slight breeze upon his forehead as it approached. Still, Mike made no effort to get rid of it. Instead, he simply smiled—an act which he had not performed in a long time.

Mike pulled himself up and proceeded to dress himself. He could tell that the sun was shining brightly outside, even with his hut entirely shut up. *That's a welcome break,* he thought, *especially since it does not seem to be freezing out there.* Up to this point, the weather had been turbulent. The cold days had been overcast, and the warm days had been rainy. *Today is different,* he mused, and he smiled again.

He finished dressing and opened up the door to his hut, only to be met with a full-fledged invasion of spring. He had been right. The temperature exuded its mildness as the sun rose slowly in the east, drying up the grass which remained a bit spongy beneath his feet. Above, the sky glistened in a tame blue and was graced with a few wispy clouds. All signs of the rain had departed sometime in the night.

After turning the corner, away from the center of the huts, his eyes met a sight that stole his breath away. Mike stared in silence with his mouth ajar, and the disbelief that initially overcame him slowly transformed into a sort of mild-mannered ecstasy. There before him, intermingled with grass of the most beautiful green, shone tens of thousands of daffodils, opening themselves up to the new season, soaking in the yellow sun, and reflecting it back in their petals. The entire hillside down to the line of trees below, which Mike was sure had been silent of such an orchestra just a few days ago, filled itself with the little tokens of joy, altering its color with a gloss of white and gold.

Such an orchestra called to him, beckoning him forward to experience it from within its midst, and he could not help but heed its call. Mike walked forward, entered, and proceeded to envelop himself in them. As he moved along through it, he reached down and felt their velveteen heads bounce off his hands. They gave way for him then moved back into position behind him, unoffended at the minor disturbance.

A tremendous welling started inside of Mike, disengaging him and forcing him to sit down, then to lie down and bathe himself in their serenity. Mike looked up into the sky and found himself on the verge of tears. It had been so long. He had not felt so alive in what seemed like a lifetime. He had just made it through the worst season of his life, a cold darkened Hell which had seemed to have no outlet. *Things are going to get better from now on,* he told himself. *They have to.* He knew it. With the clear skies came a clear perception of what he held in his hands. His life had broken down to dust, and now he was faced with the opportunity of constructing what he could out of it.

Mike turned his head and watched a colony of ants busily working in their hill. Suddenly, he felt for them. He knew that, time and again in the following year, that hill would be destroyed by outside forces. He also knew that, time and again, they would rebuild it. They would continue rebuilding it until their lives were wasted out.

Suddenly, the events of the past week looked down on him, events that had, up to this point, meant next to nothing to him. He had shut such events, as well as the conversations that attached themselves to such events, out of his head. Suddenly, though, things were seeming to change. He found himself allowing them back in for further consideration. Mike reviewed, once again, all that had happened.

About a week ago, Mike had been in his hut, passing the evening as he often did, writing a few words in his journal and daydreaming about anything but the existence he presently held. He had been lying upon his bed in a sort of stupor when a crashing din resounded outside. Mike perked up his ears to hear angry yells being passed back and forth between two young men.

At that moment, Julius had entered Mike's hut. "Mike," he sounded with anxiety, "Cassius and Arthur are fighting each other. Cassius has sworn to draw Arthur's blood."

Mike remembered jolting up and grabbing his weapon to follow Julius outside, not knowing what he was to do, but knowing also that he was the biggest, strongest man in the community, and the one most able to make any sort of resolution.

He had run out to the center of the huts, where a small group gathered with nervous faces around the two men, who had their spears drawn and were lashing out with savage jabs. As Mike approached, he could see fire in their eyes. Anger soared in both of them as they parried each other's blows and reeled back with some of their own. Even as Mike approached, he heard them swearing out curses and oaths against the other that made Mike's stomach curdle with distress. Mike wanted to avoid it, just as he had avoided other scuffles in the past winter, just as he had avoided just about everything in the past few months, but this had been too intense. Both had been intent on impaling the other, and Mike had known that if he did not intervene, one of them would succeed.

So he had rushed forward, booming out an order to stop. The two, if they caught note of it, paid it no heed, for they had continued to fight. Mike had entered the ring of fire, drawn his spear above his head, and brought it down on the two weapons, just as they made contact with each other. Arthur's spear had been ripped from his grasp, and Cassius' had been brought low enough for Mike to bring down his foot and snap the shaft of it. Mike recalled kicking the two points away and staring at both of the men in the eyes.

Both had been too shocked to be angry at Mike. Arthur had looked to be in fear. The crowd looked on in silence, curious to see what was to unfold. "What's this all about?" Mike had asked.

The two had simply stood there in silence for a moment, struggling to catch their breaths and cool their adrenaline. Cassius had been the first one to speak up, and when he had, he pointed an accusing finger at Arthur. "That man," he seethed, "is a thief. I found him in my hut, stealing the rabbit I hunted down."

Mike had glanced over at Arthur, and Arthur had not denied it. Rather, he had hung his head down. "I needed the meat for my daughter. She's sick and needed the broth. I wouldn't have done it for any other reason."

Mike had decided it was best to take them both aside separately and talk to them. After ordering the gathered crowd to disperse, he had told Cassius to let the rabbit go. Cassius, feeling that his side had been just, had donned a victimized look.

"Have some compassion," Mike had told him, "the man's daughter was dying."

"He didn't even ask, though. How am I supposed to know he wasn't going to take anything else?"

Arthur did not deny the accusation when Mike had talked to him. "Why didn't you ask?" he had inquired of the sullen-eyed man. Arthur had not had an answer to that one, and Mike had thrown up his arms at the entire situation. He had walked away from the two after having made them promise that the situation was over, and luckily, the two had possessed enough respect for him to agree, but he felt like little else had been solved. In all, the whole situation had been a mess, and Mike's energy had been depleted by the time he was able to return to his hut.

Mike then recalled the conversation he had had with Julius the next day. "You were the only one that could have pulled that off," Julius had told him.

"I doubt that," he had replied, "I was just the only one with enough initiative to do something about it."

Julius had disagreed with him adamantly though. Mike remembered staring him directly in the eyes and seeing a burning sincerity in them. Although Mike had not agreed with Julius on the matter, he had not contained enough energy to challenge him on it either. Instead, Mike had waited for Julius to continue, because he had been able to tell that something else, something deeper had been on Julius' mind. Then it had come, stepping right in rhythm to how Mike had predicted.

"I think you know that planting time is right around the corner, Mike."

"Yeah, what about it?"

"People will be looking to you for direction."

Mike recalled his feelings at those words. The feelings had not been positive. "Why do they need anybody to direct them? They have been farming their entire lives."

He recalled watching Julius roll his eyes. "Don't be a fool, Mike. You know as well as I do that that never works. Have you forgotten what happened just six months ago? All of us would have been destroyed, right alongside our huts if it hadn't been for you. One of those men out there would have been dead if it hadn't been for you. You've led us out across the countryside. You've helped us build a new community. You've hunted for us. Without you, this community would be nothing."

He had known where Julius had been leading the conversation, and he shied away from it. He wanted to hide from it, hide from Julius, but, at the moment, Julius had commanded his attention, had held a power over him with his boldness just like his daughter had. Still, like an obstinate child, Mike had wanted to fight it. He flailed anything he could at his aggressor. "What about you, Julius? Why didn't you step up at all of those moments? It was you that should have been taking the lead role in the first place."

Julius had not had a direct response to that. It was his moment to turn away. Suddenly, the boldness had disappeared. "Again," he quivered, "I think you know as well as I do that that would never work." He had turned back to Mike. "Please, Mike. Step up. If you don't do it, nobody will. We can't afford that any longer."

Mike remembered looking at Julius' pleading eyes. They had been eyes of desperation powerful enough to melt the solid shell that Mike had built about himself. Mike had felt it disintegrating; he had felt his resolve breaking down, yet still, he had somehow stood firm.

"What if I don't want it?"

Julius had given Mike a look that had tied a knot in his stomach. Without saying anything more, he had retreated from Mike's hut, leaving him again to his dark and unsettled silence.

His journal had been left silent of such occurrences. Thinking back on it now, in the midst of the fields, Mike realized why. The truth of Julius' words had cut deeply into his soul—he had known, from the very beginning, that the time would have to come where he would have to take on the role. He had wanted to run from the necessity, he had wanted to pretend it was not even there.

His reasons for refusal remained ambiguous, but Mike had his guesses. Perhaps his hesitance stemmed from his first failure at leadership. The mission was still the prominent ghost in his life. Mike figured, by the way things were headed, that it always would be. He had held a chance to do something great—the responsibility to bring it forth had been placed in his hands. It had been his offspring to raise, and he had crushed it. The failure had not been due to his lack of care—he had invested his entire soul into it—but due to his own innate weakness. The results had been devastating. They had caused the death of a great man and the ruin of his own young life.

Or perhaps the hesitance stemmed from his desire to remain in somber solitude. He knew that this was not a healthy excuse; he was aware that the pit in which he was presently caught held him back from the sun. For some reason however, he had refused the assistance from the ladder that had been handed down to him a few days ago. He was held captive, no longer by his physical circumstances, but by his own defeated mind.

Things seemed worlds different today, though. Somehow, grace had lifted him out of the pit anyway, regardless of his lack of effort. The sun shone on his face in full luster—it had seemed like forever since he felt its warmth to such a degree. Mike shed his winter cloak from off of his shoulders as he lay in the daffodils so all that separated his body from the light was a loincloth. The cloak slipped off readily and easily, and became no more than a ground cloth for him.

Julius' consideration now emanated a different light in Mike's head. He still did not want it; he was still scared to death of it, but he knew, all the same, that it needed to be done. And now, the task seemed a little bit more plausible, though by what power, he had no idea.

Mike knew what he needed to do. He pulled himself up and walked back to his hut to pull out some more weather appropriate clothes to put on. He only took as much time as he needed, though, before directing himself straight over to Julius' place.

He found Julius taking advantage of the warm weather as well, performing a few repairs on his hut. Throughout the course of the winter, cracks had formed in his walls, cracks which had made the hut deftly inefficient in heat retention. Julius patched the holes with a mortar of clay and grass so that when the summer heat came, he would not face the same discomfort.

"Ah, Mike," he started as he caught sight of Mike approaching. From the way Julius hailed him, he seemed to be in a quite good mood as well. "Have you come to help me on my repairs?"

Mike chuckled at the hopeful look on Julius' face. "After I speak with you."

Julius put down his tools and wiped his hands. "You want to speak now, then."

"Yeah, while the ideas are fresh in my mind. Let's go for a walk. We won't be long."

Julius hopped down from the log stump he had been using as a step stool and joined Mike at his side. The two then began down the hillside, through the sea of flowers. It held Julius' attention captive, and he moved his hands across their heads just as Mike had done. Mike decided to give him the moment before he started in. Julius took it, but only briefly before finally turning to Mike and saying, "What's on your mind, Mike?"

Mike folded his arms as he searched for the correct niche in which to place his wedge. "I have been thinking this whole morning about the conversation we had a few days ago."

"Oh yeah?"

Mike nodded. "I feel like I was not in the right state of mind to make such hasty comments." Mike pursed his lips. "I think you were right, though, Julius." Out of the corner of his eye, Mike caught a smile forming on Julius' face. "I hope you are aware, however, of what it will take for you."

Julius' attention was perked. Mike answered the question he knew was going through his head. "You have to promise me your full allegiance. I cannot do this without your support, as well as everyone else's."

"You've got it," he answered without hesitation. "What do you have in mind?"

"If we work as a community, then we will not only have a more plentiful harvest, but life in general will be more tolerable. But we need to unify in order for that to happen."

Julius nodded his approval.

"And we need more people. We need to gather up all the people within the area and bring them to Newhaven. We need artisans, blacksmiths, shepherds, millers, weavers. We cannot keep living without outside contact, but the greater variety of people we have within our community, within our trust, the less we'll have to depend on people we don't know. Also, the more members we have, the higher our chance of survival. Our community cannot survive solely with the people we have, regardless of whether the Saxons find us again or not."

Julius stared at Mike, but Mike did not mind. The feeling he got as he spoke was exhilarating. He had opened his mouth and the words had come. He had not felt such feelings in a long time.

"That's going to take some work," Julius stated. "That's going to take time out of plowing and sowing."

Mike, feeling surer of himself the more he thought about it, replied in confidence. "That's the thing, though. The more people we have, Julius, the more will be produced. If we do not initially take time out to make our lives better, we will never have the time to do anything."

Julius mulled the ideas over in his head. Mike looked on in silent curiosity of how he was getting through to him.

"You pledged to me your support, Julius. Now I need your help in carrying it through. I need you to trust me. I need you to go out and gather everybody you know in the area. Without them, without you, I cannot do what I know needs to be done for this community."

The two stopped walking. Julius sized up Mike and how his countenance backed up his words. Mike did not waver in his presence. Rather, he waited, unchanged in his resolve and waiting for Julius to come up with his. All of these ideas had materialized out of what seemed like nowhere, but Mike was willing to stand by them with strength. He prepared himself to further fight for them, but he did not end up having to.

Julius looked at Mike squarely and assured him of his support. Mike patted him on the back and embraced him.

"When would you like me to go out?" Julius asked him as they walked back up to the huts.

"Right away," Mike answered.

Julius nodded.

"Take Cassius and Arthur with you as well."

To that, Julius did not agree so readily. Instead, he stopped and questioned Mike's sincerity with a furrowed brow.

"I'm serious. Those two need some time together. Their lack of interaction will only split this community apart."

Mike had other reasons too. He wanted to test Julius' loyalty to him, and putting him over two men who, a few days ago, had wanted to kill each other was the best test he could think of. He studied Julius carefully as Julius hesitated, waiting and wondering whether he would try and question it more. He could tell that Julius' lukewarm apathy fought against his word of honor, for Julius knew that he had pledged a whole lot more than he had, up to this point, been willing to put forth. He realized, at this moment, that Mike would be asking him to sacrifice more than he had ever anticipated. Mike waited patiently, unwilling to back down to Julius' hesitance.

After a moment, though, Julius conceded. Mike thanked him for it and continued explaining what he had in mind. "I want everyone eating together," he stated. "There will be no more ownership of food, regardless of who hunts it down. We'll all work six days a week, and rest on the seventh as a community." Mike took a breath. "And every man will learn to fight. We cannot simply continue hiding."

Julius seemed to agree with everything. For the next few days, the two continued speaking of plans. Mike was at first a little worried on Julius' level of commitment, but the more they talked, the more he realized that Julius was only glad someone else was taking the lead role. It was a boon that he had not felt he could possess, regardless of how necessary he knew it to be. Mike winked at the weakness and took on the boon as his own. It seemed that even with the mission shot, he was destined to walk before everybody, leading them while in the throes of a loneliness that only came to those in similar shoes.

The plan was set to gather everyone together for a feast, the night before they were to start breaking ground in the fields. Mike approached Julius and asked him to present the situation before everyone and to call for their support. "You would rather not do it yourself?" he asked him.

"No, I wouldn't," Mike stated.

Again, just as he had with everything else, Julius accepted the assignment. "You want me to set out after that then."

"Yeah, the next day."

"Okay. I'll do that."

Mike watched Julius. He ushered a slight smile of approval, which Julius received with gravity. "Do you think that it will work?" Mike asked finally.

Julius ushered a reassuring smile of his own. "I have no doubt. These people need you, and if they have not realized that yet, I'm sure they will soon. We wouldn't have survived this winter without you, Mike."

Mike tried to accept it. He could not fully do so, however, until he saw it. And he did see it: the inhabitants of Newhaven gathered, they ate, they listened to Julius' words, and they gave their pledge of allegiance. Mike sat at his spot on the table, looking out on all the standing faces in amazement.

Somehow, as Julius departed and the town struck out into the wild fields to tame them, the feeling that had welled up in Mike that day of daffodils lingered with him, even when the weather backpedalled. *Things are going to get better. The sun will come back again. In the mean time, I have its memory stored in my soul, as well as in all the souls around me.* Mike watched all of them as their muscles reacquainted themselves with their agrarian tools. He knew, at that moment, despite every monster that lay lurking in the corners of the land, that he could still make something of the dust in his hands.

Chapter 21

The sunshine beamed down through the partitioned sky as the clouds moved across the landscape. Mike could not help but elicit a slight smile as he leant upon his dirty hoe and looked up at the aerial panorama, for it looked as if more rain would be coming soon. The spring had been gracious to them; it had given its fair balance of blue skies and rainy skies, which was only helping Newhaven out in their industry. But Mike's smile also stemmed from the mild air. Spring had come to stay, and Mike sucked it into his lungs with relish.

He turned down from the sky and directed his eyes back at the dark brown earth where he resumed work. He felt his muscles tense and relax, flex and stretch as his hoe broke the surface. Since he was breaking into fresh field, the work was strenuous, much more so than he ever experienced. *Who knows whether any man has ever delved into this earth before?* The thought coursed through his mind. It was virgin land, and Mike had a sort of transcendental feeling in dealing with it. For all he knew, it had never felt contact with the mortal or its woes, shortcomings, or stains. Aside from the wild game that still was very evident at various times, its only other contact with intelligence must have been the Maker Himself. Mike felt drawn to the place and its corresponding task. He embraced the hard work and sweat that it required, for it seemed a small price to pay in exchange for acquaintance with such a hallowed thing.

Mike had specifically confined himself to the groundbreaking, along with two of other strongest men of the community, because the work was so tedious. Other areas that had already been cleared and tilled were already starting to receive seeds, but Mike left such tasks to the women and children. He had ascended the hill each afternoon near to *rigor mortis*, especially during the first six days of performing the task, and he had spent almost his entire first Sabbath in his hut simply surviving, but in the weeks following, his body had adjusted, either to the requirement of the task, or to the toleration of pain.

"I also know... that we must cultivate our garden... it is the only way to make life bearable." The words of Voltaire reprised in Mike's head, as they had for the past three weeks of similar labor. That Candidian phrase, read so long ago but never fully appreciated until now, had made itself fully manifest at the beginning of the tilling. For although he had come home with muscles begging for mercy, he had felt completely free of the severe depression he now could admit to having had during the winter. The stagnancy had been torturous; all of his energy had been directed to thoughts of where he was not, with whom he was not, and what he was not doing. The seconds had passed away as hours and the days as lifetimes. He had fallen into a rhythm of inertness and had survived it at the time, but all he could look back on when those days came to mind was darkness. Mike shuddered again as the still very fresh memories panned across his mind.

In contrast, the days now seemed to be soaring past, for he had not possessed any excess energy to put his mind to the darkness that still loomed. He knew of its presence; it was palpable enough to never completely depart, but it was weak and sickly. Any remainder of such thoughts only existed in shallow feelings.

"Life *is* bearable," Mike reminded himself as the metal end of his hoe struck a fairly large-sized rock with a ding. Mike reached down and moved the dirt away to reveal its face. With the hoe, as well as his hands, he proceeded in uncovering it, and it proved to be much larger than he originally thought it was. He struggled to pull it out before tossing it off to the side with its brothers.

"But am I happy?" Mike's hands released the rock and welcomed the absence of its weight. The question, of course, was not new—he had asked himself that question his entire life. It held, however, a different shade from a very different viewpoint. From the perspective of his previous life and his life in the Realm, the answer would have been easy. The present perspective was different, however, in this reincarnated life, as was the standard of happiness, and so the question was sustained in theoretics. Mike looked around him; he looked up to the hillside where multicolored wildflowers were starting to replace the daffodils; he looked out on all the people who worked together to provide the community with food. It was no Hollywood glamour story; it was no Elfish Realm. It was not even the simple life he had possessed back in Idaho. But Mike, for some reason, did not even consider those places as his own anymore. The winter had done well to sever that connection in his mind. Mike was no longer an American, nor was he an adventurer, but a fifth century peasant, completely submerged in a sea of survival like everyone else. Mike considered the standard such a life held. *I have enough to keep me going*, he concluded, and that satisfied him.

Mike took a gulp from his water skin and continued on hoeing for a little bit longer before quitting for the day. Across the field, others were starting to head in, for the sun was high in the air, and shining boldly on the land below. It was not hot—it was actually quite pleasant now—but his muscles were quitting on him. Mike placed his hoe over his shoulder, his skin over the other, and proceeded to walk across the field and up to the huts.

The afternoon progressed, and with it, the clouds. The rain began to fall in an even rhythm and continued on through the evening. The evening meal was cooked, brought together, distributed, and everybody retired again to their respective huts; the rain had put the communal meal out of the question. Mike knew, as he chomped away at his food in solitude that he and the men would not be able to spar tonight. Although he usually enjoyed the activity, he was glad for the extra time. It freed him to sit down and pick up his journal for the first time since planting had begun.

Dipping his quill in his ink, Mike started in.

As of late, I have not been very good about writing in this journal, but I attribute that as a good thing, for life has been so filled with tasks lately that I have scarce had the energy at the end of the day to make the effort. My mattress has become, more than ever, a welcome friend this past month, for it seems as if it is the only place where I can take a breath. As soon as that occurs, however, I seem to fall asleep. Again, I am fine with that, for it only results from the general smell of industry in the air. How pleasant it has been.

Mike looked up from his writing at a disturbance on the doorway of his hut. He felt hints of agitation, for it was an interruption to his thought process, but upon seeing that it was Julius, his countenance brightened.

Mike put down his quill and looked up at his peer. "Julius—good to see you back. How was your journey?"

It had seemed like forever since Mike had sent out Julius, Cassius, and Arthur to enlist people to join the community. Mike had given strict instructions to them, commanding them to keep the location secret until the people understood and made the same oath of allegiance. He had told Julius, "The secrecy and seclusion of our positioning was our original intent in coming here. We cannot let that disappear simply because we are becoming more inclusive." Julius had agreed to do so and had since been gone for three weeks.

He now stood before Mike wearied and wet.

"It was long," Julius stated, though his tone and countenance had already said it. With his words, he plopped down onto Mike's bedding.

"I assume the rain's still coming down steadily?"

"No, it's clearing up. There are patches of blue sky off to the south which I think should be coming our way."

Mike sat back down beside him. "Did you come here to give me a report?"

Julius shrugged. "If you want one, but I came here to tell you that there are newcomers outside in the common area waiting for direction on where you want them."

Mike elicited a slight smile. "I'm glad. I'll catch up with you later. Why don't you go back to your hut and rest up? I want to meet these people."

Julius nodded and pulled himself up. Mike followed him outside to where he found the party of soaked vagabonds. They stood there in a group, suspended and silent like refugees, and looked much like Mike had felt just a few months ago. It was a sorry sight to see them, drooping with their clothes. Luckily, the rain had ceased, but the air was still quite saturated, and there was no hope for their clothes drying. Judging from the fatigued look in their eyes, Mike would keep the welcome brief. He approached them.

"My name is Mike," he stated. The people looked back at him with unchanged faces. "Please," Mike continued, "Introduce yourselves; tell a little bit about what you do and why you are here. I assume that Julius has already explained a little about us. We'll start over here."

Mike had pointed to a young man on the end. He seemed to be alone. "My name is Lucius," he began with surety in his voice. Mike was taken a bit off guard, for his tone did not match his appearance. "I was a musician for Sergius, a Patrician whose villa used to be northeast of here. I have been farming for the past two years, ever since his villa was sacked and he and his family were killed. When Julius came along to our group of huts," Lucius motioned to a few others in the group, "We answered without hesitation."

Mike nodded toward him and motioned for the next group, who ended up being a family of pottery makers, to continue on. Mike then went on through the group until everyone had introduced himself and his kin. There were about thirty people in all with a wide array of trades. Mike felt overjoyed as they mentioned all of them. There was everything from weavers to blacksmiths to shepherds to more farmers. All were humble, all were scared, and all were ready for anything that might prove a better resistance to the pending threats around them, for all had dismal stories to tell. Mike felt caught between sympathy and nervousness. All had seen their wintery hells; all had heeded the possibility for a better life, and they sought it out in him. At the same time, however, he was glad for their addition. They would most definitely be worth it.

Mike spoke to them for a bit, giving them a superficial background on himself. By now, he had mastered the history that he had created for himself and gave it like it had been true. He spoke of his displacement from his farm, as well as his wanderings. He related the background of The Haven. He reawakened their experiences in leaving The Haven and establishing Newhaven. He then spoke of the winter they struggled through and their plans for the future. Mike reviewed the way the community worked and asked for a second confirmation on their loyalty. Nobody disagreed with anything, and Mike was pleased to accept their oaths.

"We'll put you all up in various huts tonight, but tomorrow, we'll help you start building your own."

Mike solicited the hospitality of several families to lodge the newcomers before heading over to Julius' hut, where Julius had said Mike could find him when he was ready. Julius sat on the hearth, eating a bowl of soup that Aeola had kept from the evening meal. He welcomed Mike in.

"You're feeling a little bit better?" Mike asked feebly as he sat across from Julius on a small stool.

Julius nodded and swallowed a gulp of soup. "I had hoped we would have been able to make it back before the rain came, but the going was a little bit slower with all the people. Gaius, the shepherd, had his flock of about a dozen sheep as well."

"Where are the sheep now?"

"Down by the stream. One of his children is going to watch over them tonight."

"We should probably search out the best pasture land for them. Those sheep will be a great benefit to us."

Julius agreed, sipping the broth. "It will give the children another job to do as well."

"So were you able to make it to every dwelling around the Haven?"

"Pretty much. Only about half responded to our call. The other half chose not to come."

"Chose not to come?"

Julius nodded. "Yeah. Many, including Marcus, who you met, did not feel it necessary."

Mike nodded. That was fair enough. "Do you think, though," he continued, "that if we went back there in a little while, say, in a month, that some might have changed their minds?"

Julius did not seem too keen on the idea. He shrugged and said something about Celto-Roman stubbornness. Mike decided not to press the issue. Julius had done enough for now.

"How about Arthur and Cassius?"

Julius chuckled and shook his head. "As you already know, they abhorred the idea at first, but things mended out between them. I really did not need to intervene. By the end, they seemed to form a fairly decent relationship."

"That's what I had hoped. Thanks for doing that Julius."

Julius simply grunted. He still seemed to hold the unemotional lethargy Mike had always noticed was characteristic of him. Mike could look past it, though. At the moment, he was eternally grateful for what Julius had done, and surprised that he had done it without question.

"So you did get to all the places you knew of, then. There weren't any places that you might have missed?"

Julius gave off a short nervous laugh. "There are a few huts that I did not go to, but it's too dangerous. You know that man, Lucius, the farmer who used to be musician to Sergius the patrician?"

Mike nodded again.

"Well, the Saxons ransacked and took over Sergius' villa two years ago. They killed Sergius and his family as well as Lucius' family. Lucius was able to escape, but the tenants were not. The Saxons kept the tenants alive as slaves, and, for all I know, they continue to work the estate's land. Their huts are too close to the enemy to go near, though."

Mike rubbed his chin for a moment then got up. "Okay. Well, thanks again for what you've done, Julius."

As Mike walked back to his hut, where Lucius was put up along with Gaius and his family, those huts lingered in his head. Mike did not dismiss Julius' excuse—his yield of newcomers gave evidence of its legitimacy—but still, the thought stuck to him like an itchy burr. He felt, for some reason, his vision of the community was left as an uncompleted mural. Those huts were a task hovering above him, buzzing in his head until he at least reached out for it. *Is it just pure and simple sympathy for those who are stuck in slavery?* Mike told himself that the people that he had helped were already more than his share, but that did not get rid of the thought. Memories of those slave girls back at The Haven haunted his mind. He decided, in the mere thirty seconds it took to walk from Julius' hut to his hut, that he would ask Lucius more concerning the situation. That helped him breathe a little more freely.

All six of Gaius' children, except the oldest, who was tending the sheep, were settled down on the floor of the hut to sleep when Mike got back, even though the sun was just barely setting. Gaius and his wife, whose name was Damaris, sat side by side, arm in arm on the hearth watching them silently. As Mike entered, they looked up. Mike nodded to them and glanced over to Lucius, who had gotten a hold of what Mike noticed was the emblem of knowledge. He seemed intrigued by it. "What is this?" he asked.

Mike shrugged it off. "Just a gift from an old friend. It's nothing."

"Hmm," he said and put it down. He then picked up Mike's journal, which was sitting next to the emblem of knowledge. Mike felt instant discomfort at the sight of a strange man thumbing through the pages of his most intimate thoughts, but he reminded himself that it was written in English and would not be understood. Almost at the same time, Mike realized from the way Lucius was looking at it in curiosity, that even the characters themselves did not mean anything.

Upon looking up, Lucius set the journal down. "Is that Latin?" he asked.

Mike shook his head. "A different language. You haven't heard of it; it's called English."

"How do you know how to read and write?" Lucius asked. The question was directed more in a manner of curiosity than accusation.

"In my home land, on the continent; my parents taught me."

"Were your parents Patricians? Senators?"

"No, just farmers."

Mike glanced over to the other two and noticed he had diverted their attention. Meanwhile, Lucius let the fact soak in. "I was not aware that a place existed where regular farmers could learn to read and write."

Suddenly, an idea formed in Mike's head. "Well, I could teach you. I could teach all three of you if you wanted."

"But why? Why would you do this?" This question was posed by Damaris.

"Why not? It's been invaluable to me." Mike directed this last comment while eyeing his own journal. Lucius refocused his attention on it.

"What do you write in it?" Lucius asked.

"Whatever is on my mind at the time."

As the conversation continued, Mike could not tell how interested Gaius and his wife were, but he could tell that Lucius was enthralled. He expressed, more than once, his commitment to learning. His eyes intensely focused on every word that Mike said and seemed alive with desire. The topic opened Lucius up and presented Mike the gateway to this man's life for which he had planned on searching. Lucius opened that gate and invited Mike in as he explained the reason for his desire to learn.

"My patron's family knew how to read and write. They were well educated in Latin and Roman law. I would often hear of them speaking of such things at the dinner table while I let my voice rest. I yearned to be a part of it. I even drew as bold as to ask the daughter—a beautiful, but prideful young girl about one year my junior—if she would teach me. She laughed and mocked the idea, explaining that such privileges were not for people like me."

Mike listened with increased attention. This was the opportunity for which he was looking. "Tell me more about what happened to that family and its tenants."

Lucius' face suddenly changed, leaving Mike to wonder if he had made a mistake. "The family is no more," he answered with despondency. "When the invaders came I was returning from an errand to York. I approached the villa only to hear a terrible din coming from within. I saw blond hairy giants running about the house and heard bloodcurdling screams from within. I had heard stories of these men. I had heard that they were ruthless, that they never took any prisoners. I ran from the scene as fast as my legs could take me, until I could run no more."

"And the tenants?" Mike inquired.

Some of them escaped, like me—those are the ones who are here now. Unfortunately, we were the lucky ones. I returned a few days later to see what had become of the place. Instead of pillaging the villa and moving on, I found that they had taken up residence in the place as if it were their own. I stuck to the trees to avoid being seen and dared not go closer than a few hundred yards, where the line of trees ended. I did notice, however, that the fields were indeed still occupied with workers. I can only assume that these were the remaining tenants, and rather than killing them off too, they were kept to till the fields."

Mike already knew all of this from Julius' account. He wanted a second opinion, however, on the chances of helping the tenants out. Humbly, he posed the possibility to him. To this, however, Lucius shook his head. "Your idea is noble, but the task would be unthinkable. Their huts are situated well within sight of the villa, and I'm sure that they're well-guarded. You would most likely lose more men in the raid than you would acquire. Even if you did succeed, it would be guaranteed that those men would scour the country until they found both them and you."

Mike saw the logic in that, but for some reason the thought did not die. It haunted his dreams that night and even as he set back out to work in the fields the next day, reminding him of what was still out there.

Only the process of time served to gradually dull the thought, simply because there were other, more concrete things upon which to dwell. They were building a new community, with new huts, new people, new fields, and new experiences. Mike began teaching Lucius, as well as a few others, Latin during the afternoons. The evening meal became a colossal feat, as there were almost double the amount of mouths to feed. The evenings were filled with sparring and weapons making. One event gelled smoothly into the other, day after day, forming their weeks into a sort of machine. Mike got caught up in the multi-faceted normality of life, and such thoughts no longer found room in his consciousness.

The newcomers were, indeed, a welcome addition. Their added strength did a lot to move the work along, and Mike could feel that the productivity of the community was on the rise. The blacksmiths made a few trips to York, where they were able to barter for ore, and more tools, as well as more weapons, were forged. These made the tilling worlds easier and the fields were all sown and yielding small plants well before the summer solstice occurred. The weavers helped fit the members of the community into more comfortable summer clothes, made from the wool of Gaius' sheep. Mike looked out on the entire operation with great satisfaction. *This is the way it's supposed to be,* he told himself.

There were a few occasions, a few arguments that were brought to Mike's attention, but that was to be expected. These people were finding their place in the family unit of Newhaven, and a few felt that they had had to fight for that place. The misunderstandings were resolved quickly, though, and without the intensity of Cassius' and Arthur's fight.

Mike settled into the entire routine, satisfied when it did not deviate, and gladdened when it did. He grew accustomed to waking at the first hint of lavender in the sky, then getting up and heading out to arrive in the field by sunrise. He found it pleasing to work alone, the silence only being broken by the semi-voluntary grunts and exhalations that came as his muscles strained against the work. At times, he also found it pleasing to work alongside others, where even hints of jovial conversation made it into the scene.

Mike became satisfied with how the Latin lessons progressed, for most of the people attending them were able to recognize the individual characters and the sounds each one made. Some were beginning to write them out with hunks of charcoal on slabs of bark. Lucius progressed especially quickly. He would occasionally even come to Mike in the morning in the fields to proudly present the characters he had written the night before. Mike complimented them enthusiastically, even if the characters looked shaky and distorted, for it was good to see someone in such meager circumstances smile. That smile appeared more than once, and on more than one person. One could not help but begin to notice it. Truly, it seemed that an epidemic was beginning to break forth in Newhaven.

Chapter 22

Mike took full advantage of the fresh forest air blowing about him as he squatted and held his bow.

The day seemed as close to being a holiday as Mike imagined would cross his path from here on out, for his days normally showed up as nothing but a monochromatic canvas. They filled themselves with waking up, having a bite to eat, heading for the fields, sweating, heading in, and finding ways to both improve people's lives in the small compound and relax so he could find it somewhere within himself to do it all again the next day.

It was not that the monotony was torture. Agricultural work was progressive, however slow it seemed to be, and although it required the same daily tasks, such as weeding among other things, it paid dividends in the form of the growth of the grain. The afternoon and evening pursuits, both in weaponry and in language, paid dividends as well, for he had been able to witness the participants increase in their abilities. They were all clearly more adept and confident than when he had started. The improvement in weaponry was especially satisfying. It allowed Mike to breathe easier at night, knowing that they were no longer free game for whatever hunters lurked out there.

This week, though, Mike decided that they would be the hunters, though not for men. Up to this point, the hunting and trapping had been excluded from all but three or four persons who knew what they were doing and could almost always guarantee success. Mike had wanted as much help as possible to stay on the farms so they could guarantee enough grain to last them through the next winter, but the time had arrived where Mike also wanted to test the skills of his subjects, and the only real way to do that was to use live targets.

Almost a week ago, they had set off up to the north of Newhaven in order to find fresh hunting ground and had nomadically moved little by little each day. Each night, they had gathered together at an appointed place to rest, eat, and share of their successes. Mike had been pleased with the results, for the twelve men and five women that had come along with him had already hunted down seven hares, two foxes, five deer, and one wolf. It was a good deal of acquired skill put into play, not to mention a grand acquisition of meat and fur that would benefit the community.

Mike sent most of the men out in pairs, but had decided to go off on his own throughout the week. He did not even have intentions of killing anything. Already, he had had two deer in his sights before lowering the bow and clapping his hands to ward them off. The thrill alone of wandering out in the wilderness and following a trail was enough for him.

The entire week had definitely become a bright orange stroke across the canvas of gray.

Mike sucked in the moment as he sucked in the fresh breeze. A distance back, at the edge of the forest, he had caught sight of a fairly distinct hoof print in the mud. It had led into these trees, where he figured, at the bottom of the gulley in front of him, lay a small stream to which the deer had directed himself. Mike had entered a break in the brush and noted that it consisted of newly broken branches, still moist and still quite alive. He was not far in, for the brush was thick, and since the deer was most likely close by, he would not be able to get very far without making a ruckus sufficient to scare it away. So he had crouched down where he could get a good view below him. Mike now held his breath, listened, and focused his eyes.

His ears were able to hear absolutely everything. Everything sat in silence except for the steady rushing of wind through the young oak leaves and the slight bubbling of the brook that he could now see below. Mike's eyes scanned the trees alongside it, straining in the dying light of the day, looking for any sign of a brown hide amongst the bark. If the deer was still close, it was likely that it was aware of him as well and was staying as motionless as possible. Mike's eyes moved from upstream slowly downstream to the south, and there, he caught sight of a mass that broke the continuity of the brush. It was brown and, indeed, motionless, but he did not have a good enough view to verify if it was his target or not.

Very slowly, almost unmoving, Mike allowed himself to slide down the hill, taking care not to make too much noise or allow any rocks to go tumbling down. Keeping his body low, he swung one leg, then the other, over a fallen, rotting tree trunk and into a spot where he would have a better view. As he had guessed, it was the prey—a young buck about thirty meters off who watched his surroundings with cautious intensity. It stood at the stream with the intent of taking a drink, but the possibility of Mike's presence had disturbed it. Its ears and white tail were perked up, ready for any more evidence to dart away. Mike stayed as still as a stone. He considered himself fortunate to be downwind of it, for that was all it would have taken for the thing to dart away. The buck continued in its vigil for a moment longer before settling in to drink.

Mike was free to take his shot, had he wanted to. Just for sport, he drew an arrow out of its quiver and pulled it into his bowstring. *This deer would be dead where it stands*, he noted to himself in triumph. *Right through the heart*—he had it in his sights for a good minute.

Then the deer pulled up. It glanced upstream, raised its tail, and darted away. Mike furrowed his eyebrows. The deer had not looked at him. He had not been the one that had startled it away. He looked upstream but could not see anything. Whatever it was, it must have been temporarily out of sight. Mike retuned his ears. There was nothing but the constant sounds of the wind in the trees and bubbling of the brook. Far off, Mike could hear the chirping of a frog, but that would not have startled the deer. Mike listened even more intently. Then he heard it. It was faint, almost unrecognizable, but present all the same. Mike slowly descended the hill to the stream bank, keeping low and out of sight, to see if he could get a look at the source of the noise.

The disturbance was a sort of splashing, uneven and unnatural, as if there was another animal, maybe a predator upstream. *Or*, Mike realized as he slowly approached the stream, *it could be another person, possibly another one of the persons in his party*, though he had thought that he had ventured far beyond to the east of the others so as to allow them to be on their own. Then, with trepidation, that same trepidation that had long been all but dormant, he realized it could have been someone far less friendly than one of his own people. The weather was warm, and Mike was positive that the monsters were back on the move again, gleaning out anything they could from whomever they came across. Mike did not think he was near any sort of road or habitation, but this was unfamiliar country. Mike suddenly felt the necessity to crouch down near the bank, reset his arrow, and strain his eyes upstream at what could be his next target.

Then, he caught sight of it. What he saw made him jump back, not out of fear, but out of surprise. It was not at all what he had expected. The forest was now full of shadows, and Mike's eyes had adjusted accordingly, but for what lay before him about a hundred meters off needed no adjustment. It was such a surreal experience that he wondered if his eyes had been straining for too long and were materializing the image. What he saw was neither predator nor prey; it was neither a member of his party nor a monster. It was a woman. Not a roughly clad woman either, but one in a white sort of dress, maybe even something like a toga. Her body was young and limber, and moved gracefully through the forest like a ghost. She was up, out of the water on the bank on his side, and Mike realized that the splashing must have resulted in her crossing, that the deer must have heard her making way through the bushes.

Mike eyed her curiously. He could not tell what she was doing—she seemed to be going back and forth among the bushes slowly and methodically, as if looking for something. Mike raised himself up and started walking up the stream, taking care to keep quiet. The light was fading fast, but that white garment stood out distinctly amongst the branches and trees. By now, the feelings of anxiety had turned to those of intrigue, and Mike could not help but grow more careless and less quiet.

She seemed to hear him, for she stopped, looked over, and donned an expression of fear. Mike, who had stood motionless in reaction, now stepped out into the open, revealed himself, and cried out in Latin, "Wait!"

She disregarded his plea and went splashing through the stream and crashing through the bushes back up the opposite bank, not waiting around to discover whether he was friend or foe. Mike obeyed the urge within and went chasing after her. She had a good start on him and was up the hill by the time Mike reached point of her crossing. Still, he followed up the trail she blazed, and could tell from all the slip marks in the mud that she had made it up in a quite frazzled and awkward way. Mike's feet had learned to be surer from the repeated ascents of his own hill, and he gained ground on her. By the time he reached the clearing above, she was no more than thirty meters ahead of him.

He caught up quickly, saying again in Latin, "Wait! It's okay," but upon touching her shoulder, she reeled around and lashed out with a sharp rock. Mike instinctively dodged out of the way, but not enough. The point of the rock grabbed hold of his cheek and put a large gash into it. Mike felt a surge of pain well up on his face and let go of the girl, or demoness, whatever she was, to grab his wound.

"Get away from me!" she screamed in rough Saxon as she darted away. Mike looked back at her only to feel the exploding thud of the same rock striking his forehead. He yelled out in pain, stumbled back, and fell to the ground. Without looking back, the strange apparition ran away across the field and into the dying light.

By now, all the fight had left him, and he pitifully watched from the ground as she disappeared. Mike sat there a moment in disbelief before he found the presence of mind to check his wounds. His cheek was bleeding, but not badly, and he pulled out a piece of rabbit fur he used as a handkerchief to put pressure on it. He checked his other wound for blood with his other hand, but there was only a lump that had started to form where what must have been the blunt end of the rock had hit him. Mike slowly pulled himself up and started walking back toward the stream. He stumbled awkwardly along, holding the fur to his bleeding cheek with one hand and holding the pulsing bump on his forehead with the other.

As he walked, his consciousness offered a perplexing mixture of pain, confusion, and haunt. He tried to make sense of all that had happened. The girl had run for the opposite side of the field, but all he could see over there was another cluster of trees. *Where did she come from?* he wondered. She was obviously in Roman garb, but either did not understand his words, or did not heed them as others had in the same situations in the past. She had spoken Saxon to him but from the way she cut with her words, Mike could tell it was not her primary language. *She must be a Roman,* he surmised, *she had that noble air in her countenance.* But she had also fought back like a savage. Apparently, his presence had provoked her even though he did not have any weapons drawn and had presented himself as harmlessly as possible. He supposed that his appearance had surprised her, and that chasing after her and touching her on the shoulder may have seemed aggressive, but her backlash seemed too great of retaliation for such an act.

For the first time, Mike consciously admitted to himself that her features had been striking. Her presence had been captivating in a way that had drawn him in, almost as if by a power more than mere curiosity. *Perhaps*, he thought, *that was the reason I followed her in the first place.* Immediately, Mike recalled the stories of demonesses and goddesses Lucius had told while accompanying himself on the harp. *She's got to be one of the two,* he decided. He remembered one story in particular that told of how a demoness roamed the woods at night, acting as if in distress and luring men into her power. Lucius had told another one of a goddess whose anger toward mankind led her to seduce men through song, then touch them and send them down to the underworld.

Such events did not quite fit—she had done nothing to seduce him. He had not gone to the underworld upon touching her shoulder, though her reaction had given him enough pain to do so. Nothing supernatural which he would have thought would have accompanied such beings had occurred. Yet the stories still seemed the best explanation for the queer occurrence. Mike had originally passed them off as fable, despite Lucius' oath that they were true. Now he was not so sure Lucius was not correct.

As Mike left the field to ascend down the hill to the stream, he looked back once more toward the opposite trees. He half expected to see her haunting, white figure standing at the edge watching him, but she was not there. All he saw was the dark green, almost black silhouette of the grove in the dying light of the sun. The woman, or goddess, or demoness was gone. The hunter instinct almost drove him to chase after her again, this time with more caution, but Mike thought the better of it and descended the knoll to return back to camp.

While crossing through other trees and across other streams, he had almost expected to see another such figure appear and shuddered more than a few times. To his relief, however, he had seen nothing when he arrived in camp almost two hours later.

Mike plopped himself down and grabbed a piece of meat that was sizzling on the fire. "This done?" he asked one of the others as they each worked at their own piece.

One of the men shrugged. Mike looked at the meat, not even knowing quite what it was. He realized, though, that at the moment, he did not care. It was golden brown on the outside, and, as he found out, a little raw on the inside, but cooked enough for his appetite. Mike dug into it like a lion, relishing the taste of the smoke inside the still juicy and rather tender meat. He remained silent while he did so, lost in his thoughts.

Mike then decided to make light conversation, paranoid that his silence revealed too much, and he did not want to speak of his experience at the moment. "Who got this one?" Mike asked, raising the remainder of the morsel in the air. A young man of about seventeen years who sat across from him looked up and smiled. "What is it?"

"Fox," the youth replied. He held an air of pride in his voice. He had not taken anything down all week.

Mike smiled. "Good job."

This short conversation had caught the direct attention of a few others, and for the first time, Mike's face was noticed. "By Juno," Lucius stated, "what happened to you?"

"Slipped and fell on some rocks." Mike stated with a toss of his hand. "It's nothing." The look he gave only to Lucius whispered otherwise, though, and some unspoken communication let Lucius know that he would tell him the truth later. Lucius seemed to understand but still said in response, "Those rocks really got you good. You sure you're okay?"

"Yeah, fine." And that was the end of the matter for that time.

Mike got a chance to talk to Lucius alone later that night when most of the camp was bedded down. They were lying down on their respective mats when Lucius turned to Mike and asked, "What was it really, Mike?"

Mike motioned for them to arise and go somewhere else to talk, to which Lucius agreed.

"It was the weirdest thing, Lucius," Mike explained. "I was down there in the forest with a deer in my sights, when something upstream from it disturbed it, and it ran away."

"Tough luck," Lucius interjected.

Mike shrugged. "I wasn't worried about the deer—I wasn't even going to take it down—I was more curious about the disturbance."

Mike then related what had happened to him, from where he first caught sight of the woman to where he had painfully watched her run off into the darkness. He periodically looked up at Lucius and found he was listening in great earnestness to all he had to say. Afterwards, Mike waited for a response.

Lucius simply returned the matter with a sincere look. "Sounds like a woman worth pursuing."

Mike gave off a sort of half laugh, not quite knowing what to think of such a comment. Lucius' face slowly turned up into a smile, though, and he nudged Mike playfully on the shoulder. Mike exhaled sheepishly and shook his head.

"So what do you think about all of it?" Lucius asked, reinstating his sober attitude.

"I don't know," Mike replied. "The images have stuck with me quite boldly since they've occurred. You ever had that happen to you?"

"No," Lucius answered, shaking his head.

Mike pursed his lips. "It's almost as if that occurrence was more significant than it should have seemed to have been."

"Well you did see a beautiful, violent, ghostlike lady in the middle of nowhere," Lucius responded. "I should think that such an event would rattle your brain like that."

"No, but it's something else. I just don't know what."

"Well," Lucius concluded, "let's both go check it out tomorrow, you and me, during the day. We'll go see if we can determine what she was doing in those bushes, then check out what could be in the cluster of trees she ran into."

Mike felt comfort in that. That seemed to be what he had wanted to get at, though he had not known it at the time. "We'd better go grab some rest, then," Mike said, and they headed back toward their bedding mats.

The next day, Mike announced that they would camp in the same place that night then head back to Newhaven the next day. After eating some leftover meat, as well as some bread brought from Newhaven, the party separated, and Mike and Lucius retraced the trail Mike had taken the day before.

They set out in silence, allowing each other ample space to enjoy the solitude. That was one thing that Mike had grown to like about Lucius. He was witty and fun to talk to, but at the same time, he did not speak when there was nothing to talk about. At least he was that way with Mike. In the time of their acquaintance, Mike had noticed that Lucius had adjusted himself according to the person with whom he attached himself. It was a likeable attribute, and Lucius had seemed to become friends with most everyone in the community. Mike was one of those. In a matter of only a few weeks, Mike had grown to be more comfortable around him than anyone else.

They walked on through the morning, taking on a casual pace which allowed them to enjoy the peace of the fields. The birds, who were singing cheerfully despite the rather overcast day, combined in a sort of call and answer choir that surrounded them and filled Mike's heart with gladness. The air was mostly stagnant, though at times, it would remind the world of its presence with slight bursts of breezes that moved Mike's hair in rhythm with the grass. In all, the setting did not seem capable of harboring haunts—it seemed too innocent, too undefiled. Mike was surprised at the change, but was willing to accept it readily at the same time, for the images still coursed in clarity through his consciousness.

Though the light was different, Mike soon recognized the cluster of trees in the gulley that soon appeared ahead of them. "There it is," he signaled to Lucius, and the two proceeded over to it. It took about half an hour to find out where exactly he had spotted the strange woman the day before, but Lucius was patient. "Take your time," he stated. "If we don't start from the correct spot, our perspective on where she went will be thrown off and make this whole trip a waste."

Mike nodded and searched until he found the line of disturbance in the underbrush. Already, the plants had begun healing themselves, bending back into place like grass springing up after it had been trodden underfoot, but there was still enough evidence of the woman's presence from the day before.

Out of curiosity, Mike proceeded over to where she had been shuffling around to see what her interest had been. The answer was obvious—there grew several bushes already yielding rich ripe berries, and the woman had come down here to partake of them. Whether she had known about this spot previously or not was obscure until he tripped over a bundle that ended up being a basket. The bottom of the basket had contained berries before Mike had spilled them out. *So she did know,* he surmised. The realization, however, was of little consequence, and Mike immediately turned his attention to where she could have gone.

As he began climbing the same trail that he had ascended yesterday, he called out to Lucius behind him. "She rushed up this way after she saw me." Lucius followed after him. When they got to the top, Mike stopped again. "I caught up to her about halfway across this field here. That was when she sliced me with the rock and threw it at my head." Mike messaged his wounds again in recollection. They still tortured his senses.

"That's when you lost track of her?"

Mike nodded. "I didn't see quite where she went, but I imagine that she continued on in the same line that she was traveling when I caught her. That would place her right about there." Mike pointed over to a spot in the trees opposite them, which looked a lot less daunting than they had the night before, a thought that made Mike almost laugh at himself.

The two continued on their trek out toward the girl's estimated point of entry. Upon arrival, they quickly walked along the edge to search for another disturbance. They found none, but there seemed to be a definite break that would have served as an obvious doorway. They shrugged to each other and entered. After looking around, however, they found that the grove was much like any other grove they had witnessed, and there were certainly no signs of human civilization. After searching around in the trees for a good half an hour again, they were able to find another trail of broken branches.

"She must have continued on to the other side," Mike pointed out.

Lucius nodded and the continued to follow the trail. Beyond that, Mike expected to find some sort of dwelling or settlement, but, much to their dismay, when they arrived at the clearing, they saw nothing but another field. There were no houses or huts or any signs of civilization. Nothing was present to upset the sea of grass except for a small stream that wound through the middle. Mike sunk his shoulders which had been raised in anticipation, and his countenance fell. There seemed no way of knowing which way the girl would have gone from here.

He looked over at Lucius and saw, to his great surprise, a quite different look on his face. Lucius seemed perplexed by something, though Mike had no idea what it could have been. There were no distinguishable details about the scenery that would have caused such a thing. It was just another English countryside setting. Yet there was something in Lucius' eye that caused Mike to nudge his friend. "What is it?"

Lucius did not seem to consider Mike's question at first. Instead, he simply muttered, "It can't be."

"What?"

Lucius continued to ignore him, continuing on in his own world of thought. "Yet I've seen such a scene hundreds of times." Lucius began forward in a definite direction. Mike had no choice but to follow after him. Lucius began running, quickly. Mike struggled to catch up to him, which did not happen until they reached the stream.

"What is it?" Mike asked as he felt the coolness of the water soak into his shoes.

"There can only be one field that looks completely like this one," Lucius stated with a hopeful smile on his face. "If I'm right, as soon as we top that rise to the north of us here, we should come upon the villa of Sergius Gothus of Gaul."

Lucius was right. As soon as they topped the rise, a beautiful and large country villa entranced their eyes. It was painted white, with hanging gardens delighting various porches on the roof as well as a diversely vegetated sort of courtyard in the middle. Beyond, to the north and east of the villa, lie vineyards and orchards. Between them and the villa was a field of planted barley swaying in the light summer wind. The whole sight was picturesque to Mike, but Lucius looked on it as if it were a sepulcher. It was a sight in which Mike had frequently heard was a skeleton of what it used to be, for horrors had befallen it that Lucius rather desired to keep obscure. Mike turned to Lucius as he looked down on his old dwelling. Mike imagined that Lucius' last moments had been unspeakably terrible—much more terrible than anything Mike was sure he had ever experienced. To come back to such a place could only bring such memories back to life.

Yet Lucius had still come back.

"Tell me again," Lucius probed, "what did the girl you saw look like?"

Mike reviewed everything about her that he could remember, including her size and her coloring. He described what he could remember about her face, even though the light had been fairly dim by then. He concluded by explaining, "She was young, fit, and attractive and had wild eyes that seemed to draw me in. She was also wearing a toga."

Lucius took it all in with gravity. "I don't believe it," he said almost in a whisper. "She's alive. Diana's alive."

"Who?"

"The daughter of my patron, Sergius. She must have been the one who you saw." Lucius suddenly wore a restless look in his eyes.

Mike knew what was coming. He did not fight it either, for the girl, this Diana, had notched a wedge in his mind for which there seemed no other repair. The anxious energy it had given him last night had not diminished, even while he had slept, for she had dominated his dreams as well. There was something behind this girl, something that had carved her out deeper than she had cut him. Her wild eyes cried it out like trumps. There was fear and suffering and terrible injustice in the cry. It vexed him—that savage look that must have once been tame. He turned over again toward Lucius and nodded his head. Lucius understood—they both understood that they would not be leaving on the morrow. The entire situation frightened Mike more than damnation, but backing down was certainly out of the question, especially when the emblem sat re-energized and glowing in his hand.

Chapter 23

Mike and Lucius waited off in the trees until dark. Slowly, the windows of the villa began to illuminate with candlelight. Mike and Lucius did not say much during that afternoon, but were content to silently watch the compound and observe all the movements of the inhabitants that they could. The sights of Saxons were frequent—they gallivanted about the place with no direct purpose in mind. Mike observed a few of them gathered in a circle playing some sort of game, perhaps gambling. Others sat around, polishing their weapons. Some sparred. Others simply lounged in gluttony, sipping at their wineskins, ripping meat off bones and gorging themselves. They would call out, in what Mike guessed were Saxon obscenities, to various slave girls, who ran about performing various tasks.

Mike tried to get an idea of how the compound was set up and of whom it composed. It seemed as if there were about twenty Saxon mercenaries that resided at the place, as well as about five slave girls. Of course, Mike could not see everyone who was inside, and there could have been much more, but he doubted it. There were also about twenty peasants who were held in servitude and worked the land. From what Mike saw, a good half of them were grown males.

Even though Mike and Lucius lay at a safe distance, the feelings of fear were ever present during those long hours. Seeing those men resurrected memories—dark memories of almost a year ago of when he had been forced to encounter them. He still remembered meeting them face to face and having to strike out first or die. Every time he had practiced with the men of Newhaven, the thuds of the weapons connecting launched him back to those moments, where a false move would have ended up in death or severe, painful injury. He had made several false moves in practice since then, and each one had sent fear pulsing through his spine. It had been a fear that one day, there would be no room for such things. Mike could not help but think, during those hours, that that day was on his heels.

It was amazing how Mike still held on to the prospect of life so tightly especially when the concept in itself was sadistic. His existence right now was a novelty that had already seen its glory days. He seemed to keep it around simply for the sentimental value. It was amazing, too, how much power it still held over him, for as he faced the alternative—death in combat—he clung to it like it was his only friend. Indeed, they were intertwined in their grips on one another. The bond was innate in his body, his muscles, his mind, his instinct.

Mike often wondered if he was alone in these feelings, or if the other inhabitants of Newhaven felt the same way. *Are they happy?* he wondered. *Do they live because they enjoy life, or simply because they're like me—obligated to subsist? Maybe their standard of happiness is simply lower. Maybe I've been spoiled for the first twenty-five years of my life.*

Random shrieks arose from the villa down below. They were a woman's shrieks. Mike snapped out of his trains of thought to look down on the shadow of the villa. It was a horrifying sound, which, had it been constant, would have almost been more bearable. But it came sporadically, intermingled with angry Saxon words that Abe had never taught to Mike. Each time those shrieks came, or each time they were intermingled with the cursing, Mike's soul took a plunge. He did not know what nightmares were unfolding in there for that woman, and he did not particularly care to find out. He had his imagination, and that was more than enough.

"Let's do this," Lucius suggested as soon as he felt it was dark enough. "Let's walk around to the orchard. It's probably better that only one of us goes to check things out in order to avoid being detected. I'll go see what I can find since I know the layout of the house. You wait behind."

Mike agreed readily. He was perfectly willing to let Lucius take the brunt of the risk. The longer and farther he could stay away from those men, the better. He would always do what was necessary, and not shy away from it, but when others were willing to take the lead, that was fine with him.

The two kept to the edge of the woods and crept along to the north side of the clearing. The shadow of the orchard lay out before them in a comforting sort of way. Mike recalled having seen such settings as haunting and dangerous, but now he was the aggressor, and the perspective was completely changed. Now and again, as they walked, they again heard the shrieks, but they were less frequent now. Mike bit his lip to keep his head. He could barely stand being here these few hours let alone experience it firsthand like the slaves had for years.

About halfway through the orchard, about fifty meters from the villa, Lucius motioned for Mike to stay put and continued on by himself. "Keep your ears open for any unusual din," he whispered almost inaudibly. "I may get in a scuffle and need your help."

Mike nodded in understanding. The danger was therefore not beyond himself. As he waited alone in the orchard, watching Lucius disappear behind the trees, he did not move a muscle. It was almost harder putting his trust in someone else's stealth for his safety than doing it himself. The night again became deathly still and his ears attuned themselves to the slight summer breeze for any unusual sound. Still, every once in a while, that shriek would rise above the silence, driving his heart to the bottom of his ribcage. *That is not the din I'm to listen for,* Mike repeated to himself with disdain. *Oh, I wish that shrieking would stop. But please let there not be any other sound.*

It seemed like Lucius was gone for a lifetime. But the moments were creeping by, and in reality, the time may not have been more than half an hour. Mike had taken note of the position of the moon when they had arrived down in the orchard—it had just barely shone its face through the trees to his left. Time passed and it seemed stalled in its course. The entire world seemed caught in this dark rut of a valley, and Mike knew he had no power to do anything but continue standing behind his tree, peer around its trunk, and resist the urge to abandon the scene.

He ended up enduring, though, and when Lucius finally came running back, Mike gave an exhale that he felt like he had held since Lucius had left. Mike took a few more breaths to console himself. There had been no din (other than that occasional shrieking), the reconnaissance was done, and Mike readily followed as Lucius continued running. They ran for what must have been a mile before they reached the same stream of Mike's first encounter with this Diana girl. They were a little bit to the north, but such a detail was of little consequence in Mike's mind. For the first time, Mike questioned what had happened, whether Lucius had been able to find Diana, and why she was not with him.

"I made a decision," Lucius answered between breaths. They had slowed to a walk after they had reached the descent to the stream. Mike looked over at him. "And I hope that you agree with it, because there is really no going back now. I don't mean to usurp your authority on the matter, but I saw the situation and could not do otherwise."

"What happened?" Mike asked. The feelings of anxiety that had previously left him as they had put ground between them and the villa were suddenly returning.

"There're seven slave girls in there, and we're going to rescue them all."

Mike stayed silent. Lucius looked over at him for a response, but Mike did not have any words for the moment. He felt so overwhelmed by the thought that he was rendered speechless. He did not disagree. He did not feel like he could. There was no justification in liberating only some of them. Besides, Lucius had explained that there was no going back now. Mike was not sure what he meant by that, but, luckily for him, Lucius proceeded to explain.

"I told them to set their quarters on fire, escape out the back window, and then to set the orchard on fire behind them."

Mike was starting to see the supplementing implications of the plan. "We then have to face the Saxons."

Lucius nodded apologetically. "All of them. We have to massacre them."

Mike's body recalled the sickness he had felt when he had rescued another girl almost a year ago. Bile churned in his stomach simply from the thought. Nobody had ever included that detail in the fairy tales he had heard as a kid. Slaying dragons to rescue princesses had always been romanticized. Nobody had ever mentioned the emotional side effects on the knight. Maybe there had been none. Maybe he was the exception. Or maybe the writers had always been so caught up in the heroic act of the knight they had forgotten to wonder about his own well-being.

Mike also suddenly felt like a hypocrite.

"We aren't like them, you know," Lucius added, reading Mike's mind by the light of the moon. "These men killed my patrons. I was a witness to that." He grasped Mike's shoulder. "You heard the shrieks tonight. *You were a witness to that.*"

"What was causing that?" Mike asked.

"You don't want to know," was his only response. The answer, obscure as it was, seemed vivid enough.

Mike would have liked to say that the next twenty-four hours of intermission took their time, but the moon, then the sun, then the moon again seemed to suddenly speed up. *They're fiends,* thought Mike, *they seem to love to torture me.* They seemed to hurry up so that Mike again found himself in that formidable clearing hardly before he realized it. *They can just continue at that pace now.* Mike wished that they would just skip over the entire next cycle. As difficult as last night had been, this night would be different, this night would most definitely be worse. This night, he crouched with the rest of his men (the women involved in the hunt were stationed to receive the escapees). They waited in the darkness which seemed especially devoid of sound. There were no crickets even to break the tension in the air.

Mike looked behind him at his compatriots who also crouched with sullen stares. This was their first battle. This was his first battle. They were going up against seasoned warriors. The only advantage they possessed was the element of surprise and the act of aggression. There was one main entrance into the villa, which meant only one exit. The brutes would flee the burning complex, and Mike's men would be waiting there for them.

They had not complained when he had announced the change of plans. They did not question Mike's instructions. They had not abandoned him at his words, but had stood and continued to face him, eye to eye. They had followed him out early that day when he had headed the opposite direction of Newhaven. From what Mike had seen, they had not looked back as they moved forward. Somehow, they had found it in themselves to follow Mike to the precipice of the underworld. Mike hoped to heaven that he could keep them from slipping in.

They waited still in the trees in order to avoid detection before the opportune moment. Lucius and another man had run off to the peasants' huts to fill them in on what was going on and then were going to light their torches and cue the slaves to light theirs. They were to then aid in setting fire to the place. That would be the signal for Mike's men to advance.

Sooner than Mike would have wished, he heard the crashing of windows and watched as the darkness of night was interrupted by violent, cavorting flames. Pushing his feelings to the back of his throat, where they collected as a lump, he turned back to his men, and motioned them forward. His bow was drawn and his hand surprisingly steady, for the remainder of his body seemed to be shaking. Mike reached down to where the emblem was hanging in his tunic. It was glowing warm. That gave Mike a surge of comfort and he began advancing steadily forward down the hill to the villa entrance.

Off on either side of the villa, he could see two dark figures running forward and could only assume it was Lucius and his partner. The two met up with the battalion just as Mike halted them fifty feet shy of the entrance, spread them out, and told them to get down and ready. Bowstrings strained and charged the air with their tension.

In a matter of moments, the first Saxons rushed out of the complex, falling directly into Mike's plan, directly into their sights. Two arrows were fired, two arrows struck, and the two men went down. The two men who fired restrung their bows just as the main barrage came running out of the now blazing building.

The night then fell into pure havoc. Mike had no other way to describe it, even as he would reflect back on it. Shots were fired, men went down, but the enemy was more prepared after the first two casualties. They got past the doorway; they charged at the group. Mike felt himself drawing and swinging his club like a dragon slayer, tapping into a strength unfelt in a long time. Mike looked at the beasts in the eyes—fierce, unfeeling, ghoulish eyes which donned a sound determination to kill. Twenty seemed to be a million when in battle, especially when each one sold death. A shadow came at him with a club of his own, swinging down upon Mike. Mike swung back, met the man's club, and felt the surging pain emanate from his wrists. Mike winced, let out a blood curdling yell, and witnessed himself side kicking his opponent in the stomach. The shadow fell backward. Mike struck down, but the motion was dodged. The shadow rolled away and rolled back up. Mike did not give him a chance to reset and swung out at him. The shadow parried the blow, but not well enough. It lost grip on its club. In the midst of this, Mike could hear the cries of men off to the side of him. He could not look to see, or even wonder whether they were of the enemy or of his own, for he had to focus on his target, which was scrambling for its weapon; he had to gain some deciding advantage over it or he would find himself as the one dead. Mike swung again and delivered a disabling blow directly on the head. The shadow went down, eyes closing, though not before giving a locking stare on Mike. Mike winced, then took the challenger's blade off his motionless body and claimed it as his own.

    Mike was then able to look over to his side. Two of his men were still engaged in fighting. Mike drew his bow, took careful aim, and took one of the opponents out. He was taking aim again on the other when he felt a tremendous force crash down upon him. The bow and arrow fled his grasp as he went to the ground. Some monster had a hold of him, some small, but extremely powerful monster. Mike saw a blade glisten in the moonlight, and threw up his hand to parry the striking arm. They froze in a stalemate of opposing strength for only a moment, but in that moment, Mike again caught sight of its pair of glowing blue eyes. They were not the eyes of a monster, but the eyes of a man. It scared him to the point that he almost gave in. Again, though, some savage part of him had taken control. He rolled the man over and wrestled with him, struggling to gain some sort of edge. The demon was strong and determined to win however, and Mike felt his strength waning. He managed to shake the blade free from the oppressor's hand, and noted it was the one he had just acquired. Mike pinned the man down but was struggling to hold him. The man managed to get a hold of Mike's neck and tried to choke him. "Help me!" Mike yelled out in desperation. The man was beginning to wriggle free and was getting a stronger grasp on Mike. Mike reached for the man's throat as well. "Someone, get over here!" he choked again.

    Then, just as Mike's vision was starting to go, he sensed a wisp sweep in and felt the body below him grunt. His enemy's muscles suddenly tensed up, and his grasp loosened on Mike's neck. Mike felt a warm gurgling come from within the man's throat and saw crimson blood spew out his mouth. The man's hand dropped, and, as Mike's vision resumed on the man's blue eyes, he saw fear. "Dear gods, take me safely," he choked out in Saxon, and then he went limp. Mike's eyes dilated wide, and he threw himself off the corpse in horror. A figure caught him as he stumbled back, but with friendly hands this time. They were Lucius's, who moved to stand his comrade back up.

Suddenly, the fighting ceased, and with just as much surprise as it had started. Mike took a deep breath, and took note, for the first time, of the scene. He would have liked to say that all was silent, but all was not. The groans and the cries pierced constantly through the air while the villa burned in a full roaring blaze. Behind it, though Mike could not see it directly, the orchard blazed like the sun at midday. Mike studied his proximate surroundings. The Saxons all lay on the ground, either dead or injured. It was the injured that haunted the air with their cries. Mike turned away and turned up the bile that had before gathered in his stomach.

The night appeared to be far from over, even as the men retreated into the woods to find the others. Mike massaged his neck and tried not to recall the horrible scene as his steps impacted the forest floor with silent, heavy thuds. He failed miserably at the attempt. He recalled the moment directly following the moment his stomach failed. He had found out that the boy that had been so proud of killing the fox had been severely injured in the abdomen with a knife. He had rushed over at the sound of the boy's groaning voice, holding his still very queasy stomach to him and looking the boy over in desperation and in tears. The boy had died in the next few moments, and Mike had not had any words of comfort for him. He had just crouched there over him, looking down on the waning face and wiping the sweat off the boy's forehead until he, too, went limp.

Mike thought back on what had needed to happen after that. He sickened again at the thought, but he knew nothing else could have been done. They would have died anyway, but slowly and in agony. Mike's stomach had worked itself up again each time his knife stained itself with its merciful act, but there had been nothing to give off anymore. When all the cries had been silenced, Mike had collapsed on the ground and turned his head down. He had not gotten up until Lucius pulled him up.

"Come on," he had told him soberly. "You must lead your men back."

Mike had nodded and slowly pulled himself up. He had tightly grasped the handle of his bow he had recovered and ordered Lucius to tell the men to carry the boy's body back with them. The boy had been the only one really hurt, but that was all it took to make the evening a nightmare.

As they marched through the woods and left the orange glow behind them, all was quiet. There was no cry of victory; there was no glory upon their countenances. The men simply stumbled back in exhaustion. Mike, himself, maintained a silent, blank look. The peasants, who greeted them in the woods, gave off shouts of praise, but Mike's piercing stare, which seemed to cut blindingly through the dark night, silenced them. Lucius reunited with them in a modest manner, embracing each one as they walked, and Mike allowed that, but he wanted nothing more.

A little further up, they met with the women of their group as well as all seven slave girls. The five women of Newhaven approached their respective husbands and loved ones and embraced them. Mike simply stood there, halted, and thought about how he would have to tell the boy's kin. He imagined Julius' reaction when he found out that Mike had gone and done what Julius had dismissed. They had done it regardless of his warning. It was accomplished, but only with the expense of a life.

As the party sat down to rest for a few minutes, Mike pondered on the situation in its entirety. The past two nights had been polluted with unspeakable horrors. One had been replaced with the other. Shrieks had been replaced with screams. Unsettled oppression had been replaced with blazing fire and blood. A complex filled with disgust and filth had been replaced with massacre. All would be quiet the next day, and the ruins would be polluted by both scenes. Mike wished that he could destroy it all, but the memories were indestructible. He knew that they would be diluted with time, but right now, they were so pungent, so concentrated, that he was not capable of thinking on a time when they would no longer cause him pain.

He had been involved in a massacre. He had instigated the death of twenty men.

But there could have been no other alternative. Mike forced himself to reassure his conscience of that. By approaching the villa yesterday, Mike and all involved with him had crossed a threshold. Their veil of ignorance had been shed and they had suddenly become responsible to put an end to those shrieks. They could not return to their God-graced lives of freedom with their new knowledge. The act would have been inhumane—more inhumane than the slaughter they had performed.

That still did not take away from the despicable nature of the ordeal. He had pledged himself to help people, to help build a society. In order to do so, he had had to destroy one, to force hearts to stop beating. Mike had shot two men and held two as their lives left them, not to mention the three deaths he had finalized. These last five stuck out most vividly in his mind. He had been up close, in physical contact as the life had left them, especially the one he had wrestled. He thought back on that, on the man's words, *Dear gods, take me safely*, on the muscles that tensed then relaxed—a whole system devoted to an existence stubbornly struggling, then feebly failing. He thought of the man's life itself. That man had a story, just like Mike had a story, just like everyone he had ever met had a story. That story must have been filled with loves and pleasures and pains and heartaches and aspirations and dreams, moments of triumph and moments of needed comfort. It must have been a story cut short by Mike's raid—dreams snuffed out, plans destroyed, smiles and laughter neutralized. *He could have very well done such things to others, to more innocent victims*, Mike told himself, *but then again, he might not have. He may have been a family man out to seek a better life for his kin, just like everyone in Newhaven.*

Dear gods, take me safely. The words haunted him, and could very well haunt him as long as his breath still moved in and out of his body. *Did those gods hear their subject, whoever their subject considered them to be? Does the God I believe in possess the mercy to hear this man's cries, even after the horrors he has probably committed?* The answer, like an apparition, seemed to rise above the pit of confusion that was Mike's gut.

Mike finally understood why murder was one of man's greatest sins.

His eyes were drawn up from the ground by some comment or movement or something, and when they did, he met the eyes of Diana, the demoness that had drawn him into this entire mess. She was staring at him, and seemed to have been for at least a few moments. Their stares only overlapped for a second or two, but a world of substance seemed to open up during that moment. There was something in her eyes that Mike would spend the entire trip back to Newhaven analyzing, for she did not speak one word to him, nor to anybody for that matter. Analysis produced a few phrases that seemed to decipher that stare: it had been one of surprise... intrigue... recognition... respect... remorse... gratitude. She did not need to say them; the stare seemed to communicate them, and once Mike had decrypted them, they were crystal clear.

But those eyes whispered of more than these words. They whispered of things of the past, things that Mike could not so readily figure out. Had they been one thing, even one emotion of agony, understanding would have been easier, but the eyes were more convoluted than that. This Diana—he only knew as much of her as what Lucius had told him and what he could guess of her life as a slave. Everything else, every private thought or attitude or childhood essence was unknown. *But they've all got to be hid somewhere in those eyes.* Mike again found himself smitten.

As they ascended the hill to Newhaven, as the first violet streaks of dawn began to appear on the night's horizon, Mike looked out toward her figure moving methodically back and forth up ahead of him. The back of her head was somewhat less revealing than her face, but Mike knew it was only the leeward side of a world of emulsifying secrets. Thinking about their possibilities alone ground at his consciousness.

"She's the one that initiated this," Mike thought to himself, "and look what emotional torture I have put myself through because of her. She really is a demoness."

Chapter 24

Life after the Dark Holiday fell back to its usual self, which was something that Mike readily welcomed. It was busy as usual—especially since new huts needed to be built and the farming had felt the effects of their week long absence. Mike had decided to send the newly arrived peasants out to work the land, since those already at Newhaven, especially those who had been there the longest like he and Julius and a few other men, had become almost professional in building huts. As they faced the colossal task, they all settled in on their respective duties, down to some of the teens carrying up rocks from the stream for the hearths. Within a few days, the huts were up, and Mike noticed for the first time that their conglomerate of dwellings had started to take on the form of an actual community.

Mike was glad to get back in the fields after that. They were his domain; they were where he felt like he most belonged (as it always had been. Agriculture was one of the few constancies between the two time periods of his life that he had known). For that reason, as well as the fact that he did not have much else, farming had become a passion for him. As time had perpetuated, he had actually found himself looking forward to soaking up the sun like living water; his attitude had metamorphosed from dread, to drudge, to listlessness, to acceptance, to enjoyment, to zeal. It felt good to go home each evening, to kick off his boots, loosen the belt about his tunic, and crawl into bed to fall asleep to the crickets outside his hut, but only as a temperance to his passion.

And right now, his passion was starting to yield results. Newhaven's expanses had not wanted for rain this year, and, as a result, the grain was growing tall and lean. The grain was already up past his knees and looked like soft, green velvet from up on the hill. It boasted light and dark wave patterns in the wind, flaunting its color and thickness in full luster, and looking out on it was only bested by being within it.

The fields had acquired lots of weeds, however, while they had been gone, and they found themselves with a handful of labor. Mike was not angry or frustrated; he could not be. He knew that the fields were simply regenerating what had they had grown there for thousands of years. They had been paddling upstream from the beginning, and Mike had expected the digression when they had pulled out of the current. Grasses had been especially prone to come back quickly, and they upset the continuity of the field fairly generally. The people were waging a battle to keep their food clear of such pests, especially the vegetables they had planted, for they were the most sensitive, but Mike led a pretty good work force now, and they were making headway.

"I have to say, Mike," Julius mentioned about a week after they returned as they stood in the fields and drank and poured water over their bare chests, "that you were right about the acquisition of extra people. Look at all of this." Julius swept his hand across the panorama of the fields with a smile. "I have never seen such a community in such good order."

It was the first time they had really talked since Mike had returned. "Yeah, but at the cost of the life of a boy."

Julius nodded, taking another sip of water. Mike looked at him to see if he could note any sort of reaction out of him. Julius' face, however, remained unchanged from its usual self.

"I don't know," Mike continued. "Maybe I should have listened to you. He wouldn't be dead now if I didn't send them into battle."

Newhaven had ceased work the day after all the huts had been built to hold a funeral and a burial for the boy. It had been the end of a terribly somber episode. Mike had loathed the moment when he had had to face the family and give them their son's body, fearing what sort of reaction they would have, but they did not show any malice toward him at all, only quiet sorrow, complemented with silent tears when his body was finally laid to rest. They had not dealt one word of criticism to Mike though, even despite his explanation, despite his repeated apologetic sobs. Still, Mike continued to feel like a murderer, even after the boy's body had lain in the ground for three days.

"From what I hear, though," Julius countered, "you saved those peasants and those slave girls from quite a nightmare. Don't tell me you haven't noticed that in their faces."

Mike had been so preoccupied with the horrors that had come of the battle that he had to admit that he had not.

"Yeah," he continued. "They talk about it quite a bit too, how living here is heaven compared to where they were. They don't have taskmasters, they don't have oppressive drunk warriors looking for any excuse to beat them senseless. And the slave girls. You can only imagine what they don't have to deal with anymore."

Mike realized that he had thought about that as he and Julius resumed working for another hour or so. In fact, the thought had been on his mind a lot in the past week. He had thought of Diana in particular. He had only caught glimpses of her since she had arrived, which did not give him much more information about her. *She's different than the other girls, though; I can sense it.* Mike strained to pull a small tree out of the dirt. It struggled then lost its grip on the soil, coming up to be thrown off to the wayside to be burned. The other girls seemed to be rebounding, enjoying their freedom with relish: smiling, laughing, even flirting with some of the young men who worked in the fields. They were reservoirs of sunshine, bursting forth after being bundled up in their own personal clouds for so long. They brought a life to the community that had not been there before.

Diana was, indeed, different. Her manner remained stagnantly overcast. She did not go around dancing and laughing and flirting like the others. She often kept to herself and never came out to eat with the community, even after the explanation Mike had given concerning the understanding. She seemed to actually avoid him in specific, for although they had locked glances several times, she never allowed herself to be in a position for him to talk with her.

Though she kept her distance, Mike still noticed the convolution of emotions in her eyes. He desperately wanted to decode it, but her distance never gave him an opportunity. It was all very frustrating.

Mike nodded in agreement to Julius' statement. "What about Diana?" he asked, since it was on his mind. "Have you talked to her? Did you, like Lucius, know her before?"

Julius shook his head in the negative to both questions. "I had only heard of her. She was the daughter of Sergius, whose villa was a good place to barter for stuff without having to go into York. The stories were that she was quite the wild charmer, and as you can see, she certainly had the means to do it."

At least as far as her looks go, Mike thought to himself. "That's weird, then, how she is so reclusive."

Julius stood up with a pulled thistle in his hand and straightened the strain in his back. "Things change, Mike. She saw her family massacred. She became a slave and must have suffered unmentionable things. How would you react to such a thing, if you can imagine?"

I don't want to imagine, Mike thought to himself, but instead of voicing that he answered, "I guess probably the same way. It just intrigues me, though, that she is different from the others."

Julius walked over to another area that had not yet been cleared of weeds. Mike followed, for it seemed as if Julius was mulling the idea over in his head, trying to come up with a conclusion. "We don't know the backgrounds of the other slave girls, but I suppose they were not of a very high class—probably more native farmers, like ourselves. Diana is a Roman citizen, the daughter of a rich patrician. She went from a life of luxury to a life of horror, and lived the two in the same house. Can you imagine what that must have been like for her?"

Mike did not say anything but proceeded weeding the new area while tossing the thought over in his head. Julius seemed to have a point. The tragedy did rest much harder on her, no matter what the others could have witnessed. The thoughts immediately led to the question of what could be done for her, which Mike decided, after a moment, to run past Julius.

Julius looked at Mike in the manner which he had looked at him many times before. "You're a unique person, Mike."

Mike was left wondering what Julius was implying as Julius stated he needed to go refill his water skin and left him standing in the fields alone.

As Mike packed up his tools and headed back to his hut, he resolved in his mind that he should just go talk to the girl—invite her personally to come to the evening meal with the town. It had been a task he had been mulling over for some time, but after thinking today about her state and desiring to know more about the history of it all, he was pushed to actually do it. Any sort of conversation with her might reveal something else of her nature, regardless of the topic, and he would also be able to see what sorts of feelings she offered toward him now, seeing that their last direct contact had been that first day he had seen her.

Mike had seen Lucius go into her hut at various times—a hut shared by two other of the former slave girls—but he had not had the leisure either to see how long Lucius' visits lasted or to ask him of the nature of them. Lucius had been the only one that had really known her before the Saxon attack on her house, but from what he had said, it did not even seem like they had been close friends. The girl had seemed arrogant, from what Lucius had spoken of her, and whether or not all that had changed with the raid was hard to say, but Mike could attest that even Lucius had not been successful at integrating her into the community.

Gaius was sitting in the shade of his hut, sipping at his skin as Mike passed him on the way to her hut. "Mike, how are you doing today?"

Mike stopped his course and turned around, smiling. "Good, how are you? How're the sheep?"

Gaius laughed. "Good, good. Those lambs are funny little critters. Their playfulness never gets old to watch."

"I'm sure." Mike replied. He figured there was a story associated with the comment, but Mike was anxious to carry out the task in his mind. Gaius seemed to notice.

"Where're you headed so urgently?"

"Oh, I was just heading over to speak with Diana about a matter of business."

"Oh yeah?" Gaius returned, setting down his water skin, stretching on his stool, then shifting positions to face Mike more directly. "She's a quiet one. She's been a great help to me, though, for the past few days with the sheep. She is awfully good with them, and they've already taken a particular liking to her."

"So she's been down there with you, then?" Despite Mike's rather casual tone, he found himself quite intrigued by this detail. He had not known she had been involved in any of the work of the community.

"Yeah, been pretty faithful too. She's not opposed to watching them at night, even alone. My kids have been able to sleep more because of her."

"Hmm," Mike was growing more and more interested by the moment, but Gaius seemed to have said all he was planning on saying, and so Mike simply asked, "Do you want me to pass on any word or compliment to her?"

"If you want to express my appreciation, be my guest." Gaius reacquainted himself with his water skin. He took a draught then swallowed. "I haven't gotten much chance to talk to her, but my kids have. She seems to open up better to them."

Indeed, Mike thought to himself as he nodded farewell to Gaius and advanced toward her hut on the far end of the complex. The more he learned about this girl, the more everything became convoluted.

Mike paused in front of the doorway of the hut. Based upon what Gaius had said concerning Diana's nocturnal habits, he was not sure if he would be disturbing her sleep—a grand start to a conversation aimed at friendliness—but as he clapped to signify his presence outside, a voice from within told him to enter.

Mike stepped inside and found all three of the girls inside. One was laid down and napping, but it was not Diana. Diana and the other girl were sitting down, though doing what, Mike was not sure. They both turned to face Mike as he walked in, and it was obvious from their positioning that they had not been conversing.

"Hello, Mike," the one girl said with a warm smile. Diana simply stared up at him with neither a look of welcome or disdain.

Mike returned the smile. "I hope I wasn't disturbing anything."

The girl shook her head. Diana had since looked back down. It was apparent now she was fiddling with a string of beads. Mike looked over at her then awkwardly stated, "I came here to talk to Diana. Would you mind me stealing her away from you for a few minutes?"

"Whatever it is you want to say, you can say it right here," Diana spoke up. "It is okay if Constantia hears it, whatever it may be."

Mike bit his lip in feelings of sustained awkwardness. *This is not a good start.* He was determined, however, to carry through his intentions, so he shrugged and agreed to the terms. "I came by to meet you, to get to know you a little bit better since the only time we really met was down by that stream, and I feel like a slight misunderstanding got in the way there."

If Mike had expected even a slight smile to emanate from the memory of her defeating him, he was to be disappointed. Diana's lips did not break upward or downward as she retorted by saying, "Your manner of making acquaintance was a little headstrong, and you also cannot deny that you look like every other one of those dogs."

Mike let out a laugh in spite of the frank comment directed toward him. "I'm sorry that I can't help looking like a Saxon, but I can assure you that I have no relation to them," (a fact which probably was not entirely true, since he was largely of English and German ancestry, but mentioning such details would have made things more complicated right from the start and would not have helped his cause out at all). "I hope our acts of a week ago prove this to you."

A slight nod escaped from Diana's head, but after recovering herself, she added, "You burned down my father's villa."

Mike was already losing his patience; this one seemed determined to make waves under his boat. The other girl, Constantia, had deliberately turned her attention away from the conversation and occupied herself with organizing some sort of arrangement over in the corner. Mike considered leaving right then, but his determination drove him onward. He decided to ignore the comment.

"I just hope you can picture me, as well as everyone else here, in a friendly manner. I wanted to formally welcome you to Newhaven and let you know that you don't have to worry anymore. We killed your oppressors. Even now, Lucius is gone with a party to rummage through the wreckage and bury the bodies."

It had indeed been true that Lucius had gone back with a few men. He had mentioned the idea to Mike just three days ago, after he had figured that Mike's emotions had steadied a little. Lucius had brought the idea forward with enthusiasm, stating all the benefits of having the extra weapons, armor, and metal in general. "We need more metal for extra tools," he had explained. "Plus the peasants tell me that there were several livestock in the complex that will most likely die if kept in their stables for too much longer." Mike had been hesitant about the trip, feeling it disrespectful to the dead, however vicious the enemy had been, but he could not deny that the benefits Lucius had presented were legitimate. He had consented for him to go, as long as they took the time to bury the dead. To this, Lucius had been hesitant, but had finally agreed.

Mike turned his attention back toward his subject. Diana could not hold eye contact with Mike; she had turned to look away as Mike had mentioned the death of the Saxons. The beginnings of tears began to well up in her dark eyes, though Mike liked to think they bled out of gratitude rather than anger or sadness. Such an emotion struggled to soak through, though she still made no effort to verbally convey it.

Mike continued on. "You will find we have a wonderful community of people here. I am sure you are aware that we eat our evening meals together."

"I am aware," she stated, still looking away from him. As she blinked, a tear fell down on to her cheek and slowly started making its way down to her chin. It seemed to mirror the pain in Mike's heart at seeing such a being in such a state. "I have helped cook the meals since I have been here."

"We would like you to join us," Mike added, his voice now as sober as a monk's.

"I am sure you get along just fine without me. You seemed to have no problem with it up to this point."

Mike felt himself more lost concerning this strange girl than ever. "I'm not inviting you for our sake, but for yours. There are many wonderful people here to meet."

She finally turned to Mike again. In her teary eyed face fought a thousand contradictions. Mike thought he could see a desire to accept the invitation struggling its way to the surface. She wanted it, or at least a part of her wanted it. It was the part to which Julius had been referring. It was the part that still seemed to live despite every dark sheet that had been laid over it. Mike's eyes widened at the realization. Then slowly, her lips parted. "I appreciate your concern, but I am fine. Is that all?"

Mike exhaled all the hope he had pent up in his lungs. "Yeah that's all," he responded, deflated. He got up to leave, but as he reached the doorway, he remembered to add, "Oh yeah. Gaius says he really appreciates the help you have given him in tending his sheep. He is really impressed with their taking to you."

At that, Mike noticed a slight change in her expression. Again, her face did not expose much, but Mike could tell it was something new, something almost unexpected even to herself. There was a slight pause before she muttered, "Tell him that it is my pleasure."

Mike mustered out a slight nod before leaving the hut to the sound of Constantia's farewell. He walked away from the hut with slow steps. He had not felt like this since Abe had first explained the mission to him almost two years ago. Despite that sprout he had thought he had seen in her eyes, he was sorely disappointed at his intentions to discover anything new about this addition to their community. He felt like one would after eating a meal that left him hungry. Mike kicked out at a rock that lay in his path in frustration; he knew that he had done all he could for now.

Mike spent the afternoon forgetting about the whole episode by visiting the various huts to wish everyone a good day. This raised his spirits a little, since the remainder of the community seemed much more elated at his appearance. Mike was happy to talk with all of them and to hear about their happenings.

"So I hear that Lucius has gone to retrieve the weapons of those dogs," the blacksmith by the name of Cai mentioned to him.

"Yeah," Mike confirmed. "We'll probably use some of the weapons and armor as they are, but give the rest of the metal to you to make into tools, especially plows. Lucius told me that there was also livestock up there that he was going to bring back. Both will make tilling much easier for next year."

"Excellent. How did you do it this year?"

"With hoes. It worked, but it was extremely slow and tedious."

Cai chuckled. "Well, I'm glad I came after all that was done. I don't envy you at all."

Mike shrugged. "It'll just make next year seem all the more easy."

"Yeah, well, that is trusting I even do this for you."

Mike studied him, knowing this man to be lighthearted despite the circumstances in which he, and everyone else, found themselves. "Cai, did

I ever tell you how much we appreciate you and your comrade Dylan?"

Cai let out a bellow that would have fed any of his fires and slapped Mike heartily on the back with his bulging arm. "Ah, it's good to see you, Mike. Let me know when Lucius gets in."

The very event occurred that evening after the meal. A cry came ringing out of a child's voice and aroused many of the people out of their huts. Mike, too, stepped outside to get a look at what the child described as "an army of animals" approaching the hill. At first, feelings of desperation struck in Mike's stomach, but those feelings were immediately replaced by wonder when his eyes met the sight that had aroused the child's attention. Out among the fields, Lucius and the other men with him were riding horses and driving forth a herd of animals consisting of about nine more horses, five oxen, and two mules.

Mike ran down the hill, barefoot as he was, to meet his friend. Lucius greeted him with a smile and motioned for him to get up on one of the horses, for they were all saddled. Mike did so and helped drive the herd of animals up the trail to the huts. By the time they reached the top, the whole community was gathered in the commons, and was greeting the army with cheers. The people finally seemed to feel as if they were getting the victory celebration they felt they deserved. Mike did not do anything to squelch the cries of joy, but looked over at Lucius with a smile as they swayed slowly back and forth. Lucius returned the expression readily.

"We can probably keep the animals down in the pasture with the sheep," he stated as he sopped leftovers from the evening meal inside of Mike's hut soon afterwards.

"Yeah, that sounds good," Mike answered with a nod. He took the moment to glance over at his friend. Lucius looked tired, and seemed content to be back in the comfort of the huts. "You sure had the people excited out there."

Lucius shrugged. "I'm glad."

He said nothing more as he continued to consume his bowl of stew. Mike could tell that despite the joy of the victory march, something was on Lucius' mind. Something had been bothering him. Mike was about to ask him about it when Lucius pulled a sheet of rabbit skin out of his tunic. "Last night, just before we left the ruins, I wrote a journal entry about my past few days. I was wondering if you'd look it over and see how I did on my writing." Lucius stood up and handed Mike the piece of skin. Mike took it, agreed, and watched as Lucius proceeded to leave. "You can get it back to me in the morning. I'm going to get some people to help me guide the animals down to the pasture and arrange for a few extra people to look after them tonight. Then, I'm going to go to bed."

Mike nodded, thanked him again, and acknowledged his departure. As Lucius disappeared into the evening, Mike lit a candle and looked down at the skin. The handwriting was fairly legible and easy to read:

I don't know what I was expecting when I told Mike I would come up here to salvage what I could find. Perhaps I thought that it would be useful to the community, and it turns out that I underestimated the truth of that. However, the emotional stress this trip has laid on me has driven me to write my experience down. Mike said that always helped him ease his stress.

It was extremely hard for me to bury the men that killed my family—almost unbearable. It does not seem just that I should be so civil to men who slaughtered my wife and two little daughters right in front of me. I am now afraid that their fair shadows will come up from the underworld to haunt me about it, but still, I take pride that I have defended my honor in going through with it. I recognized one of the dead men I buried as being the very murderer, and felt such a mixture of hatred and sorrow I almost collapsed. The man deserved to be chopped in pieces and it took all my strength to keep from doing so.

But all of them are buried, and tomorrow I will leave this terrible graveyard forever. I never want to see it again, and I think that if I don't, the scars will eventually heal. But this trip has reawakened the nightmares I thought I had finally conquered, and I am afraid that one more day here will plant them in my dreams forever. This trip has been successful, but again, at a very great cost to my own emotional well-being. I feel like I need to recover all over again.

Mike lay back on his bed and sighed, wondering if Lucius only gave it to him for the purpose he stated. He was glad tomorrow was a day of rest, for it signified the end of a very long week.

Chapter 25

As the pouring summer rain drenched the night and threatened to flood the fields below, thoughts flooded Mike's mind. He pulled his hood tighter over his head. They were thoughts of what had happened in the past few days which brought him to the top of this newly erected tower. He was keeping watch to make sure those who had come in the vicinity of Newhaven did not come any closer. The rain dripped off his hood and onto the tip of his nose, only one of the many wet parts of his body. His toes were soaking now too. His thoughts reverted to Julius and his comrades who were experiencing the same thing, but who would not get the same comfort of going back to their own huts after a few hours. They had set off on a sort of recovery journey—a recovery of any survivors of the recent storm.

Mike had begun to wonder whether their expulsion of the Saxons from Sergius' villa had taken care of the issue for the entire area. He had been convinced the idea was true until just a few evenings ago.

A few evenings ago, Mike had noticed the eastern sky glow in a blotchy sort of orange. He had figured out its source without too much effort, for the thought had never been too far from his consciousness and resurfaced readily. The itchy burn of anxiety surfaced along with it, especially when he noted that some of the blotches were close—maybe three or four miles in the distance. Mike recalled warning those trained in the weapons—his soldiers in a sense—to be ready for action in case their place was discovered. Fires had been extinguished, livestock had been taken up to the top of the hill, and all had been told to be ready for an attack.

After that, Mike's eyes had remained glued on that horizon and the fields that lay before it—the fields that they had spent a whole season cultivating. He had waited for those torch-bearing shadows to appear out of the trees beyond them and set fire to them before charging up the hill. His stomach tensed in anticipation, all feelings of sleepiness fled, and a fear that he would again have to rekindle his murderous nightmares began to re-emerge.

They had not come, though. Dawn swept from horizon to horizon, east to west, from the fires to their hill, and did not bring along those foreign men of war. Mike's feelings of anxiety simmered, but only a little, for he knew that they were still in the area. In the matter of a day, he had a tower erected for men to keep watch, a tower tall enough to give one a three hundred sixty degree view of the countryside miles around Newhaven. A constant guard had been placed up there ever since.

In the end, the attack had not been a burden other than the reminder of fear and the minimally extra weight of the weapons the men were told to have on their person at all times. They had been seen heading out to the fields laden with slings, stones, and bows and arrows, burdens which some of the men seemed prone to shed, especially when life seemed to turn back to its normal course, but Mike had been strict on the matter. The speed of progress would have to be sacrificed for the strength of security.

The fields, on the other hand, seemed oblivious to the entire situation. They had happily filled out to a luscious blanket that spanned the expanse before Newhaven's hill. A succulent summer sun and liberal moisture had yielded a plentiful crop with the help of industrious hands and soon, it would be time to reap. The blacksmiths had been hard at work and had all the sickles ready for when the foray was to be made.

It had been the third day after Mike had seen those eerie blotches that Julius approached him, which was two days ago. Mike had been napping during the heat of the afternoon and started as Julius had entered the hut. "Don't worry; it's just me," he had spoken at Mike's reaction.

"Oh, hello Julius. What's going on?"

"I wanted to come in here to talk about those attacks."

Mike had nodded. "What's on your mind?"

"Well, earlier this year, when I went out in search of all the people

I knew around The Haven—remember how I said that not everyone responded?"

Mike had recalled the conversation as well as Julius' general feelings toward further action.

"Well, I think, considering the attacks, their opinions might have changed and we may be able to get a few more persons."

Mike had been surprised, not at the prospect of the change in the people's opinions, but in the change of Julius' opinion. He had not seemed too keen on the idea of going out on another journey beforehand. Mike had never known Julius to be a man of much compassion for others but a man with focus on his own survival. Even all the help he had given Mike in his leadership of Newhaven had been for his benefit. Mike had found it hard to believe that Julius had suddenly changed. He had stared at Julius at that moment and wondered what the cause of the change could have been but decided against asking about it, for he was pleased at Julius' desire and did not want to do anything to squelch it.

"Okay," Mike had responded. "What do you propose?"

Julius had seemed to have had a plan already laid out, which he voiced to Mike. He would take the same party he brought the first time, allowing Mike to stay in Newhaven and prepare for harvest. Mike agreed to the plan, provided Julius charged them with the same oath of allegiance, and was thrilled more and more at the idea that Julius was being more proactive and willing to help the community out. He hoped that would help the others adopt the same attitude as well.

To such things, Mike's mind also reverted on this stormy night. It had been harder than Mike had thought to establish such goodwill in the community. These people did not think like his neighbors in Southern Idaho thought, for he seemed to be the only common thread between them. Indeed, the communal meals that they had each day were slowly making progress, but they still consisted of groups of kin eating exclusively and taking home only what they had contributed. There had been no even spread of things; there had been no giving and sharing. It was, in many regards, a little bit frustrating, but Mike did not know what else he could really do.

And in many other instances, such an atmosphere was not completely descriptive of the case. These people did know how to work together. When it came to farming and other modes of labor, these people had it all figured out. They were interdependent on each other as they had been their whole lives. Their poverty had brought them to that. They did not have the independence that Mike had grown up thinking was the norm. Without the others, they simply could not survive.

The other place Mike noticed it was in his soldiers. He had started referring to them as such only because they had started referring to him as their captain. They spent so many of their evenings together, helping each other, trusting each other with themselves, that there was a certain sort of brotherhood. That was why, Mike supposed, he had grown so close to Lucius, even though he had known Julius for so much longer. Ever since the raid on the Saxons, he and Lucius had taught each other the art of swordsmanship to as great a degree as they could. They had sparred with one another on countless occasions, pushing the other to the brink of his ability, yet, at the same time, never crossing its fatal line.

That raid too, though Mike cringed to think about it in such a way, had been beneficial in uniting the men. They had depended on each other for their lives. All feelings of self-preservation had seemed to ironically disappear when the primal battle instincts kicked in. They had not moved as individuals, but as a unit. The danger of one had been the danger of all. Men had stepped out of their shoes to save those of another, and the bond of brotherhood had continued on since then, much to Mike's elation. Ever since that raid, the soldiers had spent time together—time that was their own, when they were not tied to the field or the communal dinner table. They would be seen working together, relaxing together, and hunting together.

But, as of now, they were the only ones that did such things; everyone else more or less kept to themselves.

Which was why Mike did not know why he felt so strongly about focusing on incorporating Diana into the community. She was only another example of everyone else. The sole difference was that she still did not come to dinner. *But even then,* Mike pondered, *she would be alone, since she has no kin to associate with anyway.*

At that moment, Mike caught something out of the corner of his eye, some foreign movement in the turbulent darkness. Mike squinted at the rain as he turned into it. As his eyes met the source of his arousal, he suddenly found the subject of his thoughts hauntingly appropriate. There, walking at the edge of the trees, he caught sight of a figure walking that could have only been Diana's. A moment's glance confirmed the conjecture not only with the sight of a toga that only she ever wore, but in the elegant manner in which the figure walked, as if each step were a performance, well-practiced and perfected. Mike wiped his eyes and took the moment to stare down at her. He was her only audience. The rest of Newhaven was sound asleep, lulled now through several hours of darkness by the steady rain.

She was not far off, maybe about fifteen meters from the base of the tower, and Mike could tell she was drenched. His first impulse was to shout out at her, to ask her what she was doing, but instead he kept silent and continued to stare. *Man*, he told himself again, *she is stunning.* Maybe he kept silent for that reason; maybe he knew that once he spoke up, she would disappear again into the night. *But she has to know that I am up here.* If so, Mike had to wonder what she meant by it. That conjecture simply lacked sense, leading Mike to wonder about her real intentions.

Mike laughed at himself. His mind was racing again. He passed over the same thoughts that he had encountered in high school, the same pathway of thoughts that led all men off of their avenue of self control. Mike had never seen that road to the end, for he had never ventured farther than daydreaming. He wondered, for a moment, if this apparition was nothing more than just that as well.

No, he told himself, *this is still different. This must be real. But why on earth is she out in this rain?* She was soaked. His curiosity soared, and he continued to watch her. She never once looked up at his position, but had since moved closer to the tower, almost as if she was toying with him. *But then again,* Mike argued, *why would she do that when all she has said and done to me has indicated spite?*

It was then that she did something quite out of the ordinary, something that snuffed Mike's thoughts completely out. He watched in wonder as she turned her head back, spread out her arms, and let the rain fall on as much of her as possible. And she was smiling. Her voice let out a few short laughs as she stood there in stillness, and, as Mike looked closer in intrigued disbelief, he discovered that she was breathing hard, almost as if she were forcing her entire body to masticate the moment.

Mike shook his head in disbelief. This was a breakthrough. This was something big, something that caused him to almost forget to breathe. *That laugh.* It was not a crazed laugh—though it may have been more appropriate to the occasion had it been—nor was it an unnatural laugh in any way. It seemed to fall into place like an event of a well engineered play. Mike knew, despite his previous unfamiliarity, that this laugh was Diana—the true Diana that he had never yet seen. Somehow, though he could not understand the math, it cancelled out all of her seemingly normal expressions of coldness, bitterness, and hatred.

What's the difference? What made the difference?

Mike remembered Julius' words. "She was quite the wild charmer."

He remembered wondering how that could be so when not a hint, not even a half smile had been directed toward anybody in the entire community. She had been anti-social: a self-imposed outcast in the community. It had been common opinion. Mike knew; he had heard the talk over the last few weeks. They had all been talking about her, spreading terrible rumors about her, about her loyalty to the community as opposed to her loyalty to the Saxons. Mike had stunted the talk when it had surrounded him, for it had hurt him to hear such mocking laughter about someone else and knew that it was not healthy for the community. But the train of gossip had ultimately retained its course, and, he had had to admit to himself, with legitimate reason. They only spoke of what they had seen, of what he had seen as well. He had realized that the only way it could really be stopped was for her to come out of the shell she had built herself. Since she had not, the talk had continued, and she remained, in the eyes of the community, a simple mouth to feed.

What he was seeing changed things, though, at least in his mind. "Quite the wild charmer," Mike repeated to himself very quietly, but no longer in as much disbelief as in wonder.

She was now retreating slowly back toward her hut, seeming to have had her fill of whatever religious experience had just taken place. He wished he could break that shell and see more of what was really inside.

He wished he could call out to her retreating figure and simply ask her about it. This glimpse, the stories of her shepherding, the fondness Gaius' children had for her all struck against the notions he and the rest of the people had gleaned of her. She was not who she seemed to be.

As she reached the door of her hut, she turned her hands slightly up to the sky to feel the rain in her palms. She paused. Then she did something that made Mike catch his falling heart in his stomach. She turned around and seemed to look right up at him. Again, Mike was not sure she even knew he was up there. The tower was dark; only the dim glow of the hearth fires within the huts saved the hill from complete darkness. Yet her eyes seemed to lock on to his and catch him, draw him in to their millions of secrets, bringing him almost to the threshold of understanding, but halting his progress at the gateway. She did not smile; she did not frown. She simply held that look for a moment, then turned and walked into her hut, leaving Mike wondering the distinction between truth and fantasy.

When morning finally broke, the rain had cleared out to reveal a sunny and relatively temperate day. The remains of the storm existed only on the damp and drying ground and in the memory in Mike's whirling head. He told himself it was from the lack of sleep, but he knew better than that. He sat out in one of the fields all but completely useless, for all of his energy was directed toward his racing thoughts. Even his eyes seemed to yield their faculty, for he did not notice Lucius until he was almost on top of him.

"Hey, you look a little tired." Lucius laughed. He seemed to be in a particularly good mood this morning and completely oblivious to Mike's strings of thought. Mike decided to humor him in the best manner he could. It was at least better than trying the alternative.

"Yeah. That rain didn't help."

Lucius laughed. "What a storm, eh?" He looked to Mike for a reaction but did not get any further response. He then sat down on the ground and faced Mike. Mike could tell he wanted to talk to him about something.

"Hey, what do you think about Aeola?" he asked.

The question snapped Mike out of his trance. He chuckled, thinking that almost the same exact question had been asked to him almost a year before, first by Julius, and then by all of his long lost colleagues.

"What?" Lucius asked. "What's so funny?"

Mike gave out another short chuckle before responding with, "Nothing." He then sobered his face. "She's a great, able-bodied, beautiful girl. Why?"

Lucius smiled. "Yeah, so she seems to be, huh? I think I'm going to go after her. She seems to want it. I've caught her eyeing me."

Mike gave Lucius a sardonic look. "Yeah, that doesn't surprise me."

Lucius did not quite know how to take such a comment. "Well, thanks. That's really flattering."

Mike could not laugh though, for a knot in his stomach impeded him. He looked his friend straight in the eye for an accurate reading. "What are your intentions, Lucius?"

The question, however ambiguous as it seemed, was understood. Even so, Lucius only shrugged before muttering, "I don't know."

Mike bit his lip. "Be careful what you do. Aeola is also young and foolish, but her father is not. He cares a lot about the welfare and future of his daughter." Mike then proceeded to give the history of his encounters with Aeola, a diversion which he had not originally planned on giving, but something that he realized needed to happen. He spoke of her seduction, and also of Julius' approval at it because Mike seemed to be a worthy object of marriage. Mike spoke of his rejection, knowing that he could not commit to such a thing, as potently alluring as it had been. He also spoke of how, in time, Julius had seen the lack of affection Mike had had for her and had not pursued the issue any further.

"Well, I guess we'll have to swear ourselves to secrecy, then," Lucius concluded. "I'm glad you warned me of that Mike. That will save me a lot of trouble." The statements were conclusions of facts that would have been understood by all. It had not taken long for Mike to realize that, for some reason, Julius had never much cared for Lucius. Mike had concluded that the only reason Lucius had been informed to come here was that Julius had not known that he had lived with the people that he did. Out of pure decency, Julius had allowed Lucius to come along since he was part of the group. But the two had never said more than a few necessary words to each other, and those were only in times of dire circumstances. In consequence, Mike had asked Lucius about it, but Lucius had simply shrugged ignorance. Mike had then casually brought it up with Julius, but

Julius had promptly changed the subject. Mike could only suspect that there had been some unpleasant encounters in the past.

Mike saw, now, however, that Lucius' mind was set on something that Mike would not be able to change. He longed to argue it, but felt inadequately empowered to do anything. He longed to keep him and her apart, for he knew that Aeola's power was great and Lucius' heart overpowered his sense, but his mouth could not get the words out. So instead of arguing the idea, Mike pitifully uttered once more, "Be careful, Lucius, please."

Lucius slapped him on the back and ran off, leaving Mike continuing to sit in the field, mindlessly caressing the blades of grain, hoping that the present blue skies continued at least through harvest.

Julius returned later that day during suppertime. Mike was sitting with a few others, discussing the logistics of the reaping that would begin in three days, when he heard a boy up on the tower exclaim, "He's back! Julius is back!"

Mike rose up from his spot and walked the short distance out to the trail, where a promontory offered a perfect welcoming spot for arrivals. Julius approached with his party, marching up at the edge of the eastern field. Mike had not known what to expect from this second recovery mission, but was quite surprised to see that the party was not much, if any bigger than the one that had left. As Julius ascended and caught sight of Mike, however, he hailed him with a grand smile. He, at least, seemed happy with the results.

"Julius," Mike said as Julius approached him and gave him a hearty embrace. "Good to see you back. You're just in time for supper."

"Perfect," Julius said. "That was what I was hoping for."

The party approached the table, and Mike turned to Julius. "How..." A sudden remembrance of the situation between Julius' daughter and Lucius came upon Mike, and he faltered in his sentence. In consternation, Mike quickly scanned the table, and, just as he had expected, Lucius and Aeola were seated right next to each other, involved in a spirited conversation.

"Huh?" Julius inquired.

Mike winced at the situation, but tried to do nothing more. Julius had not seemed to notice what Mike had. Mike forced his focus back on his question to keep Julius ignorant. "How did your trip go?"

"It went well," Julius reported. Mike steered Julius over to where he had been sitting, away from the two. "We were only able to summon one man, but I promise he will be a great asset to our community." Julius directed Mike's attention across the table, and, for the first time, Mike noticed a face that he had not seen in a great while.

"Marcus," Mike stated almost in disbelief. He forced a smile through the surprise. Out of anybody, Mike had expected Marcus the least, for he had rejected the notion of joining them twice already. Mike reached over and grabbed his hand in greeting. Marcus smiled back warmly. "It's great to have you here in Newhaven. Where are your father and your flock?"

Marcus resumed a straight face. "My sheep will be coming in a few days. A few of Julius' men offered to linger behind and drive them. As for my father, well he is dead now. He caught a fever about a month ago and did not survive too much longer."

Mike expressed his apologies.

Marcus, however, shrugged. "He was not going to make it too much longer anyway."

"Well, we're glad to have you here. I'm sorry we won't have a hut for you for a little bit, though. We are just getting into harvest and need all the manpower we can get."

"That's fine," Julius assured. "Marcus has accepted my offer of hospitality and will stay in my hut. He is like a son to me anyway." Mike looked over at Marcus, who smiled and gave his nod of approval toward Julius. Mike let the matter rest, glad that the problem was solved so directly.

"So Mike, how have things been going here?" Julius then asked.

"Oh really well," Mike responded quickly, thinking all too much about his recent conversation with Lucius.

"That tower seems to work pretty well. That boy saw me coming from a long way off."

"Yeah." Mike was relieved that there was something else to talk about. "I was up there last night in the rain."

Julius stole a bite of food. "Quite the storm, that was. Luckily, we were staying at Marcus' hut. I can only imagine your experience though. I'll bet you were wet, miserable, and bored out of your mind. Don't tell me you saw anything interesting out on a night like that. No lovers with their nightly rambles."

Mike looked sharply up at Julius' face. Julius was suppressing laughter, however, and Mike let out a sort of half laugh of his own. "No, none of that," he confirmed. Then, as an afterthought he added, "I did, however, see one strange occurrence." Mike then related his distant encounter with Diana—how she had seemed to view the night in a different manner.

"She is a strange occurrence, I'll tell you that," Julius said after Mike had concluded. "I'm beginning to wonder if something's wrong with her."

Mike, however, slowly, solidly shook his head. "I'm more prone to think there's something about her that none of us know or understand. She's different no doubt, but there's something behind that. Something intriguing." Mike was finding a slight defensive tone in his manner of speech. It was as much a surprise to him as it seemed to be to his listener.

"Mike, you have feelings for this girl?" Julius said at last, letting out a few short, surprised chuckles.

Mike furrowed his eyebrows, "No, I just..." but his voice trailed off. He did not know the direction of his words, and he suddenly tensed up. Julius' comment seemed to unearth a myriad of convoluted feelings of his own. Mike gulped and temporarily tried to recover his senses, for they had suddenly, involuntarily been racked. Julius' eyes pricked at him for his response. In a slightly pitiful, quieter tone, Mike uttered, "I'm just curious."

Several listeners had accumulated in the last few seconds, and now an eruption of laughter echoed around him. The blacksmith Cai gave out his bellowing laugh while Mike bit his lip and chuckled nervously. "Ah, Mike," he heard a voice cry out, "you do have emotions!" Mike tried to play it off the best he could, but the moment that he was finally able to get away from the ongoing comments for the rest of the meal was quite the welcome one.

As he walked back to his hut in the twilight and laid down on his bed, he shook it all off as sport, a nice entertaining conversation he had sprouted at the dinner table. But at the same time, he could not get the thought out of his head. *Why does she strike me in a way that she does nobody else? Do I have feelings for her, or am I just more sensitive to looking to others' happiness?* Such a pursuit had filled his life ever since spring had broken. It was the only thing that had kept him going in this despicable state of limbo. The establishment of this community had not only helped everyone else, but had helped him as well, because the moments of depression and despair, though they still had their appearances, did not come so readily. Mike's thoughts, like a mad carousel, reverted back again on Diana. *Do I feel it, as part of my duty, to leave the ninety-nine to go bring home the lost sheep, or would that not have made a difference in my curiosity toward her anyway?*

Sheep. Diana often watched the sheep at night. Mike found himself wide awake in the darkness and found himself dressing and heading out to the pasture. Without hardly thinking about the illogic of what he was doing, he was heading down the trail that suddenly seemed foreign. That did not seem to matter to his legs. The stars shone especially vibrant tonight, and Mike looked up at them in conjunction with looking out on the fields. He took special notice of every calm silent scene around him, everywhere but ahead of him, where his body was involuntarily leading him.

Mike cleared the trees and caught sight of the flock. His eyes scanned the scene before being drawn like a magnet to the rock off to his left, where, perched in the moonlight, she sat, dressed in a long, soft, blue toga with her hair let down around her cheeks, staring out on the still figures of the animals sleeping, her thoughts seeming involved either in nothing or in a world of things. Mike paused in his steps, realizing for the first time what he was doing, realizing for the first time that he had no idea what he was doing. All commands of his logical mind seemed to have stayed in his hut, asleep. Something else had driven him here.

All at once, she turned her head sharply and caught him standing there, staring at her. The alarm in her face lingered a moment before giving away to her usual, stern front. Mike stood transfixed at the nature of her face, however, for she had been caught off guard. In that moment, he had, again, caught the same glimpse of the same world of things with which she had teased him that rainy night at the tower. They were gone in a flash, covered with her recovery of presence, causing Mike to give out a silent, inner groan of frustration.

"What are you doing here?" she asked.

"I couldn't sleep," Mike answered. "I figured sitting out here counting sheep would help me out." Mike smiled, but, of course, Diana did not catch his humor.

"Everything is fine here," she said after a moment, but as he slowly approached her and sat down on the grass beside her, she did not usher further dispute. Mike joined her in staring off into the night and the two did not say anything else for a great long while. She seemed content to stay silent, and Mike was too conscious of the nervous fluttering in his stomach to set his mind on anything else. Indeed, he concluded that he was feeling something for this girl. He would not call it love; he did not think it was that, but simply a static attraction that drew him into her presence.

Mike could not help but remember this was the same pasture where Aeola had come on to him. They had been alone just as he and Diana were now. Everything seemed to wear a different color this time, though he could not deny that it held the same vivacity.

"I will disappoint you if you are expecting any sort of conversation," she finally uttered, breaking the long uninterrupted silence and returning Mike to the moment.

Mike told her shortly but casually that he did not expect anything of the sort and returned to his thoughts. She refused to talk, though a world must have been occurring in her mind. *She notices the same energy I do,* he assured himself. *Why else would she vocally try to fight it?* Mike wanted study the situation logically, but he was spending all of his energy floundering in the sea of his emotions.

He found himself wondering what else she was thinking and of the possibility that she held the same position on the matter between them that he did. His thoughts struggled to break free from him and join his swirling feelings. Mike wrestled them down. *Most people would show a little bit more evidence of it, but I'm not sure that Diana would. She doesn't expose anything.* There must have been some wall, some dam, bottling it up. Mike was prone to think it was something in him, that it was something in everyone in Newhaven, of which he was the unfortunate archetype.

He wondered what it could have been. Many of the townspeople had seen her as nothing more than a recluse, a gray canvas with no defining shape, but he was sure that the idea was a falsehood. Her night dance in the rain had proved that. *Could it simply be the experiences she has gone through? Does she keep quiet only because she feels that nobody can sympathize with her?* She had not been the only one to go through such atrocities. Mike desperately wanted to ask her about it, to find out about her life, to help her in it. *I cannot simply ask, though. That would do more harm than good.* While his mind raced like a derby, his mouth, his body all sat in stalemate for many long moments.

They passed, however, and next thing Mike knew, he was opening his mouth and reinitiating conversation. Even as he did so, he wondered what he was doing, for the action was involuntary. The emblem, which still faithfully accompanied him, gave him a warm reassurance about it, though, and so he let the words fly according to their will.

"You know, I'm not from here either," he started. She looked over at him, surprised either in his break of the silence or in the words he spoke. He continued. "I was not originally part of this world." She did not speak, but made eye contact by means of those beautiful dark lenses that had first captured him, those lenses that now commanded him to continue. Mike obeyed. "I guess that's why I look more like our enemies than our friends, but it is only by coincidence. I hope you notice that my Latin is almost perfect."

"I've noticed," she stated. "You speak like an educated citizen of the Forum."

Mike nodded. "I was educated by the best. His name was Abe."

"Like the prophet Abraham?"

"Yeah. Like the prophet Abraham. He and I were sent on a special mission up here to see if we could help restore order to society. There had been talk of invasion, and as you know, Rome is not doing so well itself. Abe, however, was betrayed by another member of the party and died. The betrayer ran off, and I have not seen him for almost a full year."

Mike paused, shook his head, and laughed in spite of his world. "You see, I'm stuck here, just like you. I don't belong here, just like you. I had everything, just like you, and it was all taken away from me."

Diana remained silent for a time. She looked out on the pasture, where everything was serene. The near full moon shone down on it, making it almost light enough to see the depth of green in the grass. The white wool of the sheep contrasted with it and made the scene quite picturesque. Mike, too, looked out on it, but waited in grand anticipation for Diana's response, if there was to be any.

"I did not know." She silently spoke finally. "Where are you from?"

Mike bit his lip and decided, for the first time, to tell the truth. "I'm from a far off land. I doubt you have ever heard of it."

Diana looked over at him to question his doubt, but when he mouthed the word "America," a slight smile escaped her as if her pride had been mildly bruised.

"It's far beyond the borders of the Empire, but from my land's very beginning, we have felt of its influence. Rome is so culturally important to us that we are inseparably tied to all of its best interests."

"So how did you come here, then?"

Mike looked over at her. He had caught her interest. "Do you believe in a higher power, Diana?"

"I believe in the religion of the state."

Mike nodded. "So do I. That higher power has brought me here through this." Mike showed her the emblem which he still held in his pocket. "Now whether he knew that I would be brought here only to see my friend die and my other supposed friend betray me, I don't know."

Diana stared at the emblem for a moment, without revealing thoughts of either wonder or skepticism. Mike watched her as he held it out. He watched her as she silently reached out and touched the emblem. It continued to glow warm at her touch. Nothing about it seemed strange or extraordinary to her. Her mind rather seemed to be elsewhere.

"I don't know, either," she agreed after a moment, but said nothing more. Mike was left wondering what exactly she meant by it, or if she meant anything at all.

The silence resumed, leaving Mike back to his thoughts, which were still quite active, though no longer frenzied. Regardless of the fact that none of his questions had been satisfied, Mike knew that he had made progress with Diana. Amidst stealing glances at her as she looked out on the night, Mike noted that she seemed a little less tense. There seemed less of a storm in her eyes. *That's good,* Mike told himself, *though right now I don't know how.* Mike sat there a while longer, and suddenly, like a wall of bricks, sleepiness hit him. He wanted to remain there longer to see if conversation would resume, but it did not show any hint, and he could no longer keep his eyes open. He got up, telling Diana that he was going to head out if that was fine with her. She nodded, and, as he walked away, he heard her call out, "Mike." He turned around. It was the first time she had ever addressed him by his name. She was staring him down with those captivating eyes. "Thanks for telling me that." Mike nodded and turned around, only realizing as he ascended the dark trail to his hut what those words actually meant.

Chapter 26

The sun spoke of a late summer afternoon. Its rays still boasted the warm glow that drew up sweat from the community members' faces as they slashed away, but the rays had seemed to slowly turn from the whiteness of the solstice toward the light goldenness of the equinox. Indeed, the land in whole seemed to be yielding gold on a day such as this. The yellow rays touched the grain like Midas, and in joy, the remaining blades shimmered as they danced in the breeze, showing off their rich, lush heads. The trees, too were succumbing to the color, though it only rimmed their otherwise still very green leaves. It was only a whisper of what would bloom in full later.

Certainly, Newhaven had pursued its harvest as such a precious commodity. Sickles dove in and came back up for air amidst the flying dust, only to dive back in again with the same vigor. The gods controlling these creatures smiled as they did so, even after a month of such action, for each dive yielded more food to lay up in store at the end of the harvest. They remained renewed in zest, having broken out of the midsummer dip of passive effort. The days were shorter and the nights were cooler, and summer soon would be no more, but its memory was happily lived in the grain falling before its cultivators.

Mike gripped his sickle tightly as he leaned into his work. With a great sweep of his tool, an extension of his hand, he felt the blades resist then give in to the sharp edge. They fell like a defeated enemy before him, and he triumphed in his victory while repeating the motion for another front. A great sea still stretched before him, but Mike did not consider it, or the work and the sweat and the scrapes and the aches that would still be involved with it. He simply took joy in what he was accomplishing at the moment, what had already been done. He had been working since light had first touched the sky, and the mass that had stared him down this morning was lying motionless under his feet and behind him, having danced its last dance in the wind. Its fall was noble, though, for it would soon be realized for its full, life giving potential. He smiled once again as he thought of it.

Perhaps part of that smile arose from the memories the actions and the sights and the sounds and the feelings of harvesting brought back to him. Mike could not help but recall last year when he found himself doing the exact same thing. He had been in The Haven then. He smiled mostly at himself and the scared, inexperienced pawn he had been. *My*, he thought, losing his smile, *how things were different back then—how much difference one year of experiences has made.*

Abe had been with him then. Mike chuckled a sort of nostalgic chuckle. Abe had been here along with all of his strange idiosyncrasies. Mike recalled Abe with his matter-of-fact communication. He seemed to never have learned how to express emotion. Mike recalled the intense intellectual conversations in which Abe had jumped with anyone who dared jump with him. He recalled Abe animatedly speaking to Arwulf of Celtic traditions while on the road, or Abe and Magnus discussing the ideals of Rome. Both Abe and Magnus were dead now, just like the ideals of Rome.

And Arwulf. Arwulf and Virgil. Mike recalled how much fun he and the two had had while harvesting last year. They had been the only ones to have seen it as a time to enjoy each others' company. They had interrupted the atmosphere with wrestling matches ending up in gut-wrenching laughter. They had found themselves in water fights with their skins, much to the annoyance of the drones around them. Mike laughed again at all the good memories they had created.

But it was a shallow laugh that, even then, had not existed for very long. They had been overshadowed by the darker moments—the moments when Virgil seemed drawn away from Mike and Abe. Mike could not but help recall the moment up on the moor above The Haven with Virgil, the moment Mike realized there was no longer any more room for laughter and games. Mike recalled the fear. He recalled not only the fear of the Saxons, or the fear of his task, but the fear of realizing Arwulf had to go and the fear that he would not go without Mike's intervention.

Mike now rejoiced in the obsolete nature of those fears. For all he knew, the positions of the sources of those fears were unknown and far off. Arwulf and Virgil were gone, and he had not caught sight of the Saxons since they had built the tower over a month ago. The time would again come when he would have to face them, but it would not be today. Today he could wash away the thoughts of death and focus on his life instead. After all that Mike had lost, he retained that one possession, and, for the moment, that was good enough for him.

Mike wiped the sweat of his brow off with his forearm and continued thrashing. Although he was physically tired, his will was not. He had to continually remind himself to acquiesce to his muscles, for they were exhausted and falling behind—a task which was difficult, for the strain of work helped cleanse his mind. Such cleansing was hard to give up, even when his body cried out for it. It flushed out any old, depressing thoughts that had been lodged in his consciousness in the past year and allowed it to start afresh, ready for whatever mysteries lie ahead.

There would be pains, no doubt. There would always be pains. But there would also be joys as well. Whatever was to come, Mike was determined to face it without looking back; he was determined to leave this dark year behind him forever.

"Mike," he heard Lucius call out. Mike looked up to see him running over with a great smile on his face. "Mike," he called out again.

"Hey, Lucius."

Lucius approached him, breathing hard. "How're you doing?"

"Tired," Mike said, again wiping the sweat, which relentlessly kept returning. And as he said that, the fatigue hit him all at once, as if his muscles finally beat out his mind. "I think I'm about done for the day."

"Yeah. I know the feeling." Mike could tell that something was brewing in Lucius' head. He wasted no more time in coming out with it. "Hey, back in the time that I worked at Sergius', we had a big celebration with music and dancing and wine at the autumn equinox to celebrate the harvest. I have asked around, and people around here would like to have one. Of course, we don't have any wine, unfortunately, but I have been teaching a few of the others to play instruments and we can provide music and dancing and food. What do you think?"

Mike was glad that there could be no wine. Glimpses of the past crept into his consciousness and almost made him shiver. "Yeah, that sounds fine. When is the equinox?"

"Five days."

"That soon, huh?"

"Yeah, but there doesn't need to be much preparation. Just a little more food preparation than usual."

"Okay. Well, it looks like that will be about the end of reaping. Do you think that we can finish off these fields by then?"

Lucius nodded. "Yeah. I'll tell them that you said if we finish reaping in the next four days, we can celebrate."

Mike smiled. "Yeah. Tell them I said that."

Lucius slapped him on the back and ran off, leaving Mike to chuckle at the lightness with which he ran. Mike still worried about that lightness, though, for he knew from whence it sprung. Whatever directly passed between him and Aeola was very well hidden, for Mike was not even aware of its nature, but something was definitely happening, something more than friendly conversation at the supper table. Its evidence revealed itself in the elevated mood that Lucius, and Aeola for that matter, carried. Mike wondered how long they would be able to hold it in.

Julius had been back a week and still seemed oblivious to the situation. He still seemed preoccupied with the arrival of Marcus, who looked to be quite the close friend. The two were always together, despite the distinct age difference. Mike figured that Marcus was closer to his own age—maybe a few years younger—but he and Julius associated with each other as counterparts.

Mike, in fact, ran into the two as he ascended the hill. They, too, were coming back from the field, and although they both looked exhausted, Julius a bit more so than Marcus, they were both in a jovial mood.

"Mike. How are you?" Julius asked him.

"Good. How are you two?"

"Pretty good," Marcus said. "Looking forward to the end of harvest, though, when I can get my own hut." At this, he looked over at Julius and smiled deviously.

Mike noted the exchange with humor. "Why, you tired of Julius' company?"

"You could say that," Marcus answered. He and Julius chuckled.

"The feeling's mutual," Julius added. "I'm looking forward to not having to share my hut anymore." The two then erupted in laughter.

Mike gave a smile akin to a kid left out of the game. Marcus took note of it and slapped Mike heartily on the back

"Don't worry," he assured, "You'll be in on it soon enough, Mike."

"Okay," Mike conceded. They had reached the top of the hill, and the two parted from him, continuing to snigger. "I'll see you later."

Mike walked back toward his hut, which brought him past the commons. There, he saw the women laying out a few of the dishes. He could not help but notice that Diana was with them. He allowed himself the liberty of an extra glance at both her and the silent way in which she went about her work. As he continued on, he continued finding himself looking back. For the first time, he did not deny that each encounter he had had like this had yielded the same result. Each time, it had brightened his day just a little more. Each time, he imagined her as if she had a smile on her face—that same smile he had seen that night on the tower, for that smile had been a window to her hidden, paradisiacal world. Alas, it had stayed hidden since then; she had not again ushered that smile in his presence.

"Something interesting, Mike?" Cai said with a wry smile as Mike walked past his hut. Cai was sitting in his usual place just outside his doorway.

Mike turned back and looked over at him, his consciousness crash landing back to the ground of Newhaven beneath him. "Huh?"

"You keep turning back. I don't know what you could possibly be looking at, since nothing back there is different."

"Ah, yeah, it was nothing," Mike assured.

Cai did not let it go. "That's an awful lot of effort to be making over nothing." Cai straightened himself up on his chair as his smile grew. "You don't have to hide anything from me. I'm too old. I've seen it way too much to let it slip past me. Have you talked to her?"

"Huh?" Mike uttered again, finding himself suddenly revealed. Cai seemed to be able to see right through him. It was quite the difference, since most of the people here were too caught up in reverie to look beneath his skin. Cai was different. He saw Mike as a person with all the weaknesses that came along with it.

"Diana. You've had your eye on her for a while now, whether you've known it or not. Have you talked to her?"

Mike conceded at this point, deciding that it was fruitless to try and hide anything and also deciding that Cai was an honorable enough person in whom to confide. "She's a difficult one to converse with," he confessed. "I've had one or two opportunities, but neither of them opened her up." Mike paused and focused in on her again. "She strikes me, though." He turned to face Cai. "What do you think?"

"Well, I don't want to make any comments because I want to leave her all to you."

Mike rolled his eyes as Cai let out one of his bellows.

"No, but really," he started, this time with a straight face. "Keep your course—talking, that is—though staring is not necessarily a bad thing. Just makes 'em figure it out faster."

"You think she'll eventually open up?"

"Who knows how long it will take with her, but yes. She'll open up, especially when she sees who you are."

Mike took the advice in for a moment, then, nodding his head, thanked Cai and started moving on.

Cai shrugged. "We need more of that around here anyway."

Mike smiled and turned around to verify that Cai was joking, but, to his surprise, he saw that Cai was serious. "Really," he explained, "especially with you. The success of a community can be measured by its output—in people that is, not just in crops. We need to see new marriages and families in this community, especially from our leaders. It'll give us the sense of hope for the future that we need."

Mike stared at him a moment, then retreated, thrown into a flood of thoughts.

To no one's dismay, the end of the week brought, with lightning speed, the evening of the festival.

Ever since Mike gave Lucius his approval, the word of the event spread like wildfire. By that evening, everybody knew and anticipated it with great earnestness. The days following were filled with a greater vigor in harvesting, and the laughs resounded in the fields more predominantly. The stench of toil of Newhaven was suddenly sweetened by a reawakened energy, an energy that had seemed to be dormant for as long as Mike had known these people. Mike had walked through the village that night to find more people out of doors, with more association going on than was usual. He had smiled. *This is going to be good.*

The day of the festival had been filled with cooking, tidying, and setting up for the grand events that were to take place that night. Mike busied himself with helping with the skinning and tanning of skins of a few animals that some of his men had hunted earlier in the week. He then helped with the preparation of a boar that they had hunted down so it could be cooked for the feast. In the background, Lucius and a few others could be heard playing their instruments, warming up for the night's festivities.

And the rest of the people, in between all of their respective duties, could be found running around, joking, laughing at each other, bringing to life any festive spirit that their souls had hidden deep within. The former slave girls were especially entertaining to watch. As they washed garments outside their hut, they could be seen slapping each other with wet clothing, fighting jovially with each other, and waving and flirting at all the men that walked past, young or old, single or married. Mike caught sight at one moment, when they lured a boy of about twelve over to them. He innocently did so and found himself caught in their traps. One of them grabbed him, forced him onto her lap, hugged him, and kissed him on the cheek, to the laughter of all the others. The boy stumbled to get away as fast as possible, and Mike could not help but laugh as well.

It was all stimulating to see. Any sort of quiet desperation the people held in their eyes on usual days seemed temporarily snuffed out. They sat down to eat, and the hilltop was filled with the sonorous chaos of animated conversation. For the first time in a great while, they were able to put a lock on the closets of their minds that held their monsters. The key was cast aside, out of sight, and readily forgotten for the moment. The people's full awareness directed itself to the plentiful food on the table and good company all around. The toil of life could be recovered in the morning.

And the feeling was addictive. Mike found himself digging with relish into the freshness of the various vegetables from the garden and the juicy meatiness of the pork in between exchanges of conversation with those around him. Later, Mike would not be able to recall the subjects of the conversation, for he hardly knew of what they talked even at the moment. Such a thing really did not matter, though, for the subject matter, whatever it was, was delightfully trivial for a change.

Mike tore into a large piece of pork and heard Cai's bellow rise up above everything else from somewhere down the table. He remembered the man's advice to him and wondered if Diana was somewhere amid this beautiful din. Mike took a moment to look down the table to see whether he could spot her. He could not, but that did not mean that she was not here. People were getting up and moving around every few moments, making the whole party very fluid, even while everyone ate. Mike shrugged, then took a hunk of dark, heavy bread out of the middle of the table and sank his teeth into it.

The games and dancing materialized soon after that. As soon as Lucius and his group of musicians came out and started up the music, people dropped their meals and formed a circle. The table was instantly cleared of all but a few of the people, including Mike, who sat back and watched as the rest started moving to the music. Mike did not linger in his spot long, however, for the girl called Constantia drew him up and guided him over to the moving circle, giggling as she did it. Mike looked back at Julius, who was still sitting at the table, and shrugged. Julius smiled and nodded a temporary farewell to him.

The dancing continued on through dusk, retaining the same bounce that it initially held. It caused Mike to recall the dancing that had occurred so long ago at the wedding in the Realm. This did not have the same intensity or grandeur. The music was simpler as well as the dancing. These people could not move like the elves did, but the spirit was the same, and after each song, the multitude turned, faced the musicians and applauded them heartily.

After a while, Mike slipped away to go see what some of the others were doing, for only a portion of the town was in the circle. At the dinner table, Mike found a few of the older men such as Cai, Dylan, and Julius, lounging around, involved in some sort of conversation. Many of the older women were doing the same thing, clucking like hens in various groups near different huts. Another group off to the side revealed a few of the younger teens gathered in a circle. At various times, the circle would let out a cheer, and Mike assumed it was some sort of game of chance. At the edge of the hill, Mike could hear the laughter of children down below and could see figures running out amidst the conquered fields. Mike looked up at the tower to see that a few of the women were silently keeping watch, not only on the horizon, but on the children as well. Somewhere out there, there may have been an enemy who thirsted for their blood and subjugation, but they were far off tonight. There was nothing to worry about tonight.

Again, Mike's mind moved toward Cai's advice as he wandered the complex. In all of his wanderings, he realized he had still not caught sight of Diana. Mike moved toward the outer edge of the complex where Diana's hut was located. In the background, Mike could hear the music relentlessly continuing, contrasting deeply with the silence of his vicinity. All the light from the candles over in the commons was a sharp disparity when compared with the darkness of such an area. There was, however, a candle lighting Diana's hut, and so Mike approached.

He clapped outside the doorway to announce his presence, and when no verbal indication of disapproval resounded, he walked in. There, amidst the dancing orange light produced by the flickering candle on the hearth, Mike found Diana lying down with her eyes open, staring up at the thatch roof. She lay still, other than the occasional blink of her eyes. On her face she wore the same blank look she always had—not of happiness or despair, but of neutral grayness. Mike stood there a moment witnessing the scene without catching sight of reaction. After a moment, however, she did turn her head and look at him.

"Mike," she stated. "What can I do for you?"

For the first time, Mike felt exposed, for he had come here not really wanting anything other than to see her. He silently cursed himself as an idiot, not having even come up with a superficial reason to hide his true intentions. All he could really do was shrug.

"I was wondering where you were," he found himself uttering. "I didn't see you outside."

Diana did not answer for a moment, but resumed staring up at the roof. Mike looked at her quizzically. Only after he was left wondering if he was being intentionally ignored did she say, "Did you expect me out there?"

Mike did not say anything. She continued. "I assumed that you knew me well enough to figure the alternative out on your own." Her stare did not break even after she finished.

I don't know you at all, Mike thought to himself, but he did not voice it. Instead, he stood there silent, feeling incredibly exposed and awkward. He wanted to do what Cai had advised. He wanted to talk to her but realized that he was failing miserably at it here, in the midst of Diana's lair. He wanted to get her out of her element, out in the open. Mike found himself saying. "Well it's a really beautiful night. Will you at least come out for a walk?"

Mike could have slapped himself in the face. He wished that he had thought about his words before they came out. He was about ready to retreat before her piercing stare, which had resumed upon him, but she silently consented, getting up and putting on her sandals. Instead of retreating, Mike silently watched her, in mild surprise as well as mild trepidation at what would unfold in the next hour or so.

The night seemed, indeed, to be celebrating with the rest of the town, whose sounds of music and laughter seemed to fall gently behind them as they commenced walking. The stars were all laid out in their proper order, shining out brightly and illuminating the shadow of the majority of the moon, for it only shone a slight sliver tonight. The night blew a mild breeze which delighted Mike's skin where his leather vest and leggings left him exposed. Slowly, the sounds of the night took over, replacing the fading din behind them. The crickets rapidly chirped, singing out their own celebration of the beauty of the night. Off in the distance, Mike could hear the hooting of an owl.

The two wandered in to the very midst of this gentle orchestra, though neither of them made any effort to disrupt it with words. That was fine with Mike for the moment, for any time he had struck up conversation with Diana, it had ended up in discord. Beside that fact, he noted that Diana's expression was peaceful at the moment, and that gave him a grand reassurance that she did not expect anything different from him anyway.

The two reached the bottom of the hill, crossed the stream, and walked out into the fields. Diana reached out and felt the grass brush off of her hands. Mike watched her. He wanted now to say something, feeling, all at once, the desire to better know this figure before him. He mentioned the first thing that came to his mind.

"The weather's been good to us all year. We've gotten a plentiful harvest."

Diana nodded and seemed to have nothing to say in response. Mike fought for something else.

"You looked deep in thought when I entered your hut," he mentioned. "What were you thinking about?"

Diana shrugged and continued walking. She was about a step ahead of him and so he could not see the expression on her face. He instantly regretted having tried bringing that question to the surface, and wished he had tried for something else more trivial. This was a tough battle that he was fighting. He fell back and waited for the next thing to come to mind. When he did, he checked it to verify that it was a better idea than the last attempt at conversation. When it seemed to pass his inspection, it came out of his mouth.

"Thanks for all you do for the community Diana, for helping out with the sheep and with the meals. You produce and do not ask for anything back in return."

She looked over at him. "These people don't have anything to give back." Then, after a moment, she softened her tone and added, "I appreciate your gratitude."

"Well, it is well deserved. Gaius is more than thankful of your service, of staying up all night with those animals. He said he's seen traces of wolves in the area." Mike could not help but catch a slight prideful smirk on Diana's face, a smirk which almost seemed to verify the rumor. Mike took a moment to stare in awe at this figure, who now walked beside him. Gaius had not mentioned that any sheep had been lost. Surely she had something else yet unfathomed underneath her skin.

"What do you like most about tending the sheep?" Mike asked.

Diana pursed her lips before evenly stating, "I like being alone, being able to meditate and dream away from everybody else. I cannot get that anymore anywhere else, even in my hut."

Mike thought at first that this was a direct reference to his disturbance of her tonight, but realized soon enough from her expression that the comment was directed to a different time and place than the present. He exhaled calmly, and felt like he understood her better than ever.

"I'm sorry that we can't give you the life you once had. We've given you what we could. And the company may not be of Roman citizenry, but they are good people."

Diana gave another wry smirk at this. Mike decided to ignore it.

"The people. The people celebrate, but for what? Their lives are doomed. One day it'll catch up to them just like it has to me."

Mike knew all of that, better than she would have thought, better than anyone in this world would have thought. Still, he found himself shaking his head. "Yeah, but you're still alive to make the best of what you have left. That's what those people are doing up there," Mike pointed back up to the hilltop, "that's what I've done. That's what I want for you."

Mike realized that may have come out wrong. Diana looked at him queerly and finally seemed to say what had been on her mind the whole night. "I am not going to give you what you want of me, Mike, no matter what you do or say to try and get it. You are a respectable man, much more respectable than I've met in a long time, and I appreciate the means which you take to get what you want, but that does not change my decision. I've had enough of that already."

Mike was confused at first, but understanding came to him soon enough to realize that there was a big misunderstanding. "That's not at all my intention," he defended indignantly. He reached out and took hold of her shoulders so he could look her in the eye. She tensed up instantly and wore a look of shock, almost fear, before she retaliated and swatted Mike's hands off her shoulders. Mike realized his forcefulness and backed off, but noticed that she continued facing him directly. "My intentions are pure," he continued. "I simply want to see you happy, from one human being to another, and I cannot help but notice that you are not."

"Forgive my frankness," she maintained, "but you are a man, just like the rest of them, and I find the bounds of your words a little bit hard to believe."

Mike about gave up in defeat. "What will you have me do, then, to change that?"

Despite Mike's frustration, Diana's defenses seemed to be breaking down. Her features were slowly, slightly softening. Still, she stared him down hard, trying to unsaddle him. Mike's stern look held its position, and the two succumbed to try to burn holes through the other with their eyes. Mike seemed, for the first time, to hold the upper ground on the battle that they had raged between each other ever since the beginning and continued rejuvenated in his foray. In that brief moment, he could tell that she was losing her footholds. He could not help but relish in the moment, for she could finally know how he had felt in trying to read her.

Then she entreated, with disarmed finality, "Swear to never touch me, ever again."

Mike conceded with palms upturned. "Fine with me. You have my word." It was a fair enough proposal which she stamped with a slight, broken nod of the head. The two resumed walking in silence for a bit longer, but because of their treaty, there did not seem to be as much discomfort. Certainly, Mike was not as frustrated with the situation as he had been before. He strained to think of what had changed, since he had not seemed to make any progress toward discovering this demoness, but the feeling may have lain in the more settled perception she now held toward him.

Light conversation resumed, and this time, she was the perpetrator. She asked him of life in America, and he explained it the best he could so that she could understand. He told her how life was much different, much more advanced, much akin to Rome. He spoke of indoor plumbing, of the various tools they had to make work more efficient and give them more leisure time. He spoke of the widespread educational system, how everyone was taught to read and write. She then asked what his vernacular language sounded like and when he spoke a few English phrases to her, she stated, "It's a beautiful language—there're lots of similarities to Latin. I wouldn't mind learning it someday." Mike promised to teach her some, to which she agreed.

Overall, Mike was amazed at the transformation that gradually took place. He had never heard her speak so much. She was quite the pleasurable conversationalist when she let her guard down, and a few smiles even escaped from her when she least expected it. Mike watched her at these moments, smiling himself, but more at the delight of the beauty of her upturned features than at the subject at hand. It was an involuntary reaction, for the sight filled his soul with a whiteness that mirrored the summer moonlight.

Mike still could not get her to talk about anything in her past—every time he steered their words toward her villa and the life that had existed there, she steered them away—but that was okay for now. Cai had said that would happen.

One day, Mike hoped, it would be different.

As they turned back toward Newhaven, it was hard for Mike to keep his thoughts harnessed, for they struggled again to run away from him. He kept telling himself that he was glimpsing the delightful girl he had always innately known her to be, and with that, he felt strong natural urges to want to hold her close. During their conversation, he kept reminding himself how beautiful she was, and each time he did, it was much to his dismay. He almost wished he had not promised what he had. But there was no possible way to take such a thing back, and there had been no other way around it at the time. Though he had worn out her defenses, he now realized that she had still effectively put him in checkmate, and for now, she was the one in control. She had confined him to his honor, and he had no doubt that that was the way it was to remain. In an effort to win Diana's friendship, he had lost out on any possibility for anything else. And so it was, he told himself—they would remain friends.

As the two made their way back, crossed the stream, and started heading up the hill, they heard a rustle in the bushes upstream from them. Mike silently motioned for Diana to crouch down in the bushes, then followed her. He directed and strained his eyes in the direction of the disturbance and was surprised to see Lucius standing in the dark on a grassy bank. Approaching him about ten meters away was another figure, and until she spoke up, Mike could not make out who it was.

"Lucius," the voice stated breathlessly. It belonged to Aeola.

Mike was not sure if Lucius had heard or seen them coming. He had seemed intent on watching Aeola's approach, and since the path up to

Newhaven had since become well packed, hard earth, any sound he and Diana might have made would have been drowned out by the rushing of the stream. Mike was curious with dread to see what would unfold. Diana did not object and continued crouching down beside him to watch.

"Lucius," Aeola stated again and ran to his arms. The two embraced for a moment before she pulled away. "I cannot stay long. My father will get suspicious. He thinks I have come down to take a quick bathe."

"And what a fine idea you had there," Lucius responded in unfitting wryness. "You don't have to be a liar."

"You don't understand," she stated. "He intends for me to become Marcus'. That is the main reason why he was so intent on going back for other families. That is why he was so eager to lodge Marcus in our hut."

Lucius now pulled fully away, beyond the reach of Aeola's grasp. "Mongrel! Has he been with you?"

Mike shifted to find a comfortable position and strained his ears to catch everything that was being said, for he could not believe what he was hearing.

"I have held him off for about as long as I could. I cannot do it much longer, though. My father is intent on his purposes. If he were to find me here with you, I would be beaten and you, I don't know what he'd try to do to you."

Aeola approached him again and wrapped his lips up in another kiss, much as she had done with Mike. Lucius, however, accepted it with zeal and lingered on a moment before again pulling away from her and saying, "Your father would be sorry to try to do anything to prevent you and me from being here tonight. And as for Marcus..." Lucius thought a moment before he chose his next words, "... I'll have to figure out what to do with him. Believe me, though, Love, you won't have to worry about it too much longer."

After that, the two came together a third time and did not separate so readily. No more words were spoken. In the midst of Mike's horror, he heard Diana's voice whisper, "I'd rather not witness any more of this."

Mike agreed. The two stood up and stole away as quietly as they could up the trail. Lucius and Aeola did so seem to notice. If not, they were too lost in each other's presence to care. Mike and Diana did not say anything more as they parted ways in the reawakened darkness of the village and retired to their separate huts.

Chapter 27

Mike awoke to the sounds of loud voices in the night. They were not in direct proximity to his hut, and so he could not make out quite what they were saying, but they were close enough for Mike to be able to note the desperation in one of the parties. Mike threw on a tunic and his sandals, grabbed his sword, and walked outside to see what was unfolding. The voices were coming from the tower. Upon tuning his ears, he deciphered that the woman who was keeping watch on top of the tower was speaking to someone below.

As Mike approached, he saw that the person down below was actually a pair of persons, Julius and Marcus. All at once, the pieces of the puzzle came together and Mike knew exactly what was going on. *Oh no,* he blurted to himself. He approached the two men in greater haste.

"Mike," Julius cried out when he first noticed him. "Aeola is gone." Mike did not react as Julius continued. "A few hours ago she went down to the stream to bathe and she never came back. When I sent Marcus down to check on her, he couldn't find her."

Mike stood there, retaining his composure, though inwardly his stomach was curling. He was sure the same was true for the other two with whom he was speaking, though he knew it was for different reasons. Even in the darkness, Mike could see that Julius' face was white, and Marcus' face was red. They had no idea what was going on, what had been going on even since before Marcus had arrived here. Unlike them, he knew that Aeola was safe. It was the balanced temperament of the community that he feared. *This will set things off.* He knew it for sure. His mind instantly raced for solutions, but his practicality told him that there was not enough information to provide one. Calmly, he turned up to the woman in the tower. "You didn't see anything?"

"No," she called back. "I'd imagine, though, that it wouldn't be hard for one person to sneak away, especially if they had no torch."

"Or two," Mike said aloud. He knew that although the remark would open a can of worms, there was no hiding it anymore. It could not be hid. It was bound to come to the surface at one point or another, and the information he had gathered just a few hours ago concerning Julius' plans for Marcus and Aeola made the surfacing all the more violent.

"What do you mean, two?" Marcus demanded, suddenly exposing his undercurrent anger.

"I saw Lucius and Aeola last night down by the river, though I don't think that they saw me. I'd imagine that she is with him now."

"Lucius!" Julius roared. He excreted a string of Latin cuss words that made Mike cringe and stormed over to Lucius' hut. Mike rushed behind, his hand ready at his side, prepared for the worst. Julius threw open the door to Lucius' hut, and right then, Mike waited for the screams and the yells. Anxiously, he peered in behind Julius, but the place was lifeless. Lucius and Aeola were nowhere to be seen. It was a relief to Mike, seeing Julius frantically search every inch of the hut without success, but only slightly so. He stepped back as Julius crashed out of the place, then watched as Julius paced around, searching desperately for some way to vent the rage that had possessed him. Mike still found himself gripping his weapon, almost more for personal defense than anything. He glanced over at Marcus. Marcus simply stood off to the side in stewing disbelief.

Lucius and Aeola were clearly far away from Newhaven by now, having fled the entire issue altogether. Mike did not know what to either do or say. He could not consult with either of these men right now, for both of them were not in states of rational thinking. Nothing could be done tonight, *but how can I tell them that, especially as they are at the moment?*

"I'm going to kill him," Julius stated. He looked wildly about him, like a caged lion, seeming eager to go somewhere, but not knowing where to start. He might as well have been in a giant box, for clouds had moved in and obstructed the stars, and the night was now black enough to make any search near to impossible, even if they had known the direction of the pair's departure.

"Julius," Mike said, placing his arm on Julius' shoulder to calm him. "We'll work on it in the morning. Go back to your hut. What are you going to do tonight?"

"That dog is with my daughter!" Julius knocked Mike's hand off him and lashed out at Mike, catching him in the cheek with his fingernails.

In an instant, Mike's sword was drawn and directed toward Julius. Mike's jaw turned down to a threatening scowl and mouthed the words, "Get back to your hut. We'll take care of it in the morning."

Mike watched Julius' and Marcus' eyes widen at his violent reaction. The aging man lost grip on his look of rage and slowly retreated back to his hut under the power of the fire in his leader's eyes. Marcus followed like a dependent little pup. Mike stood there watching them turn and walk back with sword still drawn, but instantly the weapon felt like it weighed a ton and the thing drooped and fell from his grasp, clanking dully on the ground.

If Julius and Marcus had been surprised by Mike's reaction, they were no more surprised than Mike had been. When they were gone, Mike stood there blankly, breathing heavily at what had just happened to him. Then slowly, he bent down, picked up his sword, and headed back to his hut. Upon arriving there, he shed his sandals, sword, and tunic and lay down, though he did not fall asleep for a long time.

The next morning did nothing to shed the terrible feeling that had since welled up inside of Mike's chest, and the first thing he did was head over to Julius' hut. He signaled his arrival and Julius bade him enter. Mike poked his head in and caught sight of the man. He looked horrible—like he had not slept all night. He sat pitifully on the edge of his mattress with red eyes and downcast spirit.

"Hey, I wanted to come apologize for my actions last night," Mike uttered somberly. "I don't know where they came from. I also want to let you know that I am going to do all I can to work this all out."

Julius looked up at Mike before again averting his eyes. He did not respond, but Mike could tell that he did not hold any anger toward Mike. Instead, after a moment, he mumbled, "I don't know what I am to do, Mike." Julius tossed up his hands. "What should I do?"

Mike stepped forward. "Don't worry about it. She'll be okay. Lucius is an able-bodied man."

Julius angrily pounded his fist on his mattress. "That's just it, though. She's with *him*."

Mike sat down on a stool opposite him. "Julius, what happened with him and you? What would make that so bad?"

Julius' face had become stern as he faced Mike. "He is not worthy of such a mate. I knew him when he was younger. He was a wild boy. All the peasants around Sergius' villa knew him for seducing women and taking them off on romantic escapades, then pretending he did not know them the next day. In bartering with the villa, I only heard talk of the boy, but never met him until one day when he faced me as my barterer. He said that the usual barterer was sick and had sent him in his place. I handed him my grain, and in turn he offered me a vat, telling me that it was the best wine in the area. I got all the way back to my hut to find that instead of a wine vat, I got a chamber pot. I dashed the pot against the wall in anger and took an extra day to go back to the villa to demand my grain back. The usual barterer was there and refused it, as well as a new vat of wine since I did not have the chamber pot to prove my story. I asked if I could see Lucius, and he told me that Lucius had gone back to his normal duties and could not be disturbed. I then asked to see Sergius, and the barterer threw me out."

Julius paused in his narrative. Mike could tell that the situation still made Julius fume. He concluded by adding, "Lucius is a liar and a sweet talker. He does not take things seriously, and I will not have my daughter, my only remaining kin, attached to him."

"Have you considered that it was all a big misunderstanding?" Mike asked. "Or have you considered that he's at least changed? He did have a family at one time."

"I'm prone to believe it wasn't a misunderstanding," Julius argued, ignoring Mike's last inquiry. "How do you mistake the two? He is irresponsible and has no regard for anybody but himself. I mean, look at what he's done with my daughter."

Mike had no argument concerning that. Concerning that, Julius had a point. Mike decided that talking about it further would not do any more good. He stood up and said, "I'll do all I can to fix the situation."

"If you find that boy, you can tell him that he should disappear if he knows what's good for him."

Mike, who had been heading for the door, turned around and faced Julius again.

"And you'd better hope," he added, "that you find him before Marcus does, because he'll kill Lucius when he finds him."

Mike exuded a frown. "Where is Marcus?"

Julius sat up and looked at Mike straightly. "He's already out there. He left almost right away last night."

Mike exited Julius' without saying farewell. He marched directly back to his hut and got dressed in his hunting gear. He grabbed his spear, bow, quiver, and sword, as well as a few side bags into which he put leftover morsels from the feast last night. He filled them to last him the next 72 hours. Even though it was the Sabbath, there would be no rest for him today.

Mike immediately directed his course over to Diana's hut. He promptly announced his presence, to which he was invited in. The girls must have read the look on his face, for they did not waste time in asking him what they could do to help him.

"I need to talk to you, alone," Mike declared, pointing at Diana.

His tone held such authority that Diana did not object, but put on her sandals and exited with him. As they walked away from the hut, she did not question him, but allowed him to talk when he was ready. That time came as soon as they were out of range of hearing from her hut.

"Lucius and Aeola have run off together," Mike told her. "I need you to help me find out whether they took any horses or not. You're the one that knows best how many there are."

Again, Diana did not object, but walked beside Mike down the trail and out toward the pasture. They walked in silence, and although Mike's mind was preoccupied on other things—on the community, on the wavering stability of all that he'd built up, on the potential disastrous effects that could occur if Marcus and Lucius met up before Mike intervened—although it was preoccupied with these things, Mike could not help but note how he and she had walked this way just hours before. The difference in comfort level between him and her was astounding, and perhaps the pending situation helped in that, but Mike was still amazed at what difference that hour and a half last night had made.

But he could not think of such things right now. Other, more important matters were on the line and ready to fall. He pushed the thoughts of him and her out of his head and continued in his paces. They crossed through the stretch of trees that separated the northwest field from the pasture and were met by the sight of their flock. As they stepped out into the open, a few of Gaius' children noticed them.

"Diana!" the youngest girl, a short, curly dark-haired four year old yelled and ran to Diana's side with arms outstretched. Diana smiled, picked her up and hugged her. One of the older boys, a lad of about twelve, asked, "What are you guys doing here?"

"We were coming to find out if anyone borrowed some of the horses last night," Mike said.

The lad bit his lip and shuffled a bit. Mike instantly knew what was going on and had his answer. "Lucius did come by here last night didn't he? We need to know anything you know."

The boy, the same boy who had just before been the confident, assertive shepherd of the flock, seemed suddenly disabled. His head sunk, and he did not dare to speak, not out of fear, but out of something much more confining. Mike knew what had happened; he knew the boy had given his word to keep silent. In any other situation, he would have backed down from his request, but he could not do that now, as horrible as it made him feel. The information was too crucial.

Mike took a moment to glance over at Diana. *Why did I come to her anyway when all I really needed to do was come ask this boy?* The thought had gone through his head before he had even visited her hut, yet he had still progressed over there. Maybe he wanted someone with which to share this burden, and she had already been partially drawn into it.

Mike looked back at the boy. *Maybe I should leave him out of it. Maybe I should tell him to keep his mouth shut.* Mike knew he was watching raw integrity breaking down before him. It created a sort of anti-energy that sucked the life out of the air. It seemed to be sucking the proud, self-respecting air out of the boy. It wrenched Mike's heart to watch, and he was about to pull back his words, but the boy opened his mouth before he could. "Lucius and Aeola came by in the middle of the night," he blurted with a trembling voice. "He gave me his bow and quiver of arrows to keep my mouth shut. They took off on a horse together."

Mike felt his stomach roll and crash. Still, he found himself asking, "Which way did they go?"

The boy dejectedly pointed toward a break in the trees on the opposite side of the pasture.

Mike felt wretched at the guilt he had caused to show in the boy's eyes. He watched as the boy slowly took the quiver off his back and handed it and the bow to Mike. "Here, take this," he uttered. Mike stared at the objects a moment before he realized that he did not have a choice. He took the objects, hesitated a moment more, then unsoldered his own bow and arrows. Placidly, he offered them to the boy. "Here. Consider them not as a replacement, but as a reward for potentially saving a few lives."

The boy looked at them, considered the situation, then accepted them with a teary smile. Mike patted him comfortingly on the back. He then wasted no time in making his way for the horses. He heard Diana following behind him.

"Where are you going?" she asked, trotting to catch up with him.

"Go find that fool of a friend before Marcus."

"How're you going to do that?"

Mike turned and faced her inquiry, as well as her piercing stare. "Ride hard. I doubt Marcus thought to take a horse." Mike seized the first horse he could get his hands on and jumped up on top of it.

"You have no idea where you're going."

Mike looked hard at her. She had a point, but Mike had no alternative. "What are you proposing?"

"What if I could tell you that I can almost guarantee where Lucius and Aeola are right now?"

Mike silently listened on.

"Remember that I lived in the same household as that man for most of my lifetime. I know his ways better than anybody, including where he used to go with all of his romantic escapades."

"Where is that?"

"I could tell you, but I guarantee that you would get lost."

Mike looked down at her with such a terrible mixture of emotions that he struggled to think straight. "You know I didn't mean to pull you in this far."

Diana nodded in understanding but held her footing. "Just let me go back to my hut to get a few things." Mike nodded in agreement. "And find yourself a different horse," she added with boldness; "the one you're sitting on is mine."

Despite all that was unfolding, Mike could not help but emit a smile.

His mind was a flurry as he followed Diana's galloping mare out away from Newhaven. At any other moment, he would have seen such an opportunity as more than he could have ever hoped for. For the past few months he had struggled to get a five minute conversation with this strange woman, and just last night he had been proud to have spent an hour and a half with her. Now he was on a journey with her. He never would have thought such events as today's would occur.

Yet the thought did not emit the feelings he ever imagined it would, for there were other, darker events today that had even made such an opportunity possible. They cast too dark of a shadow on Newhaven's hill for Mike to feel ecstatic. He could not help but wonder if everything he had built up there in the last year was crumbling right before his eyes. *All because of the actions of two imprudent people blinded by lust,* he mumbled. Mike could strangle the guy. If Lucius had been some fool with no capacity for temperance or higher thought, Mike would have been less angry. There would have been nothing he could have done about it. But that was not the case. This was the same man that had learned weaponry and reading and writing with tremendous tact and skill. This was a man in whom Mike had confided throughout the entire summer.

His opinion was, of course, different toward Aeola. He did not feel like he could blame her too much. That girl had her mind set on attaching herself. Mike knew. Mike also knew, with frustration, how good she was at it as well. He had dealt with it. When she had come on to him a year ago, he had pulled away, but not without his more base self screaming out objection. She had a power in her, and it was a different power than

Diana. It was a frightful power which had shown of late its true strength by transforming a calm, temperate man into a reckless, love-struck juvenile.

The beautiful, green countryside rushed past on either side of him, but Mike strove to keep his eyes forward, on the leader of this two person army. Although Diana's horse kicked up a fair amount of dust, he could still see her clear enough to watch her smoothly glide up and down with the rhythm of the gallop. *Man, she is beautiful*, Mike again thought to himself through the clouds of dust rising up around him. *Maybe she does have the same power as Aeola.* Maybe all women had that power over men to one degree or another. Mike wondered again if it would have been just as hard to keep away from Diana as it had been from Aeola if Diana used her power as flauntingly as Aeola had, if Diana acted just as foolishly as Aeola had.

Don't touch me, ever again. The words screamed out at Mike in tones of irony, and Mike could not help but shake his head at the two encounters he had had with women in the past year. He admitted now that he wished there was not quite so large a gulf between the two. He had to assure himself that friendliness was good enough. He had to reassure himself that the opportunity to talk with her, to level with her was most important to him anyway. He could not think of what he did not, what he could not have.

As these thoughts careened through his head, Diana slowed down to a walk to give the horses a rest. Although there was a world of things Mike would have wanted to say as he caught up to ride beside his companion, he kept it to the thing that was pressing down hardest on his mind. As they crossed one of the many hills carpeted with tall, autumn grass, he turned to her.

"So what can you tell me of Lucius' lifestyle growing up?"

Diana gave a short exhalation and a smirk. "Lucius was a wild and foolish boy. He grew up in my father's house as the son of a Celtic bard. The bard was an old, kind, wise man who I loved almost as much as my own father. He would tell me stories that took me to different worlds. My imagination was allowed to roam free because of him, but he did more than just tell me stories. He also always made sure I was well cared for. I felt like he was one of the best men on earth.

"Lucius was different. He is a year older than me, but you would not have been able to tell it back then. He couldn't sit still and would always be getting into mischief, letting the animals out of the stable or stealing from the vineyard. Later on he would run off with servant girls or peasant girls. He was quite smart, though he used his wits for all the wrong pursuits."

"Would he have, say, switched a wine vat for a chamber pot at the bartering table?"

Diana smiled at the thought, but shook her head. "No. Whenever he was assigned a specific job, he always took it seriously. After my father learned this, he took special care to make sure he always had a surplus of duties. He was responsible when it came to things he had been given charge over, and when he got a girl pregnant at the age of seventeen, he married her at my father's advice and started a family with her. After that, his wild days ended, and he started realizing his place in life. He worked harder than ever to learn his father's trade and took over after he died, the last year of my father's life."

Diana trailed off here. Mike had once again reached the threshold with this woman. His spirit led him onward as he surmised, "That's when Lucius left—when the Saxons attacked, right?"

"I watched as they sliced him across his gut. He fell to the ground, and they took him for as good as dead. They killed his wife and his two daughters, only four and two at the time, right in front of him. He tried to scream out—you could see it in his eyes—but he had no strength to do so. They then threw his body on top of theirs out in the woods to be eaten by wolves."

"And you—your family?"

Diana had quickened her pace to a trot, moving ahead now of Mike. She did not answer for a moment, but to his surprise, finally came back with a simple, somber request. "Ask me again some other time, Mike."

Mike kicked up his steed to follow after Diana. Soon again they were galloping through the countryside, leaving the enlightening conversation behind and moving in the direction of its horrible setting. Mike's soul was shaken by her communication, spoken and unspoken. The unspoken communication was the most haunting. *If Diana could have so easily communicated the horrors she did of Lucius, what hell-forged events does she hide of herself?* Mike thought on it with a shiver. There had been mountains of frustration put into his breaking of this woman, but he was finally getting an idea of why she still maintained her icy stamina. He did not understand the horrors through which she had gone. She knew he could not understand. He figured only God could.

Yet there was evidence that she wanted him to understand, at least someday, which cooled Mike's churning aggravation. For now, she either did not have the emotional strength to talk to him about her family, or she felt that in time she would be able to confide in him more.

Their destination was distant, but the galloping horses empowered them to endure it. In the next few hours, the landscape changed between moor and fielded hill, and though Mike saw all of it as beautiful, he also noticed that it all blended together without distinction. Mike could have seen how he would have gotten lost, no matter how good Diana's directions would have been. She seemed to know where she was going, and so Mike continued to follow her, tracing her every step with utmost precision.

It was in the heat of the afternoon when Diana slowed to a walk and began descending a hill. Diana stopped a time or two to look out on the scene, and Mike held no objection. The view from the hill from which they descended was breathtaking. Way off in an easterly direction they could see the stone walls of York. Mike peered in wonder at them, and felt drawn to one day visit them. In closer proximity, outcroppings of rock popped out on either side, and below, Mike could see a green river winding down amidst trees. Mike wondered what memories this place held for Diana and whether any of those memories had been with Lucius. A story began to rise in his head, a story that would have included both of them, playing off in this wilderness as children, before, as Lucius had explained to him, Diana felt it underneath her station to associate with Lucius. They might have discovered this place and declared it their secret hideout, their secret paradise. They might have had countless adventures here which Diana was now remembering with saddened nostalgia, for the memories were of days of innocence, before the pains and toils of life caved in, down on top to smother her.

The floor of the valley was narrow, but the river that had carved it out was also winding. On various bends sat small peninsulas of deep, green grass intermixed with thickets of trees. The water itself rushed calmly but steadily on, interrupted only by rocks or sawyers which stubbornly held their ground. Occasionally, the jumping of fish moving up the river could be seen. They popped up through the coursing surface, keeping Mike's attention riveted. Mike broke his attention toward the scenery only to glance at Diana. He discovered that she was smiling.

"This place," she uttered. "I haven't been back to this place in ten years."

"Does it have lots of memories?"

Diana looked at him and let out a short laugh. It was the first time Mike had ever heard her do so in front of him, and what a sonorous ring it created. "It's obvious isn't it?" he heard her lips say. Mike could only nod.

"Our fathers used to bring us up here to play when we were younger. Some of my best memories were here."

"It's close, then, to the villa?"

"About an hour's horse ride," she answered. "My father would place me in front of him, and we would ride fast through the trees and over the moors. I would chide him to go faster, and he would, until he'd claim that his horse had reached its limit. We always raced Lucius and his father, and we always won because my father had one of the fastest horses in all of Northern Britain."

Mike smiled as he listened to Diana speak, and for a moment he forgot the very different reason they had come up here. In the mean time, Diana had turned upstream, dismounted, and begun walking her horse. Mike did the same, and, finding the old trail only allowed them to walk single file, the conversation ended until they came to a picturesque waterfall. Mike had heard its gentle, steady roar for a minute or two before they came within sight of it, and the sight definitely did not disappoint the hopes that the sound had created. It was multileveled, with several eddying pools at differing heights. Beneath the clear water, smooth, dark rocks could be seen, rocks that were not cold and hard, but inviting. In the air, the scent of fruit was caught. Mike and Diana walked out into a grassy clearing. And there, lying beside each other on the ground fast asleep, were Lucius and Aeola.

Chapter 28

As mad as Mike was with Lucius for refusing to come back, he certainly could not blame him. For as the sight of Newhaven's hill grew before Diana and him, his anxiety grew as well. Lucius' getaway was beginning to hold more and more luster. The carefree life devoid of all responsibility or worry contrasted mockingly to the toils and fears and structures that he, himself had created in Newhaven. That said nothing of the barrage he was about to face.

Lucius and Aeola were still back basking in the clear pools, tasting the sweet berries, and lazing about in the soft grass. They had no desire to come back. Mike, in turn, was faced with bringing the news back to Julius. One of them had needed to face him, whether it was Lucius telling Julius that he wanted Aeola for his own, or Mike telling Julius that Lucius was standing his ground. Lucius had deferred to Mike. Mike had recognized the injustice of it. He had felt tempted to forget it all and join Lucius rather than face the unwarranted fire that would most definitely come. For a moment, Mike had actually considered it, but the moment soon passed and he knew that he could not. In the end, his integrity got him back on his horse and sentenced him to face the wrath of Julius for his friend.

Mike and Diana's pace was much more casual on the way back than it had been on the way there. He was no longer worried about Marcus. After being enlightened to their location, Mike was now assured that Marcus could never find it on his own and that Lucius and Aeola were at least safe from him.

As they walked, Mike found himself wondering whether Diana would have stayed with him. Instantly, he shook the thought from his head. Not only would she have utterly refused, it would have made him a complete hypocrite. Lucius had done wrong; Mike knew it. Mike was about to face the consequences of it. Even as he walked hesitantly toward them, though, he felt like he could see through Lucius' eyes. In the end, he was a man, just like the rest of them, just like Diana had said, and he understood exactly from where both Lucius, and now Diana, came.

"Well," Diana spoke, breaking the silence as they rode side by side, "I do not envy what you have to do."

"Yeah, I'm not so crazy about the idea myself." Mike had stopped and sat there on his horse, looking out as Newhaven's horizon appeared before him. It seemed to him a dark battlement with a fire-breathing dragon at the very top. He had no choice but to face that dragon. The survival of his community depended on it.

Diana was quiet for a long enough moment for Mike to look over at her. He could tell that she was tossing an idea around in her head. "Would it be easier if I accompanied you?" she inquired.

Mike let out an uneasy breath. "No. I can't imagine it's going to be very pretty regardless of what is done. We might as well leave that unpleasant experience to as few people as possible."

"Mike," she stated. Mike looked over at her. "I've experienced enough to be able to handle it. You, on the other hand, look like you need some support."

Not much more was needed to convince Mike. The two, in turn, rode up the trail just as the hill held on to the last rays of daylight. Mike was already tired, not only from the physical wear the traveling had taken on him, but the emotional wear as well. The day had been a rollercoaster to an individual who had grown used to remaining well-grounded. He longed to simply retire to his hut and leave everything behind in sleep, just as he had done all of last winter. Unfortunately, such could not be the case, despite how much he wanted it. An unfamiliar beast lurked in their village, and he had been the one chosen to slay it. It was a job that could not wait, for even his peace of mind bound him to action. There would be no rest until it was dead.

Julius' hut appeared and Mike felt to be approaching his death. He was now terribly glad that he shared his fate with another, and felt all the more affection for that person because of it. He dreaded seeing Julius' face, and how its usual placid color would turn as Mike related the events of his discoveries.

His face, indeed, came into sight, just as Mike got close enough to announce his arrival. Mike jumped inside as he saw him. "Mike," he said, "You're back already." He looked over at Diana then back at him. "Did you find her?"

"Let's go inside," Mike suggested. Julius nodded. As the three of them went inside, Julius turned to Mike. "What's Diana doing here?"

"She accompanied me on my search."

"I was the one that led him to her location," she defended.

"You did find her then," the desperation in his voice lost a little bit of its edge. "Where is she now?"

Mike suddenly recalled what Lucius had founded right before he and Diana had left to return to Newhaven. Mike had begged him to come back but only received a shake of the head in response. "No, Mike. We are staying right here, at least until winter sets in. Aeola and I are happy here. There are too many complications back there right now. Julius needs time. In time he will have to come around, because we are not going to give each other up."

Mike gulped as he laid it out to Julius. "She and Lucius are up north of here. They are not coming back."

Mike waited for it to come. And come it did. But the way in which it came had him staring in trepid confusion. If he had possessed fear in anticipation of an angry outburst, he had no reason right now to feel afraid. Yet the fear was there, and it was more potent than expected. The tense expression on Julius' face grew suddenly calm. He clinched his fists. Mike furrowed his eyebrows. *What am I witnessing?* he questioned. *Am I witnessing the face of a man in subjection to fate?* It could not be. It seemed more likely the face of a man gone completely mad. Mike shook inside.

Mike desperately tried to put on as courageous a face as he could and continued his defense. "I tried to convince them. They would not listen to me."

Julius' face remained unchanged. Mike had no idea how to read it and therefore had no idea what else to say.

"I want you to know, however," he continued, "that Lucius has not harmed her in any way. He loves her and is committed to her."

Julius remained silent. More flashes of Mike's conversation with Lucius popped into his mind.

"I want to speak with you alone, Lucius," he had told him. "Come ride out with me."

Diana had handed her reins to Mike. "He is not to ride my horse." Mike had switched horses, not wanting to make anything more difficult than it had to be. Lucius had gotten on the other horse and the two had ridden downstream, wherein the beauty had suddenly become dirty to him. It had seemed all too much like Lucius' friendship at the moment, which Lucius had tried to sustain through casual, unrelated small talk. It had owned a pleasant nature to itself, but the idea which it represented and supported was destructive, and Mike had hardly been able to tolerate its proximity.

Mike had looked over at him to see his usual, contented smile. Again, there was something similar, yet strangely different in that smile. He had thought back on the friendship that he and Lucius had held for each other. They had shared lots of experiences together that had made them like brothers. Suddenly, they could not look each other in the eye. Mike remembered not being sure how to view him anymore. He had certainly been the same Lucius—same features, same silent, yet sincere temperament—yet suddenly, he had seemed different. That difference had depressed Mike to a previously unfelt degree.

"I know how you found me," Lucius had said, dropping his previous conversation on account of Mike's expression. "I don't understand, though. Even if I'd remembered that Diana knew of this place, I never would've thought she would've revealed it to you."

Mike had had no choice but to be cold. "She and I saw you last night. When I told her what had become of you, she offered her knowledge."

Lucius had been silent a moment before sighing and saying, "Well, I'm glad it's you and no one else."

After a moment's silence, however, Lucius' expression had again changed to a smile. "You and Diana, eh? You must have been out walking, away from everybody, just like us."

"It's not what you think, Lucius," Mike had said.

Lucius had continued as if he had not heard Mike. "I'm surprised you never said anything about it before. Last you told me, she was as cold as winter. I thought we were friends Mike."

Mike had sighed. After a moment he had pulled it back to the real subject at hand. "You know I cannot support your actions Lucius."

At that, Lucius' expression had changed. "So you're going to support Julius and Marcus?" He had grown defensive. "I'm not going back, Mike. I'm not going to watch Aeola be given away to Marcus. He was planning their marriage."

"I know; I heard."

"She doesn't want that. I can't watch that."

Mike had pulled his horse out of the stream and stopped to face Lucius. "I don't need to tell you that Julius doesn't like you, Lucius. But I must tell you that he doesn't trust you, or your intentions with his daughter. He spoke of a reputation that you had. Diana confirmed it."

The ends of Lucius' mouth had turned down. "I'm sure they would've. But what about you? You know me. We've been through worlds together. People change, Mike, and you've seen the person I've become since they knew me."

Mike had been able to see the destruction occurring on both fronts. Still, he had had to continue on. "Lucius, I need to hear it. What are your intentions with Aeola? Is this another game with you?"

Lucius had looked at Mike at that point with a look that had stabbed his soul. It had not been a look of anger, nor of even spite, but a look of pain—true, sincere pain. Lucius had felt slighted by Mike, a man he had perceived as his friend. Mike had instantly felt despicable. It was obvious that Lucius had felt the answer had needed no verbal confirmation, as if Mike should have already known. It had set Mike's mind at work, evaluating whether he had been wrong to question his friend as far as he had. Still, Lucius had had enough respect for Mike to answer, "If Aeola wants commitment, she has it."

Mike faced Julius. "He did not force her in any way. It was her choice to go."

Mike had also pulled Aeola aside to speak with her. Her thoughts had made Mike a little more nervous.

"Your father is worried to death about you," he had told her.

A look of concern that she had hurt her father had flashed on Aeola's face before she emitted a look of defiance. "Well he should not have tried to force Marcus upon me. He'll learn from his worries."

"I've talked with Lucius about it. He is willing to go back and see if we can settle things."

"I doubt that things can be settled. We would just be going back to the same thing. My father would continue to try to force Marcus upon me, and Lucius would have to continue to hide everything. It is much better here where we don't have to hide from anyone.

Mike recalled the feelings of frustration he had felt, as well as the bitter taste of irony in her words, which he had decided to let pass untried. "As the leader of the community I have the power to authorize your union with Lucius, and then Marcus would be bound by the law of the community to stay away."

"I would rather stay here with Lucius." She had seemed firm in her resolve. Mike had turned to Lucius for help, but he had offered none. His weak integrity had crumbled under the weight of her allure. They had crumbled together and had become intertwined in their disintegration.

"You realize that until you do as I say that you are making a choice. It's Lucius or your father. You cannot have both as you both are."

To this she had hesitated. Mike had been able to tell that such a thought had never passed through her head. Mike had wondered whether commitment to Lucius had even been a consideration. He had wondered on what logic she had taken action, if there had been any logic at all. He had wondered whether she was going to change her mind and agree to Mike's proposal, or even denounce Lucius to be with her father. Aeola answered all of his questions with an unwavering resolve to walk no farther with him.

"Did you ever consider," Mike now asked Julius, "that your daughter did not want Marcus?"

Julius looked up at Mike. Very calmly, he stated, "Aeola does not know what she wants." Julius was shaking slightly. Mike could sense a frightful tension in his voice, as if something were about to snap.

"You seemed to think she did when she came after me. I can agree with you only to a point. Aeola is, indeed, foolish. Her means of securing men are shaky. I do not agree, however, on you forcing someone upon her against her will. Did she, or did she not, tell you her feelings?"

Julius looked Mike in the eye with a piercing stare. "She did not."

Mike exhaled slowly. "Well, I guess you realize her feelings now. I'm sorry you had to learn in such a harsh manner. Unfortunately for you, however, there is nothing that can be done about it."

"I believe there is, though," Julius continued. "You can lead me to her."

"To do what?" Mike countered. "She is with Lucius. You can have no power over that, even if I led you to her."

It was then that everything snapped.

"I can!" he said, standing up suddenly and facing Mike. Mike was able, somehow, to hold his ground. "I am her father. You have no rule over her!"

"He does," a voice came from off to the side. Both Mike and Julius turned to face Diana. "He is your leader. He is the leader of all of us. Mike has the power to decide all matters in this community, including matters of who is considered married and who is not."

Julius made an advance at Diana. Mike seized his arm. Diana held her ground. Julius reached for his knife with his free hand and Mike reached for his sword. In an instant, the two were separated but directing respective weapons at the other.

"There will be order in this community," Mike affirmed threateningly. "That is twice that you have lashed out at me."

Julius realized he was beat, again. His knife and waning strength were no match for Mike's sword. His anger was dropped and a fear began to arise in his heart. Mike had a feeling that it stemmed from something deeper than the threat of the point of his sword, though. Slowly, Julius backed away. "We are not like them," Mike continued, sword still drawn. "We are not barbarians, but subjects of Rome and its ideals, if that means anything to you anymore. Drop your knife and sit down."

Julius was a perfectly pitiful wreck. The knife fell from his grasp, thudded dully on the earth, and he stumbled back. Tears came to his eyes as Mike looked on and re-sheathed his own weapon. "They've abandoned us for good," he blubbered. "They're not coming back." Julius hid his face. Mike watched him. "I'd lost hope for a long time, Mike. My only hope was for my daughter to remain safe. You had proved your skill in her protection. You were a subject which had been easy for her to pursue. You denied her. I had to find another. Marcus was the most able-bodied man I knew. He could fight, but he never had to. He was safe with the Saxons. I wanted that for her. I wanted her to live under his protection."

Mike had slowly begun to see what that look Julius had displayed had been. It showed again in the way that Julius sat there before him slumped on a stool, shedding tears and not bothering to wipe them. He stared blankly at the dull earth as if it would be taking him soon. In a sense it was a subjection, but not the subjection which Mike had intended for him. Mike fought back his own tears at the sight. He looked over at Diana, who seemed to be doing the same as him.

The words seemed almost futile, but still, Mike delivered them anyway. "What about the protection of the community? Does that give you any sense of hope?"

Julius interrupted his blank stare to turn up to Mike. There was still no life in his eyes. "You know the truth, Mike, just as well as I do." Mike felt a lump in his throat. "We're eventual victims, just like everybody else. We may hold them off for a while, but they'll get us in the end."

Mike had nothing more to say to Julius. Julius seemed to have finished presenting his case as well, for he simply sat there staring at Mike and Diana for a moment, refusing to back down from the potency of his words. Mike turned to the doorway of the hut. "I'm sorry, Julius. For everything."

Mike walked out of the hut and Diana followed. Mike, however, barely acknowledged it, and definitely did not think about what the past twenty-four hours had meant for him and her. He did not think about their walk. He did not think about her willingness to accompany him on his journey to find Lucius. He did not think about the gleam in her eye upon reaching the canyon of her childhood. He did not think of all the help she had offered in a burden that was solely his. Last of all, he did not think of the implications of Diana's verbal oath of loyalty to Mike. All such things would be analyzed later. All he could think of now was getting to bed.

Mike could have very well taken a week off after all the drama the preceding day had brought him, but work was still to continue. He found out, the next day, that Julius had taken ill overnight and was incapacitated. That left the community down three men in the midst of harvest. There could be no breaks.

So Mike headed back out to the fields at the crack of dawn with his sickle to once again begin the motion that would consume his life for the next several hours. He started off slowly—he was dog tired. He found it amazing how many more physical aftereffects emotional strain produced than physical strain. Julius had made himself sick. Mike, though not as in bad of shape, felt sluggish. The sickle seemed to have a weight to it that required more energy than usual, and the thought that yesterday had been the day of rest did not help matters any. He would have to survive another few more days of rigorous harvesting before his break could come.

After a while, however, the work actually made him feel a little better. His energy was re-channeled to things which were predicable and consistent. The grain fell before him just as it had last week, just as it had last year. The grain was courteous—he did not have to worry about it fighting back. It knew its superior and was obedient.

Mike made sure he sweated. It almost seemed like the more he sweated, the better he felt. Drips of perspiration poured down his face, cleansing him of the feelings of discomfort and darkness that had fought to consume his life. He took long gulps from his water skin. He took deep breaths after short bursts of thrashing. His lungs toiled, his muscles ached, and his skin burned. Mike welcomed all of it with exhaust and gratitude, for it helped him remember that he was still alive, and that some things still fell in their proper place.

The next few days were uneventful, monotonous, and wonderful. Mike got up, ate, went out into the fields, sweated, took a lunch break, sweat some more, came back in for the evening meal, visited a few people's huts to socialize, then went to bed. He only caught glimpses of Diana during these days—she was most likely involved with Gaius and his herd, which had been joined by Marcus' herd—but he was okay with that. His pursuits and hopes with her had been part of his stress, and he appreciated the break from that. Besides, they were only to be friends. She had made sure of that.

Mike did not see much of Julius either. That was okay as well. Julius needed time and space. Mike had threatened him twice within twenty-four hours, which could not have been good comfort during his time of greatest stress. Mike felt bad for the guy, and wanted to give him some real comfort somehow, but he knew it was best to stay away.

So Mike filled his life with the usual, and once again, the usual felt, at the very least, satisfying. All the while, though, Mike knew that the issue lingered, frosted with a very thin layer of dust. He certainly had not killed it by any means. Underneath every aspect of Newhaven's seemingly normal days, destruction still glowed like a hot ember in a smoldering pile of coals. Mike knew that it had to reignite; it certainly had with Virgil and Arwulf. What he was unsure about was the time table of it all. Four days after the episode, though, it surfaced and struck, and did so in what would end up being the cruelest manner.

Mike had had enough of being disturbed from his sleep, for it had seemed to be the only thing that offered escape from absolutely everything. So when he felt a cold, stone blade on his neck and heard the words, "Wake up, Mike," his first thought was more of anger than of fear. His eyes opened to see the silhouette of a man standing above him. It was Marcus.

Mike did not move. Instead he seethed, "What are you doing, fool?"

"Making sure you talk to me."

Mike's hand moved like lightning to seize Marcus', a gesture Marcus did not expect to come from a recently awoken man. Mike's senses were full though, and his seasoned instincts caused him to use them. Mike employed a combination of gravity and leverage on the side of his bed to pull Marcus to the ground. Marcus fell and dropped the knife, which Mike grabbed. He then pulled Marcus to his feet, and directed the knife at him.

"Why don't you sit down," Mike suggested. "You didn't have to pull anything stupid like this to come talk to me."

Marcus massaged his arm slowly and stared Mike down. Mike could see the hardened expression that controlled his face. He could tell that Marcus' anger far exceeded that of his own, even as frustrated as he was at being woken up in such a brutal manner. Just like Julius, though, there was nothing Marcus could do about it, since Mike now had his weapon pointed back toward him. Mike had indeed practiced and near perfected his combat skills, and they seemed to have come in handy in the past week. Mike silently waited for what Marcus had to say, though he had a relatively good guess as to what it would be.

"I doubted that you would give it to me any other way."

"Well your stunt backfired on you, didn't it? How well can you expect what you want now?"

Marcus glared at him. There was reckless rage in his eyes. "Don't make me swear an oath to kill you as well. Just give me Lucius' whereabouts. Aren't you confident in his skills? You've seemed to favor him above everybody else in this community."

"You're speaking like a man drunk by rage, Marcus. If you retire now I will forget this whole thing happened. Cool off and we'll talk more in the morning."

"I will have you give me that information!" he yelled. He lunged forward, swatting Mike's hand aside and went for Mike's neck—a colossally stupid move. Mike was thrown off guard for only a moment, but he regained control in time to lunge out and slash a shallow cut in Marcus' left cheek. Marcus shrieked and retreated, grabbing his face.

Mike was going to take no more of this. He approached Marcus and lightly tapped him on the same cheek with the knife. Marcus grimaced, even though his hand had intercepted the stone face. "Don't think I won't defend myself Marcus," he warned, staring him straight in the eye from point blank range. "Get out of my hut now." Marcus stumbled out of the hut and Mike followed.

"I swear, Mike," he pointed with his free hand as he tripped backward, "that you will feel my blade cut your flesh yet, and it will not be as cowardly as the cut you gave me. I snuck into your hut once, I can do it again. And if you will not let me know of Lucius' whereabouts, I'll have you begging for mercy. I was promised Aeola and I will do what I need in order to get her."

Marcus had thought he had had the last word and had begun to stumble away, but Mike yelled out to him, not caring anymore if he woke anybody up. "Why don't you fulfill your oath right now, Marcus, if you feel man enough to call me a coward?" Marcus stopped and turned around. Mike stood looking on at him. "Go grab yourself a weapon or get out of Newhaven this instant."

Marcus smiled devilishly and retreated toward his hut, leaving Mike waiting in fury for his opponent. Mike watched him, feeling that sick feeling returning to his body, yet not backing down from it. He knew, even in the semi-rational state of mind that he was in, that there could be no other way. Despite what he wanted to think, he knew Marcus had been good enough to get into his hut. He could succeed in his oath. There was no room for such treason, especially in a community like this.

Within moments, people had come out to view what was to ensue, having heard the exchange of yells. A crowd gathered around Mike as he stood in the midst of the huts. Some of them asked him about the ensuing occurrence, but he did not answer them. The only words he spoke to them as they all waited for Marcus to come back from Julius' hut consisted of a commission for someone to bring him his sword.

Marcus returned with his spear. Mike had heard stories about how skillful he was at it. He did not let himself be intimidated by it, though. Instead, he stated, "You have one last chance to leave this community, Marcus."

"On the contrary, Mike, you have one last chance. All I ask is the information to Lucius' whereabouts. I swear that I will clear my last oath toward you if you do so. I cannot do the same for Lucius." Marcus progressed closer to Mike. Mike held his sword out defensively.

"You have made lots of oaths, Marcus, but you have broken your primary oath to us—your oath of allegiance. How are you going to answer for that?"

Marcus' teethed bared as he seethed, "I never made any such oath. I refused to make it until I was given my end of the deal, Aeola's hand in marriage."

Mike stood his ground against Marcus, who was still pacing toward him. "That is impossible now. Even if I could convince Aeola and Lucius to come back, I would never authorize your marriage with her."

"Your will won't matter when you are dead and I take your spot."

Marcus advanced in a sharp attack with a jab of his spear, but Mike had been ready. He dodged the spear and knocked it aside with his sword, then counterattacked. Marcus parried, and seemed to know how to do so without allowing his spear to be snapped in two. The two went at each other like gladiators, issuing blows with impassioned strength and energy.

In the background, people were silent. They very well could have disappeared as far as Mike was concerned, for he locked his eyes on his opponent, studying his movements, his expressions, and wild, flying emotions. Marcus indeed, lived up to his reputation. He understood how to use the superior length of his spear to his advantage, and was bold in his handling and freakish in his bursts of energy. Mike patiently, levelly played the defender until he could find a weak move. It did not come for several moments of sweat and yells.

Mike finally found the opportunity and grazed Marcus' shoulder. Marcus yelled out in pain, then struck forward with fury, again catching Mike slightly off guard. Mike dodged the point of the spear, but not without feeling some of the flesh on his side get caught and tear. He, too, let out a yell, but the fighting continued.

"You deserve to die, you know that?" Mike cut as he parried a blow directed at his head.

"I am a man of promises, Mike, and my end of the promise was not kept. I am set on concentrating on it until it is, though."

Mike attacked his opponent, aiming for the stomach. Marcus defended himself. "For that purpose, Marcus, I give you my word that all of this will be forgotten if you swear allegiance to this community like you were originally supposed to. That includes allegiance to me since these people have dubbed me their leader."

"I will not, unless I have Aeola."

Mike swung forward and was parried again by the spear, which had numerous chip marks in it by now. This time, though, the swing had been strong and the blade caught fast in the wood. The two paused and Mike looked Marcus piercingly in the eye. "You don't deserve association with *anyone* here."

Mike swung the two weapons around, jammed the spear into the ground and snapped the weapon in two. He then flung his head forward at Marcus' and sent him crumbling to the ground. Mike yanked the half of the spear Marcus still held from his grasp and held it at Marcus' wheezing neck while pinning him to the hard earth with his foot.

"Get out of here," Mike commanded. "Don't try to come back. Our guard will be watching to let me know, and then I will not hesitate to kill you."

For the first time, Mike noted several men standing around them with weapons at their sides, ready to defend Mike. Mike ordered them to guide Marcus back to Julius' hut to let him gather provisions for three days then see that he was led out. He then grabbed his sword from off the ground and waited at Newhaven's foremost promontory until he saw Marcus stumble off down the hill and into the darkness.

Chapter 29

At the first sight of dawn, Mike dragged himself down from the tower. Knowing that he would not have been able to sleep, he did not even go back into his hut. He had headed directly over to the tower and told Arthur, the watchman, that he could be relieved. The young man had said, however, that he had seen the whole fight and that it would be an honor remain with him the rest of the night.

Mike had stood up there in relative silence, staring blankly off into the black night. He did not even have a desire for sleep, although he was emotionally wasted, for his mind was still in a flurry, still in disbelief at what had just happened. He had fought Saxons before, he had defeated them and watched them fall to the ground, but he had never had to fight a member of his community.

I will not hesitate to kill you. The words darkened Mike's world. He had meant them at the time. Mike could not help but remember the feelings that had been felt at that moment. They made him sick. He had wanted nothing more than to slit Marcus' throat. It had been a lust so real and so potent that he could not bear to think of it without squirming. Of course, his virtue had won out, and he had given the knave a last chance, but it had been a task much more colossal than anyone looking on could have ever supposed. Marcus' knife had been in his possession at the time. All he would have had to have done was pull it across his neck. Nobody would have stopped him. Many of the people would have gone through with it themselves—there was no law either supporting or denying them the right. Had Mike have pulled the blade, he would not have been punished, but praised all the same.

But he would not have been praising himself. Even now, Mike kicked the ground mindlessly, over and over, as if the feelings he had harbored at that moment stuck to him like tar on his shoe. He was not raised to feel such feelings, and the reality of them frightened him more than anything ever had, including facing death himself. *I'll kill you.* Just about everybody in his time had said those words at one point or another, but it had always been with an insincere tone. Mike had meant it. His words had been sincere. *How many people, including criminals, have actually reached the point I did?* Mike had heard that most people would not be able to pull the trigger; he doubted he would have been able to think of doing it two and a half years ago himself.

Here he was, though, and everything was entirely different. He had killed. The count was now at six, and four of them had been close enough for Mike to feel their last wheezing breaths. He had seen several more die, not even to mention the countless animals he had slain for meat. For the first time in a great while, Mike took the moment to mourn his lot and the person his lot had made him.

Life went on, though, and the problems did not cease with Marcus' departure. Marcus' words lingered behind him in Mike's mind. *I never made any such oath. I refused to make it until I was given my end of the deal, Aeola's hand in marriage.* Mike did not understand the possibility of that. Marcus may have been a knave, but Mike did not think him a liar. *I am a man of promises, Mike.* Mike believed that. He believed that for everybody here. There had been foul play elsewhere, which was why Mike left the tower at the crack of dawn for the hut of Julius.

"Julius, are you up?" Mike called out upon arrival at his door.

There was no answer, but Mike could hear movement from within. Mike entered. "Julius, I'd like to talk to you."

Julius was standing at the hearth, warming some food. His back was turned to Mike and remained so, almost as if he was deaf to Mike's words, but upon hearing them, his shoulders sunk and he sighed. "I was wondering when I would hear it. I see you wasted no time in coming to condemn me."

Upon approaching, Mike had felt mild anger building up in his heart, but now, looking at a man in this state with whom he had closely associated for a year, all he could feel was pity.

Even so, he knew that he could not step down from his firmness. Mike took a deep breath and put his sorrow in check. "I can tell that you already see the serious nature of your faults," he stated. "So I won't come here to condemn you further than you have done to yourself." Mike saw Julius' shoulders relax slightly. "I want to know, however," he continued, "what was going through your head."

"Like I told you a few days ago, I wanted protection for Aeola."

"So what did you have in mind for them after they were to be married?"

"They could stay here. If the Saxons attacked, he could escape with her. They could then become subject to the Saxons just as he had before. He knows their language on account of a Saxon traveler that stayed with his family as a boy."

Mike furrowed his eyebrows. "You knew all this?"

Julius still did not look Mike in the eye.

Mike exhaled roughly and paced about the room. All he could do was shake his head repeatedly at the entire situation. He was caught in guile at the man slumped over in front of him. Everything with which Mike had praised him during the past several months had all summed up to nothing. Julius had canceled out every good thing he had done with his selfish intentions. It stained his white mantle. Mike walked about the hut until he stood in front of Julius. He gazed down in silence until Julius was forced to look up at him. "You realize what this means?"

Julius looked down. "Punish me how you like, Mike. I am just as much a traitor as Marcus."

Mike could not hold in his fluster now. "Julius, I have bigger issues on hand than punishing you." Mike tossed up his hands. "You do realize what Marcus is going to do, right?"

Julius' eyes met Mike's. There were tears in them. Mike knew he understood, but he decided to spell it out anyway. "He's going to come back with them, Julius. He's going to come back with enough of them to take control of this place. He knows everything about us. He knows how many able-bodied soldiers we have."

"What'll you have me do, Mike?" he blubbered. Julius looked to be no more than a pitiful schoolboy. "I'll do anything."

Mike tried to calm himself. He sat down and took a few deep breaths.

"We need to put off the threshing, and the gleaning will have to be lost. We need to set to work right away on building ourselves a fortress instead. We've already got the hill to our advantage, but we need to add a strong wall with pickets and towers. Work must start today. Help me spread the word to everybody to meet in the commons area instead of going out to the fields." At that, Mike got up and left the hut.

The people of Newhaven did not question Mike's command. In a matter of minutes, their industrious attitudes shifted from harvest work to forestry and manufacture. Mike enlisted Cai and Dylan, along with a few assistants, to set to work on making axes and saws, for the village only had enough for the menial building that had taken place since its birth. The remainder of the village was split up and given various tasks. Those with axes and saws were set to work at felling trees—the trees that surrounded the hill, beginning at the top and working down on the least steep side. Others were to start digging a deep trench just around the outside of all the huts, where the wall was to be. The majority of the people were sent to the stream to gather rocks and stones, which would be useful support for the fortress.

Mike and a few ingenuitive others set to work on the blueprints themselves. Mike had built fences for his farm before, but those and the huts he had built since arriving here had been his only construction experience. He had never taken on something so colossal before. It needed to be done, though. Their hideout was revealed, and it would not be long before every monster in the land would be rushing at them.

"Right now, anything we can get up will be better than nothing," Mike told his planners. "I would like to get the trench dug and the towers built first. Then we can get some temporary pickets up in the trenches. If we can get that done in two weeks, we can worry about the rest later and finish up our harvesting." After assigning the different men to take charge of the various tasks, Mike dismissed them to see that they were accomplished.

Thus, Mike was engaged in the next few days to see that everything was running as smoothly and efficiently as possible. After putting the plan together, Mike realized that the need for shovels and picks was much more pressing than axes and saws, and so he re-commissioned Dylan and Cai to make the shovels. The problem regarding the lack of metal then came up, and after much deliberation as to whether they needed to go trade for more or melt down weapons or farming tools, Mike asked them to make what they could out of bone and rock and they'd work with what they had.

With the scarce supplies, the work was hard in its progression, but the people were industrious. They seemed motivated for one reason or another, possibly due to the concern that had underlain Mike's voice when he first redirected them. Mike had not told them about his conversation with Julius—he had kept Julius' transgression private—but they seemed to make some sort of connection. Mike caught wind of the chatter wisping its way among them as he walked past and worked off to the side of them. At one point, when he was digging with a bone pick and scooping out the loose earth with his hands, he heard one man a little bit down the line say, "Surely Mike's scared of something. Why else would he be putting off harvest for this?"

"I'd wager he is," another agreed. Mike wondered whether they realized he could hear them. "Maybe something with Marcus. It was the night before we started doing this that he fought and banished him."

"Yeah, but why would he be afraid of one man who he already beat?"

"There's got to be something else. He's got to know something that he's not telling us."

"Yeah. But you know what? If he feels like this is necessary, that's good enough for me. He's gone out of his way to save us once, I'm confident that's all that's on his mind now. I don't care to know the details."

The conversation had given him comfort. It had not been the first time he had heard such comments from the people. Confident, faith abiding utterances had blanketed Newhaven's hill the entire time, not leaving any room for criticism. Hearing such remarks of confidence was the one positive thing that issued forth during the following days of stress.

After much deliberation, Mike decided to still observe the Sabbath. Two days had already yielded a fair amount of progress. Two of the towers on the southeast part of the town where the hill was least steep were completed as well as the trench in between the two. The trench was about three feet wide and three feet deep, and the displaced earth had been interspersed with rocks on the inner side to form a four foot earthen wall. The people had, indeed, worked extremely hard, and despite the impending threat of invasion, they needed the break.

Work ceased, yet Mike continued to be restless. He wished he could simply sit down and daydream on the menial things of life again, but in just these few short weeks, so much had changed that he had forgotten how. He relaxed by hunting for young, straight wood, and spent much of the morning and early afternoon making more arrows. The task, in reality, did not allow him much of a break. Although the task was much less physically demanding, it kept the pending situation burning at the forefront of his mind. He knew, all too well, that these arrows were not intended for furry flesh.

The arrow manufacture could only be done for so long anyway, though, and by mid-afternoon, Mike was up and walking around the complex again, seeing what other people were doing, talking to them, but not being able to sit down long enough to have a good conversation. After acknowledging a few others, he found himself walking up to Gaius, who greeted him with a smile.

"I always seem to find you sitting down drinking outside your hut," he told him, greeting him as well. "And you always look so relaxed."

Gaius let out a short chuckle. "Come join me, Mike. You look like you need to take a seat." Mike obeyed. Gaius then continued to sit, not finding it necessary to do or say anything. Mike turned toward him and stared him down curiously. He seemed to be entirely at peace with everything, despite the mayhem that was presently unfolding. Gaius noticed Mike's stare and gave him a questioning look.

"How do you do it, Gaius?" Mike asked in response.

"Do what?" he inquired.

"How are you able to just sit around like this? This is the day of rest, but I don't seem to be able to do that anymore."

Gaius let out a casual chortle. "I've sat around my whole life, Mike," he answered. "Being a shepherd requires a lot of that. You have to learn to relax and take the moments easily."

"Even with the threat of wolves?" Mike thought back on Gaius' reference to the enemies when he had been praising Diana.

Gaius nodded. "Even with the wolves."

Mike shook his head in frustration. "How do you do that?"

Gaius shrugged. "It comes in time, I guess. There's not one particular moment where I can say I learned it." Gaius took another sip from his skin. "I'll tell you one thing though; I never could have learned it without the wolves."

Mike turned away and sat back, pondering on the wisdom of the words. Unfortunately, he knew that they were all too true.

As Mike looked out, he noted Diana walking past. She noticed him, gave a cordial smile, and waved. Mike was not sure whether it was directed toward him, Gaius, or the two of them, but Gaius seemed to be sure of his opinion.

"So you've spent some time with that girl in the past week then, eh?"

Mike turned to him. "How did you know?" He looked on at Diana, who had sat down across the way at the commons table with a Constantia and a few other girls.

"It's pretty common knowledge around here. Plus, my children told me that you came to them together."

A smile escaped Mike's lips. "She's an amazing girl."

"That she is. And you're really the only adult that she's opened up to. That's quite the accomplishment."

"Yeah, well, that next day was the last time I talked to her. She helped me out, that was all it was."

Gaius smiled widely. "I doubt it, Mike. Any of those girls over there would give anything for you to call them yours. Diana may have had some nightmares in her life to disable her emotions, but inside, she is just as much, if not more, of a woman than any other girl. I think she is starting to realize that again. It shows in the way she looks at you. If you like her back, take every opportunity you can to spend time with her."

Mike nodded.

"Besides," Gaius added, "you need a female counterpart to tame that wild soul of yours. You're bound to get yourself killed without it."

Mike laughed at the description. "Thanks for the advice; I'll look for those opportunities."

The first of those opportunities came only a few short hours later, when everyone had sat down to the evening meal. They had just started eating when Mike noted Diana's figure appear in the commons. Mike's mouth ceased chewing, for this was the first time he had seen her make an appearance at the evening meal. She did not hide the fact well, either, for her eyes slowly and uncomfortably perused, looking for a place to sit, a place to fit in. Upon catching sight of Mike and an empty spot beside him, she directed herself over to him. Mike felt slightly surprised but made room for her.

"Hello, Mike," she said quietly, and slowly started filling her plate with food. Mike decided not to say anything about her presence, not wanting to shake an already unstable chair. Instead, they engaged in entirely different conversation, mostly about the work that had been going on and how the weather had cooperated stunningly well so far. The conversation evolved over time, only finding itself in temporary lulls, and Mike was surprised to find it still engaged as the party began cleaning up and walking back to their huts. Mike, himself, followed Diana back to her hut with her portion of leftover food. As she paused at the door, Mike was not sure what to do. He muttered a quick thanks to her for sitting next to him and was about to take his strides back to his own hut, but he paused and allowed himself a direct look into her eyes. She was placidly staring back—a privilege with which he had not frequently been allowed.

"Take a walk with me," she requested, "unless you have some other pending task at hand."

Mike chuckled in disbelief. "No," he returned, "I have nothing."

They walked silently over to Mike's hut so he could shed his food, then they headed out toward the trees on the south side of the hill. As they walked, the foundations of the wall they were building lay before them. In the light of the set sun and rising moon, they passed in between the two shadowed towers that stood watch for the community. Mike already felt a greater sense of security from them, almost as if they were parents, their giant figures standing before them to protect them from harm. They would soon surround the community and complete the feeling, but for now, this was good enough.

"You've been hard at work with these people," she commented as they awkwardly traversed the hill and ditch.

"Yeah, and the work that still needs to be done seems overwhelming. I hope that these people can keep up their motivation."

Mike did not look over at his partner in this stroll, but he could almost feel her out. Her steps were calm and steady, as if she did not hold the same worries as Mike.

"I think they feel you're a good leader," she posed, and she paused. "*I* think you're a good leader."

Mike took the opportunity now to glance over at her. Her face held nothing but sincerity. "Thank you," he replied, "it feels good to hear that from you."

They walked on and along the darkness of the trees. "You seem to put too much blame on yourself, though," she continued, "unnecessarily, too."

"What do you mean?" he asked.

"I haven't been able to help but notice that you've seemed downcast the past week. You can't blame yourself for others' actions."

Mike could feel the dam of his suppressed thoughts cracking. Diana had found the niche and was driving one of Cai's wedges into it. He allowed it to happen. "It tore me apart fighting Marcus," he confessed, "He was one of us, Diana, and I wanted to kill him. I've never felt like such a tyrant in my life."

"He was not one of us," she assured, "he was a traitor. Your actions were taken in necessity, not in privilege."

"How do you think the people felt, seeing me like that, though?"

"They respect you more for it, Mike," she assured without delay. Mike looked over at her. It was good to hear her call him by name; it seemed a grand reminder that through everything, at least one person saw him in the same light. Diana continued. "They need that from a leader right now. You cannot always be the nice guy in these times. I've seen that attempted before." She paused slowly. "That's how my father was."

Mike hesitated in his step, caught off-guard at the sudden change in meter in the conversation. Just a moment ago, she had been playing the doctor and him, the patient, but now she seemed to be begging for the opposite. *Ask me again some other time, Mike.* She seemed to be calling out those words right now. Mike jumped at the opportunity.

"What happened with your father?"

The words were out, just like they had been several times before. Several times before they had been shot down, but there, as the two locked eye contact at the edge of the darkness, she seemed to be saying, *Alright, I am finally ready to tell you.* Diana started in.

"My grandfather's father was one of the primary lawgivers in Northern Gaul. When he was fairly young, he was commissioned to come up here to ensure order amidst the threats of invasion. He was given charge of the northern military unit in York, which he ran from the villa he built in the country, where his family would not have to deal with the harshness of military life. The Romans pulled out of York about fifty years ago, but my grandfather, who had just taken his father's spot, asked to stay along with about 100 other soldiers. Permission was granted and our family remained.

"I grew up just as any other Roman noble. You can only imagine what that was like for a young girl such as myself. At the age of 19, I fell in love with one of the soldiers, a young energetic Roman by the name of Fabian. He was one of the best men I ever knew. He was strong, yet kind, rugged, yet refined, wild, yet mild mannered when appropriate. We started seeing each other and he started courting me. Things were soon all lined up for our union.

"That was when things started happening. Word got to my father that several of the native chieftains had called on barbarian mercenaries to give them extra protection. They were beginning to come to the shores in response. Fabian told me of the nature of the various meetings the soldiers held, how everyone was worried about their influence and what they would try to do. My father, on the other hand, wanted to form an alliance with them. He wanted to trust in their goodwill, and he had the final say in the decision."

"Word soon got out that several Saxon men had come ashore just down the coast. My father invited them to his villa to work things out. Fabian was not present during the meeting, and so I don't know what happened in there. I just remember watching and taking note of the Saxon leader's savage grin as he passed me."

"One night, Fabian and I were out walking in the vineyards when we heard the sound of crashing come from the villa. Our attentions were diverted over to see the same Saxons attacking the place. I cannot forget the fear I felt at that moment. I would later find out it was only the beginning."

Diana resumed walking again. Mike followed.

"Fabian unsheathed his sword and told me to run to the forest, that he'd come back for me. I disobeyed, and as he ran off, sword in hand, I followed. I approached and saw Lucius and his family cut down. I could not believe my eyes. I wanted more than anything to obey Fabian and run off to the forest, but I had to find him and my family. I hid behind a woodpile only to witness my father and Fabian fighting off the hoards side by side. They were greatly outnumbered and I realized, even from the start, that there was not much hope. I wanted to scream out but had no strength to do so. I watched that same leader, who had acted so civil before, cut down my lover. He collapsed, and I screamed out. He looked at me one last time with more love in his eyes than I have ever seen in a man before.

"The leader heard me and directed his pursuit toward me. I tried to flee but he caught me. He stated some words in Saxon, which I remembered clear enough to be able to later understand. He stated, 'you shall be all mine now, but first I must finish my business here.' He left me in the trust of two of his henchmen and made me watch as he dragged out my father and beat him to death. His business then seemed to be at an end, and he turned back toward me. That was when the real nightmare started.

"The Saxons took complete control of the villa. I was soon told what happened to my mother, and would rather not relate the tale. I hoped that they would kill me too, but the leader had other ideas in mind for me. For a while I fought, trusting that the company in York would come for me. I soon found out, however, that they had all either been killed or had deserted. Gradually, all my will to fight died out, and any resistance I initially showed slowly waned away into hatred and, at the same time, utter helplessness."

Mike looked at Diana's features. He was astounded to be hearing what he was, and even more astounded to find that her face now only held hints of detached soberness. Diana seemed to have no more to say concerning the subject, and Mike figured that she had reached the point where he had jumped into the story. Had he known this preamble beforehand, he would never have seen her as a demoness, but simply as a broken shade.

"I hope," she concluded, "you can understand that I had planned on keeping this story untold." She struggled to swallow the tears in her eyes. "You've become Godsend to me, Mike."

Mike was so dumbfounded that he was only able to give her a nod.

Chapter 30

The next month and a half yielded much more joy. The people continued in their industry, and the fortress began to take shape. True to Mike's schedule, they were able to get a skeleton framework laid out before he felt like they could not put off the threshing any longer. The mornings and evenings were getting cooler. Fog appeared more and more prevalent in the morning. The clouds started threatening rain more frequently. The air, indeed, was saturated with autumn and could no longer hold back in raining down upon them. Mike and the others got soaked more than once as they worked, but Mike just looked on and smiled at the brotherhood that was definitely becoming exposed.

The agrarian mode resumed, but just like everything else, it came to an end in its own due time. As the last of the grain was separated and stored, Mike looked out at the fields in satisfaction. Many would have called them dead, but Mike saw them through brighter eyes. The land was simply retired for the season. It had served its time and yielded its abundance. It had been the community's greatest friend, along with the ideal weather that they had still been experiencing late into the season. Because of it, Newhaven would again survive the winter.

The next several weeks were spent in continuing to fortify the fortress, a task that proved much easier than the initial framework, for the community had had to learn about structure as they built, and although they finished according to the time Mike had originally intended, it did not come without having to tear down and try again. The intensity of work had necessarily increased and the days had been lengthened, yet Mike never had to take the time to motivate the people. Although Mike had kept the details of Marcus' situation discrete, the people still felt the urgency to fortify. Their trust in Mike still held strong, and their growing faith in their own security moved them along.

And, for the first time, Mike felt a true bond begin to form amongst the community. There had been times in the past where a bond had been evident, such as the feast at Equinox, but this was more solid, more permanent. There seemed to be an unprecedented amount of light shining down on Newhaven, even in the waning season, for there was no longer a need to apportion it individually. And the difference reflected in the people's countenances. While a portion of the air, indeed, was filled with trepidation at the prospect of attack, the majority of the air was charged with joviality and laughter, with flirtatiousness and song, and with increased intermingling at the meal table. Mike could not help but be overjoyed at the sight.

He could not help but notice, either, that there was a true bond forming between him and Diana as well. Fate brought them together at one point or another most every day. She no longer hesitated to approach him or talk to him, and she no longer hesitated to smile and laugh. Mike could not help but notice it was the same laugh he had seen from the tower that rainy night which now seemed so long ago. The laugh had seemed distant then; now it was readily at his disposal. His opportunities came, he took them, and he never tired of them.

They frequently took walks together, more often than not in close proximity to the town, for there was so much work to be done, but he enjoyed even the few moments he was able to spend with her. They would converse as they walked, and what Mike saw filled his heart with life. Her speech revealed her extensive education in the Roman ways, including rule of law and ethics, and her opinions revealed that she had applied such education into her daily thoughts. She continued to press Mike to teach her some English, on which he followed through. She caught on quickly, and it was wonderful to hear his native tongue again, especially when she would repeat such idioms and slang words as "cool" and "awesome" at just the right moments.

Diana had her moments of weakness still, though they were less frequent. Bouts of anti-socialism and haughty arrogance would come through in her speech and attitude, the latter being a subject with which

Mike had subtly tried to help her. Even though it pained him to see her like that, it was hard to condemn her. Mike knew that she had grown up with everything, and had lived her whole life with the mentality of the superiority of the Romans. The rule of Saxons had humbled her a great deal, for, because of them, she had also lost more than anyone else, but at times, the subsequently easier life in Newhaven brought her childhood pride back.

Overall, though, Mike was determined to squint at her idiosyncrasies, for he found in squinting, they looked far less like stains and far more like wrinkles that could be ironed out in time. He found that the less he strained his eyes at her, the better he saw her. The same held true with the rest of the people in the community. He recalled what he had seen of Cassius and Arthur at the beginning of the season. They had changed and become solid members of the community, refusing to stand out and performing their duties quietly, but with utmost care. Mike also noticed the truth in Julius, who seemed to be putting forth more zealous efforts in the projects at hand in order to atone for his mistakes.

But most of the effort was completed now, and just in time. Cold weather was truly starting to threaten the community and had struck in small spurts several times already. The community started to descend into its normal, winter hibernation, wherein it was not as important to wake up at the crack of dawn, wherein nothing more than daily domestic activities were required. Many of the members began performing all the tasks that they had put off during the growing season, including making repairs and improvements to their huts. Others simply pleased themselves by socializing with others, talking, joking, and telling stories.

The notes of musical instruments could also be heard ringing through the air, even though Lucius was still nowhere to be found. Mike often wondered about him, wondered how he and Aeola were faring, if at all. He worried about their safety, for the world, indeed, was steadily growing colder, and he worried that they were too tied up in each other's touch to notice. The seas seemed to be washing up farther and farther inland, and he worried that they were too caught up in each other's eyes to care. Mike hoped that Lucius would soon break his trance; he hoped that they would be seeing their faces returning sometime in the very proximate future.

FORTH FROM EDEN

Mike did not over sweat it, though. There was too much beneath his gaze in Newhaven to worry about what was outside, beyond his reach. Among those proximate foci included that pair of beautiful eyes which toyed with him with greater and greater frequency. Mike was not about to let that go.

And, on this particular day, when the weather decided to please Newhaven with tame temperatures, that pair of beautiful eyes came knocking on his door once again. They enlisted him to ride out with them, into the country on horseback. Mike could not deny them. They stole away privately, for talk was now circulating around about them and Mike wanted to avoid any bantering that he could, and soon they were out upon the land, far from anything else in the world.

We are now close friends, Mike thought to himself as they dipped down into a stream and back out. He watched Diana as she rode, playfully chiding her horse through the water without hardly slowing down. Mike pursued in a sort of follow the leader fashion, which she made difficult due to the superior abilities of her horse and her horse riding.

"One of these times," he called out to her, "you're going to lose me, because I'm not going to bother trying to keep up anymore. You'll look back only to find that you're all alone."

"Maybe so," she returned, yelling out over her shoulder, "but you've said that before, and you've never followed through on your threats. How am I supposed to believe you will act any differently?"

Mike smiled, shook his head, and slowed down as he cleared the bushes surrounding the stream. She had seemed to anticipate that and slowed down at almost the same time. As Mike watched her, he again acknowledged the excitement that he still felt at being around her. He had often wondered whether she ever felt the same. Her actions and mannerisms, at times, even her comments reflected this attitude, but he had never been sure. Mike bit his lip at the situation even now as he pulled up beside her and caught her smiling at him. He wanted to ask her about it, now, while she was captured in the moment, but he knew that he would not. He knew that he would keep silent and honor himself by honoring his past oath to her. That would only change on her accord. Then and only then he could allow himself to rethink such things with earnestness.

They were riding side by side now, with no sound but the hard breathing of the walking horses exchanging between them. Mike was about to re-engage in light conversation when he noticed a cloud of dust being kicked up beyond some trees to the south of them. "What do you suppose that is?" he asked, pointing it out.

Diana matched the direction of her gaze with Mike's. "I don't know," she responded in English. "Maybe deer."

Mike was not convinced, however. He still went everywhere with the emblem, although it had not responded to him in a long time. His fingers felt for it at this moment, and the reaction was quite different. A flash of warning rang loudly in his heart. "Let's go check it out," Mike asserted, trying to keep his alarm as masked as possible. This time, Mike led and Diana followed.

They quickly crossed through the trees, and the sight at the other end of the clearing confirmed Mike's dread. They were far enough away that Mike could not make anything out clearly, but from what he thought he saw, he felt like he could identify who was at the front.

His thoughts moving like lightning, Mike turned to Diana. He could not hide his dread any longer. "Go take a northern route back to Newhaven. Get everybody on alert. I'll meet you there."

"What about you?" she asked. She was yet unmoved.

"Don't worry about me. I'll be there in a bit."

Now the alarm sounded in her voice. "What are you going to do?"

"Impede them. Now go!" Mike's voice was a command. She turned and rode off quickly.

Mike focused his attention back on the mass of riders. There were a lot of them, enough to do Newhaven damage, even with its fortifications and heightened awareness. It would not be enough to simply retreat back with Diana. He had to do something now. Mike felt for his bow.

He would have hoped that he could head them off by riding along through the trees or in an adjacent field where he could have cover, but he quickly calculated that there was no time for that. They were riding too fast. Mike looked again at the foremost rider, then remounted his own horse and took off along the edge of the trees.

He had also hoped that the riders would not notice him until it was too late, but he realized that that, too, was impossible now. Two of them broke away from the group and came chasing after him. Mike's head was surprisingly clear as he took them by surprise and kicked his heels into his horse, chiding it on toward the front of the group instead of away. The emblem seemed to almost pulse inside his cloak. He had almost headed off the group, in position to attack the entire army, when he drew an arrow back in his bow. In reality, only one man held his attention; for the moment, the rest of the army meant nothing. Mike shot and his arrow sailed true to the heart.

Everything after that seemed to occur in slow, but reawakened, motion. Marcus fell, watching Mike in disbelief as he did. The army halted and also stared at Mike in disbelief. They then began advancing slowly towards him. Mike realized that there could be no escape now. Death was a probability, its chances only slightly reduced if he opened his mouth now. Mike found himself grasping at the opportunity.

"Saxons," Mike yelled out in their language, standing his ground amidst their advance, "you see your guide is dead. The secrecy of our location has been preserved."

Mike watched as one of the Saxon leaders motioned for him to be taken. Mike did not resist. He had done all he could for the people of Newhaven. Whatever else happened to him did not matter now. One of the soldiers swung out at his head and everything went dark.

Chapter 31

Darkness enveloped Mike's head as he awoke with a splitting pain in his temple. It took a moment for him to properly focus his eyes on his surroundings, and when he did, his head cried out in objection and pleaded to him to stop the torture. He closed his eyes again and lay back on the hard ground below him. There had not seemed to be much to focus on anyway, for the room was fairly dim. The only source of light was an emanation of strips of whiteness through slits near the ceiling. The room contained shadows, which looked almost like furniture, yet there either did not seem to be a bed, or his captors had not cared to place him in it.

A rock formed in Mike's stomach as he thought back on the last occurrences that he could remember. Everything had happened so fast—a thousand decisions had been made with hardly any consultation to his conscious mind. His order for Diana to leave, his riding out against the army, his slaying of the leader, a man who had formerly been a townsman—all of these things had happened so fast and all of them had contributed to destroy the few remaining aspects of happiness that Mike had still managed to maintain.

He now found himself a prisoner in some unfamiliar cell, alone. The same feelings that Mike had felt after Abe's death bade entrance to his barely beating heart. Back then, he had been lost, without friends, and without purpose. It had been a feeling of utter emptiness, as if some demon had sucked all the life out of him. He had done all he could to depart from those feelings, to gather what was at his hands and make something of it. And he had. He had formed the pieces of his life into a grand sculpture, something in which he took pride, something that kept him looking out on it with bright eyes, something that had begun to attract the eyes of another.

Now all of that was gone and the pain had returned. Diana was gone. His city was gone. Ahead of him lie only darkness.

He knew, too, that nothing would gain any definition until the enemy came and shed some light on him. He did not even know how long he had been out, let alone what he was even doing here. Despite his lifeless emotions, the pangs of hunger gripped at Mike's sides and reminded him that he still breathed. They had taken him alive, for he very much doubted that he was dead. He felt as mortal as he ever had, and that pulsing pain in his temple was just another evidence. Beyond these conclusions, he could go no further, and so he allowed himself to fall back into the distorted world of dreamland.

Mike's next recollections were of a jarring kick to his side and an angry Saxon voice yelling for him to get up. The kick came again, forcing all air out of his lungs and daring, with pain, for more to enter. Mike's head was dizzy, and he felt like he couldn't obey the order, but he defied the notion and struggled to get his feet under him—anything to avoid a third kick. A burly figure stood before him, and Mike found himself latching onto it for support as his legs struggled to find equilibrium of balance. The figure violently pushed him off, and he felt himself crashing into the doorframe. "Get off me, wretch!" he heard its voice command.

After spending a moment latched onto the wall, Mike finally felt the power to stand on his own. His head continued to swim, and with slow progress, he was able to focus on his aggressor, who now took him powerfully by the arm and ordered, "Come with me." Mike did his best to obey, not fighting the rough handling, but staring at its perpetrator instead. The man, who was about the same build as Mike, had a strange familiarity about him, though Mike could not put his finger on it in his present state of mind.

They walked down a short, torch lit corridor before turning into a very Romanesque room with a table full of food. The Saxon shoved Mike in and slammed the door behind him. Mike continued to survey the room. There were four reclining couches surrounding the table, and in one of them lay another Saxon who had seemed to be awaiting him. In the brief, primary moment that Mike was given, he looked at this man in intrigue. He wore the sandals and toga of a Roman, but was obviously of barbaric origin.

In fact, the man looked to be a still water reflection of Mike himself. He was big, with long and straight blond hair and a strong jaw line. His facial expression was surprisingly calm—a strange manner that made Mike extremely uncomfortable.

"Mike," he said in Saxon. "Come down and dine with me."

Mike slowly advanced forward. "Don't worry," he added, "it's not poisoned." At that the man picked up a drumstick and bit into it, showing Mike that he was sincere. Mike sat down on an opposite couch, paused, surveyed the food, then dug in with vigor.

"Relax," the man casually invited. "You know, when the Romans eat, they take their time. They savor every bite," the man gave a demonstration with his drumstick, biting into it slowly and passing the food around in his mouth. "They do not eat like us."

Mike paused. He looked at the Roman-clad Saxon, who was, in turn, staring back at him with a ghastly smile. "What do you mean, like us?" he posed. His stomach, though in a frenzied hunger, suddenly turned over.

The man continued smiling. "Relax," he repeated. "Lay back. Take advantage of the food before you. My men would die to have food like this."

Mike knew his body needed the nourishment, and that became the only reason he slowly reclined back and resumed eating. Yet he could not deny the overpowering discomfort he felt in this man's presence. After looking at him again, he noted that this man had been the one directly behind Marcus, the man that had ordered his capture. *What's going on here?* he wondered. Mike suddenly resolved to not give in to any coercion he offered, except the one to eat.

The Saxon allowed Mike to do that very thing uninterrupted, which unnerved Mike even more. He tried to ignore his stare; he tried to ignore the entire situation. He tried to focus solely on the fruits, nuts, wine, and bird before him. It was not easy.

"You know," he continued after a time, "the Romans really had comfort down to a science. We men of the north are always too focused on the technology of war. Maybe we should focus more on things like this, don't you agree?"

There was the same reference to relation. Mike stopped chewing and looked up from his food to again stare down the man, who felt no scruple in returning it back upon him. Mike seemed to catch a limited view of the man's soul as he locked onto his intensely blue gaze. Its details were convoluted and cryptic, but Mike was able to decipher enough of its general shade to know of its dirtiness, to know that its only intentions were to tear down Mike's self image before doing the real damage. Again, the feelings of discomfort arose in Mike's head. The Saxon seemed to read his mind.

"You cannot find my assumption absurd on any account. It's obvious that you are not Roman, and I very much doubt you are Celtic either. You would blend right in with my ranks and you speak perfect Saxon. My question is how you got mixed up in your societies."

"I speak perfect Latin as well," Mike said in Latin. Despite the change in language, the man seemed to understand.

"A language which will soon mean nothing here, Mike."

Again, there was an underlying of familiarity in his voice. "How do you know my name?" Mike demanded.

"Forgive me," the Saxon stated, diverting from Mike's question. "I have not introduced myself. My name is Edric. Edric of the Saxons." He held out his hand to Mike. Mike refused it and Edric sat back unoffended.

"I've heard about you," he continued calmly. "Marcus, our common Roman friend has told me a lot about you—about your community, about your leadership, about your skill in battle, about your fair complexion. Even if his last words had not denoted that you were, in fact, this legend, I would have known it anyway. The way you commanded that weapon was simply stunning." Edric leaned back and threw up his arms. "I just wonder why you used it against him."

"He was not my friend," Mike answered. "He was a traitor. I would not let him reveal our whereabouts."

The Saxon who called himself Edric laughed hard. "Mike, what's the point? We're going to find it anyway. I hope I can help you understand that for some reason you got on the wrong side. Marcus had it right, and he wasn't even a Saxon like you are."

"I am not one of you," Mike scowled, suddenly deciding to arise from the couch and stand before him.

Edric continued laughing. "Again, what argument do you have for that? Look at you."

For the first time, Mike noticed that he still retained the emblem. For one reason or another, they had not taken it from him, a fact that did not make sense, yet a fact that he did not question, for sense had taken a backstage role ever since he arrived in this world in the first place. Mike was suddenly filled with renewed courage. He countered his opponent stately. "My principles guide my identity, not my appearance."

Edric looked at Mike in silence for a moment before consequentially taking a different path in conversation. "Mike, the sun is set on the Roman Empire. I think you know that just as well as I do. The Romans have pulled out of Britain; the native chieftains are calling for our protection now."

Mike shook his head defiantly. "I've seen what you do here. You cannot call it protection."

Edric shrugged. "Everything has a price. The natives want our rule; we're going to help them, but we won't do it for free." Mike's blood started to boil at the comment. Edric continued on. "Keep that in mind as I make you this offer, Mike. I want you to join us on the ruling side. Your reputation and your actions have proved your aptitude. I would consider you my right hand man. Nothing has to change. You may continue to rule Newhaven; just do it with us instead of against us."

"You're insane," Mike seethed. "Do you honestly think that I could do that to my people? You know how many of their kin you have killed?"

"You realize how many of the men here want to kill you for what you've done to theirs, Mike?"

Mike furrowed his eyebrows. Edric continued. "That guard that brought you in here? You've seen him before. You disabled him just before killing his brother while on the road to York. That says nothing of the massacre you inflicted at the villa north of here."

Mike's heart momentarily stopped in horror. Flashes of those moments a year ago rushed through his memory, haunting him with the same fears which had been so apparent back then.

"I see you remember," Edric stated, taking note of his face. "You see, it goes both ways. I could justifiably allow him to cut you down in an instant, but I've preserved you instead. All I ask in return is the location of

Newhaven. You don't even have to show your face to them if you don't feel up to it. I could get you connected up somewhere else in Britain. There would be glory, money, women—anything you wanted. You would never worry of starving again. Cut your ties with the natives, Mike. You're not one of them; you know you aren't."

Mike sat silent, staring at him. He had nothing to say. He could feel the truth of Edric's words breaking his inner self down. His natural impulse told him to lash out at the being, for his hands remained free and his enemy vulnerable to his massive frame, but his rational mind was able to subdue the desire. The action, as much as it would have seemed to vent the inner battle raging inside of him, would have only ended up in disaster.

"Think about that tonight," he said. "Tell me in the morning." Then, with a clap of Edric's hands, the guard re-entered to dismiss Mike, the same guard who had seemed only a haunting ghost not two days before.

Mike was thrown into his room again and felt the pounding of the door slam behind him. He now saw that there was a bed provided him and promptly lay down on it dizzy at the pounding that still echoed in his head. It rattled his brain, mixing everything that he had placed in order into one, giant mass of relativism. Mike lay back on the bed, then got up and paced around in torment. Despite the sureness of his refusals, he found his resolve as solid as thin ice. Edric's words had sunk deep into his skin; it seemed to run in his veins and pulse through his head in periodic poundings.

You're not one of them, Mike; you know you aren't.

The words were true on paper. *Are the natives really my people?* He had attached himself to them out of necessity. He was not from this world. They were not his responsibility. *What is stopping me from joining Edric's side?* In reality, he would be among his true ancestors. *Shouldn't I adhere to them, especially since they're on the winning side?* Mike knew the destiny of the Saxons far better than any of the Saxons knew it. *What reason is there to resist? Why live at the brink of destruction when a life of ease, pleasure and luxury is within reach?* Mike thought back on the mission. He wanted to say that the mission had chosen his side for him from the beginning, but even that could not be justified. Abe had taught him both Latin and Saxon.

Maybe, he thought, *I did enter on the wrong side.* Such thoughts told him to switch, to accept Edric's offer and regain a future for himself. Mike passed the emblem quietly through his fingers. Flashes of Diana, Lucius, Julius, Cai, Gaius, and Newhaven itself rushed through his mind. Flashes of everything he had done, everything for which he had worked in the past year ground against his logos, fighting to regain the ground it had suddenly seemed to have lost. Mike suddenly longed for it to do so; he wished he could resolve that his opinion would remain unmoved. The victory would not be easy when on trial. Ultimately, it would come down to the moment, the moment when Edric gave him his choice of consequences. He prayed to God, a being who he suddenly felt he should have known better, for strength. Even so, the battle tormented him, depriving him of his sleep, for he watched as one side, then the other gained the advantage.

Dawn came cruelly, not more than a few hours after Mike drifted off to sleep, and with its rays came the same guard. Mike submitted himself to his cruel jarrings without resistance, reviewing the mental events of last night. He was different this morning than he had been last night. Through it all, he recalled one side gaining quarter over the other. And somehow, the few hours of rest that he received seemed to solidify that victory. It seemed to rejuvenate not only his body, but his courage at the consequences he was to face. His expression held no strain as he was thrown before Edric, once again.

"Mike," he said, welcoming him in with a gesture of his hand. "How did you sleep last night? Most definitely better since you were able to discover that bed, eh?"

Mike did not answer.

"Come down and eat with me."

Mike let Edric's entreaty fall to the ground. "I'm not hungry," he declared. "You may as well dismiss me now; my decision is set."

Mike assured himself with his words that the victory, had, indeed, been definite. The battle was over, leaving his resolve as solid as a rock. He could not determine how or why, only that it was. Mike stood himself up a little bit straighter as Edric got up and approached him, then placed his hand on Mike's shoulder as if he were his friend. Looking Mike in the eye, he stated, "I had hoped that you had thought this through."

If Edric's pause and stare was for a change of mind, he was

disappointed. "You do not seem to me to be a man of shallow thought, Mike. Marcus told me of what you had done with that community. He told me of the richness and abundance that you produced in a matter of only a year. He told me of its ideal central location. He told me how good of a control station it would be for enterprising commanders like me."

"Marcus told stories. His description of our abundance is exaggerated."

"I highly doubt it," Edric said. "I think you give yourself less credit than you deserve. You see, Mike, I did some rethinking myself this past night and am frankly impressed by your stamina. You are a great leader, Mike, and despite my hopes, I would have been surprised if you had given in so easily. I would love to have you as one of my top men, but I realize that that is impossible. I'll therefore give you another option. Let's do battle, you and me. I'm giving you the opportunity to go free and lead your men against me on fair grounds. I will not make you promise to keep me alive if you defeat me, but I swear that if my men defeat your men, you will not be harmed—as long as you swear allegiance to me."

Mike paused. For a moment, he felt that that was a more than fair agreement. For a moment, he felt confident that it would work, that they could beat Edric. His men were trained in battle. They had beaten Saxons before. They were organized. These men were not used to fighting organized armies. The emblem had helped him before, it would ultimately help him in this case as well.

Mike felt uncomfortable at the thought, though. He wanted it to work. He wanted to be set free, to be able to lead his men in battle, to destroy all hope that these men would ever bother him again. He craved to be with Diana again, to share her laughter, to continue life with everybody with whom he had grown so close this past year.

It was not right, though. Mike stood his ground in regal silence. Edric reached out his hand. Mike looked at it but did nothing.

"You realize I cannot offer you anything more," Edric stated soberly. Any hint of casualness was no longer in his voice.

"It would do you no good anyway. You will not receive any information out of me."

Edric slammed his fist on the table, rattling the various plates of food. Mike blinked, but did nothing more. "Mike, don't you get it? My men will find your city. They are searching the countryside right now. How will your people stand up to us without you?"

"My people's fate cannot be changed. I will not, however, be the one to condemn them. Nothing you can do can shake me."

Edric suddenly resumed his composure. "I guess we'll see about that. I hope you realize that up to this point, I have been your protector, your protector from these men. I see now that I can no longer be that. I still have a hope that I can get what I want out of you, and so I will not allow them to kill you. But what I will allow will make you wish that they could."

With another clap of the hands, Mike's sentence was passed and the same guard came in. Mike could hear him chuckling evilly. It was obvious that he had overheard the entire conversation. Mike could not think of what was to come. He forced such things out of his mind. He forced himself, instead, to stare down his prosecutor as he was roughly led out. Edric turned away. He could not look at Mike. Mike suddenly became the one to emit a smile—despite everything that occurred around him. It was the smile of a victor.

Victory would not come easy, though. This fact was made plain in a dark room of the prison about which Mike soon learned to have nightmares. Unless one had ever experienced such pain, one could never quite understand the stamina Mike discovered he had. Every inch that felt the oppressor's tool screamed out to Mike, shrieking with shrillness, wrenching in convulsions of fastidious curses toward his resolve. Body made desperate pleas against soul, begging for mercy, begging for the pain to be over. Screaming was abandoned almost immediately; the agony fell far beyond that. Instead, Mike found himself holding his breaths, closing his eyes, and waiting helplessly for the moment to be over.

Edric attended silently, leaving all of the cursing and horrid laughter to the man who had once fallen before Mike's blows. The tables were turned now and this time, Mike found himself to be the one strapped down to them.

Pain was rotated with nightmare. Each evening, Mike found himself caught somewhere between sleep and stupor—too drained to keep himself awake, too much in pain to lose consciousness. It was at this edge that Edric's monstrous figure always hovered, offering his outstretched hand.

"Come with me," he would say, "and all of this will end. You don't have to feel this anymore. Let the fates of your friends fall where they may. Save yourself."

Day after day continued, each day leaving Mike to wonder when he'd finally break one way or the other. Death seemed to hover just above him, just out of reach. His body seemed yet unwilling to give up its status of life, and his principles remained unscathed. They were the only things left unscathed. Mike yearned to be able to look back and say it was all a dream, but the putrid, black scars or the sharp hisses of flesh sizzling were too real, to ever-present to be an imagination. It was a pain that did not depart, but lingered as a scar, reminding Mike's mind of what had been done, and what would return with the following day. The comparably milder nightmares raced like seconds while the minutes of pain were prolonged for lifetimes. Every moment processed a million messages of hate to Mike's soul, telling him to give up, to give Edric what he wanted. Still, they somehow remained ignored. Each time he made that death march to that room, his confidence in his strength waned, but each time he returned, he found himself without shame.

After one terribly long night, the door to Mike's cell again opened. Mike submissively got up—all part of the routine—and prepared to give himself over to his torturer. He was surprised to find, however, that Edric filled the frame instead.

"Stay where you are," he ordered. Mike obeyed. Edric silently stepped in and shut the door behind him. "I would ask you how you are but I already think I know the answer." Mike simply scowled at Edric's sadistic humor. "You have done it, Mike. You have convinced me that you will not be shaken. I am surprised at you."

"You would be," Mike simply declared. "You could never understand."

"I think I do, though." Edric held out his right arm. Mike noticed something that he had not before noticed. Edric had no right hand. "I lost it when I was younger. Britain hasn't been the only place to be invaded during these times. It's a different pain than yours, but I still feel it to the same degree. I don't know that you realize how hard life is without a hand, Mike."

Mike stared back at Edric, trying to figure out what he was getting at. Whatever it was, Mike now knew that he could stand it.

"I'll bet you wonder," he continued sitting down next to Mike, "why we kept your body intact, why we did not break any bones, poke out any eyes, or cut off any limbs. I'll tell you why. It's because I respect you too much, Mike. A true soldier's greatest nightmare is incapacitation. I could never do that to you."

Mike still could not tell where Edric was headed. He continued to stare at the man. Edric opened his mouth, once more. "I am, however, losing my confidence that you will be of any worth to us. That is why I am giving you an ultimatum. I am giving you one last opportunity to reveal the location of your community to us. Otherwise, you have two days to live. You choose to work with us, you go free. You choose to remain silent, you die."

Mike stared at Edric, and slowly, the blankness in his expression turned to a small but firm smirk.

"What?" Edric inquired, seeming agitated. "What are you smiling about? Have you heard what I just said? Why are you smiling?" Edric squirmed, as if Mike's stare was now the one doing the burning on him.

Mike, on the other hand, was calm, stunningly calm. When he opened his mouth to speak, his voice was even, sonorous. "I am smiling because I have won. You think death is a threat to me anymore? Edric, you have sent me to Hell and back; Heaven is a welcome option. I am smiling because you already know this. You know that after all you have done to me, I have still come out on top. I am a man of my word, Edric, and when I told you that you couldn't shake me, I meant it."

Edric stared back at him in a pitiful state for a moment before lunging out with a scowl and striking Mike across the head, sending him into full unconsciousness for the first time in many days.

The two days passed quietly for Mike. There were no interruptions; there were no more visits from either the guard or Edric. There was no food, though that did not matter anyway anymore. Mike was allowed to spend this time in silent reflection. He remained grounded in his calmness. In fact, he had never felt calmer in his life.

Edric had never once set his hands on the emblem for one reason or another, and Mike spent his days turning it over in his hands. He thought back on the first time he had seen this, over two years ago now. It seemed ironic to him that the tool made to save the world had destroyed his, but that was of no consequence now. Mike pondered on all the experiences he had met with this thing, as well as what still lay ahead of him. If memory was, indeed, preserved in the next life, he would have a world of them on which to look back. More had happened in these two years than the rest of his life combined.

Would I have given it all up to be living safely back in Idaho now? The answer to the question was not hard. The pain and the heartache, other than the comparatively dull burning he still felt on his skin, seemed to sink into oblivion while the exhilaration of accomplishment and camaraderie remained powerfully distinct. All had combined to make a sound daydream come to life, and Mike turned the condemning piece of metal around in his hands in nothing but gratitude.

The emblem returned Mike's feelings for a glowing warmth of its own. That sensation alone brought back a flood of memories. Mike recalled all the times when he had been on the right track. The emblem had glowed. Now it was assuring him the same thing. He had, indeed, done right. He had stayed on the path. The emblem seemed to comfortingly whisper an assurance that the degree of what he had actually done did not matter, but the correctness with which he did what he had had the chance to do. Mike smiled at the thought, and when the door opened several hours after the second dusk fell, he felt ready for the mysteries that lay ahead of him.

The guard led him out into a hallway, and then into a courtyard. The entire complex seemed to be empty. As Mike walked, he tried to do the math in his head, trying to determine whether it had been a full two days. Edric had given his ultimatum in the morning, and the present sky did not even hint of dawn. Mike wondered whether the execution was to go off early. Mike welcomed the thought just as much as the alternative. The change really made no difference, for the outcome would be the same, either way.

The guard led him through the courtyard and out the other end, where Mike saw, for the first time in a great while, the rolling hills shining in the moonlight beyond him. He turned and looked around. He did not see his place of execution. He looked at his executioner, the same hateful man that had brought so much pain to his life. The monster returned the gaze, and then did something that Mike would have never expected. He shoved him off and commanded in Saxon, "Get out of here."

Mike turned back to him in bafflement. "What?"

"This is your chance," he stated. "Say another word and it'll be gone. I will cut you down despite her terms."

"Her?" Mike blurted, regardless of the threat. It came out more involuntarily than anything. Mike's head could not make sense of anything that was presently unfolding.

The Saxon drew his sword, further threatening him. "I warn you. Get out of here now or I'll kill you."

Mike did not question any longer. He turned and ran off toward the night. As he ran, he heard the sound of clanking on a gathering of rocks behind him. He turned around to see a metal knife off to the side of the gate, glistening in the moonlight. It could not have been the Saxon's. Mike's eyes scanned upward above the knife and saw a silhouetted shadow standing atop the wall. It was the figure of a woman. Mike's breath caught, and he flinched to move back for her, but he resisted, seeming to catch, in the silent night air, the whisper of her voice, pleading for him to turn away and keep running. Mike obeyed, caught in the spell of her tone as he always had been.

Chapter 32

Due to the racing of his heart, Mike had not realized the coldness of the night until the moment he presently found himself. He now sat atop a horse, which had replaced him in his running, leaving his body the sole task of dealing with the icy chill of the wind rushing past him. The dark shadows of the yew trees rushed on either side of him, but Mike hardly noticed. His mind struggled to keep up, and seemed to be falling farther and farther behind him, and all he was left able to do was follow the swirling tail of the horse ahead of him.

In reality, Mike's mind very well could have been left in the first grove of trees about a quarter mile beyond his prison. That was where he ran after he fled the presence of the monster and the ghost. That was also where he had run straight into the arms of a shadow. The arms had seized him, and before he mustered up the strength to throw out a defensive punch, he had heard the tones of a familiar voice that not only pacified his fear and defensiveness, but petrified him in shock. It had been the voice of Lucius.

"Mike, Mike, it's me," he had assured.

"Lucius!" Mike had exclaimed, throwing out a thousand questions in that one utterance.

Lucius had seemed considerably less surprised than Mike had been, yet on his voice there shimmered a tone of anxiety. "Where's Diana?"

"Diana?" The thousand questions had suddenly multiplied tenfold.

"Yeah. Didn't she come back with you?" Lucius' eyes had continued to scan the bright clearing from which Mike had ventured. Mike turned back as well, now feeling a load of panic. The pieces had suddenly come together in full.

Mike's eyes had gone wide at the realization of the reality of the apparition. Turning back to Lucius, he had seen the alarm in Lucius' eyes as well. Mike had jolted forward to go back. Lucius, however, had caught and impeded him.

"No, Mike. Not now," he had commanded. "Later, yes, but not now. You aren't in a position to rescue her. We'll have to regroup." Lucius had motioned for everyone with him to saddle up. "You can use Diana's horse."

Mike had obeyed, for he had realized the truth in his friend's words. But now that he was freed from the Hell which had existed behind him, he was subjected to a new torture, the torture of knowing that his savior was now subjected to the hands of his former oppressor. Mike could not decide whether that knowledge or the shock of his change in situation tortured his mind most. Although the former fought with the support of his beaten heart, the latter sent his mind into a flurry of questions that had stemmed from the moment he was told to go free. *How did all of this happen?* he asked himself. *How can I now be free after facing death head to head? What made this providence even possible?* The sea of questions sat suspended just beyond the threshold of his understanding.

To his relief, this torture was much shorter lived than the former. It only lasted, in reality, about an hour, though it seemed much longer than that. The procession of horses, for there were about twelve men besides Lucius, slowed their pace and turned off into a grove. There in the grove was an old abandoned hut which very well could have been the old dwelling of one of the men in the group. Sure enough, one of the men rode up to the doorway, dismounted, and walked in. Lucius turned back to Mike and gestured for him to go in as well.

There was food on the hearth, which was immediately offered to Mike. After not having eaten in a few days, Mike wasted no time in delving into it with gusto and temporarily forgot all his questions. He ate for a few minutes, uninterrupted by the staring eyes that gathered around him as he filled his stomach. The food immediately re-energized him, pulling him the rest of the way out of his dreamlike state and back into the reality of his mortality.

Mike had only been eating for about ten minutes when, out of the corner of his eye, he noted Lucius staring at him from over in the shadows.

For the first time, he realized the implications of Lucius' presence. Those implications had performed obvious wear on his face. The tumult of the moment upon their first reunion had temporarily set such things back stage, but now that all the immediate drama was over and Mike's stomach was filled, the different color boldly soaked through. Mike could hardly believe what he was seeing. Not only was the presence of the figure of his friend an anomaly in itself, the state of his friend's countenance was worlds different. Lucius used to have a quiet, although proud and almost cocky, air to him. One could see now that he had dug down to his very core to find himself a complete stranger. And it shook him. It shook Mike. The man who had been with him at every bend in the road the entire summer now seemed to be hiding from him in the shadows, almost as if he were ashamed of who he found himself to be. Mike eyed him with intrigue. Lucius must have noticed, for he made an objective comment to ease the silent tension: "Despite your hunger, you seem to be fairly well fed."

Mike looked over at him, the same observations he had previously made of his friend looping through his mentality. The same thousand questions he had before felt also re-emerged. Lucius stepped out of the shadows. Mike would not need to ask those questions; Lucius already seemed resolved to bring them to light, as timid as a manner as he would carry.

"Mike, I am so sorry for all that I've done." The voice lacked strength. Mike could see from the light of the hearth fire that there were tears welling up in Lucius' eyes. "I never meant for this to happen."

Mike knew that. He silently stared at his friend as he struggled to continue. "I know that all of this was due to my foolishness."

Lucius' words resurrected in Mike's mind all that had happened since his departure. The results had been diverse, intense, and were still occurring. For some reason, though, Mike did not recall the pain. It had left him, replaced with joy that his friend was back at his side and concern at the events that were still unfolding. Mike stood up and embraced Lucius' trembling figure.

"What's done is done," Mike responded calmly. "It was just as much the fault of Marcus. He has since paid his dues."

Lucius seemed strangely unsurprised at the news of his enemy's fate.

"If there's anything I can do to pay mine, please tell me."

"You've done a lot already tonight, and you can further complete it by filling me in on what happened."

Lucius nodded, a nod which seemed to say he was going to do that anyway. He took a deep breath, wiped the moisture from his eyes, and struggled to regain strength in his voice. "Two weeks ago, Diana came to Aeola and me by horseback." The guilt still seemed to remain in his voice. Lucius struggled his way through his words. "She brought us up to speed on all that had happened in the past few months in Newhaven, including your expulsion of Marcus and resulting urgency to fortify. She told us that you two had then seen Marcus heading a large army of Saxons, how you told her to leave but how she stayed and watched what unfolded. She spoke of how you killed Marcus and how they took you prisoner. She followed you to your prison, ingrained it in her memory, and rode directly to us."

Lucius gulped pitifully. The tears were growing into larger beads in his eyes. "I did not mean for all of this to happen. I want to let you know that as soon as I found out, we rode back to Newhaven. I did what I could to raise a rescue party, but I had lost the respect of the people. It was Diana who aroused them to action. She was the one who led this party over here. We arrived here five days ago and spied out the compound, learning of its patterns. I saw you numerous times before tonight. I wanted more than anything to redeem myself, to storm the villa right then and there, but she held me back.

"Just last night, Diana told me that she was going to go do some scoping out. I insisted on going with her but she refused. I never could have predicted her intentions. Mike I am so sorry."

Mike had much to mull over, and so he dismissed Lucius from his attention. Lucius retreated feebly. Mike hoped that his dismissal was not misunderstood, for he just needed some time to himself. He wandered out to the open air of the night, bidding all the men to get their rest. The middle of the night was passing, and so they obeyed readily. He, on the other hand, was as awake as he ever had been.

Mike walked outside alone among the trees. They glistened in the moonlight but only served as a backdrop for Mike's attention at the present moment. His thoughts were turned to Diana. Mike walked about to stir up the thoughts that had collected in his head. The thoughts of what she was now most definitely experiencing made him shiver and brought back the ghostly shrieks with which he had been haunted so long ago. He knew that she must have known this would happen. The realization brought tears to his eyes.

His yoke had suddenly become hers, and that yoke was not easy. Mike, more than anyone, knew of the oppression of which that Saxon was capable, for the scars still remained tattooed on his skin. The yelling and cursing and taunting still remained tattooed on his memory. Both resided in perpetuating burning that continued to harass him. The man was a monster. He was a fiend who was not only capable, but prone to mercilessness, and Mike imagined, with a breaking heart, what his dealings now were with her, a young female in her prime.

But, again, she must have known that. She could have only assumed that, for she had most definitely used that as leverage. Mike clinched his fists as tears now streamed down his face. *Why has Diana given herself over to a renewed nightmare—her greatest fear of all?*

There was only one option for his next course of action.

Mike's legs were shaky and he turned back toward the hut. He had not eaten nearly enough to rehabilitate his body. It screamed out for rest and re-nourishment, which he would have to give it, but he would also use that time to plan for redemption. He lay down on the ground of the hut, physically much less comfortable than the bed in his cell yet paradisiacal even so, and settled into restless sleep.

Mike found out, in the next few days, that the threshold of his patience lie at the idea of knowing a loved one was suffering. He could now state that fact—he loved Diana. Every moment away from her beat against him, and he longed to be able to communicate with her, to see her pretty face, to hear her laugh, even to chide her for her occasional haughtiness, which she had always outwardly blown off. He knew all too well that she was back in the depths of humility, that she was not laughing but sobbing, that her face was bruised and her hair was matted and her body a mess. It killed him to know that she was being eaten alive at the moment, and it killed him even more to know that her meaning behind the sacrifice sustained him in his love for her. It was a terrible paradox, one that should never have had to exist. It had come, though, and seemed to swirl the life and the death, the joy and the sorrow, and the pain and the ecstasy into one great existential oracle. Mike now saw what he had never been able to before see.

This sight empowered him to be where he was at now, hidden in the trees near the villa, ready to face the devil once again. It had taken him three days to re-nourish himself, as well as build a new bow and get the feel of it. It had taken three days to discover the ways and natures of the beasts, who before, had fallen beyond his limited perceptions. The task had been colossal, for the place was well guarded, and, in turn, Mike's level of rest had been reduced to as little as it took to remain functional.

Diana's location had been verified, however, through means for which Mike would have never wished. These means, caught in the wind over the course of the nights in which he spied, fulfilled his fears by, indeed, reigniting the nightmares. Anger and desperation had boiled, better sense had been cast aside, muscles had started forward, and without Lucius pulling Mike back into the bushes, Mike would have charged forth stupid and unprepared. He had found himself throwing fists at his detainer, thinking only that he was a barricade, holding him back from ending the oppression, before he had been able to regain control of himself. Through hard breaths, Mike had wheezed out apologies to his friend, who, like always, received them without offense. "You'll get your chance, Mike," he had comforted, "Patience."

That chance had finally arrived. Lucius and Mike had it all set up. They alone were to strike forth on the villa while the others waited beyond in the groves in order to avoid risk of greater death. Lucius had initially disagreed on this point, stating first that he wanted a full attack. The option had seemed the most logical, but Mike did not want to put his men in any more danger. Moreover, he had a good feeling on an approach of stealth. Lucius had then stated that he wanted Mike to stay back and avoid any risk altogether, but Mike would not have it. In reality, Mike wanted to go at it alone, but was convinced through Lucius' pleadings to have a partner. "I feel like I can finally make full recompense for my mistakes, Mike. Don't deny me this." Mike had conceded, and now, as they waited, Mike was glad that he had.

They remained in the bushes until the designated time, when Mike's old nemesis came out atop the wall to stand watch. The butterflies fluttered in a frenzy in Mike's stomach. Nervously, he rubbed his fingers along the blades of grass beside him, occasionally plucking them just to cast them aside. The moments ticked by; the moon seemed to stand still in its course across the sky. Every moment they sat there was another nightmare Diana experienced.

"I want to get her," Mike expressed in no more than a whisper to his friend.

Lucius looked over at him, staring at him. In his eyes there seemed to be understanding. "She means the world to you, doesn't she?"

Mike returned with a nod of conviction. The comment seemed true to more than one depth. Mike half-expressed this by asking, "How does one go about repaying what she's given me?"

Lucius' face was sure and sober as he replied with words that would forever remain imprinted on Mike's mind. "It's not about repaying, Mike. You look at it that way and you'll miss the entire beauty of it all."

At that moment, a slightly warmer gust of air appeared on the night, seeming to sustain the truth of Lucius' words.

The time for redemption came. Lucius' words rung strong and true through Mike's head as Lucius slapped him on the back and summoned him to follow. They began crawling through the brush, keeping their eyes on that old, familiar monster that Mike seemed to know so well. They approached below him then hid behind a boulder. The moon shone brightly through the, again, icy chill of the darkness—Mike looked at Lucius and could see him all too well. It was the wrong time of the month to be doing this, but it was too late for such thoughts now.

Just as Mike was nodding to Lucius to break for the shadow of the wall, he heard the whinny of a horse off in the exact spot of woods where the rest of the men were stationed. Mike looked up in panic to the guard, who had been aroused by the noise. He turned and ran down from his post. Mike looked over at Lucius and they both ran for the shadow of the wall. Lucius wanted to continue in through the gate while the guard was gone, but Mike held him back. The decision ended up wise, for several torch-bearing men rushed out of the compound on horses with swords in hand.

There was nothing that Mike could do about the rest of his men, despite the desperation he now felt for them. Mike hoped with all his might that they were prepared, that they were keeping watch. He had kept them back to avoid the whole mess, now they would be drawn in anyway. Mike silently watched as they rode off through the clearing. Any minute now, the din of battle would erupt.

"We have to keep going," Lucius stated, to which Mike nodded. He was right; this was as good of a time as any. The guard had not yet resumed his spot. So with adrenaline cascading through his veins, Mike charged toward the doorway.

They entered the empty compound which was all too familiar to Mike. Off to his right, Mike noted the walk of death that he had made each of those horrible days. The corridor was darkened in its own shadow. It was hard to believe that that had occurred just a week ago. He had a different perspective on it now, though now that he did, he was not sure that it was any less nightmarish.

Mike turned away. That was not what he was to focus on. The guard's, and therefore Diana's, quarters lay to his left, on the opposite side of that hallway. Tonight he had a completely different nightmare to confront.

Lucius nudged him and pointed out into the courtyard. It was the guard, though his manner of step did not denote that he had noticed them. Lucius and Mike flew back into the shadow, pleading that he would not come their way. An alert would be sounded and they would be killed. Mike held his breath and waited in dread, but the guard climbed back up on the wall to resume his watch.

Mike exhaled and led Lucius out towards the door of the quarters, keeping to the shadows of the corridor. They approached the door and made ready to steal into it. It was then, as they reached for it, that the tense quiet was shattered and Hell exploded into its full, fiery fury.

Mike only remembered in glimpses what happened in the next several minutes. Cries resounded from outside the compound. The cries drifted to the inside of the compound. Men burst out from the closed doorways, weapons in hand. Some caught sight of them and came at them. Mike found himself and his friend fighting them off. Yells were exchanged, intermingled with the ear splitting connection of swords. They were coming fast. An orange blaze was beginning to emanate from a distance without the building. More yells, more clanking, more men coming, sweat on Mike's face. Men fell before them, but they kept coming.

"Leave them!" a voice commanded. Mike and Lucius were freed from the closing circle around them as it dissolved. There was the fading sound of their retreating steps, then the sound of solitary steps coming for them. Mike urged Lucius on to the door. Mike kicked the door in to find Diana sitting upright on a bed, her hands tied together with a rope. He ran to her and slit the rope from between her hands. Lucius struggled to shut and barricade the door from their pursuant, but was mowed back by not one, but two men.

Mike rushed forward to aid Lucius, who was now fighting with a figure who ended up being the devil himself. That same guard, his old oppressor whose room they now occupied, was right behind him. Mike met the guard head on, looking him in the eye. The only thing Mike remembered in the next few moments was the hate being passed between them. They fought, back and forth, resuming the ear-splitting shrieks of contacting swords, passing back and forth, in the shrieks, resonating memories of pain and tyranny. Mike fought losing control over his sound mind with all his might as he raised parries and sent forth lunges toward his opponent.

Then he heard a thudding and a crashing come from behind him. His opponent, who faced the source of the din, lost focus for just a second, and that was enough for Mike to deliver a crushing blow across his head to send him to the ground unconscious, yet once again. But as he took his turn to see what had happened, he, too, felt a jerk come from behind and was knocked almost senseless. Quick as lightning, there appeared a cold sharp blade across his neck, and he was wheeled around to face Lucius' sudden absence, a broken window, and a face of panic on the woman he loved.

From behind him, he heard the voice of his oppressor: a calm, yet demonic, voice. "I knew there was a reason why I didn't punish our common friend over there for making his selfish exchange." The voice was Edric's. "I find you in my hands again, Mike. How did I know it was going to turn out like this in the end?" Diana stood in front of the bed in tears. The more she moved to Mike, the harder the knife was pressed. "I'm going to make your lady over there decide your fate by striking a deal with her. Diana," he said in perfect Latin, turning to her. Somehow, as with Mike, he knew her name, "I'm going to give you an opportunity. You see that your oppressor lies unconscious over there, his sword to his side. I know what he has done to you. You know what he's done to Mike. Take the sword and execute justice on him. You do this, and Mike remains alive and with you. You cannot deny my generosity."

Diana stared back in shock. Mike's feelings mirrored her facial expression. "You seem surprised," he continued. "Don't be. He was a traitor to me anyway—taking his own actions and disobeying mine. Of course," he added, "as a result of the ordinance, you and Mike will be swearing allegiance to me." Mike struggled to get free but Edric only held the knife tighter. He could not even get any words out. Instead, he was left to watch Diana in desperate silence, wondering which fate she would choose. She stood there suspended. Mike could see the obvious hate in her eyes as she stared at the unconscious corpse. She wanted, more than anything to do it. Mike did not know what exactly had happened in the past few days, but there was apparently enough to cause her fingers to pick up the sword. Yet she stopped cold after that. She stood torn, knowing the horrid implications of Edric's offer. Mike looked on in tense silence. He knew what his action would have been. He did not mind dying. He had already come to peace with that idea once and would, in a second, choose the fatal side of his integrity. He could not, however, wish Diana's respective fate on her, a fate which she had already tasted twice, a fate which seemed much worse even in his naïve mind. Diana slowly walked over to the corpse. Still, she hesitated. Both Mike and Edric watched in anticipations of completely opposite natures.

"You don't have long to decide," Edric reminded. "In a matter of moments, he will have woken up. If you don't strike first, your destinies will be written for you." Diana looked toward the window out of which Lucius had flown. Edric noted it with a scoff. "You see that your friend has been disabled. Even if he does have the courage to come flying back through that window, Mike'll be dead before he can do anything."

Mike mourned the nature of the situation. Diana slowly turned the sword over, staring at the guard, who was now stirring on the ground.

"It's your last chance," Edric warned.

Diana stared at Edric. There was a look in her eyes that caught both Mike and Edric off guard and in confusion; it was a look that caused Mike to bite his lip and Edric's knife to loosen just a little. Her next action decrypted the look. Defiantly, she eyed Edric, took the sword, and slowly turned it toward herself. Mike closed his eyes and waited for the moment to come, for both of them.

But instead of the silent cold slicing Mike expected to feel, there arose from the courtyard a ruckus that caused Edric to turn his body and jerk Mike around. That was all it took. There sounded a sharp whizz through the air, and Mike felt Edric's body convulse in violence behind him. The grip on his neck was loosened and Mike turned and decked a wide-eyed Edric, sending him to the ground. Mike turned to see a shadow in the window, a shadow that presently sent off another arrow into the heap who stumbled forward to advance on Diana. It fell back to the ground and Lucius jumped through the window sill, his face hideously covered in blood.

"Lucius!" Mike cried in an exclamation that arose for a few different reasons.

"I'm okay!" he called back and led the two out of the room. In the courtyard, they discovered the source of the clamor. Mike's soldiers had ridden in and were giving battle with the remaining Saxons. The Saxons were a mess and were falling fast. They ran like frightened ants without order, only to be cut down by the men on horseback. Mike rushed forward and mounted up behind one of the men. "Leave them!" he ordered, "Ride out!"

Mike was obeyed. The battle was abandoned, both inside and out, and after Mike, Lucius, and Diana mounted individual horses outside the compound, the party rode off amidst the blazing light of the burning trees. They did not stop for several hours, either, and may as well have been running themselves, for when they once again arrived at the familiar dark silhouette of Newhaven, they were all well near ready to collapse.

Chapter 33

The next day, the land all about Newhaven became baptized in several inches of snow. Mike, however, slept through most of the barrage and woke up later that evening to find its presence not only surprising, but welcome as well. It had set everything at peace, muffling all noises, including the noises that had continued to ring in his head. The din of battle slowly dissipated, leaving his mind in a state of blanketed whiteness. He took the liberty and pleasure, after waking up, of simply lying in his own bed and basking in the quiet, soaking in the knowledge that it was all over, that he was able to view the morning again as a new beginning.

The Saxons had disappeared from his life, yet once again. He would not be seeing them for awhile. Newhaven's baptism had guaranteed that by covering the people's tracks. One day, they would be back, one day, they would eventually get him. This time, though, he had slipped through their grasp, leaving him free to enjoy life until the threat came round another time.

The storm had also seemed to keep Mike's visitors down to a steady trickle. He had expected a front of welcomes to accost him, but such had not happened, even thirty-six hours after their arrival. Everybody had seemed eager to stay nestled in their respective huts, putting off their welcomes for a more favorable time. Despite Mike's desire to make reacquaintance, he had not minded. It had given him a chance to spend the evening, then this morning to sit down and catch up in writing down everything that had happened to him.

Just moments ago, Mike had written of his encounter with Marcus and the army and the feelings he felt upon giving himself up to them. He reconstructed his conversations with Edric the best he could and was surprised to find how well his memory served him. He had recorded his memory of the torturing, of the final meeting with Edric, of the sentence of death, of his meditations on death, of his liberation, and then of his rescue of Diana. He now sat back and tapped his quill on his chin, wondering how to go about explaining the next passage.

All of that had been easy to write, but the thoughts which now dominated Mike's head seemed much more difficult to get out. Mike knew what he wanted to say, but did not know how to say it. As his mind wandered, his eyes reviewed some of what he had written.

I was not afraid to die. I cannot seem to understand why people make such a big deal about the whole thing. Death is nothing but another new experience. I have encountered so many new experiences in the past two and a half years, I feel like I have already died many times anyway. Such experiences had exposed me both to Heaven and Hell. I knew I had already traversed it all.

Mike scanned over the next paragraphs—his summary of the days wherein he had waited to rescue Diana. The entries were decent in expressing every emotion he had felt during that time, all except for one. His journal had properly arraigned what had been the conglomerates of shock, happiness, restlessness, hatred, and loyalty, yet one remained which dried up the ink in his quill.

Mike soon realized why. That feeling remained stirred up and exposed above the waning tide of the others. He was still very much enveloped in that emotion and therefore could not see its nature clearly.

Mike resumed tapping the quill on his chin. He was still determined to write what he could of it. He paused a moment, scraped up any thoughts he could, then began writing words, hoping they would take him in the proper direction.

I have not had the chance to see her, let alone talk to her since arriving back in Newhaven. I had hoped that she would be one of my numerous visitors, but that has not been the case so far. That doesn't mean that I was disappointed at seeing the others—quite the contrary. I was rather pleased to speak with Cassius, who happened to be the one to lead the charge at the villa. I was able to have a long talk with him in which I expressed my deepest appreciation. He was very modest about it, stating that he wanted to make sure the men were ready for anything, and when they were discovered, everything became automatic after that. I was glad to see that, for it seems like all my training paid off. I promised to publicly recognize him, but he asked me to stay quiet on the subject.

I was also able to speak with Julius, to whom I exposed the noble deeds of Lucius. I also expressed my confidence in Lucius as a worthy companion for Aeola, despite his present reputation in Newhaven. "All of that must be forgotten," I told Julius. "If it weren't for him, neither Diana nor I would be here." Julius seemed to be willing to accept my words.

As for Lucius, himself, he came to visit as well. After he shook off all of my repeated words of gratitude, he took the moment to apologize to me one more time and assure me that he would not go against my judgments anymore. "I cannot ever repair the pain I caused you, Mike," he told me. "I will have to live with that the rest of my life." I told him that he had made his restitution, and that he did not need to feel any more guilt. I told him that his loyalty was all I wanted from him from that time forth and that the past was forgotten. He took a deep breath and nodded, seeming satisfied with the matter.

The remainder of our conversation was more casual. He told me that he and Aeola were determined to marry and asked how they could go through with that. I told him that I would perform it in the presence of the entire community and that they could start making the preparations for the next Sabbath, which will be in five days. He looked extremely peaceful after that, and informed me that with the wedding, everything would be right once again.

The ideas were flowing now, and Mike's pen furiously switched off between parchment and ink bowl as he scribbled away. He had digressed from his original intention, but he was fine with that. History was ushering forth, and an inner power drove him on.

Lucius then asked me of my plan of action with Diana, to which I did not have an answer. As I think about it now, I still do not know. I cannot deny, though, that I do, indeed, feel love for her. Everything she is, everything that she has potential to become enthralls me. She *has her flaws; her arrogance and lack of desire to be social will continue to get her in trouble; but those things simply serve as assurances that she is, indeed, flesh and blood like me. I feel that together, we could make so much of each other; we could make so much of this community.*

I'd like to think that everything that happened meant something for the two of us. What she did in order to save me was colossal, yet I still cannot justify flattering myself on accrediting her motives to me. I feel like her love for me would be too much of a fairy tale to ever come to pass.

I already feel like I have gone too far even in writing these words. I cannot forget my oath to her. I cannot forget...

Mike heard footsteps struggling through the snow outside his hut. He stood up, still holding the journal and pen in his hand, and approached the doorway. At the sight of the face, he almost dropped the journal. The face was that of his present subject, her rosy cheeks highlighting the features of her exposed face.

"Diana," Mike blurted, trying to hide his fluster. "You came to see me?"

Diana cheeks turned a little bit rosier. "If you're not busy. If you are, I can come back later. It's not important or anything."

Despite the nervousness that her timely appearance issued, Mike smiled and welcomed her company. He bade her enter and sat back down on his mattress. Diana shed her fur robe and footwear and sat down on the hearth. She wore a woolen tunic, which surprised Mike, for it was distinctly more savage than the toga with which she had always distinguished herself. Mike would have commented on it, but she had commenced staring at him with her piercing, stunning eyes, and they kept him silent with their spell.

Mike instead took the liberty of staring back into them, an opportunity upon which he had never before dared to venture. The results were immediate; he felt incredibly exposed, yet he realized, in that brief second, that he did not care anymore. *If she can read into me, so be it,* he told himself. Yet he knew, even then, that she did not even need to read into him. He felt like he was telling her everything that he felt about her in that stare. To his shock and scare, yet also to his excitement, she seemed to be reflecting the message. She smiled slightly at him, and Mike could not stand exposure any longer. He blinked, cut off the communication, and opened his mouth to speak.

"How are you doing?" he inquired, and he meant it.

Diana paused to consider her answer. "I'm getting better. How are you?"

Mike let out a half smile. "Same thing. Glad the snow came. We shouldn't have to worry about any retaliation from the Saxons."

Diana tensed at their mention and proceeded to steer away from the subject. "I didn't disturb you, did I?"

Mike shook his head and looked down at his open journal. "No. Just catching up in some journal writing."

Diana gave off a wry smile. "You looked a bit flustered when I came."

"I didn't expect you at the moment. I didn't even see you all of yesterday."

Diana was making no attempt to hold back her smile. It was unnerving Mike. Diana looked down at the open journal. She advanced toward it. "I see you write in English." She picked it up as Mike watched on in helplessness. Still, she held back from crossing any lines of propriety. "Do you mind if I read it?"

Mike stared back at Diana's piercing eyes as a thousand arguments processed through his mind. Every part of his former, introverted self screamed out in opposition, but he suddenly did not want to listen to it anymore, at least when he was with the person sitting before him. She needed to know. He wanted to let her know. Mike noticed himself wandering into uncharted territory as he conceded.

Diana did not go back but read the open page, which contained the last two paragraphs. Her eyes, slowly, emotionlessly scanned the characters while her lips mouthed the words. She had been a quick learner. Mike watched her in anticipation for some sort of response, some sort of verdict. She did not reveal anything while she read, and Mike's nerves swelled to the point of bursting.

When Diana looked up, Mike did not see anything he would have expected. There was no surprise; there was no embarrassment; there was simply the same warm look of friendship with which he had grown to be familiarized. It spurred a feeling that made Mike feel at home, yet the feeling was strikingly stimulating at the same time, like the fire that presently glowed on the hearth.

Diana advanced toward him and grabbed his hand to slowly guide him up to her. Mike followed without restraint. They stood facing each other, briefly suspended in the moment. Then, she pulled herself into him and their figures initiated contact. Mike stood there transfixed, soaking in the warmth of her body and the ebb and flow of her breathing. Hesitantly, he matched the liberty she had taken to place her arms around him. The touch of her back on his palms and fingertips seemed to fill him with life.

The moment only lasted for a second, for Diana pulled away. She stared at Mike in almost a sort of confusion, seeming to sense that something bothered him.

Mike, indeed, felt mildly ashamed. "I was bound to never lay a hand upon you."

What happened next was a moment that Mike would remember forever more. Diana stared at him for what seemed like an eternity, laughed, then pulled Mike's hands in to her waist. She rested them there and left them on their own. She drew closer and her lips mouthed the words, "You did. However, I plead with you now to reconsider."

Mike needed no more than that. What followed was a sublime liberation. The touch of Diana's form, melted into his along with her lips, filled Mike with a supreme dismissal of everything else in the world. He held her tight, and in that brief moment of physical contact, he explored the expressions of everything that had subliminally passed between them all of these months. Suddenly, everything came together and out in the open—everything that had been there before, but in a jumbled and confused mess. That brief moment, as the two stood intertwined in a hut on a snowy winter day, everything aligned and life teased perfection.

The moment passed, and Diana pulled away to make eye contact with Mike. Even then, her eyes remained half shut. "I want you to have me," she entreated. "What do I have to do to make that happen?"

Mike looked at her. That same power upon which he had previously encountered was drawing over him again—that same power that Aeola had pressed upon him those countless months ago—that same power by which he had become entranced upon his first encounter with Diana. Yet it was so much more concentrated now. She wanted him to have her. *She already has me. She could draw me in right now, mold me between her fingers, do what she pleases with me.* It was frightening to suddenly be without control, yet, at the same time, she seemed merciful in her rule over him. Rather than defeat him, she wished to unite with him; she was leaving the choice of their pathway open to him, and that made all the difference. Mike did not pull away; he did not put Diana to shame like he had to Aeola and Aeola had to Lucius, rather he smiled and kissed her gently once again.

Mike knew he was the standard by which this community would live. He knew that his actions, his course of life, would be setting precedents. He wanted to do this correctly. "Marry me," Mike entreated in return. "Commit your life to me. Prove to me; prove to the world that we do not lie in shame, nor in secret, but in glory."

Mike saw unquestioned submission in her eyes as she quietly replied, "You have me then."

And, with a third kiss, those words were sealed.

So it was that two weddings were to be planned in the stead of one. They were to be welded together to be a double celebration, and upon being made public, the upcoming event became the entire drive of the community. All of the people felt that they needed to be a part of what was to be. A simple ceremony was soon turning out to become the grandest celebration Newhaven had seen yet. There was a certain energy in the air, almost as if it were spring and it was time to come out of hibernation. In reality, the cold, damp winter drew on, but the fire within each inhabitant's heart sufficed to keep the hilltop full of warmth.

That said nothing of the fire that burned within both Mike and Diana's hearts during those following days. All the other townspeople made sure that they had nothing to do with any of the preparations, which gave Mike and Diana a lot of time on their own. They shared these moments walking out among everyone else, returning the bright greetings that came their way, walking or riding out beyond the bustling limits of the compound, or simply sitting close in the arms of the other near the hearth fire, talking about the life they would soon be building together.

FORTH FROM EDEN

On the evening before the wedding day, Mike and Diana took the liberty of a stroll on the outside of the walls of the community. The snow had long since melted with recent rain that had come, and now the air was filled with a sort of mist. Gatherings of the vapor sauntered by in the dying light of the day as Mike and Diana wandered along with hands interlocked. The security of the wooden wall beside them took a commanding presence, and though it seemed ominous from their present perspective, it evoked a comfort in Mike's heart, for he knew that behind its ominous presence was the heart of a growing society of which he was a part. The ominous presence shut out the dark, cold, misty world which lay beyond and below them and protected a warmth that continued at his disposal.

"There's something on your mind," Diana spoke. She threw a delightful skip in her step every so often to keep up with Mike's comparably large strides. Mike noticed and considered slowing down, but the skip was too good to lose. Mike smiled and sustained his pace.

"There's always something on my mind."

Mike felt Diana squeeze his hand. "No, but there's been something on your mind for a few days now; I can read it in you."

She was right. Like a book, she was able to decipher his thoughts and feelings.

"I'm just wondering," he started, answering her slowly, "at your actions back at the prison. How, exactly, did you go through with what you did?"

Diana looked at him in mild confusion. "What do you mean?" Her words were soft like velvet to his ears.

Mike tried to organize his thoughts so they came out in the manner which he wanted them to come. "I mean, you must have known what you were getting yourself into when you made the agreement with the guard."

Mike glanced at Diana for assurance. She did not deny his words.

Mike continued. "How could you subject yourself to that when you had already experienced it? When it had haunted you ever since it had first oppressed you?"

Diana shivered at the recollection, explaining just how aware she had been of the consequences of her actions. Her lips parted to speak. "I knew," she stated, "that they were going to kill you if I did not do anything that night. I overheard it. I cast aside the implications of my own fate."

Diana paused. Mike felt he could not look at her. "But I also did it because I had no doubt that you'd come back for me."

Diana stopped their progression around the colonnade, turned toward him, and, with her hand, drew his face toward hers. "And you did not disappoint me." Once again, Mike faced her. He knew that she wanted him to face her. They faced each other and both knew that they were worthy of it. Had they not then uttered their love toward each other, they would have known it just as surely.

Like it had many thousands of times before, the next day came just as surely and just as quickly. Mike woke up, dressed himself, and, upon exiting his hut, was immediately bombarded by several of the men, ready and willing to help him in any way that they could. He dismissed them all, clueless as to what they could do anyway, for he had never even witnessed a marriage outside of the twenty-first century. He told them that he just wanted a little time and space to himself and they honored his request, walking away spritely.

So after Mike paid a visit to Cai, who had followed through on a request to make a few rings, he walked out to the pasture, hopped on a horse, and rode off into the soggy countryside. The land that unfolded as he rode was now quite familiar, yet it also seemed to have an element of freshness to it. The drizzle seemed to assure that. Mike's recollections were thrown back to last year when this weather had been so common before, and he chuckled to himself. What a difference a year had made. Last year, he felt to be in the depths of hell. This year yielded quite the opposite. The chill of the rushing air bit at his nose and cheeks as the horse strode on, but it did not seem to penetrate like it once did.

The winter was only one part of the grand cycle. Mike recalled what Cai told him of the old pagan rituals done at the winter solstice to bring back the sun. After all that was being done to destroy the old ways, they still seemed to be working. Already, he could tell the progressive difference in the amount of light. It brought a message of hope, a message that the present would soon evolve into a better, warmer time. Then, a little less than six months from now, the sun would start retreating again. Just like last year, it would slowly sink farther and farther into its cold dark pit below the horizon. But he was determined that it would not bother him then, just as the darkness did not now. It could not bother him, for Mike had sworn to no longer base his mood on the weather.

There were enough people in his life to make that pinnacle an easy one to summit. The thought that Diana would be with him from that time forth had seemed to place a permanent lightness in his step. The thought that he could wake up each morning and see her, that he could come back after hunting and working in the fields to find her there for him was enough to make Mike completely blind to the storms that always seemed to threaten. She would be there to work and to laugh with him in the summer. In the winter, she would remain close at hand to share her warmth with him. Life would continue on in all seasons, and they would be there for each other to bring sunshine to each of its moments.

Mike slowed the horse to a walk as he reached a little stream. He and this horse had grown accustomed to each other in the past several months and Mike could tell it was ready for a drink. Mike dismounted and allowed the horse to pursue the steadily flowing current. While it drank, Mike walked a little way off and fell down on his knees to soak in the moment. All was quiet except the gentle trickling of the stream and occasional lapping of the horse. Mike took the time to do something he had not seemed to have done in a long time. He lifted his voice up to his God and thanked him for the life which he had been given.

The silence that existed on that little spot of ground contrasted distinctly with the joyful melee later that day in Newhaven. The whole community of about a hundred people was gathered together and struggled to hold in their energy. Truly, the entire hilltop seemed to be bustling with a distinct charge of electricity. Talking and laughing rose and fell in steady rhythm, and even after Julius raised his voice a few times, it took a moment to gain everyone's attention.

Mike had asked Julius to perform the ceremony, but in reality, it did not really matter who did it, for there was nobody endowed with authority anywhere. Newhaven was an authority to itself, and the people were its rulers. What was commonly acknowledged by the collective populous was what was set in the stones. These marriages would be perfect examples of that. The words that would be spoken would be only shadows of the understandings conferred upon Lucius and Aeola, upon Mike and Diana, and upon the rest of the community toward them.

Mike stood arm in arm with Diana, and together they stood beside Lucius and Aeola. As Julius spoke the few words he had prepared, Mike took the moment to look over at his friend. Lucius' mouth was cemented in a stoic expression. His face revealed emotion not of joy, not of excitement, but of peace and determination. He, too, stood arm in arm with his bride, who seemed to have a sober look on her face as well. Mike smiled slightly in spite of the pity he felt for them. He could tell that they lacked something he and Diana had since developed. Lucius' marriage would work out; Mike knew that for certain. He even felt comfortable in saying that he and Aeola would be very happy together. But it would be nothing in comparison to what he and Diana had. He knew Aeola; he knew that ideas of survival and companionship had always been her great motivation. She had seen in Lucius a worthy enough prospect and had gone forward in her pursuit. Lucius, too, had been motivated by loneliness, and an alluring figure had been good enough for him. She was there when he needed someone, and she would end up working fine.

Mike then pulled his eyes in to his own bride. In her he saw something completely different. They had died for each other. They now lived for each other. Had circumstances been better or worse, they would have still been standing here all the same. Mike was sure of that. He held an ongoing wonder at how they seemed to fit together like puzzles pieces. There were left no gaps in between. It was hopelessly beyond him how God or Providence or Fate or who or whatever was in charge of chance occurrence out there could bring them together out in the middle of a monstrous world, at a time about which history would completely forget. It all amazed him. He kissed his bride tenderly on the cheek as Julius spoke on.

When the words had been spoken, the promises had been made, the public declarations announced, and the rituals performed, the hillside erupted, and the celebrations began. It seemed like everyone had thrown their entire souls into what came next. Mike could not help but recall the Elfish wedding ceremony he had attended almost two years ago. The air was blended with familiarity of that time as an enormous bonfire was built in the middle of town to battle the cold. Everything reeled round and round, constant and chaotic, and once again, Mike found himself helplessly caught in a glorious blur. There was music and dancing and eating and drinking and laughing and talking and flirting. There was also Diana.

One thing Mike recalled from the night was that he could not pull his eyes off of her. She wore a wreath of dried flowers in her hair as well as her long, white toga, which had somehow remained clean after all the dirt through which it had passed. She had told Mike that it would be the last time she would wear it, that she would denote herself no longer with it. Mike was happy to see that, but, at the same time, was happy that she wore it tonight. She looked better in it. She looked so beautiful. Mike, in his skins and his furs, as tidy as they were, felt unfit for her.

Diana could not help but note his looks. At one point she chided him about it, saying, "You cannot help yourself can you?"

Mike did not blush like he would have been before prone to do. "I don't need to anymore."

To that she smiled and pulled herself in close to him. Despite all the snickers of the people around them, they embraced each other tightly. Once again, they felt everything they had created between them resonate about their bodies and within them. *This is right*, Mike whispered to himself. *This is what I was supposed to find.* Mike kissed Diana gently with all of that love that he now harbored. With the touch of their lips, they left everyone and everything behind and sailed for the mists of Avalon.

Chapter 34

That first year in Britain often surfaced in the confines of Mike's recollection. It often floated in on the gulf between wake and sleep, silently sailing, the events eyeing him stoically from under the sails. The good and the bad haunted him as one, whispering to him echoes of who he once had been and what had happened to him in a year that had changed him forever. Mike recalled the death he had seen. Always at the forefront lay the death of Abe, the man who had weaned him from his infancy in the first place. The disappearances of Virgil and Arwulf followed closely behind, for it had been the death of his self. Indeed, his entire world had crumbled from beneath him to leave him standing alone in a daunting, dangerous world.

Those recollections, however, never appeared as anything more than shimmering reflections, for they became only a blurry background to a much more emotionally intense year after that. Mike often recalled the time of the daffodils, and the moment came alive every spring following. Mike had taken the opportunity each time to sit down in their midst and re-enact that moment of his first discovery of them. Each year, he had felt the revitalizing glow that arose in his heart. They had truly been the cause of his break in fever that first year. They had brought life back into his world of death. They had promised that, though the winter had been cold and barren, spring would always bring rejuvenation. Everything had built off of that: the excitement of the growth of the community, the meals, the lessons, the sparring, Lucius' appearance. Mike recalled the moral torture he had felt in battle, then the epic journey he had taken with Diana. Mike recalled descending to his lowest pit and standing tall, then being sent to his highest peak and touching the sun.

But even those days were beginning to fall in the background.

At the time, the year before his marriage had been as real to him as he had thought possible. The loneliness, the excitement, the fear, the courage, the intrigue, the love, the pain, the fulfillment—they had all swirled together to create a grand collage of reality. He could not deny such feelings as part of a very concrete system, a distinctly tangible world that still lay, again, within reach in his dreams. That old life was gone; Mike was a reincarnated being, and the self he had become was the only reality to him now; it was the only reality he desired.

Such thoughts ran through Mike's head as he lay one morning in his bed thinking. The sky was still relatively dark outside, and Mike was reluctant to pull himself out from under the blanket. There was no need anyway, for it was madly raining. As much as he needed to get out to work—to harvest the grain that was now quite tall and ripe—the storm outside would not allow it. Mike had little problem convincing himself that he needed to spend the morning beneath the thatch of his hut.

Diana still lay asleep beside him. Her methodical breathing moved her chest up and down in a steady, reciprocating rhythm. These were the moments when she seemed most real to him. During her waking hours, Mike found himself in constant veneration of the woman, for she had seemed to be almost a goddess not only in her countenance, but in her personality, in her manners, and, above all, in her love for him. This moment brought her back down to earth. This moment was a grand reminder that after everything, she remained on the same level of mortality as him. She needed to breathe, just like him. She needed to sleep, just like him. After everything that she was, she hungered and bled and ailed, just like him. He loved her like this, her head covered in her matted hair from the pillow, her all but motionless body scented with sweat from when the hut had grown too warm last night. After everything, she was so extremely present, a speck like him, a speck with him, trying with all her might to make it in this world.

It had been a little over two and a half years since they had married, and the love they felt for each other had done nothing but blossom. Although the fires of unfamiliarity that initially had fueled their passions for one another were now under more control, there burned a new flame of unity and familiarity that shone even brighter. Mike recollected on all the things that had happened since then. Indeed there were so many times that he could not even name them all individually, but group them according to relation, as well as the related emotions that had ensued, for those were all still very distinct.

There had been times of superlative joy. Mike recalled the countless number of moments when nothing in the world but each other had mattered. These had been their most intimate times—times confined solely to the other's existence, times never meant to be known or shared with anyone else. Such times had been tempered with times among the community—happy times, times when the collective family had laughed and sang and danced and celebrated life together. Diana and Mike had slightly different recollections of those times, but their differing perspectives had built a beautiful panorama which could not have been captured through their individual lenses alone.

Then there were the times that fell in the middle of the spectrum. Mike thought back on the summers they spent together, running through the fields of wildflowers and down to the running waters to swim in the stream. Mike thought back on the moments when they simply lay down on the grass and looked up at the clouds or the stars, caring only to break the serenity at sundry moments with soft words to each other. These moments had reignited the feelings of childhood, when nothing else had mattered, when everything else seemed to fade into insignificance.

"What do you think will have become of us at the ends of our lives?" Diana had asked during one of those occasions.

"I don't know," Mike had answered, moving his hand over to touch her. "That's the least of my worries right now."

Indeed they had been. There had been other times to worry about such things. Mike and his men had continued to spar with each other most every day. He had the scars of accidental slices and jabs to prove it. He had known, when they had done battle to recover Diana, that they would not be throwing up their weapons forever. Mike had the perspective of history to prove that. In the last two and a half years, he had been proven right, for Newhaven did not forever remain a secret. Saxon invaders eventually found it in their conquests. There had been more than one occasion where Mike had organized his ranks at the walls to fend off their attacks and had waited out the night in hopes that their fortifications would hold strong. His hopes had always been fulfilled, but he was left wondering, each time, when the Fates would finally cut their line. All he could do was continue to perform to the limits of his power, and be thankful for each victory they were given.

Moments, Mike thought to himself, *they're nothing more than moments on a great canvas of routine.* Those moments had been the spices of his life. Despite what his memories would claim, most days were more of the same bland porridge. Ever were they made up of the same work and sweat and dust, of the same chores, the same meals, the same conversations with the same people. That was fine with him, especially considering how he had lived it for twenty-five years. He had always done it with a smile on his face, and that had been without coming home each night to the same loving arms.

Mike had still found the opportunity at times to steal away from everything with Lucius. Their friendship continued to grow as their dependence on each other remained a necessity. Lucius had come a long way since his return to Newhaven. He had eventually regained the respect of the citizens, especially considering how he continually proved himself on the hunting ground and in battle. He was kind to everyone, and though his quiet, yet confident attitude rebounded, he did not flaunt it.

Indeed, his marriage with Aeola changed him, as it did to Aeola. They slowly became more responsible, especially when their first child came along a few months after their marriage. Since then, they had borne one more, and both children were their greatest joy. Mike thought back on Cai's prophecy, that his marriage would be the binding force of the community. He had been right. Lucius and Aeola had joined suit, as had a dozen or so others since then, including about half of the slave girls. Newhaven's first generation had been propagated, and the entire community seemed to feed off the life that sprouted of it.

As of yet, Mike and Diana had not borne one of their own, despite their desires. Mike could not help but note that Diana had never borne any children before, even after being subjected to the Saxons for all of those years. With deep regret they realized that the possibility may have been completely out of reach, which had brought many mutual tears. They could do nothing but hope for the best, though.

Mike's thoughts were disturbed by a soft moan beside him. Diana rolled over but did not wake up just yet. Mike leaned over, kissed her on the cheek, then pulled himself out of his bed and took a look outside. The light of the sun showed up as a round white orb, low in the sky. Mike knew that the rain would not last for too much longer. It was already losing strength and was now reduced to a low, steady drizzle. Mike stood out under the heavens and let it fall down upon him. Diana loved the feeling of rain. He had fallen to the same sense. The skin of Mike's face was soon soaked, and he drew up his hands to wipe it clean of the dirt and oils that had built up. He opened his mouth and sucked the goodness of the moisture out of the air. His lungs, his entire body was washed over with a feeling of fresh cleansing.

The weather cleared up in time for the men to take to the fields in the afternoon. Mike and his fellow townspeople marched out with sickles in hand to cash in on everything over which they had sweat for the past several months. Five summers had found Mike performing this task, and each year, he had been able to see more and more yield. Despite the amount of work it required, Mike had grown to love it all simply because he was able to see that everything he had done plentifully paid its dividends.

This year was no different. Mike stood submerged above the waist in the sea of golden grain. The wind powered the waves that swept across the portions yet unconquered and lapped up against the groves of trees where the landscape beyond continued. About thirty feet behind him lay the front where most of men tended to work. Mike, on the other hand, was different. He loved to start in the middle, to be completely surrounded by the grass, and to work his way out, to ride the waves back to shore.

The air soon grew misty with the spray of chaff that splashed up before the sweep of the sickle and filled the air with gold. The gentle summer breeze swept it away, keeping it moving over the waves, but not before the industriousness of the workers replaced it. Mike caught its scent in the air and smiled.

At moments like these, Mike went into a sort of mental subordination.

His whole being became devoted to the motion, and not much of note tended to pass through his head. It was a sort of dance, not choreographed, not consciously processed, but felt out and instinctively performed. The rhythm of the sweeping did not come from his muscles, nor from his knowledge of harvesting, but seemed to emerge from within his being itself.

Mike did not know how long he had been in this mindset when he was suddenly taken out of it. Before him appeared a figure from out of the mist. At first he did not look up, for he assumed it was just another worker. Mike asked what he could do to help. The figure did not respond, but remained stationary, as if demanding some different sort of reaction Mike looked up to catch a glimpse of a silhouette floating in the sea before him. For a moment, the shade was unidentifiable, for the brightness of the sun emanating behind him held him obscure, but as Mike's eyes slowly adjusted to the light, he saw who it was. He recognized who it was. In that moment, the silhouetted, floating shadow was suddenly taken from the figure and cast upon every event that had happened in Mike's proximate recollection, every event upon which Mike had been so thoroughly pondering only hours beforehand. The figure stood there and smiled weakly, revealing to Mike that ghosts, too, harbored emotion. Though a million things flashed through Mike's mind, flooding his recent dry bed of thought, he stood there speechless.

"Mike, it's me, Virgil. I'm back, and I'm ready to carry on."